Sherryl Caulfield was born in south-east Queensland, Australia, where she currently resides with her partner. She has also spent several years living in New Zealand and Hong Kong and was inspired to write The Iceberg Trilogy following a holiday to Canada.

Come What May is her second novel.

I0615845

Also by Sherryl Caulfield

Seldom Come By

Praise for The Iceberg Trilogy

Seldom Come By is a haunting love story set against the windswept coast of Newfoundland. The story draws you in from the opening lines and takes you on a compelling journey across time and continents, through love, loss, heartache and healing. It is a beautiful and memorable story – a great accomplishment and a wonderful read.
Julie Fison, Author

Descriptive, detailed and quite the page-turner, Seldom Come By focuses on the lives of Samuel and Rebecca (and their families), the beginnings of their romance, their separations, their ups and downs. A very good debut and one well worth reading for lovers of historical fiction and romantic historical fiction alike.
Romantic Historical Reviews

If you love deep, epic, romantic stories this is one for you.
Jeannie Zelos's Reviews

Reading Seldom Come By is like taking a long hot bath or enjoying a gourmet meal. You want to take your time and savour every single word, every single moment. Romantic and descriptive, it takes you away.
Jennifer Collin, Author

Seldom Come By is an exquisite tale of love and loss, forgiveness and healing..
The Eclectic Reader

I fell in deep with the main characters and really cared about what was happening with them, but also the people around them. It sucked me in, gave me heart palpitations and made me think about them and how to get back to them when I wasn't reading. That was what I was looking for. The last half of the book was beautiful and heartbreaking and romantic.
The Book Bosses

Seldom Come By is the beautiful story of Rebecca and Samuel. I adore historical novels and this is one of the most well written ones that I have read in a very long time. This book was just like the icebergs that the author described, beautiful, breathtaking, and the story just flowed much like I imagine the icebergs do through the water.
Goodreads Librarian

I just finished reading Sherryl Caulfield's Seldom Come By, the first novel in her new trilogy. I was transported to another life, another time. I laughed, I cried, I held my breath in anticipation, I sighed with delight and ultimately felt extremely fulfilled at the close of the novel. I liken Sherryl's first novel to Paullina Simons' The Bronze Horseman in its claim over my life and heart; its beautiful and gripping story; and its wonderful writing.
Beautiful Bizarre Magazine

Three words…startling – epic – romance! This is an epic love story that tests the wills of Samuel and Rebecca, challenges their love, duty to family and willingness to forgive.
Honey Lemon Tea Blog

Come What May

SHERRYL CAULFIELD

First published in Australia in 2014 by Cedar Pocket Publishing
This edition published in 2014 by Cedar Pocket Publishing
PO Box 654 Coorparoo 4151 Australia
www.cedarpocketpublishing.com

ISBN 978-0-9923759-3-5
Cover design by Sherryl Caulfield and Mark Squires.
Cover image purchased through iStock.
Photograph of Sherryl Caulfield by Lucid Photography.

Discover other titles by Sherryl Caulfield at:
www.sherrylcaulfield.com

For my dear friends,

Karen Howitt (d. 1986) and Leah Sparkes,

who loved their fathers

First Impressions

Montreal, Canada, June 1951

1

In the emotion of her farewell, Gene could not remember the name of the co-pilot. All she could think of was sunshine. When Jonathan introduced them, the young man had taken off his aviator sunglasses and smiled at her with soft brown eyes while his short, fair hair glinted and flattened in the downwind of twirling propeller blades. To her right sat Joan, dark-haired and dimple-cheeked, a nursing sister whom Gene put in her mid-thirties, the excitement in her eyes so palpable as if she were going on a Hemingway safari rather than a medical expedition to the edge of the Arctic wilderness.

'Looking forward to it?' Gene asked, practically yelling above the drone of the engine.

'My dear, I love everything about the north except for the insects.'

'How many times have you been before?'

'This will be my fourth trip. Second time with your brother.'

It was pointless to talk any more. They would have days and nights to fill with conversation. Ten weeks in fact – they weren't due back till mid-August, just before Gene's eighteenth birthday.

Three weeks ago when her thirty-three year old brother, Jonathan, had asked her to be his assistant, her heart had leapt at the chance. Months earlier, Morton, her twenty-year old brother, had abandoned her – that's what it felt like – moving west to Lumsden, to start a new and very different life. Gene had been inordinately upset over his leaving. Now she was about to have her own adventure and she couldn't be more grateful. It had been six years since she had been on holidays with Jonathan, six years since they had been airborne together, back in 1945, before he married Annabelle and became a father.

'What I wouldn't have given to be flying off on a three-month journey when I was seventeen,' enthused her mother, Rebecca, when she hugged her goodbye at the Montréal Boucherville Water Aerodrome.

'Jealous?' Gene teased.

'I am,' said her mother, 'and proud. Not proud to be jealous,' she laughed. 'Proud of you!' She squeezed her tightly as she kissed her cheek.

'Thanks, Mom.'

Gene was like her mother in many ways: the same height, the same teal blue eyes, her hair also blonde but more golden than her fifty-one year old mother's. Today, like most days, Gene wore it in a single plait at her back. She was like her mother in other ways too. Once, when she was younger, after she'd done something she'd long forgotten but which had clearly delighted her father, he picked her up, kissed her on the cheek and said, 'I love you, Genie. You remind me of your Mom when she was young: eager for life yet hesitant about it at the same time.' And on that day Gene had thought, 'That must be a good way to be.'

Now, on the first summer Saturday of 1951, she was more eager than hesitant. They were flying in a six-seater floatplane – a first for Gene and the experience a little off-putting. The plane, or rather the pilot, leant the craft to one side before lifting one float out of the water and then the other. She hadn't been expecting that, and her sense of surprise and unease only grew as the plane motored towards the bend in the river. To her untrained eye it looked as if the plane wasn't going to clear it. But although it was much slower taking off than the other flights she'd been on, the plane did eventually rise. Once airborne it flew slower because of the drag resistance on the floats, which Jonathan had already warned her about. As a result, they would stop more frequently than had they been in a plane with flat tundra tires. That suited

Gene fine. Flying was tremendously exciting, but being cooped up for hours had its limits.

Their first destination: Amos, four hours northwest. Below her, the landscape of the Canadian shield drifted by: irregular-shaped lakes, brown bogs, slabs of quartzite, the occasional hut amidst the taiga forests of evergreen spruce, fir and pine, along with the unmistakable pale green of the deciduous tamarack. Wispy cirrus clouds brushed the sky high above on their own journey northward. Good flying weather for today but a sign of a front coming from the south.

Around twelve they started their descent into Amos. From a distance Gene could see it had a small lake next to its runway. Earlier they had taken off on a river. Surely they weren't going to land on that small lake? The co-pilot, not Jonathan, was managing all the controls and the steering. They descended and flew low over the ground – only about two feet above the grassy surface – and then across the water, with the nose tilted up as if they could take off again at any minute. Then, when she least expected it, the floats kissed the water in a shishing noise and the plane turned around in a tight loop. Throughout the whole descent Gene felt as if she had been holding her breath. In quiet relief she exhaled. She now knew what to expect of landings and takeoffs in a floatplane.

At a table outside the aerodrome office Gene unpacked the picnic lunch her sister-in-law had made for the four of them: minced corned beef sandwiches with ketchup and onion.

'Like the selection?' asked Jonathan as he slid his legs under the table.

'Hmm.' She smiled, her mouth already full. Corned beef was possibly Gene's all-time-favourite filler.

'Annabelle made them specially. It might be the last time you have beef for two months so enjoy it.'

Swallowing, Gene asked, 'What will we be eating?'

'In my experience, Gene, it's best to eat first and ask later,' Joan told her.

'Is it that bad?' She was suddenly aware she hadn't given much thought to this trip.

'No,' Joan replied. 'But sometimes I don't like to think I'm eating Rudolph for supper.'

'Oh,' Gene muttered.

As their pilot walked towards them Jonathan called out, 'Tea, Sonny?'

'Please,' he said as he walked past. 'I'll be with you in a minute.'

Gene watched his retreating back. 'He looks young to be a pilot,' she whispered.

'He is,' said Jonathan, 'but that young man has over eight thousand flying hours to his credit. He's flown over fifteen different type of aircraft including Skymasters and practically been shot down by crazy-assed communists in the middle of the Cold War.'

Gene paused before she bit into her sandwich. 'That guy?' she asked in a tone that said, are you sure we are talking about one and the same person?

'Yes!' exclaimed Jonathan.

'Where?'

'In Berlin. Ask him sometime.'

Gene chewed slowly, contemplating that fact. 'How do you know him?' she asked.

'Do you remember that first time we flew west on holiday and we stopped at Port Arthur?'

'That place at the end of Lake Superior? The lake that went on forever.' Gene rolled her eyes. There had been very little to break up the monotony of that endless grey water.

'That's right. Well, on the second day, when we were in Winnipeg, while all of you were having lunch and I was filling up our tank and doing our paper work, Sonny was doing likewise. He was in the Air Force back then but had a weekend off and was going barnstorming for the hell of it. We got chatting about the trip I did with Grandad Dalton the year before. He told me he'd been to the Arctic when he was sixteen and would like to go again

4

one day, and next time I went, maybe he could be my pilot. And so we exchanged addresses and teed things up. He accrued his holidays and together we spent two months flying around up here. Joan came too.'

'What year was that again?' Gene asked.

'1948,' said Joan, with a beaming smile. 'Annabelle came too. We had a ball.'

'He flew you around?'

'That's right,' said Jonathan.

'How old was he then?'

'Around twenty,' said Jonathan. He glanced at Joan who shrugged.

'Maybe twenty-one. Something like that,' she said.

Gene couldn't stop her mouth from gaping open. 'You felt safe putting your life in the hands of a twenty-year old?'

'Absolutely!' said Jonathan, smiling at her scepticism. 'He wasn't your average twenty-year old. It had nothing to do with age, Gene, but flying hours. He made his first flight when he was twelve years old. His father was one of the original wilderness bush pilots. Started back in 1919 searching for bush fires. Flying's in his blood.'

'You talking about me again?' Sonny asked, as he sat down. Gene lowered her eyes. She knew if she looked at him right now she would blush but, if she averted her gaze till the moment had passed, she could carry off a certain nonchalance that had come with years of practice.

'Of course,' said Joan. 'You were always our favourite topic of conversation. You forgotten that?' She elbowed him gently in the side.

'Just reassuring Gene that you're one hell of an experienced pilot.'

Gene looked up to catch her brother smiling at Sonny.

'Did you tell her I was planning to use this trip to practise my aerial acrobatics?'

'Can I have parachute lessons first?' teased Gene.

'Hell, you don't need any lessons for those.' His eyes were full of merriment. 'You just clasp it on, jump out the plane, count one Saskatchewan, two Saskatchewan, three Saskatchewan and then pull the darn cord. There you go, there's your lesson.' He winked at her.

'Have you ever had to use a parachute?' Gene ventured.

Sonny swallowed his mouthful. 'Once or twice.' He raised his eyebrows. 'See, that's proof that it works.'

Gene gazed at Sonny while she kept her dubious thoughts to herself. At least she thought she had, because till that point in her life, the only person who had ever managed to read her thoughts was Jonathan, but in the next moment, Sonny burst into song, belting out *I'm gonna live till I die.*

Before she knew it, Jonathan had pulled her out of her seat and was throwing her around in a twist, singing along with Sonny, who was twirling with Joan and singing about dancing and chancing, flying and riding high.

The last time she had danced with her brother was two years ago at her sister's wedding and here she was in the middle of nowhere doing the jitterbug to a Frankie Laine impersonator, living a bit and laughing a lot. When they finished she was breathless and flushed as Jonathan pulled her in close with one arm and planted a kiss on her temple. For the faintest instant Gene felt like she was on a homeward journey to herself.

2

After lunch they flew north towards winter, towards lengthening days and dwindling temperatures. Three hours later they crossed Moose River and Moose Factory Island. Gene gazed down at the roof of a building painted white and in the shape of the Cross of Lorraine – the symbol for tuberculosis prevention. That had to be the new hospital Jonathan had told her about, built by The Indian Health Service, part of the Department of National Health and Welfare. Dotted here and there on the island was the odd tepee, plus several sturdy buildings, no doubt one of them the Hudson Bay Company (HBC) Trading Post. Gene knew from school history lessons that Moose Factory was the oldest settlement in Ontario. Established in the mid 1600s, it was also one of the first HBC posts in the entire North American continent.

They flew on tracing the wide river. Below, on the northwestern-side, was another settlement, Moosonee. Train tracks that ran southwest beside the river went all the way to Cochrane – she'd noticed that earlier on the map. This time they landed on the flowing water between the two settlements and taxied up to a small floating dock, the only sign of a water aerodrome.

After seven hours of flying, Gene stepped off the plane positively vibrating. She took a few unsteady steps along the dock then up the stairs cut into the riverbank onto terra firma, following her brother and Joan. Sonny stayed behind to do his checks. They headed towards the hospital that had only opened the year before. It was a 200-bed tuberculosis sanatorium for the Indian and Eskimo populations of Hudson Bay. Previously, those infected with tuberculosis had to be sent south. The Crees would end up in Timmins. The Eskimos further south in Hamilton, Ontario, almost as far away as Montreal.

Moose Factory, eleven miles from the mouth of the Moose River on the shore of James Bay, wasn't their final destination by any stretch, merely their starting point. Tomorrow at eight o'clock Jonathan would meet with hospital staff to put faces to the names he had been liaising with over the preceding months while he planned what supplies he needed for their medical expedition.

That night the three of them stayed in accommodation provided by the hospital – she had no idea where Sonny slept. The next morning after Jonathan and Joan had had their meetings Gene accompanied them on a tour of the newly opened hospital, which, to her surprise, was mostly full. After they finished they adjourned to the hospital mess where they met an Indian man wearing dark trousers and a brown lumber jacket, his hair short, neatly styled like her brother's. His name was Walter. Gene put him in his mid to late twenties. Sonny appeared as well carrying his maps, one of which they quickly unfolded on the table.

On the left hand side Gene could see two red crosses: Moose Factory where they were and another at what looked like about one hundred miles north, at Fort Albany, on the Albany River. With a red pen Walter put a cross almost another 100 miles north again.

'Last month,' he said, 'a Catholic hospital opened just here at Attawapiskat, for centuries a gathering place for Mushkego James Bay Cree and for the last couple of hundred years a HBC Trading post as well. Mostly a settlement of tents and tepees.'

'How many beds?' asked Jonathan.

'Fifteen,' Walter replied. 'North of there at the start of Hudson Bay is Winisk. Another Cree community.'

'Could get themselves to Attawapiskat if they were desperate.' Jonathan looked at Walter for confirmation.

He nodded in agreement. 'Yes, but there's no doctor there. Only at Fort Albany.'

On the right hand side of James Bay and Hudson Bay there were no red symbols. Gene pointed to the area. 'Are there any hospitals here?'

'No,' said Jonathan. 'That's where we're headed.'

'And who lives there?' she asked.

'Cree. Like me.' Walter smiled, his smooth, serious face suddenly transforming into a wide captivating grin. He really was quite a handsome man, thought Gene, smiling back.

'Do they speak English or French?" she asked.

'Less than five percent speak either English or French,' said Jonathan.

'Then how will we communicate with them?'

'You see that's where I come in. Ain't that right Walter?' said Sonny. '*Tanisi.*' He smiled at everyone then nodding at Gene he said, '*Iskwew.*' He touched her cheek, '*Nanaway,*' and then her nose, '*Nikot.*'

Everyone bar Gene thought Sonny was hilarious. Okay, maybe she thought he was a little bit funny. 'What did he just say?' she asked.

'Not much,' laughed Walter.

Gene looked from Sonny to Walter, perplexed, and then to her brother.

'Walter's coming with us,' Jonathan said. 'He works for the Department of Northern Affairs and will be our interpreter and trader. He'll also give us access to the fuel caches we'll need.'

Swapping smiles with Walter, Gene asked, 'Do you speak the Eskimo language?'

'A little, but I don't often need to use it.'

'How is that?'

'Because most of the Eskimos live north of here,' said Sonny. He drew a finger across the peninsula on the Eastern side of Hudson Bay, what was officially the most northern part of Quebec, along the 60th parallel, halting near a place called Great Whale River. 'We'll be hard pressed to get beyond what's the end of the tree line.'

'Oh,' Gene sighed, a hint of disappointment in her

voice. 'I was hoping to see a polar bear.'

'You'll see some polar bears. Don't you worry about that.'

She glanced at Sonny, who was clearly amused with her. She gazed back at the lines of latitude on the map. 'Who looks after the Eskimo people north of there? Are they just forgotten?'

'Ah, Gene,' said her brother, 'you'll be pleased to hear that the neglected are no longer neglected. It's amazing how it coincided with the Canadian government finally deciding to give Eskimos the vote. Just last year a coastguard ship called the C.D. Howe made its first voyage to the Arctic. It's an icebreaker design that cruises through pans of ice during the northern summer and will be back again this year.'

'Yet another thing named after that bloody chest-beater,' mumbled Sonny.

Joan laughed. 'You got me there. Minister of Everything! No one else gets a chance to make a contribution or take any credit.' She cleared her throat. 'But seriously, by all reports, it's a great ship, completely outfitted as a small hospital, has an operating room, a sick bay, a dental office, X-ray machines and a darkroom. I hear it pulls in at all the Eskimo settlements across the eastern Arctic, takes X-ray surveys and then transports any TB patients who require hospital treatment to Churchill or to Montreal when it docks.'

'Do they have interpreters too?' asked Gene.

'Yes, they will,' said Walter.

'Any other questions, Gene?' Jonathan asked.

'Just one. Do you think we'll see any icebergs?' She glanced from her brother to Sonny.

'No,' said Sonny. His sunglasses were perched on his head, and his eyes, now that she could see them at close range, were more a hazel brown. Right at that moment they were warm and very sincere. 'Just lots of ice floes.'

Gene chewed her bottom lip, and nodded slowly by way of response.

Sonny dipped his head to look more directly into her eyes. 'Does that disappoint you?'

'No,' she said. 'An iceberg is the very last thing I want to see.'

Relentless Fog

Salvage, Newfoundland, July 1939

3

It started with the iceberg, one of the most magnificent icebergs Rebecca had ever seen. At six o'clock her husband, Samuel, had rushed into the kitchen, where she and her sister, Esther, were busy preparing breakfast. He dragged her outside and up the gentle slope to the crest where she could see the ocean to her north. And there it was, its brilliant form illuminated in early morning light. She gazed in childish wonder as if it were the vanguard for a whole fleet of icebergs.

A week before on their way to Seldom Come By, Rebecca had whispered to Samuel, 'I wonder if we'll see any icebergs?'

And he had replied, 'We can only hope.' And here they were back in Salvage being graced by one the most spectacular icebergs imaginable.

Leaving their bleary-eyed children behind, Rebecca and Samuel motored towards their second close encounter with an iceberg. Their first: an unforgettable twenty-five years ago; the summer of 1914, when Rebecca had turned fifteen; the summer Samuel had come into their lives, the only shipwrecked survivor of the schooner, Madame Nightingale.

That one, like this one, like all great icebergs, had a unique and distinguishing feature. Then: a cavern at one end. Now: two pillars supporting a natural Arc de Triomphe. Under the silent yet watchful gaze of an iceberg, Rebecca and Samuel had made love. They had to – after all, they had been thinking about it for so long! Would a chance like this ever come again?

With laughter, Rebecca had said, 'It occurs to me, Samuel, that here we are in a boat, beside an iceberg and you still have your shirt on. Somehow that doesn't sit right with me.'

Ignoring the cold air, Samuel had peeled his shirt off. Grinning with all his teeth, he had said, 'and you still have yours on. That doesn't sit right with me.'

In a rocking, panting motion they had affirmed life in a paean to their youth. In those moments Rebecca felt that her body was being kissed and adored by more than just Samuel, so heady was the sense of cachet to their union.

Later, when they returned, the children clamoured over them in excitement and anticipation. Rebecca glanced at the *Salut*, borrowed from a Frenchman living in the bay. It would only be able to take four comfortably. Six of them in a boat that size would be like a can of sardines. Tempting fate, she shuddered.

'I'll stay behind. You go out with the kids, Samuel. If we've got time, I can go out again later, take any others that want to see.'

'Can I come?' piped up Anna, Rebecca's seventeen-year-old niece.

'Yes,' said Abby, Samuel and Rebecca's twelve-year-old daughter. 'I want Anna to come too.'

'Anna, you live here! You can go another time,' said her mother, Esther.

Anna looked crestfallen. Rebecca turned to her. 'When was the last time you were up close to an iceberg?'

'Never.' Her voice was laced with longing. Samuel and Rebecca eyed each other. Anna had to come.

'Jimmy, what about you?' asked Samuel. Jimmy was Anna's fifteen-year-old brother.

'Nah, don't worry about me,' he said. 'Only if there's room.'

They decided to make two trips. Rebecca would go first and take Anna, Abby and Gene, their youngest daughter. Samuel would take the boys and then, time willing, she and Samuel might sneak out again later.

When they reached the iceberg Rebecca cut the motor.

Immediately the girls began a tirade of endless questions: Where do they come from? Why are they that strange blue colour up close? How far below the water do they go? Rebecca was enthralled with the abundant joy on their faces. My God, that's what I was once like, she thought. Still like!

'Is it frozen sea water, Mommy?' asked Gene.

'No, love, it's normal water.'

'So you can eat it? Imagine the ice-blocks you could make with that!' she exclaimed.

They had called her Evangeline, after a French woman her father had met during the war, thinking one day her name would likely be shortened to Eva or Lena or Angie. But it was her brother, Morton, who got stuck on Gene and Gene she became. Abigail, named after the wise and beautiful Biblical woman, had her older brother, Jonathan, to thank for her being called Abby. He was twenty-one and had stayed behind in Montreal this holiday because – as Rebecca had told the children – he had his hands full with various things.

'Yes,' Samuel had whispered to her, 'female things like bosoms and derrière.'

'Were you into those things at twenty-one?' Rebecca had whispered back.

'No,' replied Samuel. 'I showed great restraint. I waited till I was twenty-two.'

After half an hour of being in awe of such a dazzling iceberg, Rebecca reluctantly turned the boat for home. She glanced over her shoulder, just once, almost in a silent promise, as if she were saying, 'I'll be back. Soon!' When she did she saw a dark object on one end, a seal resting on a low ledge.

The wind picked up on their return voyage. As she headed towards landfall she could see a large swirl of fog heading their way coming up from the south. She hoped it would hold off. She so wanted the boys to see the iceberg in all its glory – unobscured – in clear glittering daylight. She pressed the throttle down a bit further, her blonde hair streamed behind her; the salt spray deliciously teased her tongue and face; such an exhilarating day. Getting up close to an iceberg was the most magical event of Rebecca's entire youth and now her children were experiencing this wonder for themselves.

Windswept and exuberant, Rebecca motored into their bay. With a whoop she leapt onto the stage. 'I think I love icebergs nearly as much as I love you, Samuel Dalton.'

'Lucky I don't have to compete with icebergs that often,' Samuel replied, squeezing her arms and smacking a kiss on her lips. 'But, then again…' he murmured.

'Come on, Dad! It's the boys' turn at last.' Morton was already stepping down into the boat. It was nearly midday. After waiting all morning he and Joel were impatient to be off. There was no sign of Jimmy. Esther hurried to the house. After a few minutes she returned. 'He could be anywhere. Go,' she said, 'He's missed his boat.'

'Are you sure?' asked Rebecca.

'Yes,' said Esther. She pointed her head in the direction beyond Rebecca's left shoulder. 'That fog's coming in fast, no time to waste.'

The women stood on the stage, waving the boys off. Her dirty-blonde-headed sons were on the front seat, eyes glued straight ahead, no eyes for their mother or their sisters or their aunt. Samuel was at the stern, one hand on the handle of the motor, one hand raised in a casual farewell. His golden eyes shone warmly at her; his smile, as always, was so captivating the way it showed all his teeth.

'I'll be waiting for you, Samuel. Bye, Morton. Bye, Joel.'

When they had motored off a few hundred yards, Rebecca looked away to the distance, to the grey looming fog. It seemed nearer than it had half an hour ago. She and Esther turned towards the house. They wouldn't be back for at least two hours, three, she corrected herself. They had spent a good while staring in awe at the iceberg, circling it clockwise and then anticlockwise.

Three hours later Salvage was surrounded by Newfoundland's infamous fog. It wafted its long tentacles across the bay, revealing rare glimpses of houses on the far side of the inlet, at one with the overhead clouds. Rebecca walked down to the jetty. She peered into the mist and listened. She could see nothing. She could hear the sway of the ocean and the odd sea bird, but mostly her outlook was void. At this rate, she thought, they'll be another hour. No one ever motored quickly when visibility was low. She returned to the house grabbed a shawl and decided to amble up to the headland she and Samuel had walked to earlier that day.

By six o'clock Rebecca was doing her best to hide her unease. They were overdue by two hours but she knew, as her mother and Esther kept reminding her, they had to take it slowly out there.

'Do you know if Marty's boat had a compass stashed away somewhere?' she asked. She hadn't thought to look earlier. Esther sent Jimmy off to ask. He returned shaking his head.

'Well they're best to sit it out,' said Morna, Rebecca's seventy-year-old mother, who lived with Esther. 'Save their fuel till they can see where they're heading. That fog can be mighty disorientating.'

Rebecca knew that as well. 'I should have gone with them!' she exclaimed in frustration.

The hum of a motorboat chugging into the bay was a very clear and distinct sound. Dogs heard it even before humans. Rebecca, her senses on high alert, was outside after the first faint refrain. It wasn't Samuel. It was one of the local fishermen. She could feel her stomach churning. She could taste the bile at the back of her throat as she fought a wave of nausea. This was being sick with dread. Where was he! Where were they? Over the next hour and a half, as Rebecca paced her sister's stage, boat after boat came crawling home into the bay. Not one of them carrying Samuel and her boys.

At eight o'clock, just as the day was heading towards twilight, Esther's husband, David, turned up with their two eldest sons, Rueben and Thomas. There was no sign of David and Esther's two son-in-laws, who had their own trawler, but they were less perturbed about them. They were on a bigger boat. They were locals, but even so, Samuel had been a lot closer to shore than they had been.

The three men dashed off to dinner while the rest of the adults as well as Anna, Jimmy and Abby feverishly unloaded the boat. The fish would be salted and put away by lantern later. After twenty minutes, Rebecca climbed on board with blankets and coats, sandwiches and flasks of hot tea. David and Reuben followed with kerosene lamps and a spare can of fuel. Everyone else stood anxiously on the stage.

'Can I come?' asked Abby, her hazel eyes pleading.

'Me too,' said Gene.

'No,' said Rebecca shaking her head at them.

Gene started to cry. 'What's going to happen to them?'

'Nothing,' said Rebecca. 'They're just caught in the fog.'

'Will they be all right?' asked Abby, her voice wobbly.

'Yes,' said Morna pulling both girls to her. 'They're just going to be cold and hungry.'

From the boat Rebecca looked across at her two girls. 'Come on, you two,' she said, 'I'm sure your father has turned this into a big adventure for your brothers. You know how he can be. And in a little while, in a few hours hopefully, but perhaps tomorrow morning, when the fog lifts, we'll see them again.'

Both girls stared at their mother. Neither spoke. Rebecca did her best to smile reassuringly at them. That didn't work. She came ashore and crouched in front of them, placing a hand on each of their shoulders. 'I'll tell you one thing about your father. Your brother, Jonathan, knows this story but I don't think we have ever told you

20

younger kids. Way back, when I was a young girl, when I was fourteen in fact, and when your Dad was Thomas' age now, nineteen, he was working for his Uncle Michel. You remember Great Uncle Michel who lives in Montreal?'

'Yes,' they said in unison.

'Well, he was working for Uncle Michel one May doing deliveries to Labrador and Newfoundland. It was 1914 and they had a mishap at sea. Their boat went down but your father managed to jump on board a tiny little dinghy, about the size of the *Salut*, and live on board that dinghy for two weeks until he was rescued. He surprised everyone that he had survived that long at sea by himself.

'So remember that about your father. He's a very brave man, he's experienced and he's a medical man, plus, he knows how to look after himself and his boys. He'll be fine. We're going out to look for him but he'll probably end up powering into port before us and there will be no need for us to rescue him at all.'

'Who rescued him last time?' asked Abby.

'I did,' croaked Rebecca. She swallowed the lump back down.

Morna reached out and squeezed her shoulder. Rebecca inhaled deeply. Then she stood up, hugged her mother, and then both her daughters together, squeezing with all her might. In no time their still figures disappeared in the twilight mist.

All night they searched, up and down the coast. Every ten minutes or so, they would cut the motor and one of them would yell Samuel's name to the still moonless night. There was no wind, which was a mixed blessing. No wind meant it was warmer but damper, though to Rebecca who had gradually acclimatised to Toronto summers, it was bleak and cold and she knew her boys would be finding it likewise. No wind meant they weren't being tossed around on the open sea. But no wind also meant no concession as far as the fog was concerned. It meant their cries to the night sky would be muffled.

21

At around four in the morning it started getting lighter, a creamy white, but no let up from the fog. They decided to head home; perhaps they had missed them, perhaps they had managed to hitch a ride with another fishing boat. Perhaps, perhaps, perhaps.

There was no sign of them back at Esther's. The only news that seemed to ease their return was that the *Salut* was not the only boat missing, lost or befogged at sea. Rebecca had to remind herself that this was not out of the ordinary for where they were. The three of them would be hungry. They would be cold and uncomfortable, but their lives were not necessarily in danger. They could already be on board another boat or in someone's home, high and warm and dry. It was not beyond the bounds of possibility. They could have drifted into a bay somewhere. Samuel could have beached the boat and they could have slept ashore under some fir branches. She needed to think of all those possibilities – those possibilities that held promise.

They were going to try and grab a few hours' kip and head out again. Michael and Selwyn, Esther's sons-in-law, had already motored out having abandoned their fishing for the day. They left at five o'clock to begin searching south of their bay. As tired as she was, Rebecca couldn't sleep. All she wanted to hear was Samuel's voice. A quick phone call, a quick wireless radio message to say where they were and that they were all right. Then, she would happily surrender herself to oblivion.

If she couldn't talk to Samuel, then she was going to talk to the next best thing. On Esther's party line, with the operator helping her to connect, she rang Jonathan, her twenty-one year old son, who lived in Montreal. She didn't know if he would be home but he picked up after four rings. Her heart lifted to hear his voice.

'Hey, Mom,' he said. 'What's up?'

'Well no wind, that's for sure.'

She told him everything and all the while she was speaking to him, every few lines she kept on repeating,

'I'm sure they're fine. I'm sure they're okay.'

'Do you want me to come out?' She could hear the concern in his voice.

'No,' she sighed. 'Well, yes I'd love to see you. Everyone here would love to see you. But no, I'm sure that's not necessary. I'm sure I'll be ringing you back in a few hours telling you we found the sorry bedraggled bunch.'

'Do,' Jonathan urged. 'At once. And if you get no answer, call Uncle Michel. I'm meant to be going there tonight for dinner.'

'I will.'

After Rebecca hung up from Jonathan, she phoned Rachel, four years her senior, the sister she had grown up with.

'Rachel,' she breathed out.

'I know,' Rachel said. The word "know" full of everything. 'Mother phoned last night. No news?'

'None yet.'

'Well, don't worry. They'll be fine. They'll be okay. It's summer remember? And Mother said it was completely still last night.'

'Yes,' said Rebecca, her voice beginning to sound strange to her ears.

'Is it still calm?' asked Rachel.

'Yes.'

'Well don't worry. They won't be in the drink then. They'll be fine. I'm praying for them, I'm praying for you.'

'Thank you,' she said, almost inaudibly.

Around eight o'clock they ventured out again. Newfoundland was serving up its best pea soup; the fog was that impenetrable. Abby and Gene wanted to come with them. Part of her wanted to bring them along with her but she didn't want them looking at her strung-out face all day. Hopefully on shore there would be enough to distract them.

How that day dragged on. How she wished she could

turn off her worrying mind and be calm like the sea and the air around her. Patience! She yelled at herself. This was like those three years in her youth waiting for Samuel to return – but longer, achingly longer!

Just before four o'clock, they felt the first stirring, the slightest sign of a faint breeze from the north, thinning the cloudy veil around them, pushing it back. What a godsend. She breathed a huge sigh of relief. Everyone breathed a sigh of relief. But when the fog parted they still stared into the face of nothingness: greyness all around thanks to a profusion of clouds that the sun failed to pierce. Rebecca was doing her all to control her mounting desperation.

They decided to go to the spot where Rebecca figured the iceberg had been when she circled it with the girls yesterday morning. From there they would go further out to sea. What Rebecca feared most was in the confusion of fog and without a compass they may have motored in the wrong direction. In the midst of the vast ocean they would be far from the sighting of land. Without sun or stars Samuel would be unable get his bearings. If they were near the coast, she felt confident they would make landfall. They could row hugging the coast. They could walk for miles across headlands if they had to. Her nephew-in laws would be scouring the coastline further south where the northern current typically flowed.

After two hours and no sighting of any small boat, she asked, how much fuel they had left? We can manage another few hours, David told her as the sun started to poke through at last and the wind picked up slightly. They were now hampered by thousands of little white tops and the glaring grey late afternoon light that made moving objects more deceptive and much more difficult to detect. She squinted at the horizon. She scanned the flowing waters. She searched near and far, never ceasing despite the hollow pit in her stomach and the pounding ache in her head.

Eventually they were forced to head for home.

24

Thomas, her nephew did his utmost to comfort her. 'Now, Aunty, remember it's quite possible, more than possible, that they will have beaten us home, or Micky and Sel would have picked them up, or maybe they could have decided to hole up in some bay somewhere and camp the night and come home in the morning. Best not fret.'

Rebecca tried her best to smile at him. His voice was full of hope and optimism, like hers had once been. When was that? Oh, with Lenore, her sister-in-law who died of the Spanish Flu in 1919. She shuddered.

Back at Salvage the mystery of Samuel and Morton and Joel's whereabouts was still that. Before she walked into Esther's place, Rebecca took three deep breaths. She looked from her mother's anxious face to her sister's anxious face. She didn't say a word, just shook her head and lowered her eyes. After a few moments she asked how the girls were that day.

'Quiet,' said Esther, 'deathly quiet.' They both tensed at the word. Esther cleared her throat. 'They hardly said boo. Your father-in-law rang though. Mother spoke to him.'

Morna, her voice drawn and croaky said, 'Apparently Jonathan rang Leonard straight after he got off the phone to you this morning. Have a cup of tea dear, something to eat and then you best phone them both back.'

Rebecca nodded, but rather than sit down she went in search of her girls. They were in the living room, each stroking a kitten.

When Gene saw her she jumped to her feet. 'Did you find Daddy?' Her beautiful green blue eyes, so like Rebecca's, were wide and hopeful.

'We think they may have come ashore somewhere and decided to rest there for the night. Hopefully tomorrow we'll find each other.' Did that sound convincing? Positive?

Her girls looked sick with worry. She couldn't bear the sight of their pained expressions. 'Here, come and give your Mommy a hug.' She held out her arms and pressed their faces to her chest and stroked their honey blonde hair.

In the hallway her mother spoke softly. 'Rachel called earlier and she told me to remind you of the lost sailors from Coley Point, back in 1916. Do you remember that story? How a large liner on its way to England picked them up and when they docked they caught another liner back to Newfoundland? They were missing, unheard of for six weeks, but they turned up in the end.'

Rebecca looked at her mother. 'In 1939 we have radios, Mother. They could send a message to us. They would send a message to us.'

'Well, obviously they haven't been picked up by a liner yet,' said Morna, 'but it's not outside the realms of possibility.'

'No,' Rebecca admitted, her voice trailing off.

She went and phoned Uncle Michel. He answered after two rings, his accented animated voice galloping down the line. 'Rebecca, is that you?'

'Yes, Uncle Michel, it's me.'

'Any news?' he asked, almost impatiently.

'No, nothing at all, I'm sorry.'

'Well, just remember,' he said, back to his lively self, 'he was lost at sea last time for two weeks, so two days is nothing to him. Have faith, my girl.'

'Yes,' she said, taking a deep breath. 'I'm trying. Is Jonathan there?'

'No. He caught a plane to Gander this afternoon. I expect you'll see him very soon.'

She nearly swooned when she heard that. The Gander International Airport had only opened in January the year before. What a son! Her heart melted in relief. For a moment she couldn't speak.

'Thank you,' she murmured. 'We'll call you again tomorrow.'

She had barely hung up the phone when it rang – this time, Samuel's father. She nearly broke down when she heard his voice, so similar to Samuel's, so deep and familiar. But something inside her didn't want to surrender to tears. It was as if by surrendering to tears she was admitting their loss, welcoming the inevitability into her heart and she did not want to do that.

'Samuel's a survivor, Rebecca. Remember that. He is the cat with nine lives. And he's got his sons with him. If ever there was an incentive to keep it together then that is it. Try not to worry too much. Be strong. And make sure you look after yourself.'

'Yes,' she drawled.

'You know they could be beached up somewhere and be so exhausted and relieved to be on land that they could have slipped into a coma-like deep sleep. They could have been so out to it this afternoon that no yelling or engine noise would have raised them. There are many explanations.'

'Yes,' she said, remembering how things had been when she had first found Samuel, years before. 'Thank you. I'll call you in the morning.'

'We'll be waiting. We looked into flights today. We think we'll come out anyway because even with Jonathan there, having an extra doctor would be wise.'

Rebecca inhaled. 'Thank you,' she said, 'though I'm sure Samuel wouldn't want to put you through all that, particularly as I'm hoping he'll turn up any minute.'

'Well, we'll just have a little holiday then.' Leonard paused. 'Let's see what tomorrow brings.'

She said goodbye, hung up the phone and rested her hand on the phone box. Outside she could hear the wind blowing. She groaned – to herself and to the heavens. 'Not tonight! Another night. Please!' she pleaded.

Rebecca went upstairs to check on her girls. Her mother was with them praying for God and his angels to look after their father and brothers, to keep them warm and keep them safe. She came down the stairs with a blanket draped around her shoulders like an Indian native. She glanced at Esther.

'I'll be back in a little while, maybe a long while. Don't worry.'

She walked outside. The stars were out, as was the moon, dimming occasionally when masked by an errant cloud. Slowly she made her way up the hill, the hill she and Samuel had raced up so eagerly yesterday morning. She walked to the end of the headland. The wind whipped her flaxen shoulder-length hair across her face. She paid it no heed.

'Tonight let me be the Lady of Succour, let me calm the wind and the sea,' she whispered. 'Fill the night sky and the oceans with silence. Let my voice fly on the wings of a great seagull to the one I love.

'Here I am, Samuel, staring out to sea like I was when I first found you. Staring out to sea like I love. Can you feel me out there calling you home? Can you see the Evening Star? Come back, my husband. Bring my children home to me. Have faith that you will be delivered once again.' She paused.

Taking a deep breath, she carried on, 'We've known each other for twenty-five years, Samuel, but right now twenty-five years feel like twenty-five hours. It is not enough. Nothing is ever enough with you, Samuel. Please come back.'

She waited. She stared out to sea. She didn't cry. She refused to cry. Something inside her told her she couldn't cry. If she cried she would crumble and for the sake of her children she couldn't crumble. She took more deep breaths.

'I don't want to lose you, Samuel. I don't want to lose our boys. Haven't we lost enough you and I? Morton and Joel, can you hear me? Don't be afraid. Don't be cold. Remember Mommy loves you and that love can keep you warm inside. Daddy loves you,' her heart almost crashing on the word 'Daddy' and then the tears came, bitter tears, of senselessness, of helplessness. She tried to keep down the tears, but it was pointless.

She held her head high, looked out to the sea once

more and let everything pour out of her.

'I need to know, Samuel, what now for us? What now for me? What is it that I am meant to do? Is this our farewell, our final farewell? If you can't come back send me a sign please, Samuel. Send me a sign so I know whether to keep the faith or to bow in grace.' She closed her eyes and pressed her lips together. Then with her voice breaking, she continued. 'Were the twenty-five years we had together borrowed years? Is it now time to give you back to the ocean that gave you to me?' In anguish she cried, 'Is this what this is?'

After several silent moments, she half-whimpered, 'If it is, then, oh God, know that I already ache for the day when I can be reunited with you. I ache to wake up in the arms of the one I love.'

Rebecca stayed outside for a very long time. Till the night air numbed her completely. Till the evening star dimmed and vanished and the earth turned. And then she walked back down the hill, back inside to what was left of her family.

4

The call came ten minutes after Jonathan had arrived, ten minutes after midnight. It was, of course, relayed and relayed and relayed and wasn't quite the call Rebecca had been hoping for. A fishing trawler out of Bonavista had picked up a boat matching the description. It had the word *Salut* painted on its portside and a young boy, about seven, eight years old. Rebecca's mind went: That doesn't match the description. 'Could I talk to the boy?' she asked.

'Well YOU could, I suspect. None of the men could get boo out of him. Last we heard the wee mite was out cold. Only drank half a warm toddy. They figure they'll be back at base in an hour or two.'

Rebecca asked more questions while anxious eyes looked at her. She hung up the phone. 'Cape Shore,' she muttered. Then she shuddered. Another few miles and they would have been so far out in the Atlantic no one would ever have found them. How had Morton and the boat ended up so far southeast and where were Samuel and Joel? This was NOT good news. Good news would have been the three of them together. As the search had dragged on and the hours ticked over, part of her had always known that every hour was another sickening spiral towards despair.

Rebecca wondered what sign she had missed. What flash of significance? She was no stranger to mishap and misadventure, nor tragedy. Whenever she had reflected on such occasions, she had come to the gnawing conclusion that usually there had been warning signs – but not always, she admitted despondently – and in that short sleepless night Rebecca replayed the preceding days and weeks in her head. After paying respects to her dead father and honouring their first-born son, Rebecca thought, surely, if ever the gods were smiling down on them, if ever the karmic forces were stacked in their favour, if ever a good wind would blow her way, the time would be now. But her thoughts also leapt to another unpleasant fact…in her blissful state yesterday morning had she tempted fate? The only sign she could recall was the black seal. Was that a dark omen to be heeded? She shivered. The last time she saw a black seal it had been a sign of mystique and, oddly, reassurance.

She wanted to leave immediately in Jonathan's hire car, but David and Esther convinced her it would take hours via the roads. It would be much faster to go by boat. They set out at three, an hour before daybreak, just David, Rebecca and Jonathan in David's trawler. For some time, Rebecca stood looking straight ahead clutching her twenty-one-year-old son's hand. His was a strong hand, a strong body; six foot two. As with all Dalton men, he had matured early. His hair was almost jet-black, like his paternal grandmother's. Rebecca glanced at his profile, at his unshaven face, pensive and brave for her.

They puttered into Bonavista around six o'clock. As soon as the boat bumped the jetty, Rebecca scrambled onto it and ran towards a stranger carrying her draped son towards her.

'Morton,' she cried as she pulled him into her arms, the first of her tears flowing. 'Morton, Mommy's got you, darling. You're safe now. You're all right. Morton, can you hear me?'

He opened his eyes and stared at her.

'Tell me what happened.' Rebecca wiped her cheeks, but the tears kept coming: tears of relief, of something indefinable. 'Tell me what happened.'

His golden eyes widened in panic.

'Morton, we need your help to find Daddy and Joel. We need you to tell us what you know.'

Rebecca heard Morton exhale, she watched him close his eyes and keep them closed. Bewildered, she looked at Jonathan.

'Morton,' Jonathan said, touching his head. 'I need to have a close look at you to make sure you haven't been hurt at all.' The boy risked a glance at his older brother.

'Come, we'll set you down on that bench over there.' They pulled away the blanket and both Rebecca and Jonathan ran their fingers and eyes over his body. He was unmarked and unmoving, his clothes damp and salty.

Jonathan crouched down so his eyes were on the same level as Morton's. He reached out and held his little hand. 'Listen, bud, we don't know what's happened but we know you've been through some ordeal. And we want to help you put that behind you but before we do that we have to do our all to find Dad and Joel and you're the only one who can help us with that.'

Morton lowered his eyes and stared at their clasped hands.

'You've got to help us a bit here, Morton. Please nod to let me know you hear what I'm saying and you understand. Squeeze my hand.' His tawny eyes – his father's eyes – darted towards Rebecca and back again.

Rebecca inhaled. Whatever has happened, he can't look at me. She stroked his face. 'Morton, darling, you've been through so much, I can tell. It's taken a lot out of you, but can you find a little bit more strength inside you to help us, to help Daddy and Joel?'

He flinched and tried to pull his face away from Rebecca's hand. 'Okay,' she exhaled. 'I'm going to go in and talk to the men who found you. Jonathan will stay here. You can talk to him if you like.'

Out of the corner of her eye, she saw Morton release his brother's hand. She saw him shy away from Jonathan as well. Rebecca's mind had conjured up many terrible things in the past two days, which she had forcefully pushed away, but she had never imagined this. She went in search of answers.

Bobby Turner was the man who found Morton. Fortunately Bobby had seen Morton, because it was unlikely Morton would have ever seen Bobby. 'He had his back to us trying to paddle the boat like a Canadian canoe.' he said. 'That's what caught our attention – it was so unusual. We slowed the ship while we lowered the tender down. When I came alongside he was crying and shaking uncontrollably and he had a cake tin clamped between his knees, as if he wasn't letting go of it for dear life. He didn't. Straight away he crawled across into the dory, and brought his tin with him, hunched over it, just rocked backwards and forwards, crying, saying nothing but what sounded like a string of da-da-da-da-da-da-da-da-da-da. And I'm afraid no matter what we said or did we couldn't get anything else out of him.'

David was looking over the *Salut* when Rebecca found him. It was missing its motor, the wood splintered where it should have been.

'That explains something,' she said quietly.

'Yes,' said David. 'But how? When? And how did only Morton end up in the boat?'

'No,' said Rebecca, her voice breaking. 'The question is: where are Samuel and Joel?'

They made preparations to go to the tip of the Bonavista isthmus and search every bay between the point and the port of Bonavista but Morton wasn't having a bar of it. He thrashed himself out of Rebecca's arms, fell onto the wooden wharf and started running in the opposite direction. She caught him but barely managed to hold him as he tried to pull himself away once more. Softly she said, 'We have to continue the search, Morton,' at which point he started trembling and keening inside his throat as if he were screaming No!

Bobby, who had witnessed the entire distressing scene, came up to her. 'Take him home. He needs to be on terra firma for a while, in bed. I'll organise a boat and some men to search the bays.'

'I'll go with them,' said Rebecca.

'No, Mom,' said Jonathan, his dark brown eyes insistent. 'Bobby's men can search just as well without you on board. You need to be with Morton. I'll go if you want.'

In the end Bobby convinced them all to go back to Salvage. He would phone as soon as the crew returned – whatever the outcome.

Even then Morton did not want to put one foot on his uncle's trawler, his terror and anger amplifying his energy and determination. No encouragement or bribery on the part of his mother or uncle seemed to have any impact. Finally, Jonathan was able to placate him.

'If you went to sleep here on land, Morton, and woke up in bed at Aunty Esther's would that be okay? Otherwise, by the time we get the car round here and back to Salvage, it's going to take us two days to get you home.' Morton thought about that for more than a minute before nodding tentatively. With Rebecca's encouragement and promise not to let go of him, he submitted himself to the mystery of his brother's medicine bag.

5

Back in Salvage Rebecca did the only thing she could do in her situation. Years later with the benefit of calmness and clarity, she knew she could have acted differently but what she did at that time was this: she marched back into her sister's house adamant and revived and oblivious to sidelong glances as she said, 'We've found Morton. Now we've just got to find Samuel and Joel.' And nothing anyone would say or do would sway her.

With funds wired from Leonard they hired fishermen to help with their search up and down the coast, in every bay, in every inlet, telegraphing near and far. Rebecca could not see her own state of denial. Whether it was to give her girls something to hope for still, whether it was because she saw Morton as Samuel's sign, or whether it was because she had another deadline, one that she could not let go until she'd crossed it: Samuel's surviving two weeks by himself at sea in a small boat. He could do it again and longer, was her argument.

'Yes, but he had a boat back then,' was everyone else's argument, everyone bar her in-laws who silently supported her. They too had faith. Leonard and Lottie had arrived in a wave of vivacity and determination two days after they found Morton.

'That's right,' said Rebecca, not losing her stride. 'But they're on land somewhere this time, somewhere remote. And he is sick or injured, that I am sure of. That is why he sent Morton off by himself.' And that is what she told herself, convinced herself. 'That is why the boat is missing the motor. Samuel took it off so Morton wouldn't have to pull that weight through the water.' It made perfect sense to her.

'Why didn't he send Joel as well?' they countered.

'Because he needed Joel with him...to fetch water...to help him. I don't know!'

Jonathan stared at her shaking his head. The rest of her relatives could barely raise their eyes to her. Am I the only one with hope she thought? She didn't voice that question less they reply with a resounding YES. 'Jonathan, listen to me, believe me, trust me. Your father had such great faith in things turning out. He would have let Morton go because he believed it was his best option.'

Jonathan sighed heavily. 'I know you know Dad better than all of us but I'm sorry I don't see that. I wish I could, but I can't. I'd find it easier to believe if we knew for a fact the last time Morton saw Dad and Joel was on land, but we don't.'

On advice and warning from Leonard and Jonathan, Rebecca and everyone had been doing their best not to pressure Morton, though Rebecca had done her damnedest to coax information out of him. Infuriatingly, he remained silent, his eyes downcast. It was all she could do not to yell at him or throttle him. Three days after they collected him, with utmost restraint, she went to her son, knelt in front of him and with tears brimming over her lids, her voice catching, she whispered, 'Morton, darling, please, please, please tell Mommy, where did you last see your father and Joel? In the ocean or on land?'

He shook his head. His little face became white and sad. His eyes watered.

'Come on, darling, you can spit it out. Tell me.'

Morton closed his eyes as tears seeped out the corner.

'I can see you're upset, Morton, and I don't want you to be upset. I'm sure once you tell me you'll feel better. Tell me what happened.'

He cringed and clamped up further if that were possible.

'Please, Morton, it upsets Mommy to see you this way. Help me, help us help you!'

He cried in his throat until Jonathan pulled her away.

'Stop it, Mother.' She stopped for now. Later that day, in a brief instance of clarity, she realised that had been the one and only time Morton had tears in his eyes. She wondered if this was a breakthrough of sorts and if she should persevere.

'Jonathan, do you think it's odd that Morton hasn't cried around any of us?'

'He's cried a lot already. Remember what that man Bobby said?'

'It's as if he thinks he's done something bad and he's feeling guilty about it. Or is he angry with his father? Or at Joel for whatever has happened and he can't bring himself to speak of it.'

'It could be any of those possibilities or none. But the glaringly obvious is he's using every ounce of his being trying to not think about what happened, trying to not feel anything about what's happened, trying not to speak to anyone about what's happened.'

'And what is it exactly that's happened!' Rebecca yelled in anguish thrusting her hands out in exasperation. 'We don't know what's happened! This is what gets me, Jonathan. Morton might not even know what's happened. He knows some of what's happened and he's not talking. But he doesn't know all of what's happened as he's no longer with them!'

'And that is the blessing we have to take away from this.'

'Why are you so quick to give them up for dead? What do you think has happened to them?'

'Mother, if I had any sound theories I'd tell you, but I don't. Every possibility I work through has them missing and together, found and together. Not this.'

'Why couldn't your father and Joel be onshore somewhere, waiting for us to come rescue them? You're right. Something has happened to them. And I think they needed Morton to go and get help. And he feels he didn't do that, or didn't do that in time, or he can't remember where they were. There's so much torment tied up in his

37

grief, but if only he would open his mouth and tell us then we would know where to go and search for them. Instead we're trying to hunt down a needle in a godforsaken haystack.'

Rebecca was pacing along the stage at her sister's place. Jonathan was beside her. She didn't know how either of them got there. Last thing she remembered they had been inside sitting at Esther's table. She spun around and could see Lottie and Leonard in the distance walking with Abby, Morton and Gene along the headland. She spun round again, back to Jonathan.

'Mother,' said Jonathan quietly. "Stop and listen for a minute.'

She kept pacing.

'We need to give up the search,' he implored.

She didn't halt for a second.

'As much as I'd like for that to be true, for Dad and Joel to be holed up somewhere on land, I know and you know in your heart of hearts, that is not the case. Dad would never ever send Morton on an escapade like that and I use the word escapade deliberately. He would keep them together, as would any responsible adult, as would you. That's not what's happened. And besides, if that had happened, you can bet your bottom dollar Morton would be screaming for help before he was found.'

'You don't know that. He was in shock.'

'Granted, he was in shock but I've seen enough. I know enough.'

Rebecca half-turned away, wanting to dismiss Jonathan and the words he was saying. But his hands gripped her forearms forcing her back. 'Mom, I don't want to argue with you at a time like this. Listen to me,' he pleaded.

Her eyes quivered as she looked at him. His were secreting anguish and torment or were those her emotions mirrored in his?

'He would tell you if he could.'

On 12th August 1939, after three weeks of searching and no trace, the Dalton family – minus one father and one son – returned to Toronto.

As they left Newfoundland could Rebecca somehow manage to say goodbye to Joel, her beloved baby boy? Could she surrender him into God's hands? Could she whisper, 'Go in peace, Samuel. Go swim with our children. Look after our boys. Find Samson and Henry and be a family together and know one day I will join you once more'?

No, she couldn't.

6

Occasionally Rebecca is aware of people whispering around her. Or are they talking the same but she hears them less?

Did she eat today? Did the children have dinner? Was that Addie who handed her a cup of tea? Addie had been like an aunt to Rebecca ever since she first arrived in Toronto twenty-two years ago. Is it late afternoon or early morning?

She wakes up groggy every day, partly due to the tranquilizers that put her to sleep, partly just her. As she comes to, staring at the ceiling, the first thing she asks herself is, 'Where am I?' As her mind slowly pulls the answer together – in your home, in your bed, in your and Samuel's bed – she is sledgehammered with the realisation that Samuel is no longer with her. Samuel is gone! Joel is gone! But before she lets herself feel that brutal force of fact, she takes a flight of fancy. That's right, they have gone away, but they will be back one day.

And in this measure she keeps the pulsing pain at bay, wraps it in a thick membrane of numbness, of suspension, so she doesn't let herself feel it, but in coping this way she doesn't feel anything. She doesn't feel Abby brushing her hair or wiping her face with a flannel. She doesn't feel her children not crawl on her lap anymore or nestle up to her. She doesn't feel the wind blowing the autumn leaves to the ground. She doesn't feel anything; she doesn't taste anything; she doesn't smell anything; she doesn't see anything. She becomes mute like Morton and no longer notices his muteness.

Around the edge of her numbness is another tormenting thought: Newfoundland, that damned

Newfoundland, those damned Notre Dame Waters. They have taken my husband and another one of our sons. And mingled with that is a deep sense of self-loathing, of flagellation, of self-blame. If it weren't for her and her fascination with icebergs, Rebecca wouldn't be living this untenable life. And there she comes unstuck for she knows if it weren't for icebergs she wouldn't have this life to begin with.

Occasionally, the odd squeal, a child screaming, permeates her subdued haze.

'No! You can't leave us!'

'I have to go back to my studies, Gene, to Montreal. I'll be back in a month or so. I promise.'

'I don't want you to go!'

'I know,' Jonathan speaks softly, tenderly.

'We'll be here to look after you and help Mommy,' says Lottie, Gene's nana.

'I want Jonathan to look after me,' the child hiccups.

'I know you do, pet, and I'm sure he would want to look after you too, but he has to go back to Montreal for a little while.'

'I'll come with you, Jonathan. Take me to Montreal with you,' she pleads. 'Take me to Montreal with you!' she demands.

'Gene, listen, I have to go to the hospital every day, and next week you will be going to school every day.'

'I don't want to go to school every day. I want to go to hospital every day with you!'

'I'm sorry but you can't.'

And the child is screaming again, wailing and Rebecca can't bear it. She opens her mouth to speak – what, she doesn't know – but before she can muster a word Jonathan snatches up his youngest sister, the squirming raucous tyke, and carries her out the door.

7

All summer, in fact all year, Gene had been looking forward to going to school and turning six. She'd been looking forward to saying to Joel, her four-year-old brother, 'Ha, ha. I'm a big girl now. I go to school,' and seeing what he had to say to that. For her youngest brother, sometimes much to her annoyance, at other times, to her immense amusement, had a smart answer for everything. That was until now. Now she just wanted him by her side. She would gladly stay back from school another year, and another, till he was older and they could start together. Part of her was lost without her baby brother. With his loud fast ways, he was the centre of her world, of everyone's world, except maybe Abby's.

Abby was thirteen and starting her first year at High School. She could have been thirty she was so grown-up. She was in a different world, her own world, when she wasn't with Nana. Abby sometimes acted as if she had a special claim on their nana. Gene could never understand why.

Her grandparents were trying to excite Gene about starting school by saying, 'Abby's going to a new school and so are you.' But it didn't wash with her. Morton wasn't going to school. He was meant to be going into grade four this year, but she'd heard one of the grown-ups say, 'I don't think he's ready to go back to school just yet.'

She heard her nana ask her grandad how long he thought Morton would remain mute.

'He could be mute for months, years.' Her grandad looked unbearably sad. 'Some people never speak again.'

'Never?' Her nana's voice was raised in alarm. 'But it's

not as if he's suddenly lost the ability to speak. He can still physically talk, can't he?'

'He can, yes. But over time if the vocal chords don't get exercised, he may lose some ability. He won't forget words, so keep on talking to him, keep on reading to him. It's important not to ignore him. I think the more we ignore him, the more we are telling him it's okay for him to crawl into his cave.'

Gene wondered what cave they were talking about, but she didn't ask.

Morton sat in silence, his eyes not meeting anyone's, his face downcast while his feet traced invisible patterns on the floor. Grandad would seek him out, ask his help with something or other and Morton would meekly follow. He'd hold a basket that they might put cut herbs into, bring the mail in, go for a drive in their grandfather's car. Some days he'd help him with something in the basement.

Since they had returned that was how they had paired up: Abby with Nana, Morton with Grandad, she with Jonathan. The mother who had come back with them from Newfoundland wasn't her real mother. Her real mother was still back there, with Aunty Esther and Uncle David, on a boat somewhere, looking for their father. She knew that for a fact for this stranger hadn't spoken to her since they'd come home.

Only Jonathan remained the same, unchanged. He was her eldest brother, her much older brother, her favourite canoe companion, her favourite bedtime reader, her favourite tree climber, her favourite everything. Now he was leaving and she would be left with no one, and she couldn't seem to make him or anyone else understand how badly she needed to be with him.

She tried to entice Morton in a game of hopscotch, in quoits, in snakes and ladders. She'd come up to him, stand about two feet away and speak softly to him, almost in a whisper. He'd half raise his head in acknowledgement then shake it, slightly, pulling his mouth in and down at the corners. No, no joy there, no play, no change.

Under sufferance she went to school. Some days she joined in games, skipped or played on the swings, but more often than not she stood to the side and just watched. She was at school how Morton was at home: distanced from everyone. She rarely laughed. She didn't think it was right to laugh. No one in her family laughed any more.

The only thing that brought joy to her day was the five-minute phone call she was allowed to place every night at seven o'clock to Jonathan in Montreal. And he was always there, waiting for her call. She'd stopped pleading with him to take her to Montreal. He'd told her that he already knew that without her having to say it and they needed to spend their precious five minutes talking about other things. But that did not stop her wanting to be with her brother.

One day when she came home from school, her mother was up, ambling blithely around the kitchen, making herself a cup of tea. That was new. Nana Dalton was there as well. Nana Dalton was always there, a beacon in their blighted lives. She'd prepare dinner for them, eat with them, some days their grandfather would show up for dinner as well, and then they'd leave after they went to bed. That day Gene stared at her mother, trying to detect if anything else was new. Gene said hello. She got a bland hello in reply and a flicker of a glance. From her grandmother, she got a: 'And how was school today, young lady?' She always got that from her nana.

Later, as she was leaving the kitchen after her milk and biscuit, she heard her mother say in a strangled voice, 'Lottie, how do you learn to live again once you've lost what is most precious and dear? When the man of your life is gone? When you can't replace the baby you've lost? With the others I always held onto the hope that one day I would be blessed with another one, but not this time.'

Nana looked down at her hands searching for the answer. 'I don't know, Rebecca. I don't know. But people

44

do. Somehow they go on and they live and laugh again. We did, after Matthew and Lenore died. We had to. At the time you don't think you ever will, but you do. I think Jonathan and you were our salvation back then.'

'We're not your salvation now.'

Her nana tried to invoke an optimistic smile. 'The young ones will be, can be, ...' She took a ragged breath. 'Losing one son was devastating, heart-breaking. Losing two is ...' Her nana was lost for words. 'I can't begin to tell you.' She paused and her face seemed to twist in sympathy. Her voice cracked. 'I don't need to tell you.'

Gene watched her mother hang her head and cry. She watched her nana fold her arms around her. Slowly, she walked backwards out of the room.

Towards the end of fall, as the days fade and pale, Jonathan returns and Gene doesn't let him out of her sight. She waits for him patiently outside the bathroom. She sleeps on a mattress at the foot of his bed. She smiles for her brother and he smiles for her. He tickles her. He cuddles her. He plays with her. Then one morning he says to her, 'I have to go back to Montreal today,' and she is beyond miserable all over again. She rails at the injustice of the situation until in an exhausted breather of a moment she has a brainwave and disappears.

Half an hour later she walks into his room with her holiday portmanteau packed full of winter clothes, her anorak draped over the handle. 'I'm ready to leave whenever you are,' she says matter-of-factly, convinced there will be no stopping her this time.

With a heavy sigh, Jonathan takes her by the hand and leads her towards their mother's bedroom. 'Mom,' he says as they walk in, and Gene thinks: this is a waste of time Jonathan. You'll be lucky to get boo out of her.

'Huh,' a dazed voice mumbles. Jonathan walks over and pulls the curtains, not all the way, but halfway to let in some daylight.

'Mom,' he says again. 'I'm going to transfer to the

Toronto General Hospital to make it easier on everyone.'

Gene is stunned but before she can change gears into excitement, her mother says, 'No, Jonathan.' In a moment of lucidity, she adds, 'you've only got eight months to go. Stay put. We'll manage.'

'Mom, if I stay put, it will be for a few years, I need to work on lining up my residency this year. If I'm going to make a change, now's the time. Really, I should have changed back in August. I see that now. I wasn't thinking clearly.'

'Who was?' mutters their mother.

'I'll be able to get special dispensation under the circumstances and I'm thinking – hoping – that maybe my coming back to Toronto will help everyone get on their feet. Maybe if we get on with being a family, Morton will join us again.'

'Yes. Oh, yes please,' says Gene, clapping her hands together. She can't help herself.

'So, Gene,' he says glancing at her, 'you can unpack your suitcase. I'll be back again soon.' He turns to walk out the door.

'Wait, Jonathan,' their mother calls after him. 'Give me some time to think about this.'

'What for, Mom? I mean, really, I don't need your permission, unless you don't want me to live at home anymore.'

An hour later – much to Gene's surprise – their mother appears downstairs, freshly showered, clasping her handbag. 'I'm popping out for an hour. I won't be long.' She returns before lunch, with Nana and Grandad Dalton following in their car.

For the first time in months their mother speaks during lunch.

'Jonathan is thinking of transferring from Montreal to a university and hospital here in Toronto to finish his degree and do his residency. He thinks it's important that we come together as a family at this point so we can...'

she swallows, '...be more like a family again. What do you think about that?'

'Yes,' yells Gene. 'I think it's great!'

'Aha,' says Abby, not particularly phased either way.

Silence and glances from Morton.

'Morton, would you like to be closer to your brother?' asks Grandad. Gene holds her breath, wondering whether Morton will nod or shake. Once upon a time Morton used to idolise Jonathan as well. But with everyone he is now distant.

After about half a minute, he gives a faint half nod and flashes a look towards his brother and grandad.

'Good,' says Jonathan. 'That's settled then.'

'Not so fast,' says their mother. She clears her throat. 'There's another option we should consider. Perhaps our family could move to Montreal for a few years.'

Gene's head snaps towards her mother, as does Morton's. Abby gasps.

'Mother!' Jonathan's voice is full of reproach.

'Now, Abby,' says their mother, 'your grandparents and I want to tell you that if we were to move to Montreal, you are welcome to stay here in Toronto and live with them if you would prefer.'

'Why are you doing this?' asks Jonathan, almost in exasperation.

'Because, I don't want you to throw your medical career away. Your father wouldn't have wanted that.'

'She's right,' says Grandad.

'I don't want you to have this burden on your shoulders,' continues their mother, 'You have done more for me, for our family than you can possibly know and now it's time for me to do what I can for you.'

'What do you mean?'

Gene notices that her mother falters. She licks her lips. She sighs. 'Where to begin...'

But then Grandad Dalton speaks. "Jonathan. You helped us – all of us – in our hour of need twenty-one years ago. You may not be conscious of that but you did.'

'That's right,' says Nana.

'What you have offered today is appreciated, but it's not necessary,' says Jonathan.

'What's more necessary,' argues their mother, 'is that we leave this house. It's not the same without your father and Joel. It never will be. So let's start anew somewhere else.'

8

Within three months they had sold the house and bought a new one in Montreal, about twenty minutes walk from the home of Uncle Michel, Lottie's brother. Jonathan moved in. They went to midnight mass on Christmas Eve in Notre Dame Cathedral – Rebecca could not help but recall the first time Samuel had taken her there – and prayed for the souls of their father and brother, Joel. Leonard and Lottie came for Christmas and took Abigail home with them to Toronto; she deciding that was where she wanted to be for the time being.

On the 6th of January 1941, Rebecca walked Gene and Morton to the Nesbitt Elementary School where they were enrolled. After ten short minutes, a school administrator took Morton and Gene off to their respective classes. Rebecca was not invited nor did she ask to meet their teachers, see the classroom or have a tour of the facilities. She doubted she would have been able to muster any sort of interest had she been asked.

What she had, had been used up on the decision to move to Montreal, packing up and unpacking. She had entrusted Uncle Michel completely with the purchase of a suitable home and he had chosen well. Their new home was a three-storey brick duplex opposite a leafy park and not far from the river, the Latin Quarter and family. She had entrusted her father-in-law completely with the sale of their old home and he had sold well. She had not trusted herself with looking at any of Samuel or Joel's effects. Addie and Jerome, Samuel's second parents, the Dalton's closest friends, had boxed them up and taken them away. To where, she did not ask.

As fall parried with winter, Rebecca could barely

comprehend where she got the impetus to move through those one hundred days of living in Toronto and then shifting cities, the front she put up for her children, for Leonard and Lottie, the impression that she was on the up and could manage things with a new start – the extraordinary effort that cost her each day. Yet deep down inside she knew. It was the promise of being able to continue to mourn under the watchful gaze of no one: her children at school, her eldest at the hospital for twelve-hour blocks, her house to herself with hardly anyone she knew to call in and see how she was getting on. That was her motivation.

In Montreal she moves into a different stage, an automatic stage. Her days become clearly delineated. As Jonathan leaves for the hospital in the dark, always in the dark, forever in the dark, she rises to make breakfast and lunches and help the children get ready for school. And then she does nothing, absolutely nothing all morning. She takes the phone off the hook. She doesn't eat lunch. She doesn't pour herself a cup of tea or coffee. She doesn't snack on a biscuit or munch on an apple. Winter is permanent, inside and out. The days are long and dark and dismal. The ice cold invades everything, yet Rebecca seems almost oblivious to the season's bite, for she is hibernating. Or is she floating. At times she feels weightless, unmoored and naked without the lively thirty-pound boy she used to pick up and carry, hold to her front, her hip, her back, whenever he would let her. He never let her enough.

Around two she makes a move on afternoon tea, on dinner. She walks through dirty snow-cleared paths to the grocer, to the butcher, to the baker and back home, past trees that too seem beyond life. Then when the children are in the house she starts on the chores: the laundry, the ironing, the sweeping, the cleaning, working through to about ten each evening, stopping to have a hot cocoa with Jonathan before she puts herself to bed.

And what does she do between the hours of nine a.m. and two p.m.? Some days she goes back to bed. Some days she has a bath. Mostly she sits in a chair and stares out the window, oblivious to the happenings going on outside, just stares into the face of nothingness. And becomes a living monument to Duke Ellington's *Solitude*, except there is no music.

9

Unbeknownst to Rebecca a lot was happening outside in the world of nothingness.

Across the globe, Japan, Italy and Germany were waging war: in China, in North Africa, the Mediterranean, the Middle East, Continental Europe and Scandinavia. And although William King, the Canadian Prime Minister, had been able to secure a deal that kept large number of Canadians directly out of the war, the war industry in Canada was turning the nation into an economic powerhouse, hoisting it out of the depression of the 1930s.

The British Commonwealth Air Training Plan was turning wheat farms in Saskatchewan and Manitoba into hangars and runways; valleys in Alberta and British Columbia into tarmacs and fly-zones; and young Canadian men, along with others from the Commonwealth, into pilots, navigators, bomb aimers, wireless operators, air gunners, and flight engineers. Service industries were springing up around 230 new airfields across the country. An aircraft construction industry was flourishing. Factories in Nova Scotia and Ontario were turning out Fleet Finches, Avro Ansons and Cessna Cranes. They were making Lancasters and Mosquito bombers.

Ford and General Motors of Canada were pooling their engineering design teams to make hundreds of thousands of Canadian Military Pattern (CMP) trucks and army personnel cars, supplying half the British Army's transport requirements. Canadian shipyards launched naval ships, destroyers, frigates, corvettes, and other merchant vessels to protect the shipping lanes of the

North Atlantic. And where did all this material come from? From Canada's metals industries: from aluminum smelters and nickel mines. And where did all the food come from – for Canada, for Commonwealth military personnel, for Mother England? From Canada.

And while this frenetic, chaotic activity was happening all over Canada, something vastly different was happening in practically every classroom, in every province throughout the nation: a distinct shortage of men, a distinct shortage of teachers, overcrowding of classrooms, and substandard methods of education.

Had Rebecca escorted her children to their classrooms on the day of their enrolment, or paid a return visit, she would have discovered that the classrooms were packed like cattle carts. Every two-seated school desk was shared by three children, sometimes four or five. In Morton's class, a small stool was positioned on the narrow side of a desk, where he sat, his back to the window, his right side to the front of the room, next to a girl with freckles and red hair called Desleigh. He barely placed his slate on the desk, perching it mostly on his knee. He didn't want to be there. The only saving grace was that the schoolteacher, a Miss Atkinson, knew not to pressure him to answer any question. He had heard the lady who brought him into the room, say, 'He's not deaf but he's dumb. You know. Can't speak. Good luck.'

In Gene's classroom, the children were cramped on bench stools, jabbing each other with their elbows, sniffling in each other's ears and whispering in low voices if they dared, for their teacher, Mr. Archerfield was the most irritable and hostile man Gene had ever encountered in her short life. He would write letters and words and sentences on the blackboard and make them copy them down word for word. In his anger he would press so hard on the chalk that he kept on breaking it and as the pieces got smaller and smaller and he could barely write with what was left, he would turn around and hurl the offending chalk stub at the back of the classroom.

At other times, if someone were whispering – nine times out of ten to check an answer – he would hurl the chalk at the likely offender and tell them to, 'Shut your gob, Germaine Clarke." "Desist, Louise Du Bois, or it will be the strap next time." Gene had never heard of, let alone seen, someone be hit with a belt till she entered Mr. Archerfield's classroom.

At random he would ask a child what a particular letter was – was it a vowel, or a consonant. There was a boy, Alain, who always got his Bs and Ds back to front. Instead of saying big he would say dig; bug became dug. And then one day Mr. Archerfield wrote the word dog on the board and turning to Alain said, 'It's not bog, Alain, what is it?' Some children snickered.

Alain's lips moved trying out different words till he stammered, 'God,' as his hopeful response. Gene cringed. She would cringe every time he asked Alain a question. She was grateful that until the summer before last, her mother and father had read to her every night, as Jonathan continued to do. Except now she read to Jonathan. Alexander Beetle, A. A. Milne's Winnie the Pooh. It delighted her immensely that Winnie was named after a bear that had come from Winnipeg in Canada. She was grateful she knew her letters and the difference between a vowel and a consonant, that she understood subjects and doing words, singular and plurals. Mostly she was grateful that she could tell when it was three-thirty every afternoon and time for the bell to ring for them to leave. But even so, Gene lived in fear of Mr. Archerfield.

If a student didn't know an answer to a question he would take them out to the front of the class, pulling them by the ear. He'd ask the question again and if they got it wrong he'd scribble the answer on the board. Then he'd proceed to underscore it numerous times before forcing their face into the blackboard. With their eyes so close to the smudgy letters in front of them the words would become blurred and fuzzy. Then he'd practically throw them back to their seat, so violent was the manner in which he pushed them away.

One day a small, quiet boy was so terrified he peed his pants in front of the class unbeknownst to Mr. Archerfield but embarrassingly obvious to himself and everyone else. With his hands he tried to cover the damp patch spreading rapidly across his trousers. But his hands weren't big enough. Gene was mortified. Pierre Beauchamp became Pissier Beauchamp from that day on and though he may have been the first boy to do that, to Gene's horror and dismay he wasn't the last.

Through personal experience Gene knew that she, and nearly every other child, mostly knew the answers to the questions he posed. They simply became so scared about saying the wrong answer that they panicked and then, whoosh, everything flew out of their head in fear. Gene knew: once he said your name, as if by black magic, you lost the ability to concentrate. Your name on his lips became a curse.

No one could understand what he or she did to antagonise him – aside from getting the answers wrong. He simply was the angriest teacher. As if he was there under sufferance and so were they. One day in the middle of one of his tirades he barked at them, "The Germans made my life a misery once and now they are making it a misery a second time." He stared accusingly as if they were the enemy.

At other times he would break off in the middle of a sentence, close his eyes and rub his temples with both hands. His face would seem to go redder and redder and then he would reach for the bottle of Bromo-Seltzer on his desk, open the lid and throw some powder down his throat and then gulp down a whole glass of water. Then he'd make one of the children go off and get him another glass of water, ready for the next time, a few hours down the line. Heaven help the child who came back with a half-empty glass of water.

How Gene got through that first year of school in Montreal she would never know. Some days she couldn't bear the thought and would plead a pain in the stomach, a sore throat or a toothache. From her mother she'd often get, 'How bad is this ache, Gene? Bad enough to keep you away from school?' Her mother would place her hand on her forehead and say, 'Doesn't seem like you have a temperature.' She'd make her take some medicine – sometimes much worse than the supposed symptoms of the faux illness – and say, 'That should do the trick. Off to school and if it's still bad when you come home, Jonathan will take a look at you.'

Where was refuge to come from? She distinctly felt she wasn't welcome at home. Her attempts at skipping school, her fake maladies were compounded by the fact that by the time she came home from school she would be so starving because most of the day she had been too sick with nerves to eat a bite. At home in the afternoons she would start to relax, her stomach unclench, and sometimes in those easing moments she would remember Joel and her father and think of what might have been, only briefly, because that would make her stomach clench in a whole other way.

One evening Jonathan asked how she was finding school. She wanted to say, 'It's terrible. I hate it! I want to go back to my old school.' But how could she say that? She was the reason they had moved to Montreal in the first place. And, besides, if she went back to Toronto she'd have to say goodbye to Jonathan.

She said, 'I'm not sure.'

Jonathan asked, 'Have you made any friends?'

'I'm not sure. Maybe,' she offered, raising her shoulders in question.

'Give it time,' he said, pulling her into his arms. She wished she could spend all her time in Jonathan's arms.

As spring came Morton began to thaw as well. He didn't speak but he was more relaxed. He started playing games with her! His face became more animated. He'd even smile occasionally when he and Gene were nestled up against Jonathan's chest seated on the sofa, Jonathan stroking their heads, telling them something funny about his day, about a patient who was called Miles Long, another one who was called Slim Chance, Justin Case, Turner Corner, Iva Pickle. Their mother continued to move through life, her interest in their life lukewarm at best.

Gene was adjusting slowly to the ups and downs of her new life because she knew that come summer the downs would be done with. No more Mr. Archerfield. But when she started back at school in September the unthinkable had happened. Mr. Archerfield had moved class with them! She was devastated. And Gene knew about devastation. Losing her father and Joel had been devastating, a devastation that had diminished only marginally over the passing year as she had gradually come to accept that they were never coming back. She missed her young brother. She missed her father. He was like a king. He was strong and handsome, energetic and wise. He made her mother come alive. She didn't know it at the time, but now she saw and understood. Her mother had withered without her father.

Over the summer holidays she was worse than normal if that were possible. Morton and Gene spent most of their break with their grandparents and Abby in Toronto while their mother stayed home in Montreal. Since their return it was Jonathan who got them dinner every night. He'd come home at five o'clock and head off again around seven-thirty to do more rounds. It was Jonathan who took the call from Toronto every night, from their sister and grandparents. It was Gene who helped Jonathan peel the vegetables while their mother was lying down. Gene didn't think to question this change of household duties. She was more than happy to help Jonathan in the kitchen. Her mother was still in her life but on the periphery. Gene didn't have her father in her life anymore but she knew she had the next best thing. Jonathan! And with both men she had felt abundantly loved, abundantly safe, abundantly sure. With Mr.

Archerfield she was abundantly petrified and abundantly paralysed to do anything about it.

In the fall of 1940, her second year at Nesbitt, Gene contemplated skipping school. The idea pulled at her every day as she walked towards the school gates. 'Keep walking' it pounded inside her head. 'Keep walking,' the wind whispered to her as it whipped around her, blowing dead leaves in her path. What swayed her mind in the end was the fear of being questioned on something she would most likely miss if she were absent and then being persecuted for not knowing the answer.

She became a child who was nervous and on edge, thin and drawn, fastidious in her appearance, diligent with her homework, organised beyond her years, planning ahead for nearly any emergency. She was on high alert for imminent danger. Perhaps had she been prone to weeping and despair, Jonathan might have twigged that something was amiss, but as the only joyful part of Gene's day was dinner with Jonathan, he was none the wiser. And of late she was so tired that once she'd eaten dinner she'd often quietly take herself off to bed, collapsing as soon as she slid between the sheets. Could those who loved her most not see her wasting away?

They didn't see other things either. Like the double-headed carbuncle that came up on her lower back. Gene was vaguely aware of something rubbing the elastic of her underpants...or was it the other way round? But as young children often do, she never gave it a second thought. She was fast becoming gifted in suppressing her worries and trying to work a way around her own problems.

Then one day at school after Christmas, after New Year – the shortest reprieve – in the crevasse of bitter winter she was asked how the three 'theres' were spelt and what their meanings were. She could only think of two: 'there' and 'their'. She spelt and explained them. The third one escaped her. Mr. Archerfield asked, 'Does anyone want to help Gene with the third one?' No one answered lest they got it wrong.

'Come here, you tiresome child,' he spat at her.

Against her better judgment Gene walked slowly to the front of the classroom, her eyes downcast.

'Have you been sleeping in my class?' he asked her.

'No, sir,' she said.

'Well clearly you have, because we went through contractions only two weeks ago And you've either not taken it in you numbskull or you were sleeping on my watch. How many times do I have to repeat myself to you brats? Do I have to beat it into your head every time?' He poked her head six times as he said the last sentence, beating out his frustration.

All Gene could think was: what contractions? I don't remember any contractions. I don't remember ever hearing the word before. What happened a fortnight ago? Gene tried to think back...she remembered for several days their mother had not appeared at breakfast which was not so unusual: some days she did, some days she didn't. She and Morton had had their cereal with milk. Jonathan had left earlier. But then on this particular day they discovered there was no bread to make their lunches. There was butter and jam, relish and cheese. There were potatoes and pumpkin in the larder. There was flour even but that didn't help much.

She and Morton had stared at each other and then stared at the beans that they suspected were meant for dinner that night. They left them there and went to school without lunch. The next day they went to school without lunch as well after Gene had forgotten to tell Jonathan they hadn't had any lunch that day. Their mother had been unwell that night and not joined them for their meal. It was too bad, for Jonathan had made meatballs. On the third day when there was no lunch Gene was almost resigned to not having school lunches ever again, after all, she barely ate during the day.

But Morton was a different story. He took Gene by the hand and dragged her over to the phone and pointed at the list on the wall with the phone numbers for their

Great Uncle Michel, their grandparents in Toronto, their Aunty Rachel in St John's, and their Aunty Leise in Toronto. Morton pointed to Jonathan's number at the hospital, which they weren't meant to ring unless it was an emergency. Was this an emergency? She didn't think so. She shook her head. But Morton reached out and dialed the number and held the phone out to her.

Reluctantly she took the mouthpiece and when the phone was answered asked if she could speak to her older brother, Jonathan Dalton. She waited, was put through to someone, waited, was put through to someone else and then he came on the phone. To her relief he wasn't angry. He told them to go look for the biscuit tin with the cardinal on the front of it. They couldn't find it anywhere. He told them, never mind, to go to his room, to his top drawer, collect all the loose change and go to the baker and buy a quiche, a cream bun if they wanted one, then go to the green grocers and get some apples and oranges.

That night for the first time ever they heard Jonathan yelling at their mother. The words were indistinct and muffled for she and Morton were in the kitchen and their mother and Jonathan were in a room upstairs. When he came back down to finish dinner Jonathan was not his normal self and Gene wondered if she had done the right thing in calling him at work. Now, nearly two weeks later, Gene remembered how that day she and Morton were late going to school and rather than draw attention to herself, she had waited till morning recess and slipped back in with all the other students after the break, hoping Mr. Archerfield would be none the wiser. This hazy recollection flashed through her mind as Mr. Archerfield shoved her face up against the blackboard then pulled her away so she could see the word "they're". 'Short for they are,' he was yelling at her. 'Say it.'

'They're, short for they are,' she said.

Say it again. She said it again. Then he deluged her with sentences where she had to guess which 'there' he had used in the sentence. Finally after she managed to get them all right, he said to her, 'Now, Gene, that wasn't so hard was it?'

'No, sir,' she said, her eyes downcast.

'How do you spell wasn't?'

Her head jerked up. She stumbled, 'I don't know, sir.'

'You know how to say the words well enough just not how to spell them. Don't. Won't. Can't. Get out of my sight, girl.'

She turned around but before she could take more than two paces he kicked her in the back sending her spread-eagled up the aisle. Gene barely remembered falling face first on the dirty wooden floor, such was the exploding pain in her lower back, as the boil burst shooting blood and pus and plasma over her skin and school uniform. She came to, lying face down on a bench outside the principal's office. The office administrator told her to lie still; her brother was coming for her.

She thought perhaps Morton would walk her home. I don't think I can carry my school bag by myself, she moaned. But to her surprise Jonathan turned up. He disappeared for a short while and then he returned, seething. He wrapped her in an old grey school blanket and carried her to their car.

On the way home Jonathan asked her many things and she told him many things and more. She watched him closely as she talked. He looked straight ahead but he gripped the steering wheel firmly, set his mouth in a hard line, and expelled his breath loudly through his nose. At home he carried her upstairs to their mother's room and, without even knocking, marched in, set her on her feet, and walked to the large bay windows and yanked open the curtains.

'Mother,' he said in a loud voice. Gene was surprised he wasn't yelling, given how angry he was.

'What!' said their mother, bringing her hands to her face to cover the sudden brightness. It didn't sound like a question.

'Mother, we've had enough! I've had enough! Gene

has had enough and I'm sure if Morton would speak, he'd tell you he's had enough!'

'Enough of what?' Her mother's hands were still over her face but not for long. Jonathan pulled them away and pulled her half out of bed in the next motion.

'Enough of you not being our mother. Enough of your mourning Dad and Joel and feeling sorry for yourself. Do you think you have extra privileges that entitle you to mourn them for time immemorial and the rest of us be damned?'

'Jonathan…' She paused and wet her lips. 'You're only twenty-two. If you were forty-one you might understand. Some days it feels as if my life is over.'

'Well it's not! You're far from being an old woman. You're still a mother with young children. And while you're mourning the loss of one child you're ignoring the fact that you have four others. Four others that you should be grateful are still in your life, still love you and have not given up on you, despite you giving up on us!'

'I haven't given up on you all. Who says I have? You are managing fine. You're all doing so well you barely need me.'

'Your mute son doesn't need you? Your seven-year-old daughter who just passed out at school because of pain and abuse and neglect, doesn't need you?' Jonathan strode over to Gene and peeled off her school uniform before throwing the bloodied, putrid smelling garment into her mother's face. 'Gene has spent her school days dancing with the devil for the past eighteen months, in purgatory, too caring and sensitive to our needs to bother upsetting us about what's been upsetting her. Well, I've got news for you. She's not going back there and neither is Morton. You're going to have to get out of that bed and find them a new school. Look at her.'

Jonathan had pulled Gene over to their mother and pulled down her underpants so Rebecca could see her weeping wound. There was silence in the room for quite a few moments. 'It doesn't look pleasant, I agree,' said her mother, 'but Jonathan, every child gets boils and carbuncles from time to time. Gene was just unfortunate hers burst at school.' Her mother turned her around so she was facing her. 'I'm sure it hurt, honey, but it probably doesn't hurt as much now as it did before. Why didn't you tell us you had a sore on your bottom?'

'Mother! That is my point exactly. Why can't Gene talk to her mother about things? Why can't she talk to me? Why can't she talk about the trivial and the not so trivial? I'll tell you why, because she thinks we are already overburdened, she thinks we have enough on our minds. But let me tell you we are far from being overburdened. Hell, look at the poor people living in Britain in fear of their lives, in fear of being bombed by the Germans every night. Look at their children who have been sent to homes in the country to be safe, far away from their parents not knowing when they will see them again. Do they have something real to weigh them down, to fear, to worry about?'

'I have something real to worry me down.'

'You lost your husband and your son. It was terrible! The rest of us lost our father and our brother. It was just as terrible! I dare say what happened to Morton was the most terrible of all, but it was eighteen months ago. It is time to move on. It is time to turn the page. Time to put the phone back on the hook. You moved everyone to Montreal so you could make a new start. So you could put things behind you and get on with your life. So we could be a family again. But all you have done is physically move here. You haven't done a thing more.'

'I hoped I could have.'

'I hoped you could have too.' Gene could see Jonathan's chest rising and falling.

'Have I burdened you, Jonathan? I'm sorry. Has looking after Gene and Morton been a burden to you?'

Her brother exhaled deeply before answering. 'Looking after them would never be a burden to me. But seeing my mother throw her life away – that's something else. Seeing my mother neglect her children and those children resign themselves to the fact that their mother is just a person who moves around the house from one piece of furniture to the next, nothing more, that is a burden to me. For those children to not only have lost their father, but also to have lost their mother and worse, to have lost hope of ever really having a mother again, that is a burden to me, that is a moment of infinite sadness. To not have the mother I had growing up, not because she was taken away from them, but because she chose not to be here for them. I am so disappointed in you. You blatantly ignore those who have loved you – wholeheartedly and unreservedly – all their lives. Those who nurtured your life and helped make it what it once was; who can still make it what it could be. Your life wasn't all Dad! Your life wasn't all Joel!'

Jonathan paused and inhaled. Then in a low voice he said, 'I thought your life was your family – maybe I was wrong. Gene, Morton and I are a family and it's time for you to decide whether you're part of this family or not. Because, right now, you're not. And let me tell you more than me being disappointed in you, Dad would be sorely disappointed in you. You should be ashamed of yourself.'

Jonathan walked away. At the door he paused and turned his head. 'Shape up or ship out, Mom. Ship out to some place where you can get yourself together. But before you do anything, clean up Gene. I have to get back to the hospital.'

At last Gene gave way to weeping, not hysterical weeping, just the slow release of tears that were way overdue; not at the receding pain in her back; not for herself and the miserable situation she had endured at school for the past eighteen months; but in relief almost, because her brother had dared to speak the truth; and also in hurt, hurt for her brother. For in his last glance Gene saw what he hadn't said, what he had suffered in silence the past year and a half. And even though he was many years older than her, she knew that pain.

10

That day Rebecca realised she had not bowed in grace. She had not let Samuel go in peace. Nor Joel, her third son. Not her first, not her second, but her third! – lost to the vicious vagaries of misfortune. And for that and all the days that followed, especially the days that followed, she was deeply ashamed.

She ran a warm bath for her daughter, washed her golden blonde hair, bathed her, trickling warm water over her alarmingly thin body, gaunt like another body she had seen many years ago. She gently wiped around Gene's inflamed and now headless boil – a raw, gaping, suppurated hole near her tailbone. It must have been awfully painful. She patted her dry, put a salve of magnesium sulphide on the open sore to draw out any more infection then covered it with a plaster. Then she gave Gene her own mixture of Bromo-Seltzer powder sweetened with honey to swallow, before putting her to bed.

After lunch she went to buy groceries. But first she trudged through the snow to the park at the top of the Mont Royal where she could overlook the city and see the St Lawrence River stretching off in the distance towards the Maritime Provinces. If one followed that waterway one would reach Newfoundland. In the past looking out to sea had always given her comfort. And hope.

After many long minutes of silence, of the cold smarting her eyes, she took a deep breath, the gelid air almost burning her nostrils, and when she exhaled she said out loud, 'Okay, Samuel. Okay, Joel.'

Then she took a deep breath and when she let it out she said, 'Okay, Rebecca.' And that point became the line between her unbearable past and her tremulous future.

That afternoon when Morton came home from school, she poured him a glass of milk and placed a piece of homemade pumpkin and sultana cake in front of him. When Jonathan arrived she was standing over the stove, stirring pots. She heard him walk towards her and then, without speaking, he hugged her from behind. He kissed the top of her head, resting his head on her head. It sent a pang through her heart, as he was Samuel's height and his body felt like Samuel's. She released the ladles and squeezed his hands, pulled them to her lips and kissed them. In a throaty whisper, she said, 'Thank you.'

He turned her around and hugged her. She had a great lump in her throat, she squeezed her eyes, but tears still ran out the sides dampening his shirt. They both struggled with their breathing. Eventually, she sniffed before saying, 'I'll get there.'

'I know you will.' He hugged her tightly till she was ready to pull away. She wiped her eyes and through her tears smiled at her son. He stroked her face. 'See, progress already.'

To stay on the path, every morning upon rising Rebecca would have a cold shower, even in excoriating winter, flagellating herself with icy cold barbs. But it was a new covenant with herself, and one she wanted to honour – a daily reminder of her renewed commitment to her family, like how she used to have her first swim of the year on her birthday back in Newfoundland. But this was a promise of a different kind.

The next day Rebecca kept Morton home from school with Gene. They played Scrabble in the morning. After lunch, they tramped through snow-cleared footpaths to the Notre Dame Cathedral. The family always felt at peace there. Rebecca could never exactly say why. It had something to do with the way the blue ceiling was illuminated; it seemed to bathe them in a holy light. And while the three of them had sat surrounded by a blue aura

– their heads bowed, their hands held – a light came on for Rebecca.

When Samuel and Rebecca visited Montreal when the children were younger Gene's favourite all time outing was the marketplace. While the other children were goggled-eyed over what was on offer, Gene's eyes were only for the people. She would stare in fascination at the Indian woman in a patterned cotton dress with a man's black panama hat, and at the nuns draped in black with a crown of white wimple around their heads. Gene had asked who they were. Before Rebecca had time to reply, Abby had said, 'They are God's angels.'

'No they're not,' Gene had countered. 'If they were they would be wearing white.'

'That's right,' Rebecca had said, 'they are nuns. They belong to the Catholic Church.'

But even so Gene was fascinated by them. She had said to her mother. 'They look a bit like that statue back home, Mommy. Maybe they do have wings under those dark outfits.'

'Yes, they do look a bit like that statue on top of the pillar but, no, they don't have wings underneath their outfits,' Rebecca had replied.

'Maybe if I became a nun, I would grow wings.'

'I don't think so, honey,' Rebecca had replied. But now Rebecca thought: let her grow wings. She turned to Gene. 'Would you like to be taught by the Catholic nuns?'

'Oui.' Gene nodded. 'God's angels,' she whispered.

'What about you, Morton?'

He nodded, raising his eyebrows in a way that said the idea appealed to him as well. It was a direction Rebecca had resisted in the past. But for some odd and comforting reason, it now seemed the right decision.

They called in to have afternoon tea with Aunty Marguerite, Uncle Michel's wife. She not only knew every Catholic school in the city, but as Rebecca suspected, was adamant she could open the right doors for them as well.

That night Rebecca phoned her in-laws in Toronto at

five to seven. She could hear the warmth and delight in their voices. Abby was the last to come to the phone. 'When you're ready to join us, we're ready to have you,' said Rebecca. 'It would be good for our family to be back together.'

'Maybe.'

'Come for Easter at least. The buds will be on the trees by then.'

11

Gene now starts her school day with singing: *Morning has broken, How great thou art* and *Immortal, invisible, God only wise.* She enjoys the singing so much she joins the school choir so she can be part of their Easter pageant; so she can delight her mother and brothers and sister, Abby, in the Palm Sunday and Good Friday and Easter Sunday services. Sister Francis takes her under her wing – to Gene it literally feels that way – for at her new school, Gene feels lighter as if she can flutter from one group of friendly school girls to the next. She feels freer, as if she is let out of a cage, traipsing through the streets of Montreal on one school excursion after another. She feels alive, as if she can soar, so quickly does she grasp the language that her father occasionally spoke. Anyone would swear she was a native French speaker. She belongs!

And French is not the only new language she learns. Morton has taken to learning sign language and Gene is following suit. One afternoon when Gene was standing by her mother's side and Morton by the other, Morton's teacher, Sister Celine, said she would like Morton to learn sign language. He's not deaf, her mother replied.

'I know, but we have a young boy, Andrew, who is deaf, and who needs a friend he can talk to just as much as Morton does. We want them to learn the same language together.'

To Gene, learning sign language becomes an exciting and entertaining challenge; a game of skill and speed that sharpens the sense of sight. It is a game that brings her and Morton together again. Through sign language Gene and Morton enter their own secret world, untouched by anyone else. Through sign language her brother returns to her and as translator, Gene returns her brother to the rest of their family. Her mother and Jonathan even start to learn the odd hand gesture, the fingertips touching the bottom lip in a silent gesture of thanks.

At night, Morton lies beside her as she reads aloud from a book. Gene knows he knows the words. She knows he could read the story much faster than she. But he never looks at the words while she reads. He lies on his back and looks up at the ceiling, looks up into the imaginary world she is reading about. When she finishes, he sighs softly, reaches for her hand and squeezes it as if saying goodnight, then goes to his own bed, only five feet from her own.

But one night he lingers, and in a rough and distant voice he whispers, 'I like our new school, Genie.'

Gene is so excited to hear him speak! She halts for a second and then, rather than focusing on the novelty of his talking, intuitively, she says, 'Do you, Morton? Do you? I'm so pleased. I'm so happy for you. And for me. I like it too!' And this – Morton's speaking – becomes their secret as well.

12

Rebecca awakens to the realities of her life, to the realities of supporting a family. Thanks to a life-insurance policy that Samuel had, that she was oblivious to, Rebecca owned their home outright. For all her married life, Samuel had given her money each week to buy groceries and other items. He'd put it in a biscuit tin in the kitchen and every so often she'd open her jewelry box and be surprised to find some cash in there with a note from him to buy herself something special, a new dress, a new jacket. She wanted for nothing.

Miraculously, even now there was still money in the tea tin. Jonathan was the go between, for the money came from Leonard, her seventy-six-year-old father-in-law, and from Lottie, his wife, daughter of the founder of Sibonne Shipping and Traders, which, for as long as Rebecca had known, had been run by Lottie's brother, Michel – Uncle Michel – and now managed by his sons, Jean-Paul and René. They regularly dropped off food baskets for her and special treats: fine cheeses and quinces. And, for all she knew, they probably slipped Jonathan bundles of cash as well.

She couldn't keep living on handouts. She went to see Samuel's cousins. Could they give her some work? Could she clean for them, do their laundry, help in the business? Could she do filing, paperwork, anything? Jean-Paul and René told her to leave it with them.

A week later they called her in and told her about a position they knew of as an assistant in a postcard business, managing orders and fulfillment of stock. Nine to three, Monday to Friday. She didn't even hesitate. 'Yes. Who do I talk to about that?'

'No one,' said René. 'Just us. A Mr. Edouard Cadet is the manager. But we're making the appointment.'

'It's your business?' Rebecca practically stammered.

Jean-Paul nodded.

'How long have you had a postcard business for?'

'Ah,' shrugged Jean-Paul. 'Père's been involved in photography for nearly thirty years.'

'Really!' said Rebecca unable to hide her surprise. That night she rang Lottie and updated her on the photography business and how everything had fallen into place. 'Can you believe it?'

'What aren't those boys involved in?' Lottie replied.

It was the perfect job for Rebecca. She worked alongside Edouard and a team of photographers-come-sales reps, who travelled Canada supplying shopkeepers and tourist operators with postcard mementos for visitors. At the same time they would take new photographs along the way, throughout the seasons. She became an armchair traveller, a documenter of Canadian life. It took her out of herself and took her back to herself – back to the young girl who had a yearning way back when to discover parts of the world.

Two years to the day after that fateful iceberg trip Rebecca, Jonathan, Morton and Gene return to Toronto for a commemorative service for Samuel and Joel. It's at Rebecca's instigation. She is at last ready to say goodbye. She is stronger. She is capable. And she wants to set a new course for her and her children. It is the right thing. Her fuzzy numbness has dissipated. She has woken up. Her questions have turned a corner and taken on a new angle. No more, why me, what did I do to deserve this? Now she asks, what sort of life am I creating for my children? Is this the life Samuel would want for them? For us?

She no longer holds Samuel at bay, like some kind of taboo word that no one dare utter. She gazes intently into her past, into the person he was and at long last she decides the best way to honour him, to thank him, to keep his spirit alive is to live the life he would want them to live: to be the exuberant, adventurous, playful, practical person that he was; he, whom her heart loved.

On the same pétanque green where she was wed, surrounded by the same people who had attended twenty-four years earlier: Samuel's parents; his sister, Analeise, her husband, Randall, and now their grown up children; Addie – her husband Jerome had died in his sleep eighteen months ago; their son and Samuel's childhood friend, Joel, and his wife and children; Anthony Clarkson, one of Samuel's friends from his Montreal medical days; Alistair Anderson, the brother of Jonathan's birth mother, Lenore, and his family; and in front of many new faces – not just in the next generation, but in the colleagues and friends from the School of Hygiene where Samuel had worked for several years – Rebecca farewelled Joel and Samuel.

'Joel, you were born on a winter's day upstairs in our bathroom barely an hour after my waters broke. Samuel was ice sailing on the lake with Jonathan. Abby, Morton and Gene were downstairs and Analeise was on her way but you were waiting for no one. You were eager to get on with the living and live you did. You were a child full of everything, who got on with everyone. Your curiosity, your confidence, your determination amazed us all. And when you left, you, the littlest person, left the biggest hole in our lives. But you also gave us the biggest gift, the brightest example of how to live. And we will hold onto that always.'

When she finished, Abby, Morton and Gene each released a hummingbird. Rebecca had asked them what they would like to do at the ceremony to remember Joel. The hummingbirds had been Gene's idea. The way they hovered and then zipped from one thing to the next reminded her of Joel. For Samuel they had decided on a mourning dove, the Western turtledove, the dove of love and sorrow. Jonathan released a solitary bird after he spoke of his father, after Rebecca remembered Samuel.

'You gave me the most beautiful, exhilarating life, Samuel. You showed me a world beyond my imaginings. I loved you with every cell of my being, with every breath of my soul. You gave me the gift of your generous and loving family, life-saving and sage treasures that they are. You gave me the most beautiful and amazing children and though your and Joel's leaving broke my heart – our hearts – I took comfort in knowing that you were together, with family; that you were not alone. I knew you for twenty-five years when you were of flesh and by my side, but through our children, you live on and I know you still.'

And then for Rebecca the oddest thing started to happen. Samuel came back into her life not just in fleeting images but also in large technicolour episodes. It was as if by moving on she had somehow released him, set him free so he could join her at his leisure and show her memorable episodes of her past. Images that said: 'We had a good life, Rebecca. We have much to be thankful for, much to be happy about and there will be more that will come your way, our way.'

A word or a phrase would set her off, flying back across the years, her body tingling, her breath suspended and then quickening as she would vividly recall every word, every touch, every nuance of an amorous encounter.

She was in the midst of finally replying to all those people who had sent her sympathy cards and letters after Samuel and Joel's disappearance when Abby walked into the room and asked, 'Mom, when are we going to get my new school uniforms?' Abby had at last moved to Montreal to finish her senior years.

In a distracted manner, not raising her head, Rebecca asked, 'Summer or winter uniforms?' And before she knew it, she was somewhere else.

He kissed her while he unbuttoned her coat and peeled it off. Then he pulled her jumper off and looked down at her. 'Ah, winter uniform. I like the summer one best. I can see I am going to have to come another day.' But he stayed and kissed her some more, nothing chilling or cold about him.

Minutes later, 'Is this all regulation school clothing?' he asked in a throaty whisper, tugging at her vest.

'Possibly not,' she replied, her own voice husky.

'Off with it then.' The layers came off till she was wearing nothing but her white skivvy. He stroked her bare buttocks. 'In all my years at school I never got to study anything like this.' His fingers moved to her front. 'And certainly nothing like this.'

'No,' she said, her voice hoarse. Wetting her lips she ventured, 'Do you feel your education has been lacking?'

'You tell me,' he whispered against her mouth.

They gave themselves over to each other, flooding each other, flooding themselves, until they finally pulsed to a shuddering stop. After many moments Rebecca regained her breath, followed by her voice. 'What do you have to say for yourself, Samuel Dalton?'

'I don't know. How about, "Schoolgirls these days are so trying. Somehow they just get the better of me."'

'Mom! Have you been listening to me?'

Where was she? She glanced up at her daughter, then down at the page in front of her, to the words in her own handwriting: *I'm embarrassed*

She blushed. Without raising her head, she said, 'Can we talk about this when I'm finished here? I won't be much longer.'

She moved her pen and continued, *'to say I can't recall if I ever replied to your letter till now.'*

It was an awkward moment for Rebecca because mostly she wanted to forge a better relationship with her eldest daughter, the girl she had left in Toronto who was now back in their lives as a confident young lady. Often, when Rebecca felt she was on the outer circle, a distant third to the girl's dark-haired, olive-skinned glamorous grandmother and her adoring paternal aunt; when she sensed that for Abby, Montreal paled in comparison to Toronto, Rebecca had to remind herself, that Abigail wanted to forge a better relationship with her and the rest of the family as well; that she had joined them of her own free will.

The best times they had were when Analeise, Samuel's older sister, Abby's favourite aunt, came to town. For once two's company, three's a crowd, did not apply. And perceptively Analeise was the one who deferred to Rebecca in Abby's presence. She laughed openly and shared intimacies with Rebecca, legitimising Rebecca's position and smoothing the way for Abby to once more honour her mother.

Abigail got on very well with Jonathan – who didn't? – but she rarely had time for Gene or Morton, locking herself in her room and writing letters to her girlfriends back in Toronto.

Jonathan still spent a great deal of time at the hospital and when he wasn't there he spent a great deal of time at home – not that she didn't love his company – but Rebecca worried for him, fearing that he was still burdened with the responsibility of their entire family. Occasionally he'd go out with friends who included a group of young men and young women, but no one girl seemed to hold a special place in his life.

One day, completely out of the blue, she said to him, 'There was a Candace once whom you were keen on. Whatever happened to her?'

Jonathan looked up from the paper he was reading. 'I'm surprised you remember her, given the timing.'

'Me too,' said Rebecca with a smile. She waited. 'Well?'

'She couldn't wait for me.'

'Well, she wasn't the one for you.'

'That's what I decided too.' He sighed. 'Eventually.'

'Someone else will come along.'

'Oh, I'm not worried.'

Rebecca glanced at him and took solace in the fact

that when Jonathan met Mrs. Right, the poor girl wouldn't stand a chance, and as his mother, she didn't need to worry. He was something else her son; born with a perfect heart, a perfect body and a perfect face that would take any girl's breath away; tall, dark and handsome – his father reborn.

But where his biological father, Samuel's brother, Matthew, had by all reports revelled in his masculine appeal, Jonathan was a product of his environment, more akin to Samuel's steady approach, and in light of their family's tragic history, even more discerning.

'I've got other things on my mind at present,' he volunteered.

'What's that?' she whispered in the tone of a conspirator.

'I'm going to learn how to fly!' His face broke into the widest grin.

'Are you?' She could not deny she was surprised. But then she paused. 'That's right we talked about this before you started medical school. I had completely forgotten.' Suddenly she was overcome with a wave of dread. 'Please tell me you're not going off to war, are you?'

'No, Mom, I'm going to be a flying doctor. And in two years time I'm going to bundle everyone up and fly them to some spectacular location for a wonderful summer holiday.'

'How fabulous!' Rebecca clapped her hands.' This family is overdue for a holiday. Why not next year?'

'Because next year I promised Grandad Dalton I'd take him with me on my medical expedition to Hudson Bay and the Arctic Trading Company at Churchill. We're going to sign on with some bush pilots and find ourselves a polar bear!'

Rebecca squeezed her son's shoulders in delight. 'And how does he jump the queue?' she teased.

'It's the condition he set when he gave me the money for my lessons.' Jonathan looked at her somewhat grimly, before sighing heavily. 'And because he's not getting any younger and I don't want to wake up one morning and find him gone and realise I didn't get to spend enough time with him.'

Rebecca peered into her son's face to the glimpse of heartbreak he was showing her. After a few moments she leant across the table and rustled her twenty-three-year-old son's rich dark hair. 'Don't be upsetting yourself with thoughts like that. There are still some years left in Leonard yet. There better be.'

13

At forty-two years of age, Rebecca does not quite have the spirited energy of youth nor the inquiring mind of her formative years, but what she does have still sets her apart: the striking looks of one who was once uncommonly beautiful – a woman with stature, steady confidence, flowing blonde hair and stunning teal blue eyes. Occasionally, as has always been her nature, she has sombre days, but mostly her glass is half full, as are her days.

Though with her newfound lease on life, Rebecca's days are not full enough. She yearns to do more, be more. Aside from her job in the postcard business she gardens, she takes her family to Saturday night dances, she takes Abby and Gene canoeing – Morton steadfastly refusing to put one toe in any water, let alone in a boat – and then one day while looking at a new selection of photographs at work, she is compelled to do something she hasn't done since before Abby was born: she purchases a canvas, some paints and brushes, and starts to paint landscapes.

Initially from postcards, but then from memory: Niagara on the Lake, fall foliage in the Laurentian Mountains, the log cabin at Lake Temagami, a fishing boat on Parry Sound, a waterfall at Owen Sound. Plenty of images from Newfoundland come to mind, but she ignores them all. Yet, her artistic eye is piqued by the fact that what intrigues her about Newfoundland, what challenges her is its light. The unique way it warms and illuminates objects like a halo bursting through cloud – which no other scenic location, no matter how picturesque, seems to afford. Regardless, she is not swayed. Her paintbrushes are busy bringing other images to life.

And so it is one blustery spring day as she is rushing home, a roll of canvas under one arm, her hands too full with grocery bags and bread bags and carry bags of every description that something has to give, and before she knows it, there is a man racing up beside her, his felt hat raised in one hand, his other offering her rolled canvas, as he says, 'Excuse me, ma'am, you dropped this.' She looks at what he's holding as she squeezes her elbows by her side, checking that it's hers. 'You've got quite a load there.' He pauses. 'Would you like a hand?'

Rebecca hesitates. 'Thank you, they're not that heavy. I can manage.'

His eyes are deep-set, the palest of blues. For a few seconds he looks at her in silence. 'I'm sure you can. But on a day like today it's awkward, and I don't mind helping you.' In the end, Rebecca gives in. She carries his hat along with her handbag and the canvas roll while he carries everything else.

'I have an automobile,' she says. 'We have an automobile,' almost by way of apology, 'But…'

'I still prefer horses myself.' He catches her eye. 'Or a pack of dogs.'

'You don't see too many working dogs around here. Horses yes, plenty, of course. Where are you from? Out East.'

'No, ma'am, the opposite direction.'

'Are you from Vancouver?' There's a hint of excitement in her voice. Rebecca has never met anyone from the west coast of Canada.

'Do I look like I come from Vancouver?'

'I don't know,' she says, feeling little uncomfortable. 'You could be?'

'Vancouver's way beyond west,' he says by way of reply.

They were outside her place. 'In here.' She holds open their wrought iron gate so the man can walk ahead down the cement path. He stops at her front door, looks around and spots a stone bench seat on the edge of the porch.

'Do you want me to leave these here for you then?'

'That will be perfect. Thank you.' Rebecca smiles softly behind his back then something from her distant past bubbles to the surface. 'On second thoughts, can I offer you a cup of tea for your troubles and you can tell me more about the west where you come from?'

He has already put his hat back on. He looks at her as if he's unsure how to proceed. 'Begging your leave, ma'am, but I had intended to call on some other folk this afternoon. Perhaps I could have that tea another day?'

'Of course,' she says. 'You can catch me at home any day around now, four at the latest. I'm Rebecca Dalton.' She extends her hand. 'I do appreciate your assistance today.'

With one hand the man removes his hat. With the other he takes Rebecca's hand in his own, but rather than shake it once and release it, he looks down at their clasped hands then raises his eyes to Rebecca's. 'Begging your pardon, ma'am, but it was you I intended to call on this afternoon. Forgive me for not introducing myself sooner. I'm Wyatt Kingston, Wyatt from Lumsden, Saskatchewan.' He gives her the barest smile, but his eyes are soft and earnest.

Rebecca remembered one of the letters she'd penned after Samuel's service was to a Wyatt Kingston. She'd never met Wyatt. She knew of him, knew that he and Samuel were posted together to a Regimental Aid Post on the Western Front back in 1918. And she knew Samuel and Wyatt corresponded every Christmas. She'd written that her children had been of great comfort to her. He'd replied saying how he'd regretted not ever seeing Samuel after the war and wishing he had met his family after hearing so much about them over the years. But he doubted that would ever come to pass. He wasn't one for big cities. She'd sent him a postcard of Montreal telling him Montreal was a city for all seasons and if he ever ventured that far, he'd be welcome any time. She'd heard no more from him till now.

'Fancy that,' said Rebecca. 'What a surprise! A very pleasant one though, Mr. Kingston.'

'Oh no, Mrs. Dalton, you mustn't call me that. I've never been Mr. I've only ever been Dr. Kingston, except for when I was captain. But everyone else knows me as Wyatt. That's all I know.'

'Well then, you must call me Rebecca.' She squeezed his hand once before releasing her grasp.

Inside, Rebecca barely had an opportunity to ask Wyatt how long he had been in town, before Gene and Morton arrived home from school, followed shortly by Abby, who, after grabbing a snack, made herself scarce. But not Gene and Morton. They clung to Rebecca's side, cautiously observing and listening to the quiet stranger who had known their father many years before they were born.

'You were saying,' said Rebecca, 'that you've been here for just two days.'

'That's right. Arrived on Saturday and will head back on Thursday.'

'And how long was your journey?'

'Three days of train travel, ma'am.'

'Seems a pity to head back so soon, after travelling such a distance,' she said.

'Well, I will have done what I came to do.'

'What did you come to do?' asked Gene. Rebecca glanced at her daughter. Gene's question was too direct for one so young, but then that was how she had been as a child.

He told them he'd come to Montreal with his eighteen-year-old nephew, Paul, to make sure he got away to England without any fracas. As a favour to his sister, Pearl, he added. Paul had signed up as a gunner and was about to leave for England, then North Africa. 'Pearl doesn't want him to go, none of us do, but what can you do? I've come with him this far to give her some peace of mind.'

'That's very sweet of you,' noted Rebecca. 'Where is he now?'

'He's already boarded. He will have leave tomorrow evening to come ashore. We'll have dinner together. I'll say my farewells and when the Trunk heads southwest on Thursday I'll be on it.'

Morton signed a question to Gene. 'Excuse me. My brother wants to know, do you have kids of your own?'

Wyatt turned to Morton. 'No, I don't. I never married. But I do have dogs, lots of dogs – huskies. Do you know the breed? They cost nearly as much as a family to feed.' Wyatt's eyes were glowing.

Morton nodded. 'Do you train them?' he signalled to Gene who relayed for him.

'That, I do lad and some winters we go touring. Have you ever been towed by a pack of dogs?'

Morton shook his head. Yet, at the same time, he grinned and his eyes were alight.

'Well if you play your cards right, maybe one day you will.'

'Where do you keep all your dogs, Wyatt?' asked Rebecca.

'On the family farm where I was born, where I grew up. It used to belong to my grandparents. It's quite small but it's big enough. Pearl and her husband, Jed, live close by in a new house they built about fifteen years back. Jed runs the farm these days. We're hoping next year to be able to get one of those wheat combine harvesters to make it easier for everyone.'

'And you're still involved in medicine?'

'Yes, ma'am, I'm the local doctor. Fortunately there's a few locums in Regina that I can call on these days, which means I can head away a bit more than I used to.'

'So you're not opposed to travel,' said Rebecca, lightly teasing, 'just travel to big cities.'

'I don't know if you call what I do travel.'

'Wait till you meet Jonathan. He's got some journey ideas of his own. Probably not what you would call travel either.'

'I am look forward to meeting him, see if he's a chip off the old block.'

'Yes,' drawled Rebecca. 'Jonathan is a unique combination of his father and his uncle. The very best blend. You'll see. He'll be home soon.' Poor Lenore, Rebecca had thought many times over, she didn't get a look in.

'Well, Matthew was one of a kind and your Samuel was a fine man. One couldn't ask for better men.' He tipped his head slightly at Rebecca. She smiled her gratitude. Something in Rebecca warmed to this gentle man, this quiet, solitary man with a certain youthfulness about his weathered face – not too weathered she corrected herself, more tanned and lined in places. Despite his occupation he obviously spent plenty of time outdoors. His was a compact, strong face, made up of clear panes, a straight nose, straight brows and a good jawline with no sign of any slackness. She'd noticed earlier that his height was only two or three inches above her own. Underneath his checked blazer, she suspected his frame would be lean and wiry. In certain lights his short, dark blonde hair glinted silver.

As always, Jonathan was the perfect host, deftly taking on the role of head of the family. He sat and talked medicine with Wyatt. He talked Samuel with Wyatt. He even talked Matthew with Wyatt – briefly. Rebecca knew, aside from blood, Matthew had very little bearing on Jonathan's life. He'd once told Rebecca that whenever he looked at a photograph of Matthew, he did feel sad, but to him Matthew was the uncle who had been lost in the war. Samuel was the only father he'd ever known and the only father he'd ever wanted.

Wyatt had last been in Montreal in 1919 on his return from the battlefields, twenty-four years earlier. Much had changed in the city during that time and much had stayed the same. Still, Rebecca and Jonathan were quick to plan an itinerary and invite Wyatt back to dinner on Wednesday night. They even offered for him to stay in their spare room but he wouldn't hear of it.

On Wednesday Wyatt met Rebecca at her work. She wanted to show him their gallery where they featured photo enlargements of the best of their postcard range. On the way home he bought a bunch of freesias, a bottle of wine and a block of chocolate for the children.

For dinner, Rebecca served a seafood bake with salad and bread. Partway through the meal, Morton, through Gene, asked, 'Can we come and visit you one day and see your dogs?'

'You would be most welcome,' he replied. 'It would be easier to visit in the summer, but you can't go riding on a dog sled in summer. You have to come in winter for that.'

Morton looked at her beseechingly.

'I think winter is out of the question, Morton.'

'Well, can we go this summer?' piped up Gene. The girl was practically telepathic as far as Morton was concerned.

Morton was grinning and nodding his thick-sandy-coloured head at both her and Wyatt. Jonathan just sat back and laughed.

Rebecca let out a faint sigh. 'I think you two are forgetting yourself. You can't go hoisting yourself on Wyatt like that. Besides, we're going to Toronto this summer and then we're heading off to Muskoka Lake with Nana and Grandad Dalton, and Analeise and all the family. We planned it last summer.'

'I don't want to go to the lake. I don't want to go to any lake.' Morton signalled. Rebecca didn't need Gene to translate. His expression said it all. She let out another sigh.

Wyatt gave Rebecca a sympathetic smile. 'Maybe next summer then,' he said.

14

A slow correspondence began between them, a letter every two or three months. Wyatt never wrote more than a page. For Morton's benefit he always made sure to mention something about his dogs. Rebecca would write three or four pages in return.

After all, she said to herself, she had more people in her family to write about. At the back of her mind, she wasn't sure if Wyatt actually wanted them to come and visit or whether he was ambivalent. What she felt mostly was that he wanted them to feel welcome to come and visit if they chose to do so.

Then in April, as their spirits were rising with the onset of spring, almost a year to their first meeting, Wyatt wrote and formally invited them to visit him that summer. He said arrangements could be made to accommodate them on the farm to spare her expense and he had a car to collect them from the station and show them around. It was up to her. She asked Jonathan.

'Why not? You'd be mad not to. Look at how Morton perks up every time a letter arrives from Wyatt. Look at how he writes back to him with your letters. That's something we want to encourage. And besides, I'm not going to be here. Abby will want to go to Toronto and be with everyone there, so what do Morton and Gene have to look forward to? Go! Explore a new part of the country with them. Give them a different summer holiday experience for a change.'

She went. By the end of the train trip she was certain Morton and Gene knew everyone onboard. The last time they had been that excited was when Samuel was in their lives. She had made the right decision. The land leveled and flattened and stayed flat, through wheatfield after wheatfield. There was the occasional silver birch, the occasional alder, a house and a red-roofed barn here and there, and fields spotted with beef cattle. But mostly, there was one, never-ending sky. From her train seat the sky looked enormous, the land mostly a mustard ribbon to the horizon. But above was a massive blue diving bell of a sky. Ah, but when the weather turned bad, as it surely would, when the snows came, you wouldn't stand a chance, she feared. There seemed more above to come down.

Wyatt was waiting for them on the train platform in Regina. He was dressed very smartly in a shirt, tie and jacket and immediately reached for Rebecca and Gene's suitcases. Morton carried his own. Both children also had small canvas packs on their backs. They went to a café for refreshments. It was nothing by Montreal or Toronto standards, but it was homely with frilly curtains and the pot of tea was good. The children enjoyed their milkshakes. Pleasantries were exchanged, a little formal at first – not with the children, with the adults – but then they found their way, Rebecca helping when she said, 'I think I can safely say, "We're excited to be here."'

On the farm Wyatt pulled up in front of small, two-storey A-framed house. It was painted white on the outside, with a grey roof. It had a few rock gardens out front, dotted with asters and tiger lilies. Another garden stretched along one side of the house. There was a closed in porch at the front with a settee at one end, and a hallway that ran down the middle opening into the kitchen. On the left hand side was the lounge with a fireplace. On the right hand side was a bedroom with a double bed. Wyatt put Rebecca's suitcase in there and told her that would be her room. Behind her room was one with two single beds for the children and beyond that was the bathroom, laundry and another porch.

Wyatt placed Gene's suitcase in the second bedroom. 'Gene and Morton,' he said, 'This is where you'll sleep.'

Twelve-year old Morton grabbed Gene's arm and signalled a message to her.

'Can we go see the dogs?'

'I'll take you there in a jiffy. They're out the back.'

Then another message, 'How come your dogs didn't bark when we turned up?'

'They know me and they know my car. For anyone else they'd bark their heads off and maybe bite their hands off. So be careful around them. Over time they'll become your friends but you need to be wary around them and give them the chance to get to know you. Don't go anywhere near them without me until I tell you it's safe to be with them by yourselves.'

'You hear that, you two?' Rebecca said.

Morton and Gene looked at her, begrudgingly agreeing. Next, Wyatt showed them the kitchen and the bathroom.

'Where's your room, Wyatt?' asked Rebecca.

'Out the back,' he said.

It was then she realised that he'd surrendered his bedroom for her. 'Oh, but you can't,' she said. 'I can sleep on the porch. You must sleep in your own bed.'

'No, I won't bide that. We've got beds upstairs in the attic, but in summer I tend to sleep out in the barn. Did it for years before Pearl and Jed got their place.'

'I don't mind sleeping in the attic at all,' Rebecca insisted.

'Please, I insist,' Wyatt replied. 'I'm more comfortable with things this way.' And so she demurred.

Wyatt took them out to the barn and one by one introduced each dog to them. They placed the backs of their hands in front of each husky's nose so the dogs could smell their scent. The dogs sniffed between their legs as well, an unexpected move that made Gene and Morton laugh as they backed away.

For dinner they ate cottage pie that Wyatt had prepared the night before. He lit the wood stove and some time later put the dish inside to reheat. Something about the standalone house, the wood as opposed to the thick cement walls that she now lived between – and shared on one side with a neighbour – reminded Rebecca of Newfoundland, of the home she grew up in, of a home that had a lot of living inside its four walls.

That night as she closed the door on her room Rebecca noticed the newness of the patchwork quilt folded on a trunk at the end of the bed, the crisp whiteness of the embroidered cotton coverlet over the bedspread, the freshly starched doilies and the small vase of flowers on the duchess. Smalls signs of comfort and of welcome from Wyatt or maybe his sister, Pearl, whom she would meet in the morning. And then her senses became aware of something else. She was surprised she hadn't noticed it earlier. The walls were newly painted. Not in the last few weeks, but certainly not more than a year ago. That touched her: the thought of him returning from Montreal and wanting to make the place presentable for them, in the event that they ever came to visit. As she lay down, she was pleased they had made the trip; that his efforts had not been in vain.

Each morning Morton and Gene would go with Wyatt to feed his pack. They watched and listened. They stroked and ruffled. They returned each evening. Any time Wyatt said, 'Let's check on the dogs,' they would race to his side.

In the barn there were four bicycles, in reasonable condition, oiled and cleaned. All four of them went riding, down straight roads turning at right angles down other straight roads and more – like a mysterious maze thought Rebecca – till eventually they'd arrive at a picnic spot beside a stream and shady willow trees. They fished with short rods made from the branches of the very willows they had rested under.

'Are you turning my children into Tom Sawyer and Huckleberry Finn?' she asked in delight. Morton was a natural at fishing, his senses seemingly sharpened. Once or twice Rebecca heard him whisper, 'Wow', at what he managed to raise from the river and that warmed her heart. The children swam, in their underwear. Some days Wyatt would toss his Stetson-like hat onto the bank, peel off his chambray shirt, and, in his trousers, swim with them as well. Even Rebecca joined in for it was hot, dry hot, on the prairies – such was this continent of extremes.

They had dinners with Pearl and Jed. They went to the movie house. They played cards, euchre mostly. They went south to an aerodrome for an open day to watch the fly boys training in all their fancy flying machines, to see formation flying, aerial loops, spins, and wing-overs. Gene and Morton learnt the names of every type of plane: the single engine-aircrafts – the Fleet Finches, the Fleet Fawns, the Fairey Battles, the de Havilland Tiger Moths and the Fairchild Cornells – and the twin-engine aircrafts – the Bristol Bolingbrokes, the Avro Ansons and the Cessna Cranes. But the ones they loved the most, were the ace fighter pilots in their single-engine Harvards. Wyatt told them they were the most powerful and responsive machines and the very planes that would shoot down the Germans. Morton would mouth the names of each aircraft, storing them to memory, never speaking them out loud.

15

The dogs, somehow, were different. They seemed to open the secret passage to Morton's voice, yet whenever he walked away from them, it closed behind him.

Gene was with Morton when she heard him utter the second spate of words he'd ever said since the tragedy. It was late in the afternoon. The day had been cooler than most, and Wyatt had surprised them when he said, I think it might be cool enough to take the dogs out for a short run. Their mother joined them while they set up then she left to go in and start dinner.

Out of the barn Wyatt dragged a go-cart contraption: four wheels on two axles with an old tractor seat. He told them he'd built it himself for summer exercising. The dogs immediately started prancing on the spot, their ears erect, humming a soft growl in their throats. Wyatt started talking to them in a low voice. 'Yes, yes, it's time. We're going.' He released four dogs, one by one, from their chains and tethered them to his leads. He told Morton and Gene that in the winter, he'd hitch eight to the sled, but their load that night was light and four was plenty. The dogs would be exercised turn about.

'Now, you're going to have to watch from the sidelines,' he said. 'But if all goes well I'll take you both with me, one at a time, for a second and third run.'

They nodded in speechless astonishment. The dogs barked in ceaseless excitement. Those in chains barked too, something akin to unrestrained frustration. Wyatt settled himself in the chair, grabbed hold of the leads firmly and with a flick and a 'Charge' they were off, bounding down the dirt road, nothing but dust and disbelief in their wake.

When he returned Morton got to ride first. Gene thought it was only fair. After all, he was the main reason they were there. Then it was Gene's turn. She settled herself in front of Wyatt, his legs either side of her and then they too were charging down the road, the wind lifting her fair plaited hair, dust particles on her tongue, the speed and thrill like nothing she had ever experienced in her life. The dogs bounded in unison, the leads jostled and her eyes streamed. Her eagerness and apprehension quickly gave way to delirious laughter and the next thing she knew Wyatt was laughing along with her.

When they returned they swapped the dogs over. Their mother waved to them from the back porch and they waved in return. Wyatt went solo again first, and then Gene joined him next, followed by Morton for the last run. As they approached the barn, Gene ran along beside them. Morton was nestled between Wyatt's legs with his feet on top of Wyatt's and his eyes on the pack. He was completely mesmerized by them and the whole experience. And just as they slowed to a halt in a distant, unused voice, he said, 'I like your dogs, Wyatt.'

Gene's blue green eyes locked with Wyatt's pale blue. Neither daring to say a thing. After a lengthy pause Wyatt said, 'Morton, you could become a fine dog trainer one day. It's got a lot to do with signals and whistles, a delicate but firm sense of touch, and the odd word here and there.' Morton's eyes remained frontwards, his face enthralled. He nodded in the most silent of agreements.

Gene never said a word to her mother. But another afternoon when they were out in the barn, which they were now allowed to do by themselves, wandering from one dog to the next, brushing their ears back, gazing into their knowing eyes, running their fingers through their thick moulting hair, Gene heard Morton say each dog's name aloud as they came upon it: Smokey, Pixie, Blacksox, Fire, Ringer, Thunder, Condor and Sheba. And then, like her, he started chatting to each dog, though his voice was strained and faint from lack of use. 'Would you like to come back and live with me in Montreal? I'd like that. We could go riding every day after school. Andrew would like you I'm sure.'

At one point she looked up towards the door and there was her mother, her hands clasped in front of her, Wyatt behind her squeezing her shoulders as tears rolled down her mother's face. Gene opened her mouth, but her mother put her forefinger to her lips, gesturing to keep quiet, and so Gene bowed her nine-soon-to-be-ten-year-old blonde head and talked away to her dog, only every so often glancing up at her mother, still standing there, tears silently streaming down her face, clutching one of Wyatt's hands on her shoulder as she and her brother talked nonsense to Wyatt's dogs.

16

That evening after the children had gone to bed Rebecca and Wyatt sat on the back porch enjoying the cooling air, the midsummer night sky and the sounds of owls.

After some minutes of comfortable silence, Wyatt spoke in a hushed tone. 'Morton is Samuel spat out, isn't he? At least physically...that golden gaze of his, that look he gets when he's completely absorbed in something.'

Rebecca laughed. 'I'm surprised you remember him that well.' She removed a stray clip from her hair and secured it more firmly.

'Well, we had plenty of days at the front just staring at each other, waiting around before all hell broke loose.'

Rebecca sighed. 'Yes, it is a comfort to know he's like Samuel in lots of ways.' She paused. 'But he's not the carefree boy he once was, not the carefree boy he might have been had things been different. Being here around your dogs is the most spirited I've seen him since the accident.' Their eyes met. 'Thank you.'

'It's not me,' he replied. 'The dogs deserve all the credit.'

'Oh, I don't think so, Wyatt. You're very good with children.'

'Must be the nieces and nephews I've practised on.'

'Must be,' said Rebecca. She'd met some of them the Saturday night before when they'd gone to Pearl's for a family dinner.

'I'm better with dogs though.'

Rebecca chuckled. 'I imagine you're good with children when they come into your patient rooms.'

'I manage.'

'How did you end up being a doctor? Seeing you out

here, I wouldn't have picked that as your calling.'

'How did I become a doctor?' he repeated. He was silent for a few moments looking down at the cup in his hands. Then he raised his head and looked into the distance. 'It wasn't a calling that's for sure.' He paused before continuing. 'I had an older brother; Truman was his name. When I was ten, and he was sixteen, he had an accident with a horse. We don't know what happened exactly. Most likely it bolted. He fell, the horse took off but Truman's foot was caught in the stirrup and he was dragged a long way before the animal stopped. He lay there for hours until my father came across them. It was a bad injury as you can imagine. He lived for two days and then he died. My parents did the best they could but there was no help available. We were all distraught, my father especially. One day, I don't know how many days or weeks later, I tried to ease his suffering by saying, "When I grow up, I'll help you on the farm, Dad." And do you know what he said?' He paused momentarily. '"The world doesn't need more farmers, son. It needs more doctors."

'And so I decided, there and then, that I'd be a doctor because that was what maybe could have saved my brother. Saved my father as well. Though now given what I know about head injuries, I doubt anything or anyone could have saved Truman.'

Rebecca took a sip of her own drink. 'Your father, did he ever recover?'

Wyatt crossed his ankles. 'No.' He sighed. 'Something died inside Dad that day and he was a different man. It was as if he started dying from that day onwards.'

After some moments, Rebecca asked, 'Did he live long enough to see you become a doctor?'

'No.'

He said it so softly that Rebecca just managed to catch it. She cleared her throat, wanting to offer Wyatt something – a cup of solace, a breath of empathy perhaps. 'The children will say I became a different person after Samuel died. And they would be right. I did not feel like myself and there were long periods that I do not even remember.

'When Samuel returned from the war after Matthew had died, all he wanted to do was to retreat from his life and everyone in it. And he did, for six months. He went far north, practically to Hudson Bay, and lived in some old fur trapper's hut. We railed at him at the time. But it's different when the shoe is on the other foot, for that was how I became. My life no longer offered me what I most wanted. It couldn't. That had been taken away from me and would never come again. I wanted to be alone with my thoughts and my thoughts were only for him…and Joel. I was a closed shop to everybody else.'

'What are you now?'

Rebecca took a deep breath. With a hopeful smile, just visible in the moonlight, she said, 'I'm learning that when you open for business, business can be surprisingly good at times.'

A few nights later, Rebecca asked Wyatt something she had long wondered. She had been tempted to ask Pearl, but she thought Pearl might get the wrong idea and jump to a hasty conclusion. So she decided she would just have to find a way to ask Wyatt himself. They were once more on the back porch sitting on the old couch, a comfortable space between them, staring out at the silhouette of two large Manitoba Maples. The only light came from the hallway behind them and the evening sky, festooned with a thousand stars as bright as the incandescent nights of her native Newfoundland.

'I don't mean to pry,' Rebecca said, 'and you can tell me it's none of my business, but I am curious as to whether you've ever been close to marrying.' She had planned the question deliberately that way: she didn't want to ask him why he had never married.

He was quiet for a little while, before clearing his throat. 'It's a fair question.' He then resumed his silence.

Eventually Rebecca couldn't contain herself any

longer. 'Does the fair question deserve a fair answer?' She laughed.

'How about this: I've been fairly close twice, but not close enough.'

'Did they get away?'

'No. More likely, I did.' He laughed lightly, pausing for a few moments. 'No, I withdrew. I don't think I'd be an easy husband. I like my space around me, Rebecca. I doubt if I could live with someone day in and day out, year in and year out. I could do that for maybe three weeks...here and there,' he looked at her, his eyebrows raised – they had come for just over a fortnight – 'but I don't think I was one cut out for married life.'

'Sometimes you never know whether you're cut out for it or not, until you give it a shot.'

'Maybe,' he said. 'But I'm such a loner. I think any woman who hitched her wagon to me would find her life quite lonely.'

'Maybe all you need is a woman who's content with that kind of loneliness.'

'Maybe all I need is my kind of dogs.'

Rebecca laughed softly.

They sat in companionable silence for a few minutes. 'What about you? Do you think you'll ever marry again?'

'Me?' said Rebecca, somewhat perplexed. 'I've never given it a single thought.' She paused and wondered why that was so. 'Maybe, because I still feel married, Wyatt, even after, how long has it been? Four years? I'm Rebecca Dalton through and through. That's who I am.' She was quiet for a while. 'Samuel always said, never give up hope for whatever it was you were wanting. But you see, it's not that I've given up hope. I'm just not hoping in that way. I hope for different things now. That Morton will speak again, be normal again. That my children stay safe. That they will be happy, not sad. That they will not have to suffer the loss of another loved one for decades to come. That I will live another forty-four years but still die before them.' Rebecca had celebrated her forty-fourth birthday only the week before. She paused, 'I don't know what other women my age hope for, but that's me.'

'That their children will come home safely from war. That the war will end.'

'Yes, amen,' said Rebecca. 'And, soon.'

Their days in Saskatchewan that summer rolled on rapidly as summer holidays do. It was peaceful. It was quiet. It was small, hometown Canada with not a lot happening on the surface, which to Rebecca, Morton and Gene was just fine, because they had enough company and good times to fill their days. And when it came time to leave, none of them felt ready to do so. Still, goodbyes had to be said.

'Thank you for having us, for making us so welcome, for being so wonderful to my children,' said Rebecca.

'It wasn't a chore,' said Wyatt, in that dry way he had. And he looked at her in that unreadable way he had. But after a few moments his soft blue eyes sparkled and the corners of his mouth tugged until he could no longer stop himself from smiling.

Rebecca shoved him playfully on the shoulder, then stepped forward and kissed him on both cheeks. As she stepped away, he grasped her wrist and turning close to her he looked into her face, his eyes earnest. 'Anytime,' he whispered.

Two months later, as a thank you, she sent Wyatt a painting: four people riding down a country road with that great Saskatchewan sky looming overhead.

The next time they saw Wyatt came completely out of the blue, or in that case, white – a blizzardy late March day the following year, 1944 – the day before Morton's thirteenth birthday. He appeared unexpectedly in a long felt coat, packs and sacks hanging off his padded frame. And in two of those sacks were two three-month-old husky pups.

Rebecca was speechless, and delighted. Morton and Gene were over the moon, and Mars and Jupiter as well. Wyatt glanced at Rebecca. 'I thought this would bring a language you love into your life,' he said.

She nodded. She was close to tears. 'Thank you,' she managed at last. Then with a laugh, 'I don't know if I'll be thanking you when they're fully grown and wreaking havoc in my house.'

How much Rebecca's spirits lifted with Wyatt's arrival, which was odd she thought, as she didn't think she had been unduly down before he came. But then winter had a way of wearing everyone down, the melancholic routine of cold and darkness. And there were days when Rebecca went through the motions, doing her best to keep loneliness at bay. Yet now there was Wyatt, who warmed her heart. He warmed her whole family with his quiet ways – so unlike Samuel which was the blessing, because he could never be Samuel. He couldn't replace him. He never would, and he wasn't trying to, and because of that none of them resisted him or felt threatened by his presence. He was just Wyatt. He was himself and everyone loved him for who he was, and for the friendship, the comfort, and the care he brought into their lives – Morton especially. He would write to Wyatt regularly, telling him about the huskies' antics and thanking him for the latest book Wyatt had sent him. How he had loved *White Fang* and *The Call of the Wild!*

They didn't go anywhere that summer holiday. Morton didn't want to be separated from his dogs – Sooki and Flint – even though his best friend, Andrew, promised to take them and look after them. Instead, Rebecca's sister, Rachel, came from Newfoundland, with her two daughters: Mary, now twenty and Beth, seventeen, the same age as Abigail.

Jonathan, at twenty-six, had started seeing another young medical student: a twenty-year-old girl called Annabelle. One Saturday as he was walking out the house he casually said by way of explanation that he was off to help Annabelle with her anatomy revision.

'All right.' Rebecca nodded, and then lowering her voice, she added, 'Some Lovers Try Positions That They Can't Handle.'

'Mother!' said Abigail, clearly embarrassed by her mother's use of the word, let alone the thought of her mother in the throes of passion. 'What has that got to do with anatomy?'

Rebecca looked at Jonathan who stood half gaping at her, shaking his head lightly in wry amusement. 'You tell her,' she said, unable to suppress a wide grin.

He sighed. 'It's a mnemonic, Abby, that is used to remember the eight bones in the wrist which is called the carpus. It's made up of the scaphoid, lunate, triquetrum and pisiform, SLTP, Some Lovers Try Positions, and the trapezium, trapezoid, capitate and hamate, TTCH, That They Can't Handle.'

'You're both sick,' said Abigail, turning away from them.

'Abigail! If your father were here right now he'd be the one who would be horrified. Horrified that I'd raised you to be such a prim.'

'Rather a prim than a prostitute,' she called over her shoulder.

'The word lover is not synonymous with prostitution!' Rebecca called after her. 'It's synonymous with a healthy adult consensual relationship. How do you think you came into this world? Why do you think I was so blissfully happy with your father all those years? He was my husband, my best friend, the father of my children and my lover. You'll find out before you're much older. The physical union between a man and a woman is the most beautiful thing. It's almost a holy sacrament.' Her daughter was nowhere to be seen.

'I'm out of here,' said Jonathan, already at the door.

Some time later, a subdued Abigail came up to her. 'I didn't mean to rubbish you and Dad.'

'I know you didn't.' Rebecca put her arm around her

and hugged her shoulder. 'It's just your father had very firm views on the subject. A sexual relationship is not something to be abhorred. It's something to be appreciated. Even your nana would say, "Oh la, la".'

Abby managed to break a smile at that. 'So what sort of views did Dad have?'

What to tell her? That he was a master? That he wrote the book? Rebecca swallowed. 'Your father loved the naked body. He thought it important that people not shy away from it, nor be ashamed of it. What can I tell you? He was a very physical man who enjoyed carnal pleasures and through him I came to enjoy them as well.' Rebecca paused before venturing further. 'I hope all of my children find someone who pleases them in the same way.'

On their honeymoon Samuel pushed up the sleeve of her robe, kissed her on the wrist, whispering, 'Have I ever told you how beautiful your carpus is?'

'No,' she said smiling at him, 'I don't think you have.' She remembered him writing to her once about the carpus after she had broken her arm. 'Some lovers try positions that they can't handle,' she teased and raised her eyes in a challenge.

'Not us, Rebecca. I believe we can handle just about anything.'

He lay her back down and leaning over her feet he kissed her anklebones. 'Your talus are beautiful. You have such slim ankles, legs to die for, even your patella is pretty.' He kissed her kneecaps. Then he untied her robe and parted it a little way and bent down to kiss her collarbone. 'Your clavicle marks you as a princess, such a prominent straight line from one corner of your shoulder to the other, so tantalisingly.' She had marvelled at it herself, the first time she saw it in a mirror at the age of nineteen. He traced his tongue along her collarbone then pushed her robe off her shoulders, then completely off her body. He lay down facing her with one arm, stroking her back.

'Now, your scapulas, they're out of this world. They are two of the most beautiful specimens I have ever seen towering above

your trapeziums. I go weak when I'm behind you, inside you and look up at your scapulas.'

'Go weak,' moaned Rebecca as she turned her back to Samuel. He stroked her shoulder blades with both his hands and then he kissed her spine, one vertebra after the other, from her neck all the way down. 'Your sacrum, your coccyx, makes me go crazy.' He breathed moist warm air onto her and ran his tongue over her.

'Go crazy,' moaned Rebecca.

'But they are nothing compared to your gluteus maximus.' He squeezed her bottom and kissed it. 'It marks you as the daughter of Zeus. So enticing.' He rubbed his hands over and over her buttocks and then himself back and forth.

'As enticing as my breasts?' asked Rebecca.

'Oh your pectoralis majors are major indeed.' He reached around and rubbed them possessively and then let his hand trail down her abdomen. 'Perfect starlit pointers to your pale pulsing mons pubis.' She was pulsing.

'Your mons veneris, mound of Venus, cleft of Venus,' his fingers were faintly feeling the folds of her flesh. She pressed his hand firmly into her. 'Your nectar of the gods,' he whispered.

'Come whoever is thirsty, accept the water of life as a gift,' she murmured.

'Oh, I accept.' Moments later his voice thickening, 'Was this what you had in mind?'

'Yes,' she whispered. 'Yes, help me, save me! My whole body is salivating. Salivating with unquenchable craving.'

'I can't help you', said Samuel, 'I'm suffering from the same inexplicable affliction. Sit on top.' He slowly rolled onto his back and she rolled with him, her back to him.

She liked this position. She liked the hardness of him inside her pushing into her at an angle, the zing of the sensations.

'How's that?' he asked.

She moaned in answer. She reached down and fondled him while she moved up and down, groaning and moaning with each movement. Her nipples, her whole front was tingling with the need for Samuel to lay his hands on them, as she lifted and lowered herself, almost fainting at the elevated sensations.

'Samuel' she breathed out. 'You are ... this is ... so, so, so...'

'What, Rebecca?'

'Like chocolate but better. I can't get enough of you.'

'I know,' whispered Samuel hoarsely, 'this view leaves Niagara Falls for dead.'

Rebecca moaned with the pressure and the pleasure of it, and in a heavy, dripping sauntering voice, said, 'Ooh, Samuel don't stop. Please,' she urged, 'don't stop.'

'You like it, Rebecca?' He was groaning, gasping.

She was breathless and panting. 'I. Like. It. All,' she managed between each exertion. 'Oh, Samuel, keep going.' And after that she didn't have any words left but he kept going until finally she cried out, and he cried out in expiration as pleasure waves the size of Niagara Falls pounded and tumbled and coursed through their veins melting like warm rich chocolate inside them.

That was a different life, wasn't it Samuel? But it was some life, that it was. The shock of Samuel and Joel's disappearance had sent Rebecca's body straight into menopause; though she was so grief-stricken she'd barely noticed. That night however, for the first time since Samuel had died, over five long years ago, forty-five year old Rebecca lay in her bereft bed wondering if she would ever be loved by a man ever again. Would she ever be so fortunate to have those emotions, share those experiences again?

17

The following May they celebrated Victory Day in Europe, though the celebrations were short lived for many of the Canadian sailors and airmen were reassigned to the Pacific Theatre in the war against Japan.

In late June, fourteen-year old Morton and his virtually inseparable, dark-haired companion, Andrew, caught the Canadian Pacific Railway from Montreal to Toronto to Regina in Saskatchewan, hauling Sooki and Flint along with them. The huskies naturally had to travel as cargo and so too did the boys – by choice – only going through to the passenger carriages to use the bathroom and buy food when needed. Under Wyatt's watchful guidance, they were going to learn how to be dog handlers. Sooki and Flint were going to learn how to be part of a dog train towing a sled. Six weeks later, Jonathan would fly Rebecca, Gene and Annabelle out to Calgary– a first for everyone – whereupon Wyatt and the boys were to meet them for the Stampede. After four days Rebecca and Gene would return to the farm for another two weeks and then they would all catch the train home together.

But the week before they came to leave Montreal, Gene announced she didn't want to go.

'Why don't you want to go?' asked Rebecca.

'I don't know. I just think everyone will have a better time if I don't tag along.'

'What do you mean, tag along?' Pause. 'We want you to be with us. You had a great holiday last time we visited Wyatt.'

'I know.'

'So why not come again this time?'

Silence.

'How do you see it as you tagging along?'

'I don't know. Morton's got Andrew. I'll be a bad smell hanging around them. Abby's off to Toronto. Again!'

'You can go to Toronto if you wish. And I already suggested you invite a friend to join us out west.'

'And I already said no! I don't want either.'

She had and Rebecca hadn't been overly surprised that she said no. Gene had friends at school but none that Rebecca could say were close. Gene's closest friends had always been her brothers and Rebecca had never thought to question that until recently, because for Rebecca her sister, Rachel, had always been her closest friend too. But lately there had been a change in the dynamics. Jonathan was pre-occupied with Annabelle, Morton spent all his spare time with Andrew and his dogs, and Abigail was Abigail, too caught up in her own life to register the fact that she had a sister six years her junior. Rebecca hoped one day it might be different and decided to make a point to talk to all of them about Gene. But meanwhile, what about the upcoming trip?

'Well what are we going to do then?' asked Rebecca. 'Change all our plans because you don't want to go.'

'No. I don't want to you to change your plans.'

'Well you can't stay home by yourself, and you know Morton will be disappointed if you don't show. Wyatt too.' That didn't even garner a response. Rebecca let it be for half an hour while she thought things through.

'How about you and I go and have a little holiday together somewhere first? Hmm? Quebec maybe? Ottawa? Or we could do some day trips? I've got enough gas coupons.'

Gene looked at her, considering the offer then shook her head. Rebecca was becoming increasingly exasperated. She decided to wait till Jonathan came home.

'Why don't you fly out to Calgary with us,' he suggested, 'and come back with us in the plane? So you stay out there for four days like us, see the Stampede, see

Morton and Wyatt, but you don't have to stay on.'

Gene looked at her older brother, a frown on her forehead.

He walked over to her and touched his forehead to hers. 'You won't be a bad smell with me,' he said, just loud enough for Rebecca to hear. 'You never will. You know what we mean to each other.' Jonathan wrapped his arms around her. Gene returned his hug.

'Thank you,' mouthed Rebecca, loving her son more than ever. She savoured that moment: the sight of him with his dark hair and his broad arms hugging his almost twelve-year old sister, her blonde hair in a simple pony tail half way down her back, her head under his chin, her eyes closed and her face calm.

That night after Gene went to bed Jonathan pulled her into the kitchen and told her he was worried about Gene.

'I know,' Rebecca agreed. 'She's disinterested in so many things but maybe that's a stage some teenage girls go through.'

'Some, Mom, not many,' noted Jonathan.

'When I was her age, I was quite melancholic at times. Even your father noticed it when he first met me. It was like I was riding a swing of despair. Some days I would be bright and optimistic about the future. Other days I would be glum and vaguely depressed that my life was going to be just like my mother's and that thought completely bored and saddened me.'

'Do you think that's her?'

'I don't know. She's not desperately sad and she's not exuberantly happy. She's just nothing,' said Rebecca.

'She's totally ambivalent about so many things. I hardly know what she likes and doesn't like anymore.'

'At least she's got her singing,' noted Rebecca. Gene sang in the school choir and to everyone's surprise she had a very good voice. She could have been the lead. In fact, Rebecca had offered for her to have extra singing lessons, and for a while she had, but she had shied away from any performance that would put her in the limelight.

Jonathan leant back against the kitchen bench his arms crossed, staring into space as if he could figure out an answer. After some moments he unfolded his arms and turned to his mother.

'I think we have to make more of a thing about her singing, support her whenever she performs. Ask her what she's rehearsing. Ask her to sing it for us at home. Maybe you could see if she wants to bring a friend from the choir home for dinner one night.'

'Jonathan, believe me I have tried.'

'I'm sorry, Mother. I'm sure you have but we're all going to have to try harder to make a point of including her in more things. I'll ask Annabelle to do something with her one night a week, and Abigail too when she gets back. You take her to a movie on a Friday night. I'll speak to Morton and make sure he spends some time with her after school rather than with Andrew and the dogs all the time. Maybe the three of them can do some things together. And I'll try and make a point of doing something with her and only her once a week.'

'Do you think there is a serious problem?' asked Rebecca.

'No, not yet. At least, I hope not. I think she's going through a stage where she's a bit lost. Listless, perhaps. Aside from her choir there's nothing else that she's latched onto. I think we just have to keep her trying new things and something will spark.'

In the following days Gene continued in her non-defined state and even though Rebecca considered asking her daughter what the problem was she decided against it, feeling her question would result in an 'I don't know' answer, which would lead to more upset and a greater sense of paralysis.

Instead, Rebecca hoped that by acting as if things were improving, things would improve and in time Gene did seem to crawl ever so slowly in the direction of her mother's hopes.

When they arrived in Calgary, however, Rebecca

discovered another one of her children had upset their plans. Morton.

'I'm sorry,' said Wyatt. 'I tried to convince them to come but they wouldn't budge. I hope you don't mind. I couldn't drag them away from the dogs. Nearly brought them with me in the car but Paul's at home again. He's staying with them, keeping an eye on them. And we'll be back in a week or so.'

But strangely after Jonathan and Gene and Annabelle flew out, neither Wyatt nor Rebecca was in a hurry to head east to Saskatchewan.

'Have you ever been to Lake Louise?' he asked, almost hesitantly.

'No,' she said. 'Have you?'

'Twenty-odd years ago I have. You follow the road up along Bow River to Banff. It's not far from there. Banff's full of skiers in the winter, but not so much now. Just lots of summer alpine meadows to explore and the odd grizzly to keep a healthy distance from.'

'Sounds lovely,' she said.

He called Pearl and told her they wouldn't be home for another week. She told them to enjoy themselves, take their time.

It was everything Wyatt said it would be and more. Much more. There were pockets of blackberry bushes sprouting along the road. They could stop at their leisure and pick their full, giving wide berth to the black mother bears and their cubs also picking their fill.

They went to Moraine Lake guarded by the stunning and once secluded Valley of the Ten Peaks. The water was mirror-like, such a clear reflective blue sourced from Larch Creek and the Fay Glacier. They hiked into alpine meadows full of white and pink, and yellow and purple flowers: lupins, forget-me-nots, gentians and larkspurs. They had picnics. Rebecca busily sketched in her notepad while Wyatt brewed up a strong cup of tea or coffee – whatever they fancied. They saw bald eagles and other birds of prey. They spied woodpeckers busy setting up their homes for next winter. They walked through conifer trees and smelt them, sharp and pungent, reaching for the sky, bold and evergreen.

And in the evenings they made love: glorious, unrepentant love.

'I'm not Samuel. I could never be.'

'I don't want you to be Samuel. I want you to be you.'

And how had they got to this place? It just seemed the most natural thing in the world to do. Were they swept away by the surroundings? Beautiful as they were, she didn't think so. For Lake Louise was breathtaking; the rooms at Chateau Lake Louise on par with the best she had ever stayed in; the view, from her balcony, divine. The sky at night was superlatively clear; the stars, a million distant burning fires; the moon, full and tumescent – a lover's moon. They had kept the curtains open, letting the light stream in, and made love in the bare moonlight.

They'd wake up and order room service – fresh coffee and French toast. Wyatt would pull on his trousers and his shirt, but leave it undone, for on the first morning Rebecca had placed her hand on his and boldly asked him to leave it unbuttoned.

'You like looking at my fifty-five year old body?' His voice was diffident; a shy smile played on his lips.

'It's a very fine body.' Rebecca grinned in admiration. It was. He'd kept himself in remarkable shape. His body, though lean, still had muscles in all the right places. It felt so good to lay her hands on his naked chest, his naked back, to press her cheek up against his smooth skin, her lips too. His aquamarines eyes, which she once thought were sincere and lonely, she now thought were sincere and at peace. Wyatt seemed to be quietly alive in a way she had never seen before and she relished that.

After breakfast, he would retire to his own room to shower and change. And then they'd set out on another adventure: a walk up to the tea house on the Skyline Trail, reminiscent of the Himalayan tea houses, so they were told, selling only tea, not coffee, much to the disappointment of an irate American tourist; a paddle to the end of the lake and back; a stroll past the Swiss Alp-hornist playing on the lake's promenade; a side excursion to Emerald Lake and its magnificent wooden bar from Whitehorse in the Yukon; and in the evening, cheese fondue at the Chateau's European inspired restaurant.

'Do you remember it being this beautiful?' Rebecca asked, as they gazed at the glacier in the distance glowing pink in the dying twilight.

'It has never been this beautiful.' His lips brushed her ears; his arms nestled around her shoulders. 'Because of you, Bella Becca.'

They returned to their lives. The correspondence continued just as before. But not just as before, for the letters now were letters of love, of surety, of pleasures shared, of future plans. This man who was her dearest friend. This man who would write to her and, bless him, would write separately to her children, so they too had the thrill of reading about his adventures. He wasn't a man of many words, but his words were enough. His presence was enough, and too, his simple actions. After years of resistance, Wyatt finally succumbed and installed a telephone. He told Rebecca he wanted to hear her voice. She liked to hear his as well, even though she filled most of their conversations with the happenings of four children and two huskies. The fact that he was making changes to his life for her, for the two of them, warmed her heart. To hear him call her, Becca, thrilled her in other ways.

One day he wrote and told her, confirmed bachelor that he was, he would make an exception for her, if marriage were important to her.

She found that both utterly touching and hilarious. She wrote back and told him that strangely, it pleased her very much to know she was a woman in her forties with a handsome, virile lover. She added:

Even more strangely, I think Samuel would be proud of me for being so daring. We once had a fascinating conversation about lovers and virgins – way before he and I were ever intimate. It started with his take on the Commandment: 'Thou shalt not commit adultery'.

'Rebecca, Rebecca, Rebecca,' he said, shaking his head at me. 'Don't you know that Commandment was written to deny women and disadvantaged men – men without means? It was a way of wealthy men, maintaining their power.'

And on he spoke about how Abraham, Moses and the like could have numerous wives and concubines – lovers – as long as they could afford them – giving a man the right to have several sexual partners and guaranteeing that the children born to their wives and concubines would only be their flesh and blood, thereby securing their bloodlines. So they could have numerous 'legal' partners, he said, and not commit adultery. Women on the other hand were only permitted to have one partner, their husband or master.

I was fifteen at the time. So naïve. You can imagine my astonishment and awkwardness. I couldn't even bring myself to say the word, 'lover'. All I could manage was to ask him if he thought it was okay for women to have such relationships and why he thought so.

His reply was along the lines of: 'Because many men do, and have done for centuries, and it's a double standard if women cannot have the same liberties. Just like there's a double standard of virginity for men and women.'

That confounded me as well. He urged me to read La Reine Margot by Alexandre Dumas, which I did many years later.

But on that day my curiosity got the better of me. I remember thinking I would say a prayer for forgiveness that night but I gingerly asked away – I doubted whether the opportunity to have such a conversation with someone about such matters would ever come again.

Wyatt wrote in his reply:

Samuel sounds like Matthew through and through – a side I never got to fully see on the Front. Luckily he didn't corrupt you completely, but then again I'm very fortunate to know such a liberated woman.

18

Somehow, by providence, by good design, by coincidence or by opportunity, Wyatt and Rebecca managed to holiday together each year and see each other at least twice in between. Rebecca would go west with one or any number of children, Wyatt would come east: one year for Jonathan's wedding – he and Annabelle tied the knot in 1947; the next year for Abigail's twenty-first; then the following year for Abigail's wedding to Will, a friend of her cousin, Daniel's, from Toronto – no surprises there. Jonathan gave her away, while her cousin, Daniel – Analeise and Randall's second son – stood as best man. Rebecca thought that was a nice touch indeed. But an even nicer touch was Abigail, of her own volition, asking her nearly sixteen-year old sister, Gene, to be her maid of honour. It did wonders for Gene's self esteem.

That same summer Rebecca turned fifty. A few months later, in September, her mother, Morna, would be turning eighty. Rebecca had not seen her mother or her sister, Esther, since the summer Samuel and Joel disappeared. Her sisters and mother had been invited to Abigail's wedding. They sent their apologies along with their gifts. Rebecca knew it was an expensive undertaking for them to travel all the way from Newfoundland to Toronto. She was disappointed, but she understood. The people who mattered most to Abigail were there in abundance and that was what was most important.

But even so Rebecca missed them. She thought of Samuel as she watched their twenty-two year old daughter say her wedding vows. She missed him. She smiled through her tears. Sitting next to her, Wyatt squeezed her hand. He knew. She tried to console herself with the fact that she was the one who was fortunate to have lived to see this day, and hopefully many more.

Jonathan was the one who first suggested it. The thought had entered her mind but she didn't quite have the courage to come out with it: that the family visits Newfoundland for the summer to celebrate her fiftieth birthday with her mother and sisters. Plus, it had been a big year for Newfoundland. After two referendums the country had finally voted to become part of Canada. It was no longer a British Dominion. Joey Smallwood had prevailed. It seemed fitting for Rebecca to return and celebrate. Knowing that Newfoundland was now part of Canada, soothed her in an unexpected way, like how she was soothed arriving in Toronto all those years ago and being welcomed with open arms by the Daltons. She felt only good things would flow from this union.

The poignancy of both occasions, however, seemed lost on the rest of her children.

'We're just back from our honeymoon,' Abigail said. 'Sorry, we're staying in Toronto and setting up home.'

Eighteen-year-old Morton signed one word. 'Never'.

Gene looked from Morton to Rebecca clearly not knowing who to side with. In the end she declined, opting to stay home with Morton and the dogs. So they postponed the immediate family celebration till August and only Jonathan, his four-month-pregnant wife, Annabelle, and Wyatt accompanied her. But intuitively, Rebecca knew that with those two men by her side, she would get through whatever it was she needed to get through.

Part of her expected to be haunted by Samuel, but she found it was true what they said about time ameliorating past pains. There were days she wished she would find him sitting at her mother's table, so they could drink long cups of tea, trade constant smiles and catch up on life. She recalled many fine memories and her sense of loss was there, as an undercurrent, a warm sadness, but it did not overpower her. She was busy making new memories now. With her sisters, nieces and nephews, and grandnieces and grandnephews there was so much life around her, within her. She thought more of life than death, more of new experiences with loved ones, old and new – Wyatt and her daughter-in-law – and more of the future than the past: of becoming a grandmother and wondering how that could be.

Still, there was no denying her past. On the day before her fiftieth birthday Jonathan suggested they take a drive to Lewisporte for lunch.

'Shall we go in two cars and take mother, Esther and Rachel?' she asked.

'Actually…' he paused, pulling her eyes to his.

'I'd rather just take you. I never get to spend time alone with just you any more and today I'd like to.'

How could she deny him? Besides, Annabelle and Wyatt seemed more than happy for them to have some time alone together.

Jonathan drove while they chatted. She was vaguely conscious of the turns in the road, the glimpses of ocean, an odd directional sign here and there, a billboard for a motel on a crest of a hill, and then next she knew Jonathan was stopping the car outside a brown barn, seemingly in the middle of nowhere.

'Is everything okay?'

'I hope so,' he replied. 'Come on, out you get.'

When she walked around the other side of the building she discovered it was a small hangar adjacent to a relatively new airfield.

'Happy birthday, Mom!' said Jonathan, his face full of delight. 'We're going to spot us some icebergs.'

Her hand on her heart, her smile as wide as the St Lawrence, Rebecca just shook her head in delirious disbelief.

Within twenty minutes they were airborne, flying over the Atlantic, past jagged granite cliffs to their left, up above the fishing trawlers, gliding over iceberg alley. And it was beautiful. Magical. Breathtaking. Silver white structures jutted out of the still green ocean, the water elemental and emerald, transparent and new. Giant forms of icebergs, expansive underneath, revealed a whole new world. Complete illogical floating marvels. Melt pools the colour of deep midnight blue transfixed them, one so deep it was like a funnel in the ice; others had water peeling over the side in a ceaseless cascading flow.

Northbound they flew, heaven-bound. She lost count of the icebergs, of the shapes and sizes, each one different, each one seemingly alive. She was lost in a sweeping symphony of earth's creation. And on that day Rebecca knew that whatever had come to pass, come what may, icebergs were an undeniable part of her soul. It was a rare gift and her son had given it to her. A new memory of icebergs for her to treasure along with the others she held so dear. She was moved beyond words. She just put her hand on Jonathan's leg and squeezed out her heart.

19

She returned to Salvage, overflowing with euphoria.

'So, it **was** a good idea,' said Wyatt.

'Yes,' she hugged him. 'It was the best idea. You knew obviously.'

'We all knew.' His grin of delight matched her own. 'So, tell me, what was it like?'

Rebecca shook her head. 'Words can't describe it.'

'Try some.'

So she tried.

Later as they were getting ready to turn in, he said to her, 'Hard to imagine anything on your birthday topping what you did today.'

Rebecca was part way through unbuttoning her top. She halted as she caught his eye. 'What? Are there more surprises in store?'

He chuckled. 'Not that I know of, but even if I did, Becca, I wouldn't be telling. I know how to hold my tongue.' He poked it out in jest.

'Is that so?' She laughed as she moseyed up to him. 'Well, how about this for a surprise? Tomorrow, on my birthday 50th birthday, why don't we do something you've never done before, something I've only ever done once myself?'

'Okay,' Wyatt drawled, 'what do you have in mind?'

'Come on, Wyatt, humour me. I don't want to rush the surprise.'

'What? I'm meant to guess, am I?'

'Yes, have a crack.'

'Something I've never done before?'

'That's it.'

'Whale watching?'

Rebecca gasped. 'Haven't you ever been whale

watching? We'll have to do that this holiday! But, no not that.'

'Flying above the icebergs.'

'Yes, we absolutely must do that together as well. I want you to see how spectacular it was. Keep guessing.'

'Oh I don't know, Becca, some peculiar Newfoundland custom.'

'Not just in Newfoundland, but yes, in Newfoundland this time.'

He pressed his lips together then raised his eyebrows and his hands as if he were out of ideas.

'Okay I'll give you a hint,' she said taking both his hands in hers and looking into his eyes. 'It will be big. It will make headlines,' she teased, her eyebrows raised.

Wyatt just stood there smiling and shaking his head at Rebecca waiting patiently for her to spill the beans.

'Are you ready for it?'

'Yes,' he nodded, 'I'm ready for it.'

'Why don't you and I…get married?'

His eyes flared in surprise, his mouth parted; yet he was lost for words. Aha, she'd got him. 'Whose got your tongue now? Hmm? The cat? Or me?'

'Are you serious?' he asked, squeezing her hands, his pale blue eyes peering into her own.

'Yes,' she said, squeezing back, although she couldn't help but giggle. 'Yes, I'm serious.' She tried to regain her composure.

He released her hands and took a step back. 'I thought you didn't want to complicate matters. Didn't want to cramp my style?'

'Don't worry, none of that has changed. We don't have to live together permanently, maybe when Gene finishes school we could live together a little bit more. Would you like that?'

He nodded. 'Hard to imagine it five or so years ago, but, yes, I would like that very much.'

He paused.

'I thought you liked being Rebecca Dalton. You told

me a few years back that that was who you were now, who you would always be.'

'I can still be Rebecca Dalton and be married to you. I can still be your wife, Rebecca. Becca. I don't have to go round changing my surname do I? Is that a deal clincher for you?'

'No,' he said. 'Never has.' He rubbed the side of his face. 'I told you years ago, if you needed me to marry you to make things respectable between us I would. You weren't fussed. What's changed now?'

'I know you did, Wyatt, and I appreciated that. But to me that was about making things respectable for other people, not for us. This is about us. This is about me finally having the clarity, given all we have shared in the last few years, of saying, I chose you. I love you.' She reached for his hands again. 'I want you to be my husband – not as a consolation prize because I can no longer have Samuel. This trip in some strange way has closed the chapter on that. Today I think I found the last part of myself that has been missing for years, and it wasn't Samuel. It was me! What makes me whole! I almost feel reborn. And I am on the edge of a new beginning. I'm about to become a grandmother for goodness sakes! You've never had children but I want you to have grandchildren. I want you to be the grandfather of my grandchildren and in that way, you, Samuel and I can be as one. What do you say?'

Wyatt pulled Rebecca's hands to his lips and kissed them. 'I say, "Whatever makes you happy, Becca." You know I love you. Have loved you from practically the first time I laid eyes on you. I just never wanted to encroach too much on your life and your family.'

Rebecca released one hand to stroke his face. 'Wyatt, **you** are family. You have been for some time.'

They kissed and they kissed, and their kisses felt so familiar yet so new. Breaking off, he murmured, 'Would you like your birthday present now?'

'You!' Rebecca lightly shoved his shoulder.

'Well yes, that!' he chuckled. 'But, no, given what we've just talked about, what I bought you for your birthday. It's kind of fitting.'

'What did you buy me?'

'Oh, nothing much, just this little thing.' He broke off and went to his bag and returned with a small velvet box.

'You bought me a ring?' Rebecca asked. 'What were you thinking?'

'I thought a lot, trust me. What does one give a woman for her fiftieth? And not just any woman. In the end I settled on a beautiful ring for a beautiful lady. The colour reminded me of your eyes. Go ahead, open it. '

It was beautiful: a large, striking blue topaz in an old gold setting with tiny diamonds either side of the precious stone. She took it out of the box and placed it on her ring finger, next to Samuel's gold wedding band.

'Oh, Wyatt.' Rebecca dragged her moist eyes away from her finger. 'I do love it.' She kissed him and squeezed him tight. 'And you know what? I love it that my mother and sisters can be at our wedding tomorrow.'

'I'm sure they'll love that too.'

'Yes…they missed everything last time. It won't be a problem with the church, do you think? I mean it's a Thursday, can't imagine St Stephens being that busy.'

'Wouldn't think so. And we've already got the wedding breakfast taken care of – your party!'

'How economical of us.' She chuckled as she folded down the covers. 'Wait till we tell everybody in the morning,'

Wyatt unbuckled his belt. 'What about the kids? Do you think they will have a problem with us getting hitched?'

'Not at all. Banish that thought. They'll be very happy for us.'

She was right. They were.

20

Rebecca can now paint icebergs

She's not so enamoured with her first few attempts, but then with patience and practise she manages to capture the light on the white, the translucency of the water, the paleness of the sky, the muted sunrises. It is pure realism.

On one visit, Jonathan stared speechless until he finally murmured, 'It's like a photograph. Better than a photograph. There's an intensity, a richness that supersedes the natural form.' All those years spent gazing at icebergs are starting to pay off.

And the gallery that till now, has only ever taken one or two of her paintings each year, sells them as quickly as they hang them. They ask for more. They'll pay her more.

Jonathan's old room at the front of the house is now completely devoid of furniture bar one small settee and a table. It's faces the street and on warmer days the windows are thrown open so the natural light can pour in. She has two large canvases on the go so she can work on one while the paint is drying on the other.

She shuffles her hours at the postcard business so she can paint more in daylight while processing orders and paperwork at night. She goes in during the day only when they need her now. Wyatt urges her to resign from the postcard business altogether but she tells him, she needs the money. He tells her she doesn't need the money any more. She tells him she doesn't want to give up the postcard business; she enjoys looking at all the new photographs. Okay, he says.

The gallery wants her to have her own showing in December 1950. She never seems to have enough hours in the day. Wyatt comes to her that Easter – she feels bad that he is the one doing most of the travelling – but he tells her he doesn't mind and says nothing will stop him from being there for her opening. Her eighty-three-year-old mother-in-law, Lottie, an avid art-lover all her life, promises her she won't die before attending the opening. Lottie tells all her friends because suddenly Rebecca is getting cards of congratulations and best wishes months before her show.

Gene is seventeen and in her last year at school, breezing through most subjects, topping her class in French and Geography. Morton works for a newspaper as a general intern. He's hoping to secure a cadetship to train as a journalist covering sports and animals. He's already taught himself shorthand – another unusual language that he flits through with ease. He works afternoons and nights; she rarely sees him. He runs the dogs in the mornings and most days Andrew comes by and runs the dogs in the afternoon. Sometimes Gene joins him. Abigail is pregnant while Jonathan's son, Matthew – her first grandchild – is teething and crawling. Fall descends, the leaves on the trees wave amber and gold but Rebecca barely notices their presence for there are never enough hours in the days or nights as they turn into a white swirling luminescent blur.

21

At around eleven o'clock at night, a week before her mother's opening, Gene turns off her bedside light. She is nearly asleep when she hears Morton come home. He is later than usual. She can picture him patting the dogs that sleep in the downstairs hall, and if she strains hard enough she may even hear them moan in return. A few minutes later he trudges up the stairs and walks down the dark hall towards his room, but tonight he halts outside her room, pushes the door open and walks over to her bed. Part of her wants to say, 'What, Morton?' but she remains silent, her right eye shut, her left open, curious as to what he might do.

But he doesn't do anything. Instead, he bends down and whispers, 'Gene, roll over.'

Trust him to know she was lying there wide-awake. She moves across to make room for him to lie on the bed next to her. He searches for her hand and when he finds it he holds it tight. He lies there struggling with his breathing, his chest rising and falling and Gene instantly knows all is not right. They stay that way in silence for many minutes. She can faintly smell beer on his breath. Eventually she says, 'Do you want me to tell you a story?'

'No,' he says, his voice tight. 'Tonight, I'll tell you a story.'

'What's happened?' She places her other hand around his hand that is clasping hers. She has no idea what to expect, but whatever it is she knows it's going to be bad.

'Nothing's happened,' he pauses, 'to me'. Then in the next breath: 'Everything's happened to me.' She strains to understand him. She hears him first but then she has to work out the words, so foreign are his sounds.

'What happened to you tonight?' she asks, hoping for more clarity.

'Tonight I had a meal at Dunns after work.'

'By yourself?'

'No. With Andrew.' His voice breaks on Andrew and at the sound of her brother's broken voice a hole suddenly rips in Gene's stomach.

'What about Andrew?' she asks. Andrew worked as a typesetter at the same newspaper where Morton worked.

Morton is silent.

'Morton! Tell me!'

'It was the quickest thing, Gene. I still can't believe it happened.'

Slithering tentacles of fear snake their way inside her. 'Believe what happened?'

'We were walking along Saint Catherine Street when we saw one of those new Cadillac Fleetwoods, a black one, so we stopped to have a look. The hood emblem is something else, a stylised man's face in chrome with a cape, an angel perhaps. Anyway, the next thing I knew there were horns blaring, tires screeching. I looked up and there were lights headed straight towards us. I grabbed Andrew to drag him away but he just shoved me backwards onto the pavement and I went sliding on the snow and ice. I think he thought I was being impatient, as if I were saying, "Let's go!" Oh why oh why did he have to be born deaf? He crouched again to look at the emblem and before I could even get to my feet, before I could pull him away this car lost control on some black ice and slammed into him, pinning him between it and the Cadillac.'

Gene gasps and starts to cry. She brings their clutched hands to her chest as if to protect herself.

'It was awful, Genie. To see him squashed like that. His head split and bleeding. It was like Dad all over again.'

Gene…cannot…breathe.

'And for the barest moment he catches my eye, just

like Dad did, as if he too knew his life was about to be over. He had the same look, Genie.'

Morton is crying now. 'I can't keep living with that look. It kills me. I can't get rid of it. And this powerless, this helplessness – not to be able to change what happened – not to have prevented it.'

'Morton!' Gene exhales. It is all she can manage. She wants to tell him to shut up, to be silent.

'We were out at the iceberg looking at those two towers when all of a sudden this piece falls off and crashes right next to the boat. It's like an explosion. The boat is forced over by the surge of water. We are all thrown in the ocean, the motor snaps off, Dad's yelling at Joel and I to tread water, but to stay back from the boat, while somehow he rolls himself on top of it. I don't know how he does it, but he uprights it and he points to our lunch tin and tells me to swim over and grab it which I do and he tells me to get in the boat and use it to scoop the water out as quickly as I can.

He tells Joel to hang on to the boat while he's swimming after one of the paddles that he brings back and lays across the seat. Tells me I'm doing a good job, scooping the water. He's scooping water, and Joel's trying to splash the water out and then another piece of ice breaks away, crashes down. We don't even see it. It lands behind us somewhere and this wave hurls me and the boat and Dad back towards the iceberg. I don't know what happens to Joel but I'm looking at Dad and the iceberg and it happens so quickly, Genie, but it's like it happens so slowly. Almost taunting me as if…if my hands were big enough I could reach out and push us away, or reach out and pull Dad to safety. But the boat is rammed into the iceberg – Dad in between – and his head and body are squashed between the ice and the boat. I scream out to warn him but my scream comes after the fact.

He gives me this look as if he is sorry. As if he knows it's the end. As if he wants to say something but can't.

And the next moment he's collapsing, sinking and I've got his shoulders and I'm trying to hold him up, trying to pull him in, while we're bobbing around and being bumped into the iceberg again and again. And there's blood all over his head and his eyes are closed and I can't lift him up. And then I turn around and I look into the distance and I can see Joel facing us, dog paddling like mad towards us. I swear I can see the whites of his eyes. He's terrified. He's crying. I don't know what to do. I think if he can make it to the boat, then maybe he can help me drag Dad in, but he's not getting any closer, he's being towed away and I think, the only way I can get to him is if I let Dad go. But I can't. I don't want to. I'm torn. And every moment that I hesitate is a moment lost for Joel. I know that now. I could have saved him but I didn't. I stood holding a dead man. Our father. And then at some point, I don't know when, I don't know how, I knew I had to release him. I had to turn my back on him and start paddling, start looking for Joel. I tried to paddle away from the spot. As fast as I could I tried to, but it was useless. I had to stop and scoop out more water. And then I started paddling, and paddling, and paddling, but I never saw Joel again.'

Gene does not know how to respond. Her mind screams out a constant ear-piercing NO while she weeps quietly, breathes raggedly, clutching her brother's hand. After about half an hour, Morton wipes his face. 'I can't live here any longer, Gene. I can't live with Mom's icebergs.'

'They'll be gone soon,' she cries.

Hours later, he whispers, 'I'm glad you know now, Gene.'

I'm not, cries her heart.

22

Gene somehow moves through the next week. No one but her knows the weight on top of her each morning when she awakes. How she can barely push it away. How she struggles to get out of bed. How she goes with Morton to Andrew's funeral and clutches his hand throughout, and is strong and brave for him, and cries with him, for him. All her family goes: Wyatt, Abigail, everyone who's in town for her mother's opening, which is put back by a week. Gene knows people look at her despondent face and see one thing; inside she knows another.

Ten days later for her mother's opening, she puts on a dark green jersey dress under her winter coat, clips her blonde hair at the crown, and forces a weak smile for all those she knows: relatives, friends, business associates, gallery owners and patrons. But she exists in a surreal world: seemingly proud of her mother, yet utterly horrified at her, at her innocent, blasphemous act against her father. She is angry, angry at the injustice of the world that it is so callous in the way it snatches from her the people she loves.

To save herself, to save an embarrassing unforgiveable scene she detaches herself from her mother, removes herself from everyone. When the speeches are over, she and Morton steal away, the gallery is packed, no one notices, they don't say goodbye to a soul.

At home Morton takes the dogs for a run, he on his bike, the dogs on leads tied to his handlebars. That's his sanity. Tomorrow he's going to ask Wyatt if he can move to Saskatchewan and live in his barn. Her mother and Wyatt will agree. In one small corner of her heart she is happy for him. She wants him to go. Just like she wants to go. Away from this world, away from what she's heard, what she carries, to the other side where reunions happen and then she can erase all of it. She can't bear it. She goes to their bathroom, to their medicine chest, to the bottle of pills prescribed for her mother by her grandad an ice age ago. It is half empty and at least ten years old. She pours herself a glass of milk, goes to her bed and one by one swallows her life away.

Dark Days

Montreal, Canada, December 1950

23

Montreal's Victoria Hospital was built of a grey limestone that had darkened with age. Outside it may have passed for an orphanage. Inside there was no mistaking the penetrating smell of ether and iodoform and other scents that assaulted the senses as one walked the wards. This hospital had been Jonathan's life for the last decade. Rebecca wondered if he still noticed the overpowering pungency or whether he had become immune to the odours. Maybe he welcomed them as if they somehow primed him for the challenges of each day.

They had just come from Gene who had not woken throughout their entire visit and now they were sitting with Doctor Simmons, a balding man with gold rimmed glasses, discussing Gene's progress and possible treatment. It was two days after Rebecca's exhibition opening, two days after Gene had tried to end her life. That she had not was purely because of the uncanny intuition of both brothers and blessed good luck.

Morton had not gone far on his run. Three streets from home after he had passed kerb after kerb of graded snow it dawned on him that perhaps he should have asked Gene to come with him. She had been nothing short of an angel the past week. It occurred to him his sister too could do with losing herself in a fast-paced dash with the huskies. No sooner had he thought that than Sooty suddenly yelped and started limping. In one motion Morton dismounted from the bike letting it fall on its side, the wheels spinning through the air. He ran to her side to pull her bloody mouth away from her bloody foot. A jagged piece of glass had impaled in the tender web between her front paws. From the incessant licking her tongue was also cut and bleeding.

He grabbed the glass and removed it. No more running that day. If that wasn't a sign to take Gene on a walk up Mont Royal, what was?

Upon entering the house he went straight to the kitchen, pulled an old tea towel out of the bottom drawer and tightly bound Sooty's foot. Sit, he motioned. Then he bounded up the stairs. A few heart-gripping moments later he was carrying Gene back down, the mouth of the empty bottle between his teeth. Placing her on one of the lounges, he raced into the kitchen, found a copy of his mother's invitation, phoned the art gallery and in his little used voice asked to speak to Doctor Jonathan Dalton.

Eighteen minutes later the three of them were at Victoria Hospital. Morton carried Gene in his arms while he raced after his brother down a warren of corridors towards a vacant operating theatre where Jonathan yelled at him to lay her down on the table, take off her dress and secure those straps across her hips and her chest. Less than thirty seconds later he returned wearing a mask, an apron, his hands in gloves and two nursing sisters similarly attired. One saying, 'Doctor Mills will be here in a minute.'

Jonathan saying: 'Too late. Morton, You might want to step outside. I'm going to cut Gene open. Right now!'

A nurse's gloved hand lifted her singlet. Jonathan's gloved hand was clasped around a scalpel – hospital policies forbidding the operating on one's relatives be damned.

Morton turned and walked away as his brother sliced into his sister's stomach and did his all to empty it of half-dissolved, half-absorbed tranquilizers and save her life.

Why Gene had tried to commit suicide none of them knew. Or weren't saying. Morton was his non-talkative self, more in cahoots with his dogs than ever. Each time his eyes met Rebecca's they screamed in frightened alarm and worried anguish. Wyatt's gentle words of praise and encouragement: 'You saved your sister's life, Morton. What you did that day was extraordinary,' seemed to do little to settle his unease. Undoubtedly this was almost one too many deaths for one lifetime. If Morton had not turned around when he did...if Jonathan had not acted without hesitation.

Dr Simmons was telling them Gene's blood pressure was back to normal and that he suspected anytime soon she would wake wondering where she was and what had happened. Hopefully there would be no brain damage, he added.

Rebecca was aghast. 'Surely not!'

'It can happen,' Doctor Simmons said, but I suspect Jonathan intervened in time.

For Rebecca that possibility didn't bear thinking about. All she wanted to know was when Gene would be well enough to be discharged.

'Physically I'd say another week but there's a long road of recovery ahead of her. We need to understand what prompted the suicide attempt. Was it depression or something else?

'Typically it's one of two causal factors. One: prolonged depression, where the patient has endured long periods of low self-esteem and a poor sense of self-worth...lethargy, loss of appetite, a general disinterest in life, melancholia, prone to crying. Has that been Gene?'

She and Jonathan looked at each other. 'There have been elements and episodes of that, but I wouldn't say sustained,' she said. 'If anything, I'd say up till quite recently she was in high spirits.'

'What happened recently?

'My younger son's best friend was killed.'

'Well, that could be it. The second major cause is a sudden traumatic event, which could be death of a loved one; a major shock, bad news or a setback of some description, such as a failed romance; or a physical attack such as a rape or molestation where one can't handle the feelings of disgust or fear.'

'I'm not saying, what you're saying is not correct,' said Rebecca. 'She was saddened by Andrew's death, as we all were. But I think her reactions were normal for a teenage girl and would not have led to this extreme action. Had Morton been the one who had attempted to take his life then, yes, I think that might be true. He saw his friend being killed. We understand that he felt helpless not being able to prevent it from happening.'

'Perhaps though, Andrew's death has come at a vulnerable age. Some young people find it hard to accept death, to come to terms with the fact they will never see that person ever again.'

Rebecca's eyes gravitated towards Jonathan where they held for three counts before returning to the Doctor.

'He was young,' Doctor Simmons explained, 'she was young...the thought that that easily could have been her, not Andrew, with her brother. That sense of being undeserving of one's life is often very real for some patients.'

She sighed. 'Who knows?'

It was a rhetorical question but the doctor answered it. 'Gene.'

Jonathan let out the breath he had been holding. 'Sadly from a very early age my sister and my brother made reticence their own exquisite art form.'

Doctor Simmons noted that down. 'Every door has a key,' he said, looking up at them. 'Admittedly some can be like searching for a needle in a haystack. In my limited experience it's critical that the patient is in an environment where they are not forced to provide answers, where they don't feel threatened. They have to be free to explore their thoughts and feelings without any recriminations.'

'I don't threaten my children,' she said, feeling a little affronted.

'Mother,' said Jonathan, touching her arm. 'I know

you don't and Doctor Simmons isn't saying you do. You're always very encouraging. But that's not to say that at times Gene may feel intimidated just by virtue of your age and experience in the world, and the very fact that you are her mother, a person of some authority in this situation.'

Rebecca slanted her head in faint acceptance. 'Have you had any other cases like Gene?' she asked.

'Each case is unique until you get to the core of the issue. Psychiatrists can then draw comparisons on causes, possible treatments and likely results.

'I can't stress how important it is to get to the bottom of the issue that's driven her to take her own life. Because if you don't, more than likely it will resurface again, when she undergoes another period of distress. It's critical that we're able to ascertain what the best treatment is to cure her so she is no a longer a threat to herself.'

'When can we start?' asked Jonathan.

'When she's physically recovered and feels mentally strong enough to be able to talk to someone. At the same time, we will start her on a course of anti-depressants and she will have to stay on them for some time.'

'So once she's physically well and on medication, she can come home and then start to see a psychiatrist?' asked Rebecca. 'Is that what you are recommending?'

'That's along the lines of what I'm recommending, but, Mrs. Dalton, home may not be the best place for her. Her home environment might be part of the reason she tried to take her life in the first place.' He held up his hands. 'Please, I mean no disrespect – it's just all part of what we need to determine over the coming weeks.'

'So are you proposing that she stays here until it's decided she's well enough to come home?'

'Gene's currently in one of our post-operative wards. My professional opinion is she needs to be transferred to some place where they have psychiatric skills and resources to identify and manage her treatment.'

'Not to an asylum!' Rebecca exclaimed in horror.

'Doctor Simmons, my husband was a doctor and worked at 999 in Toronto for a year and we promised each other that no one we loved would ever end up there or a place like there.'

While she was speaking Jonathan and Doctor Simmons had exchanged knowing glances.

'When was that?' Doctor Simmons asked.

'1920,' Rebecca volunteered.

'I'd like to think the treatment of patients with mental health problems has improved considerably in the past thirty years, but so too have the number of people requiring medical assistance,' the doctor grudgingly admitted. 'I don't know if various psychiatric conditions are on the rise or if it's just a matter of more sufferers now seeking medical attention, but the situation is in line with the rest of the medical professions – and that is, unfortunately, there are simply not enough doctors to go round. And for psychiatric patients there are not enough institutions. I could go on…' He sighed.

'You don't have to convince me the situation is dire,' said Rebecca. 'Please just tell me what and where you recommend?'

The doctor sat back, interlocking his fingers over his stomach. 'There's a place about an hour's drive from here at Saint-Placide on the north-western shores of Lac des Deux-Montagnes, run by the Sisters of Providence. Quite a large estate with beds for 200 patients but their care and accommodation is multi-leveled depending on the seriousness of each patient. The institution likes to ultimately get their patients to the point where they are self-sufficient, living in houses on the estate with other recovering patients, and that the patient will eventually self-elect to return home. It seems to have the best success rate I've come across.'

'Are their patients all women?'

The doctor hesitated. 'They have some men, but the majority are women.'

She smiled. 'I'm pleased to hear that. Gene is perhaps

more comfortable in the company of men.'

'They have good staff and are serviced by some of Montreal's best specialists.'

'Do they have a waiting list?' she asked.

'They do for some of their beds. Others, people can buy, more or less. If you're wealthy and want the best for your family and money's no object, they will take you in. But there is a third possibility.'

Rebecca glanced at Jonathan wondering if he had any clues as to what that might be – a special dispensation for people within the medical fraternity. The doctor's answer surprised her. 'As it's run by Catholic nuns who consider suicide the greatest sin of all, particularly suicide attempts by young people, they readily accept them with open arms. To them, your daughter is a prized life, swinging in the balance. As dire as her situation is, it is fortunate for her and yourself that she didn't have a mania episode.'

'Yes, we're relieved she's not prone to gauche acts of exposure and indecency,' said Jonathan. Rebecca suppressed a small smile at Jonathan's sarcasm.

'I can make some enquiries,' Doctor Simmons offered.

'Thank you. That would be appreciated. And we don't expect charity. We would like to pay for Gene's treatment as much as we can afford. We'd also like to visit the place soon if it's possible.'

'I'm sure many things can be arranged.'

Rebecca stood and straightened her dress with her gloved hands. 'I forgot to ask. The name of this place?'

'Freshwater. Is that right?' queried Jonathan.

'Yes,' said the doctor.

Rebecca looked at her son. 'Do you know about it?'

'Only in passing.

24

Gene wakes and it is white: the room, the curtains, the bedcovers, everything, except a vase of flowers on the stand next to her bed with soft pink camellias, rich glossy green leaves and the undeniable scent of sweet daphne. Her head feels fuzzy. She attempts to clear it by sitting up and is immediately halted by a stabbing pain in her stomach. She lies back down and feels her abdomen, covered in the thick padding of a bandage. She has no memory of any injury.

A few minutes later a nurse walks into the ward. Gene calls her over. 'Excuse me. Where am I?'

'The Victoria Hospital.'

Gene is in a state of disbelief.

'Would you rather be somewhere else?'

'Why am I here? What happened to my stomach?'

'You've been operated on. You had ingested some harmful substances. Got carried away with the tranquilisers.'

A wave of dread washes over Gene as memories come to the surface. 'When is visiting hours?' she asks.

'Two to four every afternoon. Your mother and brother have been here every day.'

'Which brother?'

'Your doctor brother.'

Gene exhales deeply but suddenly wishes she hadn't because the movement hurts her stomach.

'Would you like me to call your mother and tell her you're awake? She asked us to let her know as soon as you came to.'

'Please, no,' says Gene. She wonders if she could feign sleep for two hours. Somehow she doubts it.

That afternoon her mother walked briskly into the ward with her arms outstretched and tears of relief in her eyes. 'They told me you had awoken. Such wonderful news.' She bent and embraced Gene, kissing her on the cheek and her head. Jonathan was not far behind her.

Gene tried to smile for them. She tried to make eye contact. Her eyes flickered from one to the other in Olympic time then she looked down at her chest, along her stiff still body, wishing she were stone.

Jonathan rustled her hair then bent down to kiss her on the cheek. 'Round one to Morton and Jonathan,' he said. 'I hope there's never a round two.'

Gene closed her eyes. But this time she was able to smile as she nodded in silent agreement. With his usual panache her brother had known the perfect words to break the tension.

'Gene, I want you to know we are all here for you. Everyone is wanting you to pull through.' Her mother gave Gene her brightest smile. 'How's the food? Have you been able to eat anything today?'

'I had a glass of chocolate milk and a boiled egg on toast. I hope my stomach will be all right. Did they really cut it open?'

Jonathan and her mother exchanged glances.

'Yes,' he said. 'They did. Pumping your stomach wasn't the best option given the circumstances. It will heal quickly. It's sore because your muscles have been cut and stitched back together.'

'Wyatt and Morton bought you the flowers. Aren't they just beautiful? They gave me a bunch as well. I tell you the whole house smells of daphne. Hard to believe such a few sprigs can be so pervading.'

'How long will I be in here for?' Gene asked, looking from one to the other.

Jonathan hesitated. 'Most likely a week.'

'The time will pass quickly,' said her mother. 'I brought you some of your favourite books to read.' Out of a bag she pulled the *My Friend Flicka* trilogy, her copy of *Gone with the Wind* and two books that Gene knew belonged to her mother: *The Painted Veil* and *A Town Like Alice*. 'I just finished reading that one by Neville Shute. I loved it. Set in Malaysia and Australia during World War II.'

Jonathan changed the subject and told her that Matthew pulled himself up on his feet yesterday for the first time and had just cut his fourth tooth. Soon he would look like a proper rabbit. He also told her Annabelle would send chocolate brownies as soon as she was allowed to eat them.

'Can she send them in tomorrow?' Her brother smiled at her. Tentatively Gene glanced at her mother. 'Where's Wyatt?' she asked.

'He's still here. He's vowed not to leave till you are on your feet again. Nana and Grandad are still here too. They'd like to pop in and see you sometime before they head back to Toronto.'

'Sure,' Gene nodded.

'Perhaps they can come tomorrow?'

Gene nodded.

'Abigail and Will had to head back yesterday. She left you this card.' Her mother placed it on top of the pile of books.

'What's Morton up to?'

'He's back at work and looking after Sooty. You wouldn't know but she cut her foot quite badly a few days ago.'

Her mother and Jonathan kept up a steady banter for thirty minutes until Jonathan asked, 'Are you tired, Gene. Would you like to rest?'

'I think I would.' She gave each of them an apologetic smile as they said their farewell.

25

Rebecca stayed away from the hospital the next day and let her in-laws go instead. All things considered, she thought yesterday had gone well, but she didn't want to overwhelm her daughter. She could sense Gene's guilt but she was unsure how to broach the subject. At some point she would need to, along with her planned treatment.

She started by asking Gene could she brush her hair for her. She said she imagined it would be quite painful for her to raise her hands above her head.

'Is it a mess?' asked Gene.

'It's tangled,' said Rebecca, 'but it doesn't look too dirty. I just thought it might make you feel a little better.'

Gene obliged.

Midway through brushing, Rebecca said, 'I don't know what's happened these past few months. I'm sorry I have been buried up to my eyeballs in my paintings. I obviously have missed events that have been happening in the life of my family. I want you to know I accept some of the responsibility for this. Clearly I have been neglecting you and Morton and everyone else. I'm sorry I've let my painting dominate our family life.' She paused. 'I hope to be able to manage that better going forward and find greater balance. I'm sure that's possible. I think it will be a long time till I have such a pressing deadline like the one I've just had.'

Gene didn't look at her mother but she silently nodded in acknowledgement of her apology.

'Are you anywhere near ready being able to tell me why you wanted to take your own life?'

Previously Rebecca had asked Wyatt and Jonathan, 'Do you think she was trying to send me a message, by trying to end her life on the day of my opening?'

'Don't be ridiculous, Mom,' Jonathan said. 'We all want your exhibition to be a sell-out success.'

Morton had got up and left the room. 'Shut up Rebecca,' she thought. By his actions her youngest son was telling her there were more important things at stake. He was right.

'Gene, darling, I promise, I won't get angry, whatever it is, it will be okay. I can't imagine whatever it is warrants the taking of your own life. Tell me and we'll work through it together. A problem halved is a problem solved. Has somebody done something to hurt you?'

Her daughter looked at her and then looked away.

'Perhaps you would prefer to tell Jonathan or Morton.' Gene's head swerved back to Rebecca. Her eyes were piercing, almost as if she were saying, 'How could you?' Rebecca flinched. She placed the hairbrush on the table.

'Gene, please hear me out. It may not be me, it may not be Jonathan or Morton and if that's how it is, so be it. But at some point you're going to have to talk to someone about what you did and what you were feeling at the time that led to that decision. That's not me saying this, Gene. It's the medical advice we've been given.'

'What advice?'

'Well, they tell us is it wouldn't be in your best interests for you to come home until you've worked through with a psychiatrist the reasons why you tried to end your life and learn new ways to handle any difficult situation that may arise in the future. As I understand it, once they're confident you won't try to end your life again then they'll be happy to release you.'

'Sounds like a prison sentence.'

'It's for your own safety.'

'I'm meant to do all this by next week?' Gene gave her a look.

'No, that would be ridiculous. They suggest transferring you to another hospital about an hour away for you to have your treatment there.'

'What's this place called?'

'Freshwater.'

'What's it like?'

'We don't know. Jonathan and I are going down there tomorrow to meet some people and see.'

'What will the treatment be?'

'I don't know exactly. Psychotherapies, psychoanalysis, basically what I understand a lot of talking with you to try and uncover why you were feeling so low that you wanted to end your life.'

Gene made no reply.

Rebecca waited for several moments. Then, in what she hoped was a soothing voice, she said, 'Darling, as you know a psychiatrist is a specially trained doctor and being a doctor they have to uphold the doctor's oath of confidentiality. What you tell your doctor is private. He or she will only tell us, if you give them permission to divulge anything to us.'

Her daughter gave her a dubious look.

'Trust me,' said Rebecca. 'I once told a doctor in Boston something I had never told another, not even your father. Believe me I never wanted to tell a soul. But in the end I did because I knew I could trust him, and the only way he could help me – and my situation – was for me to level with him.'

'Did he help?'

Rebecca contemplated what to tell her. 'It was the start of an important process. I doubt I would have any children today if I had not started that process of disclosure, of unlocking what was inside of me.'

She was half expecting Gene to ask her specific questions about the nature of that very disclosure, but to her surprise Gene didn't. Instead she said, 'Can you tell Morton I'd like to see him please.'

26

After her mother left, Gene lay there certain in the knowledge that her brother blamed himself for her trying to take her own life. His avoidance spoke volumes. He would see that the burden he had carried for twelve years and offloaded onto her had been too much. How could he not? Gene worried about what that might do to him. She berated herself for what she had already done to him – he who had already suffered more than anyone else – not just recently but in years gone by.

She remembered that time with lucid clarity. How could she not? It was one of her strongest memories.

Three days after her father and two brothers disappeared, one was returned.

She had sat and stared at him, not fully convinced that this could be her brother. She didn't say a word to him. And he, too, frightened by his own ordeal, did not say a word to her either. Perhaps if he had returned with her younger brother and father she might have felt different.

Another two days passed until she had sidled up to Jonathan and whispered in his ear, 'Is he really Morton?'

'Yes,' Jonathan had said. 'He's just taking a little while to come back to himself. He feels strange and lost in his world right now. Just like you. Why don't you try talking to him?'

Gene hadn't known what to say. She was too young to know what words might bring him comfort. She was too stranded from her childhood instincts to realise that maybe she didn't need to talk to him, she could just play with him like she used to.

At five years of age, she was too young to understand the weight of her silence, how it fell heavily on her eight-year old brother, almost drowning him in unspoken blame and accusation: what have you done with our father and with Joel?

But now she wasn't too young. And now she knew that her brother, who had borne too much too early, had magnanimously never retaliated against her silent charge. If anything he had owned it and nursed it in his own silent self-imposed penitentiary...until just a few weeks ago. Some sister she was. How dare she try and kill herself for the sheer knowledge of what had happened, when Morton had lived through what happened – twice – and somehow managed to come out a scarred survivor. But everything was all too much for the languor of her heart.

One thing she knew for certain, she could never tell any of her family. Why inflict on them what had been inflicted on her?

Morton came the next afternoon at three-thirty p.m. just when she thought he wasn't going to show. His head was bowed, his feet dragged, his clothes seemed to hang on him like they belonged to someone two sizes bigger. He stood at the end of the bed and barely glanced her way.

'Come here,' she said, holding out her hand. He came to her and she took his hand and looked up into his face.

'I'm okay, Morton. Really, I am. I couldn't sort some things out but now I have. A bit extreme I know. I just needed a little break from everyone to think things through.'

He pulled his hand away and immediately started signing. 'I should never have told you.'

The speed at which he moved his hands, the pained expression on his face told her he was angry with himself.

'Yes you should have,' she signed back. 'You should have told me years ago. You should not have had to carry this around inside you.'

'I should so have and I should have realised that was where it belonged.'

145

'That's not what this is all about.' She signed.

'Isn't it?' He challenged her.

She glared at him. 'Pull up the chair please, Morton,' she said out loud. 'Have you asked Wyatt and Mom yet if you can move to Saskatchewan to live with Wyatt?'

He exhaled loudly and shook his head, his eyes blinking shut.

'So I have a confession to make.' She looked at him and tried to force all the earnestness she possessed to light her eyes. She could feel her voice straining but she pushed through. 'I want you to go to Wyatt's. I really do. I want you to be happy. After what happened to Andrew I understand you need to get away. It's just I didn't want to be left by my lonesome and I have no one. You're kind of all I've got.

'Just a little while ago there was you, Andrew, Sooty and Flint. Andrew's gone, you and Sooty and Flint will be gone soon. Mom's with Wyatt even when she's not physically with Wyatt. She has her paintings, her work, her grandson. Jonathan's got Annabelle and Matthew. Abigail's in Toronto with Will and will be a mother soon. And I'm just a nobody with no one.'

'No one sees you like that. No one treats you like that.'

'I know. But that's how I feel.'

'I'll stay in Montreal. I can go to Saskatchewan some other time.' Morton signed.

'No. I want you to go! I want you to be happy!'

'How can I be happy when you do this to yourself?'

'I know. It was a dumb idea. I don't know how to excuse it. But guess what?'

'What?'

'I'm not going to be at home with just Mom.'

'You're not?'

'No, I'm going away to some hospital, a nuthouse probably, at Saint-Placide.'

'What will you do there?'

'I don't know, maybe make some new friends.' She

gave Morton a dopey smile. 'So, see, there's nothing stopping you from going away with Wyatt, cause I won't be in Montreal either.'

'How do you feel about that?' he signed.

Gene shrugged. 'I think I should go.'

'Will you finish school?'

'Who knows? I don't want to go back to Saint Margaret's now. Every girl in the school will be talking about me behind my back.'

'You're right. They will. Maybe you and Mom will have to move to Saskatchewan for a while so you can finish your schooling at Regina.'

'Wyatt wouldn't cope with that. He'd go AWOL.'

'You're right he would.' They chuckled ever so lightly.

'What are you doing tomorrow after lunch?' Gene asked.

'No plans really.'

'Can you come back and help me tell Mom and Jonathan what was going on? Can you make sure Jonathan comes with Mom? Wyatt can come too if he likes.'

He told her he would bring all three. 'Are you sure you want to go to this asylum?'

'I'll wait to see what Jonathan and Mom have to say. I need to serve out some penance for what I did to all of you. I'm sure if I don't like it then they'll let me leave.'

After he leaves Gene closes her eyes, the muscles in her lids working doubly hard to curb what's lapping at the brim but it is futile. Hot tears force their way through and she cries in anguish for her brother, and for herself, and for the lies she has told. She hates herself for such deception; for her actions in taking such a seemingly selfish, drastic measure; for punishing him now in this way and making him feel guilty for wanting to spread his wings when he wasn't abandoning her; he was just going somewhere else.

27

Freshwater, the asylum at Saint-Placide, on the north-western shores of Lac des Deux-Montagnes, run by the Sisters of Providence, was a homely hospital come estate comprising a long main building rendered in wheat colouring with big windows and several large, double-storey residences on either side that fanned in a semi circle around the lake. All the buildings gazed over the wide expanse of lawn down to the poplars, cottonwoods and willows that lined the water's edge. On the morning of their arrival it was a still winter's day, the sun struggling to light the sky in the milkiest of pale blues. A few people were outside walking in slow trepidation past small, well-trimmed evergreen shrubs. The admission sister told Rebecca, Jonathan and Gene that in summer there would be settees under umbrellas, tennis and badminton to play, market gardens to attend. Her mother said that all sounded lovely but she was hoping Gene would be home by summer.

Her first room was on the second floor of the main building that was the hospital. She was told once she had made progress with her treatment she would be moved to one of the houses supervised by one of the nuns. Freshwater wasn't the horror house it could have been yet it wasn't the revelation others wanted it to be. At times Gene heard screams and howling but mostly it was a genteel community where one could recover from breakdowns in a restful native setting and talk to God in the small chapel, attendance at which was purely voluntary. Gene felt she could have been at a tuberculosis sanatorium or a spa clinic that Zelda Fitzgerald may have frequented. They gave her a journal and encouraged her to write her thoughts and feelings. She penned not a word, not even the trifling of a memoir. What she did was remain amiable but separate from everyone including herself. Her psychiatrist, Doctor Trantham, who had tortoise-shell glasses and unruly dark hair, asked her repeatedly why she attempted to commit suicide and repeatedly she told him because she didn't want to live without her brother; she didn't want him to leave. He asked her who her friends were. She told him, my brothers and my brother's friend, Andrew, who died. He asked her, 'What about the girls at your school?'

'They're not my friends. They're acquaintances. People I sing with.'

'Do you spend time with any of them outside of school?'

'Sometimes. Rarely.'

'Why's that, do you think?'

'Well, when I was eleven, the girl I was closest to moved with her family to Baltimore. Another one, her father was an alcoholic and reminded me of a teacher I had when I was seven years old so I didn't pursue that friendship. I felt sorry for her but one afternoon at her place was enough for me. And then, in the past little while two other girls who I was friendly with have both become besotted with boyfriends and all they can talk about are their beaus and their upcoming debuts, which is definitely not me.'

'Are you not interested in boys and dating? I understand if you're not, you're still quite young.'

'No, I'm not interested,' she replied.

'One day you might be. You're quite attractive, I'm sure there would be plenty of young men interested in you.'

'I don't want to have this conversation,' said Gene getting up to look out the window.

'Okay, moving along, what do you like to do with your spare time?'

'I like to read.' She stayed staring out at the window.

'What else?'

'Spend time with my family, my brothers. Go to a movie.'

'What do you think you might like to do when you leave school?'

'I don't know. Maybe become a nun.'

'Why do you say that?'

She turned back to look at him. 'Because they seem at peace. They're in the background. No one seems to judge them. They just go about their business quietly. They don't get asked too many questions.'

He laughed. 'Maybe you'd like to be a librarian.'

'I have an aunt who works part-time in a library.'

'Who's that?'

'My mother's sister, Aunty Rachel.'

'Perhaps you should chat to her sometime.'

'Perhaps I might.'

Gene's mother would visit her every week on a Wednesday, bring with her a picnic lunch and fresh baguettes. Jonathan and Annabelle and Matthew would visit every Saturday. Gene was always friendly, though quieter than the younger Gene they had all known. When Matthew became tired and grizzly, she would put him in his pram and push it back and forward. When he dozed off, she would lean over him and gently stroke his hair before rejoining her brother and sister-in-law, all the time thinking, please may your life not be tainted.

Morton and Wyatt would write occasionally, Abigail as well, enclosing photos of her first born, whom they called Anthony Dalton Howard. Her grandparents from Toronto wrote as well inviting her to come and visit whenever she wanted. Throughout all that time Gene wondered about what she was meant to change about herself and who she was meant to be when she left. She struggled with the concept of change. What about her past could be changed? Absolutely nothing! She was mired in it. At the same time she was in no hurry to leave Freshwater. She'd already apologised to her mother and

Wyatt, and to Jonathan and Morton at Victoria Hospital before she'd arrived at Freshwater. With Morton by her side they told them of his planned intentions and she of her appalling overreaction.

The term melancholia was bandied about. How did one catch it? How did one cure oneself of it?

One day Doctor Trantham suggested that if she didn't feel like writing in her journal perhaps she might feel like drawing or painting.

'Are you kidding me?' Gene blurted out. 'No, Mom's the artist in our family. She's the one with talent.'

'Everyone's got a talent for something. Seems to me you'd like to do something with your hands,' he observed.

Gene suddenly felt very uncomfortable. She didn't like people making observations about her. 'Why do you say that?'

'Because of the way you constantly move your hands up and down rubbing your leg all the time. I've noticed even when you're reading you do that or you flex your foot up and down or from side to side. I don't even think you are aware of it.'

Gene immediately put her feet flat on the ground and her hands underneath her legs.

'Please don't see it as a criticism Gene. It's merely that I think you have a lot of restless energy. Do you have problems sleeping?'

'Sometimes.'

'What do you do when you can't sleep?'

'I read.'

'Do you make yourself a glass of warm milk?'

'No. Sometimes I go for walks around the grounds.'

He paused before he responded. 'That's very brave,' he said. 'The dark doesn't frighten you.'

'No. Not really. The walking tends to calm my frustration at not being able to sleep. And often I find I can come in and fall asleep after that.'

'Do you wake your charge sister and tell her what you're doing?'

'No. I have a note that I always leave on my bed if I venture outside.'

He suggested she go for more walks during the day so she would be more tired at night. 'What do you think about when you lie there at night unable to sleep?'

'Poetry. Music. Sometimes I wish I had learnt the piano.'

'There's still time. You can start here even. What poems?'

'Ones by Verlaine. And Victor Hugo.'

'Any verses in particular?'

'And I feel the starry gulf within my soul;

'We are both neighbours of the silent skies.'

The doctor completed the verse for her:

'Since you're beautiful and I'm old.'

'No,' she said. *'Since I'm alive and he is dead.'*

'Who is dead?'

'Many people. My father for one. It is his collection I read.'

'When did your father die?'

'When I was five.'

'Were you with him?'

'No,' she said softly.

'Did you see him afterwards?'

She shook her head. 'He disappeared. Drowned.'

'So you never got to say goodbye?'

'We had a service for him. Two years afterwards. We sent a dove up into the sky.'

'Do you still miss your father?'

'Is your father still alive?' asked Gene.

'No,' he replied, his voice mellow.

'Well then.'

Doctor Trantham cleared his throat. 'Any other favourite poems?'

'Alfred de Musset.

'My heart replied: It's never enough

We'll never have had enough of sadness:

And don't you see that changeableness

Makes past pain dearer to us, and sweeter?'

'And what does that poem tell you?'

'It's okay to be sad. It's okay to be lonely.'

'Does that sadness make you want to cry?'

'No,' she exhaled. 'It's part of me. Sometimes it feels like an old friend I had forgotten about has returned to be with me again.'

'Does this friendship feel heavy like it's weighing you down?'

'No.'

'Is it okay to be happy? To be surrounded by people having a good time?'

'Sometimes.'

'Are you happy to be alive? If happy is the word for it.'

'I am satisfied that I am alive. I no longer wish to die.' She glanced at him. 'Satisfied?'

'For now.' He smiled.

28

In April Rebecca and Jonathan had a meeting with Doctor Trantham to discuss Gene's progress. 'Your daughter seems to embrace sadness and melancholy, yet isn't overly saddened with it,' he told them. 'I couldn't classify her as a negative person with low self-esteem but rather a person resigned. She is most unusual.'

'That's Gene,' noted Jonathan.

'Quite. There have been no startling insights or revelations. Nothing to me that says she's been awakened by a particular discovery and made some firm decisions. Yet I'd be surprised if she were a danger to herself anymore.'

'What do you propose we do?' asked Rebecca.

'To me it seems Gene needs to be re-awakened to life. She needs to find at least one thing that really excites her. Something that gives her a strong reason to live. I don't believe she's found that yet. And to be fair most people her age wouldn't be able to say what their reasons for living were. But in Gene's case she has had reasons for dying and we need to make sure her reasons for living are much greater and more pervasive. Otherwise, she's going to live a life where she's constantly battling the demons of depression. She is highly intelligent. I think in part her depression is a sign of her boredom. She needs to be challenged. She needs to be engaged in activities where she's needed, where she can make a valuable contribution, where her efforts are acknowledged and appreciated. I'm not sure what that is exactly but it's what we need to put our minds to.'

The next time Rebecca visited Gene she took with her a letter Morton had written to her the month before.

Dear Mother

I have travelled back through time. The day is nameless. The year could easily be as well. By the winsome light we live by the jostle and the pull of the team. Wyatt ahead of me with his team of six huskies and me with mine, standing on my sled as we trail behind in a wonderland of white. Sooty is proving to be a fine leader and Flint is always close behind as his point. Thunder and Condor, Titan and Axis make up the rest of the team. It's hard to believe how much we are towing – easily three quarters of it food for the dogs and ourselves. Each morning and night we melt buckets of snow for drinking water for man and beast.

It was a slow trip here towing the trailer and all we were hauling. We drove all the way through Alberta through Calgary and Canmore to Quesnell in BC then onto Wells and Barkerville to the head of Bowron Lake on the western slopes of the Carriboo Mountain Range. Since Barkerville we have not seen another soul. Conifers and spruces, crowned in snow crystals the size of acorns, surround us. At nights when the dogs settle we hear the distant cries of timber wolves, hungry and lonesome, and I recall stories Dad once told us.

In summer this place is a popular canoe circuit. A classic by all reports – ten lakes, three rivers and one creek create a near perfect quadrangle of eighty miles of waterways at an altitude of eight thousand feet. We will go one way around the circuit then retrace our journey to lengthen our stay in this magical place. Black and grizzly bears, moose and caribou roam free for eight months of the year, but not now. I will return one summer and no doubt gaze in stunned wonder at the lush transformation. There are five huts on the route. Inside the one we last over-nighted were twenty mobiles of canoes that people had carved with their names on them. I have started whittling my own of a sled and six huskies. I will leave it in a hut on our final night. It will be unique – my signing of nature's guestbook.

I am learning mountains from Wyatt and equally from the experience of handling the dogs over such long distances each day. I think of Andrew and some days feel he is riding with me, whistling in my ear. Last night I experienced another first: a loud booming explosion. I was certain it was an avalanche. But to my amazement it was a tree. It is a strange concept a tree exploding in the dark, loud as cannon-fire but with no light or flames or scent of wood smoke. Wyatt as ever was non-plussed. All he said was, 'Ah, the breaking heart of winter'. The next morning in our searching we found a maple tree cleft almost in two, the bark rent in pieces on the snow – the telling sign of a severe frost and forty below temperatures. To lay awake and listen to the sound of trees exploding is something I never imagined and I have to say I don't relish. Sooty and Flint don't like it much either. That's nature for you – one minute beyond beautiful, the next brutal.

Yet I err towards the beauty. At night under the still brilliance of the full moon I take my team out for an invigorating dash across the iced-over lake. They are in their element. With no load they sprint like mythical creatures flying above a frozen land, never tiring, never wanting it to be over. More exhilarating than anything else is their sheer joy in the run itself. When it is over they lick my face, constantly, such is their ebullience. When we race I cry with the wind, but I cry with delirious happiness and think I am part dog myself. I have never felt more alive or in love with life. I wish Gene could know this feeling. Thank you for letting me go.

Love Morton.

When Rebecca wrote back to him she wrote:

This winter across the great distance of two thousand miles my son has returned to me. I could not be happier for you or for myself. I want to read about your every adventure.

To Gene, she said. 'Here, read this. And be proud of yourself for also letting him go.'

29

In a distant unknown landscape in the company of a pack of dogs and a wise man, Morton, her brother had once again, but on a much deeper level, discovered the bright lights of his soul. To Gene it was the best coded-message she could ever receive. On the scales that balanced his life, the tragedies of their father, Joel and Andrew had been outweighed by the magic of his devotion towards his beloved huskies. She had no answers for herself but the news of her brother nudged her own scale a little in the direction of optimism.

On Sunday 13 May, Jonathan came to collect Gene to take her out to lunch in Lachute for his thirty-third birthday.

'Are we meeting everyone there?' she asked.

'It's just you and me,' he replied. 'Annabelle, Matthew and I are having dinner with Mom tonight.'

The waiter took their meal order and returned with a cranberry juice for Gene and a Canadian Club for her brother. After toasting her brother Gene drank half her glass in no time. Jonathan watched her down her drink with wry amusement. 'We don't get much cranberry juice at Freshwater,' she said, smiling lightly as she reached for the napkin to wipe her lips.

'I'll be sure to bring you some next time I come,' he replied. 'But, hopefully you'll be out soon.' He took a sip of his own drink. 'Gene,' he said, 'I've got a proposition for you.'

'Yes?' Her tone was cautionary, thinking he was about to challenge her to up the ante on the information she was volunteering to the good Doctor Trantham. But what he said to her was way off the mark.

'I want you to come and work with me this summer.'

'At the hospital? Don't I need to be a trained nurse for that?'

'No, on both accounts. I'm going to do another summer as a bush doctor. Annabelle and Matthew are going to move in with Mom for a while. I'll be heading north in early June taking a nurse and pilot with me, but I want an assistant to help with all the recording I have to do. And I think Joan, my nurse, would welcome some female company. But aside from all that,' he paused, 'I'd like to spend some more time with you getting to know the young lady who is my sister.'

He had her from the very beginning. But he sealed it with his closing. How few and far between were the people who genuinely wanted to spend time getting to know her. Gene started to cry.

His arm went round her shoulder. 'Is that a yes?' He squeezed her shoulder. 'I have every faith you can do it.'

Through her tears, Gene nodded 'I can. I will.'

Against her temple he whispered, 'You know what you mean to me.' And she did. How could she have done what she had done to him, to them all?

It was early June 1951 when she was discharged from Freshwater. Jonathan collected her just after seven and drove straight to the Montréal Boucherville Water Aerodrome. Her mother and Annabelle had packed her bags and, along with Matthew, met them at the aerodrome to farewell them on their northern adventure.

Her mother gave her a card that she told her to open once she was airborne. Inside she'd written out Walt Whitman's *Miracles* in its entirety. The lines: "*sit at a table at dinner with my mother*" and "*every hour of light and dark is a miracle*" tugged at her heart. Her mother's forgiveness, her mother's encouragement to see the beauty in life and count it all as a miracle.

Inward Bound

Hudson Bay, Canada, June 1951

30

There were four of them on that plane that first Saturday in June: Gene; Jonathan; their nurse, Joan Bridges, a married, thirty-something brunette whose mother was looking after her three children while she worked on her fourth northern medical expedition; and Sonny Marlow, their unmarried, unfazed twenty-four year old pilot. It was the second time Sonny had flown Jonathan north, but not his second trip by a long stretch, as Gene would discover after he and her brother had surprised her with their impromptu Frankie Laine song and dance routine during their first meal break in Amos.

Apparently in 1942 the United States established an airbase just outside of Churchill, known as Fort Churchill, which since the end of the war had been jointly used by Canada and the United States for military training exercises and other purposes. Over the last few years Sonny had been on many a mission to the airbase and to Frobisher Bay on Baffin Island, inside the Arctic Circle, as well as other locations further north on surveying assignments. 'I'll show you on the map one day,' he said.

'Okay,' smiled Gene. On the table in front of her lay the map of Ontario that Sonny and Jonathan were following that day. She was enjoying poring over it, noting landmarks they were likely to see en route, hoping she would be able to identify them as they flew overhead.

'Do you always have a co-pilot?' she asked.

'No,' said Sonny with a single shake of his head.

'So you have to read the map yourself as you're flying along?'

'Can't exactly rely on anyone else to do it,' he said deadpan.

Gene laughed. 'You must have a good memory for landmarks.'

'I'd say it's an occupational necessity, wouldn't you, Jonathan?'

'Did you say occupation hazard?' joked Jonathan.

'Okay,' said Gene, smiling as she held the map up against her body so Sonny couldn't see any details. 'How do you know when you're coming into Moose Factory? Is there a gigantic moose standing on the roof of a factory?'

'That would be a mighty sight indeed,' said Sonny, smiling in return. 'But no. First, off when we're approaching Moose Factory there's the Moose River, though if it's a grey day, that doesn't stand out as much as you might think. But about an hour before, if we're on course, off to our left we should see a reasonable size, rectangle shaped lake, called Kesagami. It's about twenty miles long give or take.'

Gene found Lake Kesagami on the map.

'Then,' continued Sonny, 'we bear just a fraction left of due north and after about 40 minutes or so we should start to see three forks of the Moose River, the first one a lot narrower than the second two. But really, the first thing we will see of any major significance will be the red steeple of the Anglican church that will be clearly above the tree line.'

She could see the church cross on the map, wondering how high the steeple was.

'Do you want to fly up front?' he asked.

She looked at his soft brown eyes and his steady smile, realising he was dead certain of his assessment. Something about that gave her great comfort, yet it also unsettled her. For here was a man, and not just any man, but a young, experienced, fine-looking man, who seemed to know the world over and himself most of all. There were shades of Errol Flynn's bravura about him, shades of The Sea Hawk. She could see him hanging off a shroud, looking out to the horizon reconfirming his bearings.

Later that afternoon after they landed and motored up to the small dock he came round to help Joan and her off the plane. 'Did you see the steeple, Gene?' he asked.

'What steeple?' she teased.

The next morning Jonathan, Joan and Gene met the hospital superintendent for a tour of the newly opened tuberculosis hospital, a 200-bed facility for the Indian and Eskimo populations of Hudson Bay. It surprised her that the hospital was nearly full. It surprised her more when she heard there were three hundred Eskimos at the Mountain Sanatorium in Hamilton, making it the largest community of Eskimos in the entire country. To think their congregation was all because they were sick!

Gene made some comment to the effect, to which the superintendent replied, 'Well, yes, sadly the travelling clinics and mass surveys of the nineteen-thirties and forties largely ignored the great north. It's only in the last two to three years that it's getting the attention it needs. Red Cross Hospitals and nursing stations didn't reach this far, part of the complication being the language barrier. The only medical services they had were provided by the missions, which were grossly understaffed. The situation is graver than we ever predicted. At least one in five Eskimos is infected with TB. The Cree have fared only marginally better.'

'How dreadful,' said Joan, her voice full of sympathy. 'Surely it can't just be their lack of exposure to western diseases making them more vulnerable?'

'No, you're right. Environmental factors have played their part. Recently starvation has been a real issue for many Eskimos living northwest of the Hudson – the Kazan River community for one and those around Baker Lake. The migratory caribou herds either by-passed their areas or perished themselves. And when the human body is stressed through starvation, latent infections become active.'

'So what happed to all those infected?' asked Gene.

'They were airlifted by military pilots based in Churchill, passed through the small Catholic hospital and then put on the next train to The Peg. Winnipeg,' he added by way of explanation for Gene's benefit. 'Didn't come anywhere near here.

'But it's a spiraling problem,' the superintendent continued. 'Because of the distances they need to travel and the scarcity of medical aid, they don't present themselves until their condition is serious, which consequently means they have nearly always infected people around them.'

'And that delay would reduce their chances of making a full recovery,' noted Jonathan.

'Exactly,' said the super, 'and their period of convalescence is much longer than the average person.'

'Thank God for streptomycin,' said Joan. The antibiotic had only been available since 1946, providing at long last an effective treatment and cure to a disease that had killed people for centuries.

'And the BCG vaccine,' said the Superintendent. 'Vaccinate anyone under twelve. And make sure you check the inside of their elbows first. A doctor here two years ago was convinced that would create less keloid scarring.'

'What about polio?' asked Gene.

'I was just going to ask that myself,' said Joan. 'That scourge is on the rise down south.'

'It's around,' said Jonathan, 'but because they don't get the warm temperatures up here, not as prevalent.'

After they finished the tour, and meetings, they moved to the hospital mess where they were joined by a Cree Indian, named Walter, whom Gene surmised was in his mid-twenties, and Sonny, carrying maps under his arm. They lay them out as the superintendent, Walter and Sonny pointed out the medical services west of Hudson Bay between Moose Factory and Churchill.

Their attention soon moved towards the east of the Bay: north Quebec, due west of Labrador, where there were no established hospitals, only a sprinkling of schools and remnant Trading Posts amongst a few larger settlements. The land was home to the Cree people and the odd Canadian descended from European settlers: largely trappers, whalers or merchants. It was where they were headed. Well over ninety percent of the population spoke only their native Cree. Good job Walter was coming with them as their interpreter and trader.

Great Whale River, the northernmost Cree village in Quebec, located at the mouth of the Great Whale River, would be their final destination. It was on the fifty-fifth parallel, said Sonny.

Gene noticed he was always talking in parallels. She guessed that's how you looked at the world when you were forever looking at maps, judging distances and working out fuel supplies.

'What's the distance between each parallel?' she asked. She could see there were ninety parallels of latitude between the equator and the North Pole.

'Sixty-nine miles,' Jonathan replied.

Moose Factor was just above the 51st parallel. 'So only about 280 miles away,' she said.

'We'll cover an area about the size of Newfoundland all up over the next two months,' said Jonathan, mostly for her benefit. 'During that time, Sonny could be making weekly or bi-weekly trips transporting the sick to and from Moose Factory.'

She looked at her brother and Sonny, ever so slightly nodding her head in acknowledgement.

They talked further covering a mix of topics: what services were provided for the Eskimo people in the far north – there was an icebreaker hospital ship called the CD Howe named after a controversial Canadian politician; the likelihood of spotting polar bears – high! and the chances of seeing an iceberg – low!, which as far as Gene was concerned was good! At that point the meeting seemed to be winding up.

'Are we set to go then?' Gene asked.

'Not quite,' said Jonathan. 'The local Mountie wants to make your acquaintance. He wants you and Walter to record any birth, deaths and marriages for him. Walter will take you along to meet him. We'll see you back at the plane in about half an hour.'

The plane they were travelling in was a De Havilland Beaver, driven by a single propeller. It had three windows at the front – one large one and two smaller side ones – and three other windows down either side but all towards the front half. It had six seats in total: two at the front and four in the cabin. The door was midway down on the right hand side. All their equipment, food and medical supplies were packed behind them in the same enclosure accessed through the same door. Gene had never been inside a plane more fully loaded. Thankfully they wouldn't be packing and unpacking every day.

She had just buckled herself in, Walter likewise, when a child wrapped in a red tartan shawl hurled herself past Sonny through the open doorway of their aircraft. 'Please take me with you,' she cried.

On closer inspection she was not a child but a small woman, the first Eskimo Gene had ever seen. Her imploring eyes searched Gene's face and every face that turned towards her. 'You go north? I want to go north back to my family. I haven't seen them in nearly three years.'

'Where have you been?' Jonathan asked, peering through the gap in the two front seats.

'At the sanatorium way down south, but I'm clean now. My parents haven't heard from me in all that time. For sure they think me dead.'

'Where's home?' Joan asked.

'Igloolik.'

'Holy Smokes!' exclaimed Sonny. After a few seconds he said, 'I don't think they even make maps that go that far!'

'Where is it, Sonny?' asked Jonathan.

'A pinprick of an island between Baffin Island and

Melville Peninsula…inside the Arctic Circle…about the sixty-sixth parallel.'

'Miss, what's your name?' asked Jonathan.

'Rosie.'

'Rosie,' said Jonathan, 'it's not that we don't want to help you but maybe you'd be better catching a flight to Churchill and maybe from there you can score another ride to Repulse Bay or somewhere?'

'I'm here now. When next plane to Churchill? Where you go?'

'First, east and then north, to Great Whale River, Quebec.'

'You go Whale House?'

'That's the plan.'

'I go as far as I can with you and then I walk. Then I find kayak or wait for the ice to freeze and I walk some more. I not eat your food. I find my own.'

'That's not what I'm worried about, Rosie.' Jonathan inclined his head towards Sonny who was standing on the dock. 'Sonny?' he called out.

Sonny exhaled loudly. 'Mr. Howe needs some lessons in bloody repatriation.' He turned his back on everyone. Some moments later he muttered, 'What the hell?' He turned to face them. 'The more the merrier. Rosie, can you sing for your supper? I'm not talking about that throat stuff you Eskimo girls do. Something we'll all know.'

'I know church songs. I know gospel. I know *Up above my head*.'

Joan chuckled. 'You know that one?'

'Yes, ma'am. I believe in Heaven.'

'Hallelujah,' said Sonny. 'We'll just have to move those crates so you can sit down.'

'I sit on floor. Good for me.'

'No. You'll sit on the seat with the belt on. Walter will show you how. And you can put your feet on the boxes.'

'Me not want to break.'

'Me not want you to either but trust me you won't.

They're made of wood. What do you weigh? Eighty pounds if you're lucky.'

Later that day Gene learned Rosie was seventeen years old. It didn't register with Gene that she too was seventeen – eighteen in August. What registered with Gene was: Rosie was sent down south away from her family when she was fourteen, to a place where she knew no one, to a place where no one she knew could visit and worse no one she knew could even write to her, for her parents didn't know how. What kind of world were she and Rosie growing up in? Yesterday Gene felt herself sliding forwards. Today she felt herself sliding backwards.

31

For their first week they camped at Old Post, an island on the Nottaway River and a busy summer hub for over one thousand Cree. It was the site of an old North West Company post that had become a Hudson Bay Company post in the early 1800s, with the island boasting a sizeable Anglican church and an equably sizeable cemetery.

When they arrived Walter guided them to an area near a stone fire ring where they were to erect their tents. Immediately they started on the task – three doubles for everyone to sleep in – one for Joan and now Rosie, one for Gene and Jonathan and one for Sonny and Walter. Plus, they had two larger tents with screens and window flaps: for their mess and hospital room; and a smaller one, some distance away as their ablutions tent. Axes and shovels were standard equipment on bush aircraft.

Walter disappeared but returned after thirty minutes with two local lads carrying armfuls of cut spruce branches. These they laid at the base of all the tents, even in the ones they were sleeping in to provide an extra layer of insulation. Temperatures during the day were around ten to fifteen degrees, at night close to zero.

Shortly afterward, Walter took Rosie and Sonny with him to show them the local water supply: a small spring that ran into a creek that ran into the Nottaway. This became their arrival procedure for the ten other settlements they would visit that summer.

Gene went to bed in daylight and got up in daylight, the sun setting around ten and rising around four. Jonathan would climb out first and she would emerge from their tent around six. Rosie was always first up, boiling the water and making breakfast for everyone. She had taken it upon herself to earn her keep and would confer with Jonathan Sonny and Walter about what supplies were available for lunch and dinner and what they would like. Sometimes she would tell them: Tonight we have pike, or, tonight we have trout. Walleye.

Jonathan would always smile at her. 'Did you catch some fish in your traps last night?'

She would nod, her white teeth splitting her round face, hold her hands up to show him how big the fish were. Between Rosie, Walter, who enjoyed being back in his native environs, Sonny, who was a capable hunter, and the Cree patients who offered food as payment for Jonathan's medical attentions, they hardly wanted for a thing.

Only a few days in, Walter returned to camp one morning telling them they were invited to a powwow that evening.

'What's the occasion?' asked Gene.

'Goose Festival, to celebrate goose hunt. Practise your goose calling. There will be a contest and this afternoon.' He looked at Gene. 'Remind me, I'll show you something special.'

Sonny broke into honking noises.

Everyone laughed.

'How does that sound?' he asked.

'Terrible,' said Rosie. 'You scare them away. You be quiet.'

Around four after Walter finished translating for what they hoped was the last patient of the day. 'Gene, you want to come?' His eyes were alight. 'Won't take long.'

She looked at her brother. 'Go,' he told her. They would finish up.

'Where are we going?' She could normally curtail her curiosity but not in a place so foreign.

'To the meechwap,' He grinned as he led her towards a tepee some distance away, past railings of drying wads of sphagnum moss, which she learned were used for baby's diapers. 'Now Gene, when you go inside say,

"*Tanisi ohkomimâw.*" Means "Hello woman who is grandmother."'

The meechwap was a cooking tepee, warm and fragrant inside with the requisite thick layer of spruce bows on the floor. There was a rack over a fire, above which were suspended around twenty geese. Next to it an old white-haired woman in a sleeveless top twirled the glistening birds with a stick. Gene followed Walter's lead. The old lady nodded a greeting. She then stepped forward and plucked two globs of stuffing from a large bird and handed them a piece each. '*Mikwek,*' said Walter.

'*Mikwek,*' Gene copied. It was made from bannock with wild rice, nuts and herbs, laced with geese oil and something sweet. Gene smiled in pleasure at the old lady whose deeply wrinkled face gave her a cheeky smile in return, almost as if she were saying: 'I'm a good cook, aren't I?'

'Why cook in a tent?' Gene whispered.

'So the smoke is not blown by the wind into your eyes. See it goes straight up the hole. Also so they can cook away from prying eyes. When I was a kid my *mohkom* – grandmother – would twitch us with that stick if ever we came too close to her fire. But we were wise to the fire, we were just trying to steal some morsel of something, yet old as she was, she was still quicker than all of us.'

Gene smiled at Walter's confession. 'It smells so good,' she said. 'What's in that marinade?'

'I wish I knew.'

They crept outside wishing it were dinnertime already.

In northern Quebec, one thousand miles north of Freshwater, Gene started writing in her journal, recording their travels, the people they met, the food they ate, the campsites they stayed at, what they talked about at night, the cases they attended to. Within days she could identify the telltale signs of TB: chest pains, fever, night sweats, shallow breathing, coughing up mucus and blood. She'd think TB even as she was writing down the symptoms for her brother; all the while wishing the symptoms could reveal something fleeting and harmless. She and Joan, as well as Sonny and Walter for that matter, had to regularly undo buttons and manoeuvre clothing to show their TB scars – all part of convincing the natives that needles were safe and that they would leave a mark but it wasn't something to be feared.

The vaccination had mixed results amongst the adult population but if a doubting Cree mother could see that others had walked the same path they were asking her children to walk then she was more likely to let them be vaccinated. More often than not she would put her arm out to be vaccinated first. With a charming smile Joan would oblige. It was too complicated to convince them otherwise.

On the fourth day Sonny flew nine TB patients back to Moose Factory. This time some of them had to sit on the floor.

Gene spent that day wading through downheartedness at the thought of those patients, most of them young children having to spend months away from their parents. It brought back memories of her as a young child feeling lost in the world. She was still sloughed in somberness when Sonny returned. After a few minutes he asked, 'What happened around here today?'

'The usual,' Joan replied.

'What did I miss? Did someone die or something?'

'No,' said Gene, raising her eyes to his. 'Why do you think that?'

'Because of you. You're miserable. What's the problem?'

She shrugged. 'I just feel sorry for those little kids so far away from their family. How awful that is. That's all.'

'Those kids had a blast on my plane today. Something they'd never get to experience if they weren't sick. Sure it will be tough – for some of more than others. But unlike poor Rosie over there, they were not alone. They have kids from their own village with them. But here's the thing. They now have a chance of reaching adulthood, of surviving. You're looking at it all wrong. Don't feel sorry. Feel overjoyed that you have played a role in making that happen That we have medicines today to treat them.'

She looked at him and tried to smile for him. That evening she excused herself shortly after dinner. When she woke in the morning her despondency lingered.

The next night after dinner Sonny said to her, 'Gene, can you come with me? There's something I want to show you.' She got up and started following him, leaving Jonathan and Joan reading. Walter and Rosie had already disappeared. Sonny led Gene near to where the plane was docked then helped himself to one of the birch canoes dragged up on the bank.

'We have to go up river for about a mile.' They paddled in silence till they reached a sandbar that they paddled past before turning left up a side stream. After a while he pulled in close to the bank just before it turned sharply at a right angle. 'Stop paddling,' his voice low. 'Do you hear anything?' Gene pushed her paddle into the grassy side to help with their purchase. She listened and what she heard was singing, a woman singing in Cree, different to the singing they'd heard a few nights earlier around the campfire. There was no steady repetitious beat or a constant tone. It was a melody, light and playful, entrancing and soulful.

Sonny spoke quietly. 'Ain't that a beautiful sound? A young Indian maiden singing her heart out, singing out her happiness.'

He was right. Even though Gene couldn't see the girl's face she could hear the joy in her voice. 'She could be singing her version of Ave Maria,' Gene whispered.

'You know that song? Jonathan told me you sang in a choir.'

'I know it.'

'When she stops you should sing it for her, like a calling. She might sing back to you.'

Gene shook her head. 'My days of singing that song are over.' She peered over her shoulder at Sonny, looking at him through thin black gauze. The insects were so bad in the evenings she had taken to wearing a netted hat whenever she was outdoors. 'How did you know she would be here?'

'I didn't for sure. I came with Rosie two nights ago to help her set some trap lines but when we heard her singing, we just did what you and I are doing now. Sat quiet and enjoyed the performance.'

Their mystery squaw sang for another ten minutes, until they were left with nothing but the tinkling of the creek.

'Tell me, Gene, when was the last time you were happy like that?'

'Sonny!' Gene shook her head annoyed at the trap she had walked into. 'As if I could pluck an answer to that out of thin air.'

'Don't you remember?'

'What is this, the Spanish Inquisition?'

'No. I just want to know. That's all. What makes your heart sing? I know you don't owe me any kind of answer, but I'd like you to tell me just the same.' He paused momentarily. 'I'll tell you when my heart last sang. Here, ten minutes ago, with you in the boat being massaged by water, surrounded by this peaceful never-ending country, listening to that young lady. That was magical.'

'That's your version of magical?'

'Hearing other people's joy, bringing joy to others. That's magical. Every day's magical to me. I'm living the dream. Doing what I love. Flying planes, meeting new people, going to places untouched as opposed to lands damaged and scarred, being answerable to hardly anyone and those that I am, like your brother, are people I choose to work with, whose company I enjoy.'

'Well your life sure sounds dandy.'

'And why not your life? Look at you! You've got a brother who loves you so much he practically worships

174

you. I have no siblings. You've got a mother and sister-in-law who are equally as fond of you judging by the way they sent you off with that private horde of treats.' He was right. Inside her bag she'd discovered chocolate brownies and boiled fruit cake and caramel fudge that she was rationing and sharing with everyone, plus, a bottle of lanolin all the way from Newfoundland. 'Look where you are, the adventure you're having. How many other people your age would envy such an opportunity?'

'That's all in the plus column. I can see that.' Wyatt had introduced her to the concept of plus and minus columns when he worked through with Morton what to do when he finished school.

'What's in the minus column?'

Gene kept her back to Sonny and her mouth closed.

'Okay, why don't we try this another way? I will tell you one of the best things that has ever happened to me, one of the happiest moments of my life. Now I don't owe you that, but I'm happy to share it. Normally I'm happy to give without expecting anything in return. That's my way in life. But see with you, I think I'm going to have to play it different. I think you got yourself a habit there of holding things too close to your chest.

'Now normally I would say that that's not a bad thing to hold your cards like that. But not opening up and sharing can become one of those habits that are hard to break. Seems to me you've gone so long not wanting to talk about the stuff that saddens you that you've forgotten how to talk about your good stuff, what it is that makes you happy. You're hanging on to all that bad stuff and while you're doing that, it's taking up room inside you that could be filled with more enjoyable things.'

'Have you been talking to Doctor Trantham?'

'Who's he?'

She glanced over her shoulder. 'What did my brother tell you about me?'

'Not much at all really. Mostly, that he wanted you to have a good time on this trip and could I help with that.

175

But it seems to me, some days you're not having such a good time. So what's a guy meant to do?'

Gene's eyes stared ahead at the rippling current. 'Why should I tell you anything? You're virtually a stranger to me.'

'See, there you go again. Veering to the left when you could be veering to the right. After ten weeks up here on this excursion I could be one of your best friends ever.'

'How many other seventeen-year-old girls are you best friends with?'

'Well, there's Rosie.' Sonny cracked a laugh. Gene did too.

'Are you sweet on her?'

'Hell no, not in that way. What am I going to do with an Eskimo wife? But she's a ball of fun. That girl's got a spirit I love.'

'What about my spirit?'

'See that's the thing, Gene, how can I love something I can't see, or touch, or feel, or smell? I ain't seen what your brother's seen.'

He pushed the boat out into the middle of the current, doing a j-stroke to steer it around. 'I'm not a spy for your brother,' he added.

'I know that.'

'Everyone else here I know quite well or am getting to know quite well, but you're distant. I figured if I didn't say anything after ten weeks you'd still be distant. I want you to know, you can trust me. Tell me your stories and I will tell you mine.' He paddled a few strokes. 'Is there a reason why you're distant or is that normal behaviour for you?'

After a few moments Gene said, 'Both.' And then a little while later without turning to look at him, she conceded, 'You scare me a bit.'

'Me?' He sounded quite baffled. 'In what way?'

'The way you can see inside me.' She spoke very quietly. 'Keeping distant makes it easier to hide from you.'

'You don't have to hide from me.'

32

Three days later as they were setting up at a different campsite on Lake Opemiska, home of the Chibougamau Cree, Gene softly said to Sonny, 'I'm ready to tell you.'
'Tell me what?'

'My happy memory.'

Sonny stared at her for a few good seconds. 'Good. I'm ready to hear it. Do you want to tell just me or should we make it a campfire thing and everyone could tell their stories.'

Gene shook her head. 'Just you.'

'Right,' said Sonny. 'Let's go fill up the water containers then.'

They walked away from camp, side by side, their pacing evenly matched. Gene was five foot nine. Sonny was a few inches taller, just marginally shorter than Jonathan, she'd noticed. She figured he was six foot one, but he hadn't yet filled out in the way Jonathan had. 'Okay, you go first,' Gene said.

'While we are walking along? I don't think so. This telling needs a sense of place and occasion.' He looked around. 'Over there, under the spruce with half its branches missing.'

They sat down, about a foot apart from each other.

'You go first,' said Gene.

He looked at her.

'Please,' she said.

'All righty,' He paused then began. 'Would you believe that for many years during the last world war while most people were fervently hoping for an end to the conflict I was fervently hoping for it to continue?'

Gene held her breath while her eyes held Sonny's gaze. That was quite a statement.

'I grew up near the wheat fields of Winnipeg and I couldn't wait till I was eighteen to sign up with the Commonwealth Air Training Plan. Every morning when I woke up it was all I could think about. I'd mark the days off on the calendar. I could fly a plane by then, dozens of them. Already clocked up one thousand hours. But my parents didn't want me going off to war. Said they only had one son and couldn't afford to lose me. But they also knew flying was my passion and eventually they were just as afraid of losing me to anger and defiance as they were to war, so they said when I turned eighteen, they would sign the papers, giving me their permission.'

'Did they?'

'Yes.' Pause. 'Do you want to know the date of my eighteenth birthday?'

'Yes,' she smiled at him.

'May 8 1945.' He paused again. 'V Day Europe. Can you believe my luck? I never heard the end of it. My mother telling me constantly that God was listening. Even so, I signed up because in the Air Force I'd get to fly planes much bigger and faster than I would ever get to fly anywhere else. It was hard getting in because they decommissioned so many people across the ranks. I scraped in with my hours and flight record because I didn't need much training – that and the fact that I was an equally capable mechanic as I was a pilot.

They started me flying B-17s and B-24s. I'd flown up to the Arctic with my father when I was sixteen so in my second year in the Force I was assigned to fly some military photographers and surveyors up here, as far north as the seventieth parallel. When I returned they moved me up to C-47s then C-54s, which were big four-engine transports. That's the same plane that's called the DC-4, which is used as a civilian commercial passenger plane these days. So while I was flying that they transferred me to Uplands, Ottawa, to Military Transport Command, where with a co-pilot we'd fly VIPs in and out of there in all types of weather. I flew and flew and flew, on the job, on my days off, seven days a week to get my hours up so I could qualify for more challenging aircraft like the jets they were rumoured to be working on, which they were. The Vampire.' The way Sonny said the word hinted at its menacing form. Gene was enthralled. 'And when they told me I needed to take a break I said, "fine" and I went off with your brother for two months, still flying, but not every day as you can see. And then in 1948 not long after my third anniversary with the forces, Canada was asked to supply C-54s and two hundred pilots to the lockdown that was happening in Berlin. I was up here flying with your brother but when I returned I was given one week's travel leave before I had to report to Portage La Prairie and then to Rhine-Main Air Force Base in Frankfurt, Germany. I was then bussed to the 60th Troop Carrier Group at Y-80, Wiesbaden, Germany, where my Berlin Airlift flying began.'

'The place where the war ended,' Gene noted.

'Yes, except I'm sure for many people it felt as if their new life after the war had not yet begun. The destruction that you saw from the air, the streets you drove through.' He shook his head while his lips were grimly pressed together. 'Imagine Montreal being flattened and you having to live in rubble under tarpaulins or in basements, with not enough manpower, to clear and rebuild your homes. No running water in your home. No electricity. No heating. It's like an aftermath of an earthquake. Almost easier to walk away and start somewhere new. It will take years to rebuild.'

'So you saw some of the worst of humanity.'

'Yes,' Sonny drawled, 'And some of the best. The logistics for that airlift operation were astounding. Planes were arriving and taking off in Berlin every ninety seconds, twenty-four hours a day, flying from all over West Germany.

'I first flew milk and groceries into Tempelhof: butter from Denmark, coffee from Brazil, sugar from Cuba, wheat from America and Canada. Supplies came from all over the world. Then on the return trip back to Wiesbaden I would fly a load of displaced persons, mostly orphaned women and children that were then dispersed to different areas around Europe. During the winter I hauled nothing but badly needed coal from Wiesbaden to keep the Berliners warm. The plane would be so full of dust that we would open two back windows to draw it out. And in the midst of all that you had to contend with Russians in the airspace trying to intimidate you.'

Gene shook her head in dismay. 'How bad was that?' she asked.

'Pretty bad. They'd fly real close to you and shoot right next to you but never at your actual craft. They'd release balloons in our flight corridors. They'd interfere and jam our radios, shine searchlights into our eyes. They tried everything, but nothing broke us. We were men on a mission, part of something bigger, something monumental, more than that, something sacramental.

'It was two and a half hours down the flight corridor from northern Germany, then twenty-five minutes turnaround as our cargo was unloaded during which time we were given weather briefings and snacks and the maintenance crews were checking over the plane and then we were back in the air, heading north for another load. Two shifts per day. And while it was go, go, go it was the most exciting initiative I've ever been a party to.'

'Your happiest moment.' Gene mused, smiling at Sonny.

'Not quite. There was this American, Gail Harvorsen, who became known as Mr Wiggles.'

'Mr Wiggles!'

'You know this part?'

'Yes.' Gene beamed. 'Tell me your part.'

'Well he wanted to do something for the children of Berlin as you know, so he decided to drop candies from his airplane. Chocolate bars, gum, all day suckers. And to let the children below know he was the candy man, he'd wiggle his wings and the engineers on his plane would

180

throw out chocolate bars attached to handkerchief parachutes to the children waiting below. Every day the children increased and every day he would drop more. And then several of us pilots got on board and confectionary manufacturers and school children up and down America and Canada, Australia, the United Kingdom tied sweets to handkerchief parachutes.'

'That was me!' said Gene proudly. 'We did it at our school.'

'Did you?'

'Yes! Every Friday afternoon. Wow, how amazing that you were one of those pilots!'

'Believe me, it was amazing. To see those kids with their hands above their heads waving at you in gratitude, and exuberance, and sheer delight at the simple pleasure of receiving a candy – nothing has ever come as close. That is my happy moment.'

'It's a great happy moment,' said Gene, feeling positively happy inside just hearing about it. 'You know, your story has made me think of a second happy moment.'

'What's that?

'When I was eleven, Morton, my next brother up turned fourteen and for his birthday Wyatt, who is now our step-Dad, came all the way from Saskatchewan to surprise us with two husky puppies for Morton's birthday. And as you were talking about the children being exuberant and grateful, it reminded me of how those puppies were whenever we came home from school. They'd run up to us and try and jump all over us and we'd crouch to hug them and they would lick and lick and lick our face – more excited than any human ever is to see us. Whether you were gone for an hour or ten days they were always all over you with their affection.'

'Yes! That's what it was like with those kids. That pureness of spirit. That sheer delight.'

Gene sighed.

'Okay. Your turn now.'

'My story is nothing compared to yours.'

'Your story will mean as much to you as mine means to me and that's what's important.'

'Okay.' She took a breath. 'Well my story goes back to the summer of 1938.'

'How old were you?'

'Nearly five. My birthday is in August. Morton was seven, Joel was nearly three and a half. Abigail was eleven, her birthday is in May too and I think she must be the same age as you as she turned eighteen the month war ended. And Jonathan was twenty-years old at the time but he didn't come away with us. He'd gone away with friends of his from university and we were all upset wondering how he could choose his friends over us.'

'The meanie!' teased Sonny.

'Exactly. Anyway, for our summer holiday our parents took us to a place on a lake they had been to years before in the middle of Ontario somewhere. We drove for hours and when we got there we had to load our stuff into a boat and then ride in that for another hour or so, unload our stuff and then Dad took the boat back to the car to bring more stuff that we couldn't fit in the first load.

'We stayed in this secluded log cabin and had our own private little beach, a silver birch at either end with a jetty and lawn in front of the house, no other cabins in sight, hardly any other boats went by during the day. There were two Canadian canoes at the cabin for us to paddle in and inside the cabin there was one big room with four bunks around the sides, a kitchen towards the back, a big table in the middle and to one side was the only bedroom – Mom and Dad's.

'Sometime during the second week, late one night when everyone was in bed asleep I awoke to noises, voices outside. I lay there frozen and then after awhile I slowly got out of my bunk and walked to my parent's room and opened the door. Dad woke up immediately.

'"Yes," he whispered.

'"Daddy," I whispered back, "I hear voices outside.

182

There are these strange men outside."

'Mom stirred and asked what was up. And when she heard she said, "Come here darling, Daddy will go see."'

'Yes,' said Sonny interrupting. 'Daddy will go greet the bogeyman.'

Gene smiled at Sonny. 'So I climbed into bed with Mom and when Dad returned five minutes later he said, "It's just some canoeists. They've been paddling by moonlight and they wanted to pull in somewhere and rest up for the night. They'll be there in the morning and I can show you then, but there's nothing to be afraid of."

'He carried me back into my own bed and lay down with me till I fell asleep. The next morning I had forgotten about the canoeists until Mom was preparing breakfast and she said to Dad, "Do you think those campers would like to join us for breakfast?"

"'I don't know, shall we ask them?" Dad said.

'Mom said, "Why not?"

'Then Dad said, "Say Morton, Joel, Gene, do you want to come with me to say hello to the campers?"

"'Sure Dad," said Joel. That was his standard line. "Sure Dad. Sure Dad."

'We walked outside down to the tent pitched near the water's edge. Dad cleared his throat and said, "Good morning, is anyone awake?"

"'We're awake," said a deep male voice from inside.

'My father said, "Good. I've got some little people here with me, who have something very important to ask you."

"'Wait a second," said the voice again. We could hear rustlings inside the tent and then the tent flaps moved as the stays were untied from the inside. And then a man pulled a flap back and there was Jonathan. I was flabbergasted. Morton smiled the biggest smile and Joel's eyes nearly popped out of his head. None of us had recognised his voice.

"'Surprise," said Jonathan, as he came out and bent down to hug us.

'And Morton said to him – I can still remember it, "Oh, I knew you'd come. I just knew you would come."'

'That's your brother.'

'Yes. And I carry this picture in my head of that moment with my three brothers: the twenty-year old, the seven-year old and the three-year old and the delight that was so clearly written on all their faces was the same.

'And then after Joel had recovered, he wanted to know how Jonathan had gotten there and when he had gotten there. After he had told him, Joel said, "Will you be on my team, when we have canoe races?"

'And Jonathan replied, "I'll be on your team for some of the races bud and guess who can be on the other team?"

'The next moment our cousin Benjamin stuck his head through the tent flap and said, "Me." He was much older than us, older than Jonathan by about three years. His was the other voice I'd heard the night before.

'So that summer we spent our days in and on the water with Jonathan and Benjamin and whenever we had canoe races there would always be one adult with one child, they were always so much fun. Dad always wanted to give Mom a head start and Mom never wanted to take one. We'd play this kissing under the water game, where the eight of us would lie face down like an inverted sundial, our faces close together and try to pass a kiss around the whole circle before we all burst to the surface breathless and bursting for air. Apparently it was Abigail's favourite game when she was little.

'And I remember at the end of one long, energy-sapping day Joel lay curled up in Jonathan's lap, while I was in Dad's, Morton was in Mom's and Abigail was in Benjamin's and Joel in his small voice, said, "Jonathan will you promise to always come on holidays with us? We have the best time when you are on holidays with us."

'"Yes," we all cheered, even Mom and Dad.

'Then Morton piped up and said, "You too, Benjamin."

'To which he replied, "Thank you, Morton."

'And then Jonathan said, "I tell you what, I promise I will always try and come on at least part of your holiday with you. How's that?"

'Joel nodded in quiet approval before saying, "Good."'

All throughout her story Gene hadn't looked at Sonny. She'd sat beside him, her legs bent to one side, her body half turned to his but her eyes were fixed straight ahead. When she finished though, she turned her eyes to him and offered up a hopeful smile.

His return smile was genuinely warm and there was something else about his expression, something akin to wonder. 'That's a beautiful story,' he said. 'Of a beautiful family.'

In that moment Gene sensed that the one thing his high-flying life lacked was a huge loving family. Tears trickled down her cheeks. 'It's a sad story,' she said. 'That was the last holiday we ever had together.'

'Maybe,' said Sonny putting his arm around her. 'But don't let that sadness creep into your story. That came later. In its entirety, that was a beautiful holiday and nothing that has come after will ever take that away from you.' Sonny squeezed her shoulder. 'Thank you for letting me spend some time with the Dalton family. I wish I had known you all way back then.'

Gene nodded through her tears. 'You would have loved my father. He was such a fun man, yet at the same time a man of honour. And he was handsome, was he handsome. One look at my parents together and you knew what love was. His smile was his own. It filled his eyes and lit up his face. It just drew you in. All you wanted to do was sit on his lap and pat his cheeks and smile back into his face when he smiled into yours.'

'Seems like he created a man in his image with Jonathan.'

'He did.' Gene pressed her lips together. 'Our family would not have survived without my brother,' she said, almost as an afterthought.

'When did your father die?'

'The following summer. We were in Newfoundland visiting my mother's family.' Gene paused. 'He, ah, drowned.' Moments later she said, 'Joel too.'

'Bloody hell,' Sonny swore softly under his breath.

33

A few days later an Indian elder came to see them. He walked awkwardly, almost rocking side to side. Even from a distance and wearing long trousers Gene could see his bowed legs. It was a painful sight. She wondered if they operated on people like him. Certainly not here. He sat down in one of their camp chairs. Rosie offered him a cup of English tea and an Indian sweet bread.

'*Mikwek, mikwek*,' he said. Then in English, 'Rain tonight.' He tapped his knee. 'Swollen.' His voice was worn like his body. He looked at Gene and smiled.

Gene smiled back. 'Does your knee always swell up before the rain?'

'That's right. Don't need no fancy piece of equipment to tell me the way of things. I can read the clouds. But I can read my body better.'

'Do you need to see the doctor?'

'That depends. Does he need to see me?' Gene laughed while he sat stone-faced. I just come to visit. Say hello.'

'*Tanisi*,' Gene said.

'*Tanisi*,' he replied. 'Here we say *Kwaay*.'

'*Kwaay*,' Gene repeated. 'Where did you learn to speak English?'

'My grandfather. He was Scottish, but spoke our language for so long he nearly forgot. Sent me away to the nuns at Lac St Jean.'

'So you speak French as well.'

'*Mais oui*.'

'And do you like being able to speak a number of languages?'

'No.'

Gene was surprised. 'No?' She looked at him, at the droplets of spittle on his lips and noticed that his lips seemed to work away before the words came out.

'Speaking English ruined my life. Ruined the life of my people. Our home.' He waved his arm in front of her. 'Here, where we live is not safe from the *wemistikoshiw*. Never safe any more.'

'*Wemistikoshiw* is white man, not windigo,' said Sonny who had not long joined her. 'In what way did the white man ruin things for you?' asked Sonny.

'They find gold. They find silver, copper, minerals, and they tell us we have to move. They want to cut down trees and they tell us we have to move. They make us move three times in twenty years. And then when we settle some place they move the trading post.'

'That'd be right,' said Sonny.

'I'm confused,' said Gene, 'don't you move around year in and year out?'

'We have summer hunting ground and winter hunting ground but always in the same spot. Our winter hunting ground is our home but now everything is temporary. The resting trees of my ancestors are no more.'

Gene wanted to know more about the resting trees of his ancestors but first she wanted to know how his speaking English ruined everything for him.

'White man come to me twenty years ago when I was in my fifties and say, "We understand you can speak English." Yes, I nod. They say, "We are geologists. We study rocks. We like rocks. Do you have any interesting rocks in this area?"

'I say, "We have all sorts of rocks. What kind of rocks you want to see?"

'"All sorts," they say. "Show us all sorts. Where are they? We will pay you to be our guide."

'So because for many years the white man of the Hudson Bay Company was good to my forebears, last century very good, I take them for their word, that they like rocks. Not that they like the precious stone and mineral in the rocks. Why would I think that? They exclaim at the size of rocks, at the view from our cliffs, at the formations, at our caves. They try and tell me how old the rocks are. Can you imagine deciding how old a rock is? They ask if they could take samples of the rock away? And I say go ahead. Who wants to hump a bag of old rocks on their back?

'And then they come back with more men and then government men come and tell us we have to leave. "We want this land. It's in the national interest." Moral suasion is what my grandfather used to call it but there was nothing moral about it. We don't want to leave but they make us go and they move us to another area. Then seven years later they come and the whole thing happens again. And a third time.'

'Did they pay you for taking your land?'

The old man leant forward in his chair towards Gene. 'You look at the world through pale eyes. Even if we were offered money we didn't want to sell. The land was not for sale. But many white men don't respect that. I'm with Tecumseh on that one. Indian land is owned in common by all. Not by an individual. The land belongs to our ancestors, and to our great grandchildren. We are here only to look after it. Treat the Earth and all that dwell thereon with respect. Remain close to the Great Spirit. But when weak white man wave money in front of weak Indian the rot sets in.'

'Why do you say weak white man?' asked Gene.

'Because strong white man would know better. Like Mr. Watt. He was a good white man.'

'Who was Mr. Watt?' asked Gene.

'He was the head of Rupert House, a HBC post at the mouth of the Rupert River,' Sonny explained. 'We'll go there in a few weeks. I'll tell you all about him later.'

'Tell me your name, young lady?'

'Gene. Gene Dalton.'

'Well I'm Eli. Eli Silver. Fitting, don't you think, considering I'm like Judas.'

'But you didn't accept thirty pieces of silver for your land.'

'No, but I led them to our secret places and we lost what was most valuable as a result.'

'See, I have a different view on Judas,' said Gene. 'I think God loved him deeply, and saw in him a man of great character, a person who could sacrifice the short term for the long term good, a person who could do what no other man could do. I wish there was a book of Judas in the Bible for I've always wanted to read his story, his version of events. Throughout the Bible God asked men to do things they didn't want to do or made them do things that he wanted them to do. Look at Joseph. His brothers had to sell him into slavery in order for him to save his whole family years later in the famine. Jesus had to die on the cross and be born again. That's what was in the prophecy. How would his death have been had he said to his twelve disciples, "Now friends, gather round, I need you to nail my hands and feet to the cross and hoist me up and let me hang there till I die." Would any of them have acceded to his wishes? I don't think so. Judas was a man of action. He did what had to be done. I think he was more central than Pontius Pilate even, because Jesus's followers could have hidden him forever to protect their son of Nazarene. If there were no Judas there would be no crucifixion, no resurrection and no everlasting life.'

'Do you believe in the life hereafter?' Eli asked.

'If it means one day I will see all those I love who are no longer of this world then yes, I do.'

'In that Bible story is the story of the whole world, the pull in both directions. All that lies beyond what we can't see. In showing those men around I followed our own creeds. Be truthful and honest at all times. Give assistance and kindness wherever needed. Now I follow our tenth commandment. Take full responsibility for your actions. That I do. I am to blame.'

'No,' said Gene. 'Don't think like that. You are

responsible, but, for what? That, you cannot see today. But try to believe some good will come of it.'

'Though you may not see it in your lifetime,' added Sonny. He came over and squeezed Eli's weathered hand.

'Will you stay with us for dinner?' Gene asked. 'My brother would enjoy talking to you.'

'Depends. Do you have any tobacco?'

Gene smiled. 'We should be able to rustle some up for you.' Although Jonathan rarely smoked, occasionally he liked to sit around a campfire and draw on a pipe.

Later that night Sonny came up to her. 'So sometimes you do take the glass is half full approach when it comes to helping others. I'm impressed. One day you might try some of the same medicine.'

'Don't know what you mean,' Gene mumbled, turning away from him, biting down on her smile.

Eli stayed with them, sleeping in their mess tent, for that night, as he had predicted, it rained and rained hard. Next morning after breakfast Sonny walked him back to his wigwam. When Sonny returned he came over to Gene. 'Hold out your hand.' She held out her hand. 'A thank you from Eli.' Into it he placed a rough clump of pure silver the size of a man's thumbnail.

She looked at its uneven form, then reached for Sonny's hand and put it back in his. 'I can't keep this. Every time I look at it I will think of how he was taken advantage of.'

'Unbelievable. There you go again. Thinking the worse rather than thinking the best. That a revered Indian Chief thought so highly of you he wanted to give you an offering, a token of his appreciation, something that had meaning to him and what he hoped had meaning to you. You're right, you can't keep it. I'm keeping it for now. When you understand its full value come see me and maybe then I'll let you claim it.'

He turned his back on her and walked away. Part of her wanted to call out to him, to say, 'Sonny, come back.' But then what?

34

After the rain came days of settled weather. They moved onto Mistassini Post on Lake Mistassini, their largest settlement to date and the largest lake they had come across. As they unloaded Gene asked Jonathan why he wasn't doing much of the flying. Certainly he wasn't landing or taking off.

'I'll take off from this lake,' he joked. 'How about that? I should be able to manage that.'

'Well?' she asked.

'Well, because in this plane I'm the emergency pilot only. I may have hundreds of hours flying under my belt but not in a floatplane and landing a floatplane is not something I want to practice with other people on board and all our cargo. I've had a few lessons in a twin-seater but not enough to pilot this craft.'

'We can go out once we've unloaded everything for a practice run if you like,' said Sonny. 'What do you say?'

'If you're up for it.'

'I'm always up for it.'

'So, what's the difference between flying a floatplane and a normal aircraft?' Gene asked. 'I know obviously that the landing apparatus is different but how exactly does that affect everything?'

'It's like this, Gene,' said Sonny 'There's what you're landing with and what you're landing on. Floats demand a different method of flying. You can get into a lot of trouble on floats because you can't just stop the airplane. There's a brake pedal in there but it ain't attached to anything. And the plane's a lot more sensitive on water. Less forgiving. If you jerk it one way, you're just as likely to flip it over and sink your craft.

'So when you're coming into land you have to pick your water, and estimate the wind and the current to know where you should be able to stop. Landing and taking off from the ocean or a large lake is always tricky, as you have to watch the swell and the weather. Anything with a swell more than a foot high and you can forget it. No landing, no take off and worse, what are you going to tie your plane up to? That's what you've got to work out before you land in rough weather.

'Also, where will you take off because you always need more distance to take off than you do to land? You don't land and then say, "I wonder where the reefs are? Or where were the submerged logs," because you can't see them when you're down.

'Big rivers are good because they are often more protected but you have to make sure you can get out of the fast flowing current. Small lakes are typically good as well. On a big lake like this one or the Hudson Bay, if there is a storm on the east side it will create waves that will eventually work their way across to the west and vice versa. Here,' he waved his hand at the shoreline, 'you have trees around the lakes and you can get into the sheltered side. Up north there's no shelter because there are no trees – and not many spare parts if the aircraft gets damaged.

Gene tried to imagine what that must be like.

'So, as a pilot, you don't want any swells but equally, you don't want glassy water either. Perfect conditions are a light breeze and gentle ripples. You cannot see glassy water – even if you try really, really hard, even if you're wearing these things.' He pointed to his sunglasses. 'It's difficult to judge your height above something that you can't see. It makes landing hairy even with a craft as capable as this one.'

'So I take it the plane we're flying is a good float plane?' Gene asked.

'Yes,' said Jonathan. 'This beaver is a DHC-2 and was first introduced in 1947 as the successor to the

Noorduyn, isn't that right, Sonny?'

'Yep, the all-purpose bush plane of the Canadian North,' said Sonny.

Her brother pointed to the large cabin. 'Gene, see the cabin, the loading door and the high wing. They're prime requirements for bush aircraft. You don't get a plane more robust and versatile than this one. Designed and built here in Canada to operate in extreme conditions whether it be on wheels, floats, skis or tundra tires.'

Sonny took over from her brother. 'You mightn't think it but it actually has excellent STOL capabilities – that's what we call Short Take Off and Landing. On land it can take off in 600 feet.'

When Sonny described it to her it sounded like the most technologically advanced plane ever built until she discovered it had just been superceded by another De Havilland, an Otter, or as some liked to call it The King Beaver, which had its maiden voyage while she was swilling sleeping pills. That plane could seat ten or eleven people depending on the configuration. Gene looked over their plane. Her eyes came to rest on the floats.

'Now, why are we flying a float plane instead of a normal one with wheels?'

Gene's twirled her head towards Sonny. He had just spoken the very question that was on her mind. He was so disconcerting. He winked at her and clicked his mouth at the same time. He got her with that one and he knew it.

'Quite simply, because with tires we would need to land on airfields and they are few and far between. Tundra tires won't work here because the ground's got too many saplings springing up higgledy-piggledy. This is the taiga after all. Where we're going is where the voyageurs went and they used the waterways and that's what the James Bay Cree still use today.'

'So how do you learn to fly one of these? Because it's not the flying is it? It's the take off and landing.'

'You're right. You need to do lots of exercises to perfect your landings. The first one is called 'Cleared to an Altitude of Two Inches'. It involves finding a very long lake – at least five miles long – this one would be fine – and what you have to do is fly above the lake maintaining an altitude between two and twelve inches above the water.'

'It's not as easy as it sounds,' volunteered Jonathan.

'I don't imagine it would be,' she said.

'The second exercise, we call the 'Fifty Foot Hill'. It involves the same stretch of water and the goal is to land softly, take off, climb to an altitude of 50 feet, and repeat over and over again.

'And the third exercise is one of my favorites. The idea is you have to land next to a selected spot, make a full circle, while remaining on the step, and take off again.

'What's the step?'

'What happens when we take off in the plane, what do you notice?' Sonny asked.

'We power through the water and then at a certain speed we seem to rise out of the water but glide over it as if we were skating.'

'That's it. That's the step. As a seaplane accelerates for take off, it begins to hydroplane on the bottom-most edges of the floats. That 'hydroplaning' phase is called being on the step. Your floats are barely touching the water as you hydroplane at near-takeoff-speed. So that's the third exercise that we practice – learning to manage the step and turn on it – because sometimes waterways are so small that you have to be able to maintain acceleration as you go around a corner and you have to learn how to land in a small lake which often can mean turning back on yourself as part of your landing. That's different to landing on an airfield.'

'Sounds it,' said Gene.

Around five o'clock, Gene joined her brother and Sonny on a joy flight, come practice run. The first two exercises Jonathan managed fine. Then Sonny got him to join them together and then when he was a breath away from the water Sonny got him to bring it down and keep it on the step and take it off again. After they had flown for thirty-minutes, Jonathan, said, 'that's it, I'm done. That takes a colossal amount of concentration.'

Sonny agreed. 'Half an hour is pretty intense, particularly in a plane this size.'

'What about the full circle?' Gene called out from her seat behind them.

'Do you want to do the circle, Gene?' asked Sonny.

'Well isn't that the pièce de résistance?'

'Okay, hang onto your seat,' he said.

Making a turn while on the step ended up being an adrenaline rush like no other. Sonny being the master that he was turned the plane in the tightest of circles. Gene had seen figure skaters twirling on the ice on Ottawa's Rideau Canal and the speed that some of those people could do, men in particular, made her dizzy just watching. She even had lost her balance many times while learning. The feeling of being on the step and turning on the step was just that but on a grander scale. She could have been on a ride at a carnival. She felt wildly out of control yet at the same time knew Sonny was in total control. He did a circle in one direction and then did a figure eight and another one and another one, fast enough yet slow enough to ensure the waves from the last turn had dissipated by the time they came back to that part of the circle and then he looped out of the circle and started doing more figure eights but in the opposite direction before finally turning the Beaver towards the river bank where they would moor it.

'How was that?' asked Sonny.

'That ride had you written all over it,' Gene mumbled. She rested her head back on the seat and stared at the ceiling of the aircraft. 'It was good, but I don't think I can stand on my feet just yet. Where's the stretcher?'

That evening just after dinner a strong wind picked up, a cold gale from the north. They all donned their down-filled jackets. Sonny and Jonathan went to check the ropes on the plane and tie it more securely. It was too early to go to bed so the others moved inside to the sanctuary of the mess tent, and lowered the flaps covering the screen windows. Jonathan returned, followed by Sonny wearing a colourful tuque.

'Did your mother let you bring the tea cosy?' Joan quipped.

'Ho, ho,' Sonny said. 'Looks like we're in for a night of frivolity and entertainment.'

'Well I generally avoid temptation unless I can't resist it.'

'That so? What else you got knocking around in there?'

'Let me think on it. I'll come up with something.'

'What about you, Rosie? I'm not hearing music. I'm hearing blowing.'

'No problem,' she said, 'We can do that one.'

'I'll sing it with you,' said Joan. 'Come over here, love. Now you lead and I'll follow.'

Rosie began *Up above my head*. Then Joan started her round.

Gene followed the first verse with a made up verse, "*I hear beavers in the air*". To which Sonny cried out, 'Very original.' All of them joined in for the last stanza.

'Your turn, Walter,' Sonny said when they had finished. 'What do you know?'

Walter sang *The little white cloud that cried*. He sang it so solemnly they thought he might shed a tear or two in the singing. Everyone applauded when he was done.

Joan followed Walter. 'All right, here I go.' She stood and walked a little away from them all. 'Move over, Billie.' She hummed a pitch, tuning her vocal chords and then she started in a voice that was surprisingly deep and throaty, giving a soulful rendition of *God bless the child*.

She finished and took a bow while Sonny wolf-whistled in appreciation. 'How do you top that? What do you say fellas?' They huddled together. Then they stood and moved to where Joan had been standing. 'This one's for Rosie,' said Walter, nodding his head as he smiled at her.

'Are you ready?' said Sonny, looking at his male companions. 'Your lead, Jonathan. A one, a two, a one, two, three.' Jonathan launched into the *Cry of the wild goose*. Sonny sang the next verse. Gene was impressed. He was good. He was fearless. All three of them sang the chorus together and then Sonny sang out, 'Take it away, Walter.' Gene turned to look at Rosie's face in the candlelight. She was clapping as they all were, but Rosie's eyes were positively glowing as they sang about geese wingin' north in the lonely sky.

When they finished, Sonny said, 'Okay, everyone on your feet, one behind the other, boy, girl, boy, girl, hands around the waist. They snaked to *Mule train*.

Gene knew the song. It was one of Wyatt's favourites, possibly because he fancied himself as bit of a rancher too. But when Sonny sang his version he changed the words to include all those present, substituting doctor for folks, nurse for miner. For himself he sang: *Some high flying thrills for a Sonny in the hills*. When he got to the last verse he sang: *There's a Gene full of sadness but she's sweet around the border,* and Gene practically froze, thinking, my God he's quick. Not just witty but perceptive.

They fell apart laughing when the song came to an end. But Sonny being Sonny was too quick for her because in the next breath he said, 'Gene, don't think we're going to let you off the hook. You're our encore. What's it going to be?'

She looked around at the expectant faces and knew she could not deny them. She smiled but a stab of panic plunged into her heart and her mind fast became blank. She turned to Jonathan. 'Any suggestions?'

'Something from your choir?'

'No.' she said, shaking her head and biting her lip. Her choir had sung at Andrew's funeral, but not her. She did not want to be dragged back to that time.

'Something to wrap up the evening,' her brother suggested.

Every second she felt her disquiet and desperation increasing. She wished there were a genie that could grant her a wish so she could vanish into thin air. Suddenly, without words being spoken, Sonny sang the opening line to *Baby it's cold outside*, as if he knew she wanted to suddenly flee.

And from within her came the second line as if he had summoned it, *I really must go*. He knew his part and she knew hers: a pas de deux in song. Their voices danced around each other, gentle yet tousling. By the end of it Gene felt far from cold.

When they finished Jonathan clapped and yelled. 'Bravo, Bravo!' The others joined him. But Gene was almost deaf to their appreciation. She turned to Sonny, gazed into his cinnamon eyes, and gave him a rare smile, one she reserved for rare people and rare occasions.

35

That summer Sonny would go on to carry enough critical TB cases back to Moose Factory that he could fill the hospital in one short season with new Cree admissions. Each time he left he would ask Rosie if she wanted to come and try for a lift north out of Moose Factory. Each time she declined. 'I'm here now. I'm heading north,' she would tell him.

Besides the TB, equally distressing was the high number of polio patients – more than they had expected. Many of who had long suffered in silence through the splitting headaches, fevers, stiff necks and backs, fatigue and muscle pain. Some needed operations to cut and elongate their tendons in their legs and wear a leg brace. Few were interested in that, preferring to drag their damaged leg behind them. In Nitchequon, on Lake Nichicun, they came across a fresh outbreak of polio.

Located far to the east, beyond the headwaters of the Eastmain River in part of Labrador, the Nitchequon post had closed in 1943. It reopened in 1950 after the federal government in 1945 began operating an aeradio station there to provide air-traffic control and weather information for pilots in the region. The settlement had a simple airstrip but a much bigger lake.

Jonathan instructed Rosie that they were to eat only their supplies or food that she caught – no local food offered by locals. Accept it and burn it he told her. All the water had to be boiled before it was used for anything, for personal washing, for ladling more liquid into a stew on the fire, for cleaning the pots, for cleaning one's teeth. Boil it. Boil it. Boil it. The polio patients they didn't evacuate. None needed the iron lung as far as he could determine. Instead, Jonathan got the town's people to rearrange their living arrangements so victims could be in houses that were quarantined. All children were ordered to stay away – polio for some reason being more virulent amongst the young. Fortunately Nitchequon was the smallest and remotest settlement they had encountered. 'Don't travel for three months. Don't spread this,' Jonathan advised their elders through Walter. The parents were instructed in how to wrap their children in hot bandages three times a week and to stretch and massage their limbs.

Jonathan and Joan saw children with ear infections and tonsillitis, eczema and asthma; children with clubfeet and knocked knees; adults who complained of always being thirsty and hungry and peeing all the time, having to get up in the middle of the night. Jonathan made them fast for twelve hours and come back for Joan to take a blood test, which he then studied under a microscope.

Gene asked, 'Do you do this kind of thing back in Montreal?'

He shook his head. 'I had a pathologist do a refresher with me before I came up.'

'I was going to say that I thought respiratory diseases were your speciality.'

'They are.' He gasped and gasped, his hand clutching his chest like he was an asthmatic, then he broke into a wide grin.

Next stop, Neoskweska, after that, Nemiscau, and then finally the famed village at the mouth of the Rupert River known as Rupert House that Gene had been hearing so much about. It had been the very first HBC post site. This was a settlement of single and double-storey wooden houses – some of them painted, some not – largely devoid of trees, except for the conifers around the Trading Post building in the distance. Gene could identify them easily now – they were always sited on the best location with views up and down the river, painted white with red roofs. Here the lack of trees reminded her a bit of Newfoundland except the grass was much greener and the countryside not littered with large boulders.

Like a group of bedraggled survivors in some Western movie, everyone in their party walked down the main thoroughfare past women repairing fish nets and tanning moose hides, past the Jim Watt Memorial Hall towards the HBC post when suddenly she smelt the heady bouquet of freshly baked bread, something she hadn't smelt – let alone eaten – for weeks.

She stopped and gasped. 'Where is that smell coming from?'

'From the bakery up ahead,' said Jonathan. 'Do you need some help in finding it?'

'I think I can manage,' she smiled sideways at her brother while her stomach rumbled. All six of them walked into the store. A small lady, her hair in a chignon, stood behind the counter with her back to them, re-arranging loaves of bread and scones into baskets.

'Greetings, Maud,' said Jonathan.

She twirled around, her eyes scanning the males in the group for the face belonging to the voice.

'Mother of God,' she exclaimed, 'Look who's come back to visit me at long last.' Her mouth and cheeks turned up into an apple of a smile. 'Johnny Dalton and Sonny Marlow. And is that you, Walter Niles? Look at the three of you! My, Sonny, you've grown into a man. How's your father these days?'

'He's well. Thanks. Mostly staying closer to home these days, keeping Mom company.'

'He's still flying?'

'Still flying.'

'Oh look, it's Joanie.' She came out from behind the counter to give Joan a hug.

'And who's this bonnie lass?' smiling at Gene as she looked her up and down.

'Maud, allow me to introduce my sister, Gene,' said Jonathan.

'Welcome, Gene.' And in the same breath she said,

'and who is this wean such a long way from home?' She smiled at Rosie.

'Yes, small as she is, Rosie is actually the same age as Gene,' said Jonathan.

'What have they been feeding you, Rosie? Obviously not my bread. Here, help yourself to a piece.' With that she walked behind the counter, sliced some bread, pointed to a bowl of butter and a knife and said she hoped they didn't mind caribou butter.

'How long you about for, Johnny?' Maud asked.

Gene laughed. In all her life she had never heard anyone call Jonathan Johnny and in the space of thirty seconds this woman had called him Johnny twice.

She couldn't resist. 'Yes, how long we staying here, Johnny?'

Jonathan gave her a drop it Gene look, but there was a playfulness behind the glare. It seemed he was happy to indulge the gregarious Mrs. Watt and forgive her abbreviation of his name.

'A week at least, maybe two. Depending on the health of the nation so to speak. How's your family?'

'All good. Grandchildren getting a good Catholic education right here in Rupert House. What's there to complain about?'

'Many kids at the Mission or have they gone home for the summer?'

'Enough orphans there to keep you busy for a few days, don't you mind. What about you? Where's your beautiful wife?'

'Home with our son, Matthew, and another one on the way.'

'Well you just answered my next question. Will you promise to have dinner with me one night?'

'Why don't you have a night off and join us for dinner in our camp?'

'That will be my pleasure.'

'Rosie will come by one morning and invite you.' Jonathan smiled at Rosie who nodded in agreement. 'In the meantime, we'll take some bread off your hands before we head to the bar for an overdue drink.'

In a room at the other end of the building, Gene studied a sign while her brother ordered.

```
If you give an Indian something,
give him the best you have,
because he will always give you his
best!  — Jim Watt
```

Walter came up to stand next to her. 'He was Maud's husband,' his voice very reverential. 'He came from the highlands in Scotland. Very honoured man amongst the Cree. Like his wife. They saved the Cree from financial destitution.'

'In what way?' asked Gene.

'They saved the beaver.'

'The beaver needed saving?'

'Yes,' said Walter. 'When the Watts came to Rupert House in 1920 fur prices were booming. Soon more and more white trappers came north in search of the lucrative beaver fur, competing with the Cree on their own land. In less than ten years the beaver was nearly extinct. In the winter of 1928 only four beaver were brought into this store, down from 2000 eight years earlier.'

'That's a rapid depletion!'

'Yes, a catastrophe. Meant the start of hard times for the Cree. Without beaver to trade, the Cree's economy collapsed. Over the years we had come to rely too much on white man's goods – guns, wires, flour, lard. Without beaver to hunt, people starved. The Watts had to overextend credit to the Cree so they could provide for themselves. Rupert House lost money for the Company and Mr Watt risked losing his job for extending credit. He wrote to the company asking for compassion but the Company ignored him. He even wrote to the head of the Company in England and when the head of the Company in Canada found out he reduced his wage.'

'He didn't!'

'He did.'

Gene shook her head in disbelief.

'Times were bad. In one year thirteen people from one whole family died from starvation. The Watts did what they could to feed the Cree from their own food but they could not save everyone. It was then that Mr. Watt realised he had to save the beaver.

'Stop people from hunting it?' Gene queried.

'Yes,' said Walter. 'In 1929, rather than buy beaver skins from the Cree he announced that he would only buy live beavers, mating couples, and he bought them with his and Maud's own savings. Not the Company money. He was a very smart man. Mr. Watt realised that for each pair of beaver he saved, there would be ten in three years and twenty-six in five years.

'But for this conservation programme to work, he needed all of us Crees to support it. We had to be willing to locate the beaver, sell them to him and protect them. When he talked to my fathers they understood what he was doing. And he trusted them. But, they pointed out, it wasn't them they had to worry about; others would come in and trap the beaver. They were right. He needed control of the trapping. So the Watts decided to ask the Quebec government for control of the beaver for the protection of the Cree. They wanted to create a wildlife sanctuary for Canadian Indians. It had never been done, but this did not deter them.'

'So how did they go about that?' she asked.

Walter smiled. 'I was just about to tell you.' He paused. 'In the winter of 1930, it was decided that Maud, who spoke French, would go to Quebec City to plead their case. In the heart of winter she set out by dog sled with her two children, three and six years old at the time, and some local guides.'

For an instant Gene thought of her brother, Morton, but mostly she tried to picture that small woman she had met just minutes before with snow shoes on her feet, commanding a travelling party in the middle of winter across frozen James Bay. 'I can't believe she took her children with her. Why didn't she leave them at home?'

'I believe after she concluded her business in Quebec City she was going to visit her parents who lived in Gaspé. Anyway, from Moose Factory they continued south to the railway construction camp, then continued by train to Quebec, arriving one month after they left home.'

'And her mission was successful?' Gene asked.

'After she pleaded her case before the Quebec government, they approved a reserve consisting of 200 square miles.'

'Wonderful!' Gene smiled with satisfaction. 'She got what she wanted.'

'No,' said Walter.

'No?' queried Gene, somewhat confused.

'No,' repeated Walter, nodding his head at the same time. 'She thanked them for the reserve, but then proceeded to tell them it was far too small and simply would not do.' Gene burst out laughing. She could imagine that feisty woman in full swing.

Walter laughed too. 'Maud had worked side by side with her husband for ten years and was good friends with the Cree. She knew more about beavering than all of those men in Quebec put together. In the end her persistence paid off. She was given a lease of 7,200 square miles for a beaver reserve that was to be managed for the benefit of the Cree hunters who depended on the beaver population for food and clothing for their people.'

'Then she got what she wanted!' said Gene grinning in triumph.

Walter smiled proudly in return and led her to a large map on the wall where he pointed to the land between the Eastmain and Rupert rivers, and between the Bay and Nemiscau. 'This was the 7,000 square mile reserve.'

'I bet her husband was happy.'

'Yes, but the Company was furious with him. They saw it as theft of their monopoly. They came to the edge of firing him but pulled back for fear he would move to the competition. What they did instead was demand he turn over the reserve to the Company.'

Gene sighed in exasperation. 'Tyrants!'

'Ah yes, but wait,' said Walter. "The Watts had thought through this possibility well before Maud left for Quebec, so the reserve had been set up in Maud's name only, and out of the Company's reach, further infuriating the bureaucrats.'

'Brilliant,' she said, clapping her hands in delight.

'But in the end the Watts had to turn over partial control to the company when it became apparent their savings wouldn't be able to fund all the live beaver they were wanting to purchase. However by 1938, the beaver count had reached 3,300. That same year a second reserve was established and in 1940, the first reserve was opened to controlled trapping.'

'Wow! In ten years they had resupplied their stocks.'

Walter led her to another map hanging on the wall where she could see markings for a number of beaver reserves. 'The Rupert House reserve was so successful that the federal government, the Quebec government and the HBC jointly set up ten more reserves in the past ten years covering 187,000 square miles on both sides of James Bay.'

'What an achievement,' she said, filled with admiration at their efforts. 'Where is Mr Watts today?'

'He died,' said Walter, very solemnly. 'Here in 1944 of influenza. But he had seen his dream come true. And the Cree never forgot Jim. That hall we walked past earlier. They paid for that to be built in his honour.'

In her journal that night, Gene wrote down Jim Watt's motto and the remarkable story of the husband and wife who created Canada's first wildlife preserve and the pragmatic Cree who supported them. In her prayers she thanked God for the Watts and thanked God that Eli Silver had the pleasure of knowing them well.

36

The days were warmer. They were all getting round in mid-season clothing, still wearing long sleeves and long trousers to cover themselves from the insects. Truth be told the black flies weren't so bad around their camp as Rosie was always quick to throw some spruce branches on the fire if she saw them buzzing around. It was only when they walked off that they seemed to be aggressive.

Every time he flew Sonny would pull on his brown bomber jacket and his sunglasses. Gene imagined it had been his unofficial flying uniform before joining the Air Force and here he was back in it again along with his flying boots and light brown nylon air force wind pants.

Then it dawned on her: she didn't know if he was still in the Air Force or not? Was he taking another extended holiday on orders from the military?

One day when he was pumping fuel from a forty-four-gallon drum into the tank in the plane's wing she walked up and asked him.

'No, I left the Air Force just under a year ago,' he said dryly.

By the way he spoke she could tell it hadn't been a welcome experience. Normally she wouldn't pry but, for her, Sonny was a person who was comfortable talking about practically anything. 'Do you mind me asking what happened?'

'The Korean War is what happened.'

'Did you go to that war?' Gene was confused. The war had only started just over a year ago. Did he go? Was he shot down? Injured?

'No. I woke up and realised I never had any intention of going to war. I was naïve, selfish. The only reason I joined the Air Force was to fly planes I couldn't fly otherwise. I never thought of killing. I've never killed another human being and I wasn't about to.'

'I guess that was a good reason,' said Gene. She had been unprepared for his admission and didn't quite know how to respond.

'Yeah, well...strange how I didn't want to admit it at the time but after Berlin I was grateful Mom's prayers were answered, that I didn't get to fly in the war. Hell, there's no way I would want to be responsible for that death and destruction, even if Hitler was a despot that needed to be stopped. I'm glad I didn't have to go through that baptism of fire. You meet some pilots, they seem to get off on it, almost like they have a blood lust or a bomb lust, but that's not me.'

He took a break from working the hand pump.

'I felt bad about it. Still do. The Air Force invested so much in training me. I said I would stay on and train other pilots but I didn't want to stay and go off to Korea. I offered to work in medical evacuations only and they said they couldn't guarantee it and all I could think of was Nagasaki and Hiroshima so I said: okay I will have to guarantee it then and so I resigned. All my friends in the Force said I was mad. I probably am.'

He returned to filling the tank while Gene stood and watched him, not really knowing what to say. When he finished he rolled the hose back up and secured the caps.

'I'm sorry if I disappoint you, if you find my actions cowardly. There's too much pain and suffering and dying in the world as there is. I'm not adding to it.'

He turned to look at her then and it felt like he was seeking her approval or her forgiveness.

'I don't think you are a coward, not at all. I come from a family where the males were all doctors: my father, my uncle, my grandfather, even my great grandfather and now my stepfather and Jonathan. They were all committed to saving people's lives. Three of them served in wars to save people, four if you count Wyatt, though sadly one of them ended up being killed himself.'

Sonny nodded slowly in understanding. 'You know I'm surprised Jonathan didn't serve in World War Two.' He glanced at Gene to see if there was an explanation.

'I don't know if he would have liked to or not. I've never asked. But the decision was taken out of his hands. He was needed at home.'

'Got you,' said Sonny his eyes catching Gene and her meaning.

'What was your position in the Air Force before you resigned?'

'Captain.'

'Is that right? O Captain, my Captain.' Gene smiled at him then laughed to cover her own blushing as she turned and walked away. After she had taken five steps she turned again and said in a tone most serious, 'I'm glad you weren't like Walt Whitman's captain.' It wasn't till later she realised she hadn't asked him what he was doing now, other than flying them around the Canadian wilderness.

Next time they were alone she asked Sonny, 'Was your mother relieved when you resigned from the Air Force?'

'Yeah, she was. My Dad too for that matter. But they also conceded my time in Germany was, shall we say, an educational experience and they were glad I had that opportunity.'

'You mentioned the other week you didn't have any siblings,' Gene said.

'No, I don't. Apparently I had an older sister but she died of diphtheria a few years before I was born. So there was just the three of us.'

'Was that hard growing up with no brothers or sisters?' asked Gene.

'It was what it was. I would probably say our family is tightly knit because there's only been the three of us – but I don't think that's always the case.' He paused and looked at her.

'No,' she agreed.

Sonny nodded by way of reply. 'When my father was around we three did everything together. When he was away it was just Mom and I. Occasionally we'd visit Dad's brother or his sister and their families. I've got a cousin, Sylvia, who's close in age to me. We get on well. No relatives in Canada on my mother's side.'

'Oh,' said Gene, 'how's that?'

'Because my Mom was born in Norway and all her family are still there, well, except her father. He was killed during World War One. Worked as a merchant seamen delivering supplies to Britain and returning with coal. Odd, how my grandfather and I both transported coal at one stage in our lives. Anyway, during World War One, despite Norway being neutral, nearly nine hundred vessels – almost half of the Norwegian fleet – were torpedoed by Germans, my grandfather's boat being one of them.'

'That's terrible,' said Gene in sympathy.

Sonny shrugged. 'That's war for you. An absolute waste. My mother had two brothers Sven and Halen. I've never met them. She still writes to them every year. But after my Grandfather was killed her mother gave her what money she had and told her to go far away and find a husband in a place where the Germans wouldn't be able to touch him. Mom was twenty at the time and couldn't speak any English. She went to Liverpool and caught a ship for what she thought was Sydney, Australia, thinking she would go on to New Zealand but it actually came to Sydney, Nova Scotia. When she realised her mistake she decided to catch a train across the country but fate intervened. She met and married my father and never made it to the west coast of Canada.'

Gene laughed softly. 'Perhaps that was her destiny.'

'Perhaps,' agreed Sonny.

'Like flying is yours.' After a pause she asked, 'This plane you fly now, who does that belong to?'

'This baby's all mine. Bought it with my Air Force earnings.'

'Is that so?' She smiled. 'Aren't you a good saver?'

'That's me. Forever saving.'

'Who's paying you to be here?'

'The Department of Indian Affairs.'

'So you trust my brother to fly your plane?' Gene teased.

'Yep. He trusts me and I trust him.' He gave her a look that said: that's enough for me. Sonny was cleaning the insects off the windows and windshield of his much-loved airplane, balancing on the floats while he did so. Gene was helping him by throwing out the dirty water and fetching a new bucket of clean water for rinsing.

'Sonny,' she said. 'Aside from this baby that you love, anyone special back in Winnipeg?'

He halted, glancing over his shoulder at her. 'I've got some good mates, but if you mean, a girlfriend, no. Too busy coming and going, flying all over the place for a steady girlfriend, if you know what I mean?'

'Does that mean you have lots of unsteady girlfriends all over the place?' She laughed at her own joke.

'Ha, ha,' he said, laughing with her. 'Watch it, or I'll throw a bucket of water at you.'

'I'll throw one back,' she teased, catching his eye. 'So no sailor business going on then? No good times girls in every airport?'

He stepped off the float onto the bank. 'Does that strike you as me?' he asked, suddenly serious.

She held his eye. After a moment she softly replied, 'No.'

He slanted his head in faint acknowledgment. 'If you must know, I haven't had a girlfriend since I was your age.'

'Seventeen...I find that hard to believe.'

'Be that as it may, it's the truth.'

'What happened? Did she break your heart or something?' Suddenly Gene wished she could take back her question. It sounded so flippant. What compelled her to say that? That was so unlike her! There could have been any number of reasons why the relationship was no more. 'Oh, Sonny, please ignore me. I'm sorry, that's none of my business.' She went and threw her bucket of dirty water over the base of a heather bush then scooped up more clean water from the lake. When she returned she kept her mouth firmly closed while Sonny rinsed the windows then dried them with a rag. When he finished he washed the cloth, wrung it out and hung it off a windscreen wiper to dry.

With his back still to her he softly said, 'She did break my heart.'

Something about his admission touched Gene's heart. 'I'm sorry,' she said, her voice barely audible.

He turned to face her, his ready smile in place. 'It happens. It was a long time ago now.'

'What happened exactly?' she asked.

'She became a war bride. Snatched up by a New Zealander who was over here training with the Commonwealth Air Training Plan. There were hundreds of men across the prairies at the time. You'd go to a dance and you'd be lucky if there was one girl for ten guys. My poor mother never got to rest. She'd be on her feet all night. Saw it as her duty to ensure those chaps had a good time being so far away from home and all.'

'What was her name?

'Lesley.'

'And how old was she?'

'Seventeen.' He paused. 'Your age, right?

Gene nodded. 'Did you ever meet the man she married?'

'Once,' said Sonny. 'He was a decent enough chap... eight years older than us...an engineer from Auckland wearing a smart captain's uniform.' He paused for a few moments. 'I felt like a kid next to him. I was. How could I compete with that?'

'You became a captain yourself,' said Gene softly.

Sonny shrugged. 'Those Kiwis and Aussies ended up with a fair number of our Canadian women. The bastards!' He laughed at that. 'They took some of our best, that's for sure.' He took his sunglasses off and wiped them with his shirt. 'That was a lesson in life.'

'And what was the lesson?'

He looked at her with his soft brown eyes and his light brown stubble. 'Maybe it pays to be a cradle snatcher!' He grinned.

'Or a captain, with an accent.' Gene grinned in return.

37

One night around their campfire Rosie started talking about her home – what she was most looking forward to, what she missed, what she loved: in winter, the snow covered mountains of Baffin Island, rising out of the flat frozen tundra; in summer, the cliffs of Mont Thor valley, where barren women on a pilgrimage would make an offering to a rocky massif that bulged out like it was with child, hoping they would then be able to hold a baby inside them for full term.

Mostly Rosie didn't see her world in seasons but in something else: the time of white and the time of colours – the blue forget-me-nots, the pink fireweed, the purple saxifrage, the yellow tundra flower. With the great thaw came the return of birds: the gyrfalcon, the Arctic skua, the snow goose, the green-winged teal and hundreds more. Too soon they were gone again and they would descend into whiteness and into blackness. Where she lived it was daylight on average for two hours a day in winter. There was always one day where there was no light at all. But in that long dark night and the chilling whiteness, the northern lights would come to brighten their world pulsing rivers of light, flecked with stars, brilliant greens, dazzling reds, blues, whites, oranges and yellows. And just to make sure one didn't miss them, they would sparkle and crackle across the peaceful silence of the ebony sky.

'You can hear them?' asked Gene in wonder.

'Yes,' Sonny reassured her. 'They are like an electrical conductor.'

'I want to hear them one day!' declared Gene.

Rosie talked on about the great mammals that shared

their landscape: the giant muskox; *nanuk*, the polar bear, the great lonely roamer; and in summer, her favourite, the elusive narwhal. As Gene listened it struck her that Rosie's ties with her home, her identity with the place, were infinitely greater than Gene's had ever been with her home in Montreal. Without seeing first hand, Gene understood how the geography of that distant place shaped the spirit and character of the people who lived there. And oddly that revelation left her with a profound sense of yearning – for what, she did not know.

At night in their tent Gene said to Jonathan. 'We will have to take Rosie back to her home.'

Jonathan chuckled.

'We will, Jonathan,' she insisted.

'I don't dispute that. You just figured that out?'

'When did you come to that realisation?'

'The moment Sonny cursed Mr Howe for his appalling repatriation policy.'

'Have you told her?'

'No. We'll surprise her.'

'Good,' said Gene smiling in the dark. 'I'm looking forward to going there now. You don't think there will be any icebergs up there do you?'

'We'll be flying over the Foxe Basin. I can't guarantee there won't be any icebergs. But Gene we will be in a plane not in a boat. Don't let the thought of icebergs put you off.'

'If it weren't for those icebergs our father and brother would still be alive.' There, she said it. At long last she had said it: the unspeakable reason.

'You think so?'

'I'm utterly convinced. I know so. Don't you feel it in your bones?'

'Whether I feel it or not, I'm not convinced our father would still be alive.'

'How can you say that!' Gene felt sorely aggrieved.

'Look at his history,' said Jonathan. 'At nine years of age he survived being swiped by a grizzly bear. Ten years later he survived his boat going down in the freezing Atlantic and being lost at sea for two weeks. He survived being overrun by Germans in World War One. He survived being bombed at Hospital City when his brother did not. He survived an encounter with a wild wolf beyond the 54th parallel, an encounter, which I understand he only survived by the grace of that she-wolf for he was weaponless at the time. But at forty-four years of age he didn't escape another scrape with death and the way I look at it his number was up and in his final moments possibly he realised that too and accepted his fate.'

Next to her brother, Gene shuddered.

'But you know the thing about Dad, that makes me happy?'

'No,' Gene's voice was barely audible.

'Dad was like Sonny. He lived till he died and possibly each one of those near misses made him live more intensely.'

'Was Joel's number up also?'

'Gene, I miss Dad. I miss Joel too but clearly, unfortunately, Joel didn't have Dad's lucky streak. However I take comfort in the fact that they went together. Like Mom said at their ceremony, they weren't alone.'

'You think?' Gene rolled over and tried to make herself go to sleep. But thoughts of her father, his head being smashed against the iceberg, his face morphing with Andrew's, then Joel's terrified eyes cresting on a distant wave, tormented her. Rather than Morton it was her in that boat and she felt just as desperate and powerless and angry and scared. She snuck out of their tent and changed in the mess tent so not to disturb Jonathan and went walking in the breaking light but an oppressive mood seemed to hang over her all morning.

At lunch Jonathan decided Sonny should fly some more people back to Moose Factory and suggested Gene go with him.

'I don't need to go,' she snapped.

'You don't need to. But I'm giving you the afternoon off. Take it if you want. You can send Mom a telegram for her birthday. It's the day after tomorrow.'

'Pack an overnight bag,' advised Sonny. 'Meant to be a front sweeping through later. We might let it pass and fly back in the morning.'

She was midway through packing when Sonny came up to her tent. 'Gene, can I ask you a question?' he called out.

'Sonny!' She wasn't in the mood for his questions.

'Now, come on, I've been good to you. Indulge me once more.' He waited patiently outside her tent.

She backed out, stood up and looked up at him, his eyes not far from her own.

'I've just been thinking that if you wanted to, you could go home today. From Moose Factory I could take you across to Moosonee and put you on a train. You'd be home in three or four days if you'd rather. I can help Jonathan and Joan with the note taking, Walter too. We should be able to manage.'

'Well, I can easily see how none of you need me,' she said, taken aback at his bluntness.

'Wrong. You're contribution is helpful. My handwriting is shocking. Walter's is not much better. We won't be doing the Mountie any favours but what we don't need is your glumness.'

'I haven't been mean and nasty to anyone. What's your problem?'

'True, you haven't been but you're so damn gloomy. It's so unnecessary. It just weighs everybody down. We don't need it. You're like a bear with a sore head. Right here, right now, where is the pain in your life? Has one of us upset you? Are you tired of being away from home? Do you miss your mother? Are you bored with being around the Cree all day? Sick of all this?' He stretched his hands out wide and twirled around. 'Is the scenery getting you down? Are you not well? Do you have some other problem?' He stared at her. She stared back at him, her chest rising and falling.

'Can you answer yes to any of those questions?'

His cinnamon eyes reached out to hers. She closed her eyes, shook her head and lowered it.

'I didn't think so.' He waited in silence. 'Gene, is there something bothering you from way back that you want to talk about?'

She kept her head lowered as she said, 'Not that I want to talk about.'

'I've been thinking about the story you told me about your happy moment and I'm wondering if you believe your life will ever be that happy again?'

She lifted her head, stared at him and grimaced a fake smile.

'Don't do that. Just answer my question.'

'Of course I do. I have to. If not, what would be the point in living?'

'Then why aren't you living? You keep living in the past, Gene. Occasionally you flare up in the present and it's so beautiful when you do, but it's so fleeting, it disappears like a fog burning off. We see a glimpse of your spirit, but then you let whatever it is drag you back there.

'But here's the thing you're missing. You're stronger than that thing. You're the one that determines where you are and who you are. Decide to be here. Be Gene. Be now. But if you don't want to decide to do that then decide to go home. Go back to whatever it is that haunts you, whatever it is you've got so used to living with that it's a comfort. Because unless you exert some influence over that thing and yourself, none of us has a hope in hell of being happy around you.

'I'll be leaving in an hour. You can come. You can stay. You can go home. I'm sure your brother will understand.'

This time Gene didn't watch him go. But she wanted to.

Forty-five minutes later after Sonny and Walter had loaded five passengers on board – one secured on a stretcher in the back and the rest in the seats in the cabin – Gene sheepishly made her way to the aircraft. She noticed the only spare seat was next to Sonny. 'I guess I'm riding up front with you.'

'Yes, Gene. You are.'

When they were seated inside, before he started the motor she said, 'I'm sorry.'

He looked at her, his smile slow yet compassionate. 'That's okay. Apology accepted.'

With their earmuffs on they travelled mostly in silence, until all of a sudden she heard Sonny speaking through the headphones. 'Hold on, we've got company. We're going down.' He glanced her way but she couldn't see anything behind his glasses just his excited smile.

She tried to speak to him, yell at him but he couldn't hear her. His voice came again inside the earmuffs. 'Press that red button on the cord attached to your head phones when you want to talk to me then release it when you're done.'

'Are they big and white and furry, like you promised?' Gene teased.

'They are big and they are white,' he replied and grinned at her. And as they came in closer she saw them, a pod of beluga whales, basking in the sunlit shallows at the mouth of a river, a few had baby calves. Sonny banked into a descending spiral to get closer, the Cree looked out the windows and she could hear their ahs of delight before the whales turned toward the sea, struggling to cross the shallow bar away from the plane overhead.

In Moose Factory at the post office Gene sent her telegram:

Happy birthday Mom from Hudson Bay.

Love to Annabelle & Matthew as well.

Gene & Jonathan

To her surprise there were letters there for the Daltons, and Joan, and one for Sonny too.

That night after dinner they went for a walk through the town, past the Anglican St. Thomas Church, past its cross-hatched fence and prominent bell tower that Sonny had spoken about weeks before; past a house that had a small sign that read Old Cottage Hospital; past kids playing outside in the long hours of twilight. At Moose Factory they weren't all Indian, there were many white folk as well.

On the other side of the island they sat and watched naked children, maybe eight-years old, slick as otters, swimming in the river. Their copper-coloured hands would grip the long sedge grass on the bank and haul themselves back up. They would take five, ten paces, turn around then run fearlessly down and hurl themselves back in, at times trying to bomb each other with a wall of water that careened down on their friends. The river flowed strongly but that didn't deter them. They seemed to know their limits, and their own strength, and how to paddle with determination to get close to the bank and the slower flowing waters.

'They're intrepid,' noted Gene.

'That's the Cree for you. They're known for their bravery.' Sometime later he said, 'Did you know that in both world wars, the highest percentage of volunteers in Canada came from among the Cree around Moose Factory? And I'm told they signed up without hesitation for the Korean War as well.'

'Really?' said Gene. That fact did surprise her...just the thought of Indians in a foreign country fighting someone else's war – a war her father and Wyatt had participated in.

'The most highly decorated Canadian Indian in the first world war – I'd go as far to say possibly the bravest, most daring soldier in all of Canada – was Francis Pegahmagabow. Peggy they used to call him. An Ojibwa from Parry Island in Ontario. He was awarded the Military Medal three times plus bars for bravery in Belgium and France. He was the best sniper to come out of the war apparently.

'Then in the second world war this Oji-Cree, chap by the name of Boyden, was awarded the Distinguished Service Order and ended up being the highest-decorated medical officer of that war. Quite a reputation the two of them.'

'They must have had an amazing ability to overcome whatever fears they had to be such a steady shot, don't you think?' said Gene.

'Perhaps fear was their friend,' said Sonny. 'That's why they could be so brave. Unlike me.'

'I don't know. I think you're rather brave.'

'In what way?'

'The way you stand up to me.'

Gene couldn't help herself: she burst into uncontrollable laughter and fell backwards, her eyes closed, her chest rising and falling in spasms of mirth. She opened her eyes and found Sonny leaning over her, one hand on the ground on the far side of her. His face was full of merriment. 'The question is, how brave are you?'

She looked up at him, at his honey brown eyes, his fresh-face, bronzed cheeks and unavoidable grin and suddenly felt entwined in a sense of mild panic and wonder. A sense of knowing that with one move on her behalf this playful innocence could transpire into something else that while still playful and still innocent, would undeniably be a threshold she wasn't sure she was ready to cross. They gazed into each other's eyes, drew closer to the other and then in the unspoken question and the unspoken answer Sonny pulled back, jumped to his feet, reached down and gave her his hand to pull her up.

'Rain clouds coming up from the south.' He nodded towards that direction. 'Thunderstorms rolling up from the prairies. We might get rained on before we get back to the Hospital.'

'I can handle a bit of rain,' said Gene.

'Clearly you can.'

From that day onwards Gene saw Sonny in a new light, in a 'how come I never noticed him in that way before' light? In a 'how could I not notice him that way'? I wish I didn't notice him that way! For when the sun shone on his fair hair which was getting longer and wavier by the day and a glint of light caught his sunglasses and his teeth gleamed and she looked at his brown leather jacket with the sheepskin collar she longed to have it wrapped around her body and he with it. Each and every time she felt herself almost lightheaded at the sight of him and she hoped to high heaven that he couldn't tell what was going on inside her mind.

In the days and the weeks, in the going about their business, in the conversations and the plane rides and the singing and the laughing this had come to be. Any other young woman would have been nervous and excited in equal measure. With anticipation and trepidation beating in their veins they would have gone with it, said: bring it on. But any other young woman was not Gene. Gene knew she was nowhere near ready for the unstoppable force and the unhideable force that Sonny Marlow could be in her life. But more so, if he only knew the truth, he wouldn't want to be ready for her.

38

As is the case with all adventures, once you reach the halfway mark the days seem to race on ahead of themselves. Jonathan and Sonny, Gene and Joan, Walter and Rosie fly over deep gorges running the length of the Eastmain and Opinaca watersheds, to Eastman itself then Old Factory and Fort George. Sonny makes what they all hope will be his last flight back to Moose Factory with five sick TB patients requiring hospitalisation and ongoing treatment.

As he readies to leave Gene goes to him and asks him to check at the Post Office to see if there is a return telegram from their mother.

'Roger. I'll check for mail as well.'

She stands there not wanting to leave or perhaps wanting to go with him again. She's not sure.

He stands and smiles at her. 'You can kiss me goodbye if you want.'

In his disarming way he has gone straight to the heart of the matter.

Gene tries to hide behind a laugh. 'What makes you think I want to kiss you?'

'You wanted to kiss me the other night.'

'I thought it was you who wanted to kiss me.'

'Hell yes, but I could have sworn the feeling was mutual.'

Gene looked down at her boots then forced herself to meet Sonny's eyes. 'I admit there was a part of me that wanted to kiss you.' That part excited her yet it also made her feel uncomfortable.

'What was the other part thinking?'

Gene looked to the side. 'That my kissing you could

be a dangerous thing. Set things in motion that neither of us could control.'

'You think?'

Gene bit down on her lip. Her brow frowned in concern. 'It's possible.'

'What are you worried about?'

Gene closed her eyes. 'I can't explain it.'

He put his arm round her and pulled her into his shoulder like Jonathan did. 'Don't worry, the moment's passed. You can kiss me another day.'

'That's just it, Sonny,' she said, her eyes still closed. 'Sometimes there isn't another day.'

'Now, Gene, come on. I promise to come back so you can kiss me another day. And when you do you'll curse yourself for not kissing me sooner.'

She put one arm around him and gave him a little squeeze of a hug. 'I can live with that,' and she smiled in relief as she walked away.

Great Whale River – the name of a place and a river – named after the beluga whales that frequented the mouth of the river – was the northernmost Cree community in Quebec and their last post on their medical mission. Protestant and Catholic missions and a Canadian Air Force base were all part of the vibrant community. On the northern side of the river was the southernmost Eskimo village of Kuujjuaraapik, gateway to Rosie's homeland.

'Now, Rosie, you going to head home today or tomorrow?' Sonny teased. 'We all got bets riding on this. I hope you are true to your character because I sure don't want to have to pay up.'

'No, I wait and cook for you and leave when you leave. Maybe Jonathan can cross the river and be doctor for the Eskimos on the other side. I will be interpreter and Walter you can be the cook', she laughed.

Jonathan told her, if they had enough time they would do just that.

'You mind if I go across tonight and say hello to some people.'

'Rosie,' said Sonny. 'Let me do you the honour of motoring you across in the plane. Gene, you want to come for a quick look.'

The three of them sat in the front of the plane, Rosie and Gene sharing the same seat. Once they had secured the craft, Sonny and Gene walked through the streets, either side of Rosie, as she smiled at people and nodded in greeting. Her eyes were on fire. '*Chimo. Chimo.*'

'Do you know anyone here?' asked Gene.

'No. Not that I know of, but I will find some people to talk to. Don't you worry about me.'

Sonny told her she was the last person he'd worry about.

Without planning it they had walked directly north through the town and as they approached the outskirts, Rosie let out a loud cry. '*Inukshuk!*' She raced towards a collection of stones precariously placed one on top of the other. Sonny and Gene watched her run up to the structure and when she reached the rocks she pressed her body up against a vertical upright and hugged it.

When she turned round there were tears in her eyes. 'Come, Gene, come and kiss the Inukshuk with me.'

Gene went up and happily wrapped her arms around the adjacent upright and quickly pressed her top lip and nose against the stone as she had seen Rosie do moments earlier.

'So the stone you kiss.' Sonny sighed theatrically. 'Blimey.' Gene and Rosie gave way to a gurgle of laughter.

'What does Inukshuk mean?' Gene asked.

'Mean like a man,' said Rosie. 'They are all over our homeland.'

Gene took a few steps back and looked at the rocks again and now she could clearly see the figure of a granitic giant with its arms outstretched.

'We build them to help drive the caribou herds to a place of ambush. We build them as landmarks so we can find our way across the tundra all year round and not get lost.'

'They're like massive man cairns,' explained Sonny.

'That's very novel,' said Gene. 'Do the Cree have something like this? They could certainly use some because their countryside is so flat for miles with very few vantage points to take a sighting from.' She noticed the further north they travelled the more stunted the willow, and the spruce and tamarack had started masquerading as scrub, diminishing in height the further their distance from the south.

'They do actually,' said Sonny. 'That tree we sat under that night we filled up the water containers at our second camp.' Gene's eyes met his. 'Do you remember all of its branches in the middle were missing – it just had the top and bottom branches left. That was one of their signal trees.'

'I thought those branches had been cut down to use on a floor somewhere.'

'Maybe they had but the main reason was to create a landmark. They call it Lobstick. Sometimes they create them as a tribute or monument for a friend, other times a talisman.'

'Did you choose that tree deliberately?' asked Gene.

'I did,' said Sonny, his caramel eyes warming on her. 'That way you'll always remember it.'

In the almost never ending twilight Gene decided there was much to admire in Sonny Marlow: his easy-going gregariousness, his lack of pretentions, his consideration, his convictions, his unflappable, joyful approach to life. When she thought of everything that Sonny was it unnerved her and left her feeling underwhelmed with her own shortcomings. One night as she lay in the tent with her brother, she asked, 'What do people think of me? What do people see when they look at me?'

Jonathan took his time in replying. 'I can't speak for

other people,' he said, 'only for myself. What do I see? I see a young woman who hasn't entirely found her way yet and that's because she doesn't want to copy any one, she wants to be her own person and I applaud that. I see someone who is very different to many girls her age. She is strong and independent. She is not materialistic or coy or gaga. She doesn't gossip. She's sensitive and upset by the injustices of the world.' He paused for a few moments. 'I'd say, overall, this young woman is very refreshing. She's smart. She has a natural beauty. She relates well to men of all ages and she relates to them in a way that is completely above board – never wily. I would say she has the ability to have deep and lasting friendships with people she truly cares about. She is loyal and selfless. She is someone whom I'm immensely fond of and proud to call my sister.'

'I wasn't fishing for compliments,' Gene said, not wanting her brother to think she was seeking flattery. 'Thank you all the same.' She reached over and tapped him on the arm.

'I was being truthful,' Jonathan said.

'Do you think other people see that?' she asked.

'If you be yourself and let them see that, they will.'

Days later Jonathan asked Rosie what her plans were.

'I walk to Fort Chimo. Mrs. Watt wrote me letter of introduction to give to some friends of hers. She lived there once.'

'So she did,' Jonathan said. 'That's very thoughtful of her. From there, what is your plan?'

'Maybe I catch boat to American base on Frobisher Bay and from there I walk. By the time I need to cross the sea it will be frozen.'

'Seems like you have to go a fair way east out of your way to get north.'

'Me no worry. I still go north.'

On the morning of their departure, Rosie stayed with them to the very end helping with the last of the packing.

When they were all done and standing around the plane, Jonathan said to her, 'Rosie, we want to thank you for your company and assistance these past two months. You are a fine cook, and washerwoman, and made our campsites into a home away from home. A comfort we would not have had without you. And you kept the Whiskey Jacks from stealing our most precious items.' Everyone chuckled.

'I have taken the liberty to write you a reference for future employment if ever you have the need. As well, we have all pitched in to give you a little thank you present that might help with food, clothing or whatever on your journey.'

Rosie smiled and nodded at Jonathan. He handed over an envelope. She said, 'Thank you very much.' Jonathan gave her a hug. Everyone gave Rosie a hug. Then she bent down to put the envelope in her pack.

'Rosie, perhaps you want to open the envelope before you go,' said Jonathan.

'I open later. Thank you.' She nodded at Jonathan again as she fumbled with the ties.

'Normally that would be the appropriate thing to do,' Jonathan suggested, 'but today it might be best if you open it before you leave.'

'Go on, Rosie,' called out Sonny. 'We want to see your face when you open the envelope.'

Rosie gave Sonny a grin as she said, 'I hide from you, Sonny.'

'Go on, Rosie, open it now,' urged Gene.

Apprehensively she looked at their straight faces and then slipped a finger in the corner of the sealed envelope and tore it open. She pulled out the paper inside. There were two sheets. Jonathan told her to read the top one. On it he'd written:

This paper entitles the bearer, one Rosie Parker, one free airplane ride to Igloolik for services rendered. With love and appreciation.

It was signed by all of them.

In all her life Gene had never seen such a look of surprise and incredulity. It topped Jonathan turning up at the log cabin on the lake. It topped Wyatt turning up with the husky pups. In that instant Gene's heart soared high with Rosie's. Everyone was so poignantly aware of what their generous gift meant to her. Rosie started crying but she also started jumping up and down on the spot and she ran up to Jonathan and threw her arms around him and pressed her face into his chest. They all crowded round, hugging her, rubbing her back.

'Good job you learnt to read in that hospital,' said Sonny.

39

North over the tundra they flew; Povungnituk, Cape Dorset and Igloolik in their sights. Three days flying towards the pole skirting the eastern side of Hudson Bay. North beyond the tree line they flew; towards low-laying Lapland rhododendron, crowberry, and mountain cranberry flourishing in the permafrost; over muskegs thrown up by invisible muskrats; over countryside that moved with them until they realised it was a massive caribou herd on their annual migration, fording wide rivers, their antlers high above raging waters.

Images and experiences coalesced: grizzly bears standing in snow-banked streams waiting for arctic char; everyone catching their own in rivers that abounded in seafood; Sonny slipping on a mossy stone and going for an unplanned swim to their great amusement; polar bears congregating around the coastline anticipating their return to the sea ice to hunt seals; giant muskox, larger than any hoofed animal any of them had ever seen, hair two feet long, dust mops on their hooves, a herd of ten, eating plants faster than they could grow. Jonathan and Gene held hopes of seeing a lone wolf but instead were graced with multiple sightings of arctic foxes, surprisingly only the size of a domesticated house cat sporting a blue-grey coat of summer fur.

Stratus clouds, uniform and pewter, covered the entire sky. At times precipitation of drizzle and light mist screened the vista. But when the sun shone everything was more colourful than any other place on earth. As if the world was closer to the sun and the angle of the earth created new colours that did not exist anywhere else.

Far below the horizon's edge, lakes like bronze shields

reflected the afternoon sunlight. Bogs and basins gave the impression they were painted on the landscape; opalescent waters, yellow, green, turquoise, ivory and obsidian; full of plant organisms and minerals buried in a hidden sea. They soared far above a lone lake, blue as a pastel sky, shallow and placid with white swirls like dollops of cream, then another the colour of blood and rust, the oxidized metal of copper and nickel.

The kaleidoscope continued: the midnight sun; the summer brilliance of sedge and louseworts, of chamomile daisies and harebells, pasque flowers and white flowers of tufted saxifrage opening into a bell then transforming into a star that tracked the light; arctic willow, bearberry, and sura: ten times richer in vitamin C than any orange.

On they flew in the company of snow geese, and tundra swans, and gyrfalcons, enjoying the grandeur of a landscape untainted by another human being or a single building. Seemingly unlived. Untouched. Such was Gene's northern odyssey in the summer of her eighteenth year.

In Cape Dorset civilisation rose out of the wilderness: a new Anglican church. In Igloolik: a new day school. Rosie marvelled at the development that had occurred in the two years she had been gone. They declined her invitation to come meet her family, instead saying their farewells on the village outskirts, leaving her to enjoy her homecoming in private.

'You write to me. I write to you,' she said. They assured her they would.

'*Watcheeya*,' Walter said.

'Goodbye,' they echoed.

Rosie smiled and thanked everyone once more but it was Gene who felt she should be thanking her, thanking everyone for bringing her so far from where she had been. She took two steps to the side so they were in a rough circle and in the silence after their farewell, Gene opened her mouth and sang in joy and praise offering herself and her one true gift while she smiled and her eyes blessed each of the glistening eyes around her.

Should old acquaintance be forgot, and never brought to mind?
Should old acquaintance be forgot, and old lang syne?
For auld lang syne, my dear,
For auld lang syne,
We'll take a cup of kindness yet,
For auld lang syne.

New Beginnings

Montreal, Canada, August 1951

40

Although Rebecca had only met Sonny the once – that morning he flew north with her son and daughter – it wasn't until their second meeting that she had anything close to a conversation with the man. On their return to Montreal Jonathan invited Sonny to join them for dinner and be their guest overnight before heading back west. Rebecca was extraordinarily glad that he did, not just for the opportunity of getting to know the striking young man, but to observe the dynamics between him and her son and daughter. For in their laughter and their stories and their easy glances Rebecca could see how relaxed they were with each other and knew even in silence they would be comfortable together.

In one short evening four other things became apparent: one, the high regard both Jonathan and Gene had for Sonny; two, Gene was alive in the way that Morton was alive in his letters – Jonathan's idea of taking her north was the best thing they could have done; three, Gene had matured into a woman – yes, a woman, with empathy and confidence. There really was something alluring about her. Just the sight of her in a fresh white linen shirt and fawn jodhpur trousers, her sun-streaked hair brushed into a loose plait halfway down her back, her teal eyes and white teeth sparkling in her sun-kissed face spoke of an easy elegance. Rebecca was delighted and mesmerised by her transformation. And she wasn't the only one. And that was the fourth point. That evening Rebecca knew in her heart, like sometimes only a woman can know, that one day Sonny Marlow would be her son-in-law. And she found the idea pleased her very much.

That's why the following morning after he had left

and Jonathan had taken Annabelle and Matthew on a picnic did it absolutely astound Rebecca when Gene announced that she wanted to become a nun.

'Where did that idea come from? Rebecca practically stammered. 'Did you meet some overzealous nuns at missions when you were up north?'

'There were a few sisters,' admitted Gene. 'But no, it's something I've been thinking about for quite some time. I thought the nuns at Freshwater were very much at peace.'

'Well I'm afraid it's an idea that has to be deferred for quite some time. I'd like you to finish school, for your sake, more than mine. You will regret it in years to come if you don't. But I leave the choice of where you wish to study completely up to you.'

'It's okay,' said Gene. 'I'll go back to St Margaret's. No sense buying new uniforms for some other place.'

'All right,' said Rebecca, giving her daughter a grateful smile. 'Most prudent of you. Thank you.' She paused. 'And I'm sorry to say you need to be older before you make a decision like the one you're considering. At a minimum, twenty-one but I would say even older than that.'

'Mother! I'm getting the distinct impression you are not in favour of the idea when nuns perform important roles in society and their lives have immense purpose. Remember nuns gave Morton and I an education at a time when other places couldn't provide. I would have thought you would have supported such a notion.'

'I do support the notion. I'm just not convinced it's the right path for you that's all.'

'Why not?'

'Well for one, you seem reborn again after being in the northern wilderness. I think that openness and sense of freedom agrees with you. I fear being cloistered in a convent might be detrimental to your well being.'

'I disagree. I think I would quite like the structure of their days, the simplicity of their lives which wasn't that different to what I encountered up north.'

'The two are not one and the same. But perhaps more importantly, I didn't realise you harboured such a calling. That surprises me, that's all. Are you that deeply devoted that you could live an austere life and abstain from life's pleasures? I certainly couldn't.'

'I'm not you, Mom.'

'I know that,' Rebecca softened her voice. 'But just consider the possibility you might be entering a time of great change in your life. At eighteen I did, and after I married your father we went on to have a very amorous relationship. I can't imagine any child of our union not being similarly inclined.'

Gene made no comment. Well, I guess, how could she, thought Rebecca.

Ten months later Gene finished school and Rebecca held her tongue while she accompanied her to the Sisters of Charity of Montreal to understand the process known as Enquiry, a three-year period where Gene could discern her calling within the Catholic Church. Then, out of nowhere, Gene enrolled in a bachelor's degree at McGill University to study a double major in history and geography. The relief Rebecca felt was palpable. Gene told her if she didn't become a nun she fancied herself as a reporter for National Geographic. Such was Rebecca's relief she almost popped a bottle of champagne. In her excitement she rang all their relatives – anyone would have thought Gene had just graduated with first-class honours the way Rebecca enthused about the latest development in the life of her youngest daughter.

'Your father would have loved the idea!' said Rebecca in encouragement. 'I would have loved the idea, had I known about such things in my day.'

Ever since her trip north Gene had taken to buying National Geographic whenever the latest monthly edition appeared on the newsstand. She liked reading about far away people from far away places, about their culture and rituals. Rebecca could understand the fascination and enjoyed hearing Gene's stories of Eli Silver and how the

Cree buried their dead high in a tree branch so their soul could easily leave their body; of how the penis bone of a marten made a perfect needle to sew moccasins and traditional garments; and how ancient civilisations had survived for centuries without European advancements. 'That trip made me realise just how much there is to learn from other cultures,' Gene told her mother.

While Gene studied, Jonathan became a father two times over: Annabelle had a daughter they called Alison, who in no time was crawling, then walking. Shortly after, Abigail fell pregnant with her second child. Out west on the prairies Morton worked with Paul, Wyatt's nephew, learning how to be a wheat farmer. Wyatt, in his early sixties was scaling back in his doctor's practice, using locums more and more, so he could spend more time with Rebecca and one month with Morton and their dogs, touring during winter. Rebecca now painted most days, and when in Montreal worked less and less in the postcard business.

Through all this, Sonny wrote to Gene and Mrs. D as he had taken to calling her. More often than not he sent postcards from some curious destination he had visited. In return, Gene would ask Rebecca to bring home a postcard from work from some obscure place so she could send it onto Sonny to confound him. Rebecca always obliged, hoping in the teasing and geographic suspense something more binding would take hold.

And then in late September 1953, not long after Gene's twentieth birthday, a few weeks before Gene was about to start her second year at university, Rebecca received a phone call from Wyatt, different to all his other phone calls which made thoughts of Sonny and Gene's unformed union fade into obscurity. 'Morton's been in a car accident,' he told her. 'He's in a coma.'

41

He had broken ribs, a pierced lung, a snapped collarbone, a fractured femur, a broken wrist, sprained fingers, cuts and bruises, but he was alive! Driving between Regina and Lumsden he had overshot a corner and rolled the car. It wasn't until Rebecca arrived two days later and Morton was out of the coma and questioned by the police that they discovered the real problem was not the car accident but his foot, which refused to move from the gas pedal to the brake pedal on his car.

Acute anterior poliomyelitis. They suspected he contracted it a few days earlier at a pub in Davidson, where reports of other cases soon came to light.

The prescribed treatment was immersion in a warm pool morning and night to keep his muscles limber while his nerves were recuperating. This was not possible with parts of Morton's body already in plaster, so Rebecca took him back to Wyatt's and took to wrapping him in steaming bandages and massaging his limbs. The only time they weren't red was when Rebecca was sleeping. For nine months Rebecca worked with him and on him.

As his bones healed she got him up and walking to the barn to see the dogs, then down the road with her. She got him holding a piece of rope in one hand and trying to out-pull her, one hand and then the other. She got him pushing his foot into her hands while she tried to force his knee back to his chest, she turned him over and got him lifting his foot in the air behind him, she got him touching his toes and in the process she realised her own hamstrings, advanced in years, were surprisingly tightly strung, but by the end of months of working with Morton she too could place her hands flat on the ground.

Not bad for a soon to be fifty-eight year old.

In the spring of 1957, just as Morton's muscular strength was starting to return, on a cloudless, windless day with the promise of hope and reprieve in the air they got word from Toronto that Lottie, at eighty-five years of age, had died in her sleep. Analeise would delay the funeral until she got there. Would Morton be up to the travel? She knew he would want to come. Rebecca had not seen Lottie's approaching death. To Rebecca she was immortal. So many memories of her mother-in-law flashed through her mind: her *joie de vivre!* How they would miss her. She cried as she packed their bags and booked train tickets for the following morning, wiped tears from her cheeks as she cleaned the house and watered the gardens.

Hours later as the day retired and dusk approached she heard a motor like none she had ever heard before pulling up outside. She walked onto the back porch and there was Sonny walking through the field towards her, his plane several yards behind him. Before long he was by her side, saying he heard they needed a ride back east. His presence made her heart rejoice, reminding her of all the great men in her life – Samuel, Wyatt, Jonathan and now he was one of them too. And she thought: 'Gene, Gene, hurry up and finish your degree and marry this man before someone else snatches him up. You have no idea what you are missing.'

Sonny came to the funeral. Wyatt came too in the end, the first time all of her family was together since her art gallery showing years before. And now it felt that aside from new grandchildren there was another new loved one in their midst. She watched Sonny and Gene together, they were comfortable together, like old friends, but nothing of magnitude came to light. She spoke to Jonathan about Sonny, she spoke to Abigail about Sonny, and back in Lumsden, with a captive audience in Morton, she spoke to him about Sonny. The only person she didn't speak to about Sonny was Gene herself.

But with three years of study behind her Gene didn't seem to be forward in speaking to anyone about Sonny, least of all him, or spending any great time with him. She didn't apply for candidacy with the Grey Nuns either, which was something, but Rebecca was stumped as to why Gene didn't encourage Sonny – nor he her. Holding her tongue was a major feat for Rebecca but she had learnt with Gene that if she suggested something, Gene was just as likely to veer in the opposite direction. She almost felt like engaging in reverse psychology – a simple: 'You know, I get why women don't swoon over Sonny' – to see if Gene would spring to his defence and his arms. But who was she kidding?

Instead, Gene moved to Ottawa to take up a traineeship with the Department of External Affairs and after visiting her one winter Rebecca discovered her daughter seemed quite content with her life in a cosy and eclectic bedsit. She had become an ice skater of some style and endurance and had a number of friends, including a number of male friends – specifically a number of homosexual male friends, much to Rebecca's surprise.

Upon her return home she rang Jonathan.

'What do you think's going on?' she asked. 'Is she that way inclined?'

'Do you think she's that way inclined?' Jonathan asked her in return.

'No,' said Rebecca.

'Does it matter if she is?'

'I have never given it much thought, Jonathan.'

'So, she has friends who are of a different sexual persuasion to us. Her having friends is a good thing, right?'

'Absolutely.'

'Perhaps she's not that interested in or ready for a deeper friendship with a man.'

'You talk to her, Jonathan, find out what's going on.'

'Mother, it's fine, just let things be. Everything in good

time. I had a few years in my twenties when I wasn't interested in anyone in particular.'

'Fair enough,' agreed Rebecca, but beyond all that there was something else, something Rebecca couldn't quite put her finger on about Gene's life in Ottawa that unsettled her. But then from time to time Gene would call and say, 'I'm thinking of coming home this weekend. I haven't seen Jonathan and everyone for ages. Do you have any plans?' Or she'd call and say, 'I'm thinking of going to Toronto this weekend to see Abigail and Grandpa Dalton, would you like to come too?' And Rebecca would put aside those little niggles which she had come to accept as the normal worries of mothers with adult children who want their children to be happy, which mostly translated to: wanted them to be with someone – and would happily head south for a weekend with her daughters and her extended family in Toronto. By then the trips away were welcome for she no longer had the postcard work to break up her week. She now painted full time as her paintings were in high demand.

And in the summers her life took on a whole new direction.

42

It was her mother of all people who called her. 'Rebecca, you are not going to believe what that Joey Smallwood has done now.' Well into his second term, the man who some called the father of the new Newfoundland was both popular and polarising – his biggest black mark: courting German industrialists as investors in the modernisation of the province. Many people were outraged. 'Has he forgotten Beaumont-Hamel? Forgotten that ninety percent of Newfoundland's army were slaughtered by Germany during World War I!'

Rebecca listened with interest to the latest development. After her mother's phone call she went in search of Wyatt. He was reading a copy of National Geographic in the lounge room. Rebecca had so enjoyed poring over the magazine when Gene was still living at home that she decided to subscribe herself.

'That Joey Smallwood makes me feel like I'm a schizophrenic. One minute, I'm agreeing with what he's up to, the next I'm wildly against it.'

'What's he done this time?'

'He's come up with the brilliant idea of closing down the outports as a way of reducing government spending on teachers, doctors and other vital services.'

Wyatt put down the magazine, placed his silver rimmed glasses on top of it and rubbed his eyes, his three frown lines clearly visible on his forehead. His hair these days was more silver than blonde, but he still had a full head of hair which added to his youthfulness even though he was in his mid sixties. He kept it very short only about half an inch all over and Rebecca rather liked the way it caught the light at different angles.

'I imagine that's upset a few people,' he said looking at her.

'It has! And he's wanting the fishermen to retrain to do something else.'

'All the outports?'

'No, just the small ones, like Deception. Salvage is safe.'

'Well, maybe he's got a point. Maybe, they would be better off closer to bigger centres.'

'Maybe, but it should be their choice, don't you think? Not his? Mother tells me they're fighting it in Seldom Come By, in Deception. All up and down the coast.'

'Good for them.'

'Good for them, all right. He's already on the move though, offering incentives for people to move, by moving their houses for them for free! So they keep their homes.'

'How's he doing that?'

'He's floating them over the summer–'

'Floating them!' interrupted Wyatt. 'How's he doing that?' His interest was now definitely piqued. His pale blue eyes were shining bright, Rebecca noted, like a boy in a candy store.

'Oh, I don't know exactly. Somehow, they attach big floating buoys or drums to the base of houses, knock the foundations away, slide them down into the ocean, then tow them with tugs to a bigger settlement. They'd have fun trying to do that with our old home. I'm sure it would break up in the process.'

'Sounds impressive, though.'

Rebecca shoved his shoulder, 'Whose side are you on?'

'I'm just marveling at the engineering feat, that's all. It would be something to see.'

'You think? People being rounded up like cattle – that's what they're calling it by the way, "Rounding up the outports".'

'Some people will welcome it, Becca. To have their

house moved to a better place at no cost to them might be a blessing. Now that you've lived in the big smoke for umpteen years, where would you rather live year in and year out?'

She didn't have to think too long and hard about that. 'I suppose so.' But then, 'Where would you rather live?'

'Touché, my dear.'

'That's right. You would rather live as far away from the big smoke as possible. I want to stand with the people of Deception who want to stay. And I certainly don't like the thought of our house at Second Chance being knocked over.'

'If, it's still standing. You haven't been there for what, fifteen years? How do you know it's still upright?'

'Let's go and see, shall we?'

Only after a few days in what was a very holey – not to be confused with holy – old house, it was evident Wyatt was way more comfortable in the old saltbox house than in Rebecca's brick mansion in Montreal. 'We should have come here years ago!' he exclaimed.

Prescient Wyatt had bought with him a bag of tools, but they still needed help from quite a few tradesmen from Deception to work on upgrading the house, along with supplies from Seldom Come By.

'See,' said Rebecca. 'If they had been rounded up, where would we be?'

'We'd be progressing at a much slower rate, I grant you that.' He was wearing navy trousers, a tan leather tool belt and a pale blue chambray shirt. It set off his pale blue eyes perfectly. Out of everything he wore, she loved him in that shirt, or rather those shirts, for he had quite a collection. He always looked so relaxed and at ease in them. They were him. The shirts and ties he wore to his practice, the stylish checked tweed jacket he wore for dinners out, while they suited him, were not Wyatt.

They bought a kerosene generator for power, mainly for better lighting, rather than having to rely on kerosene lamps inside. They doubted, given the outport controversy, that electricity would ever come as far as their house.

Rebecca spent her days passing saws and screwdrivers, making pies and pinwheel pastries, and when she could, filling large notepads with sketches and shadings, and taking countless photographs of icebergs – from daybreak to dusk.

She and Wyatt made a pledge. They would return, if not every summer, then at least every second summer.

In early 1958, at ninety-two years of age, Rebecca's former father-in-law, Leonard passed away. A few months later in the following summer they all convened on Parry Sound for three weeks holiday. There was quite a crowd: Samuel's sister, Analeise, and her husband Randall; a pregnant Abigail and Will and their three; Jonathan and Annabelle and their four; and Rebecca and Gene. Sonny flew in Wyatt and Morton along with his parents Don and Elin and, to everyone's surprise, his new girlfriend, Kristina, a Plains Cree Indian from the Sweetgrass Reserve near Battleford Saskatchewan.

Rebecca did a double take when he said Saskatchewan thinking the beautiful well-spoken young lady with high cheekbones and long blue black hair was her son's love interest but no, she was Sonny's guest, and after Rebecca had snuck herself a quick nip of brandy in a teacup she breathed easier and thought, 'Why shouldn't Sonny be with someone beautiful who adores him? Goodness me, the man is thirty! Samuel was thirty when we went to Paris. It's high time he was married with children. Maybe it will make Gene jealous. Maybe at long last she will lay her cards on the table.' But no royal flush emerged that holiday.

Like everyone, Gene warmed to Kristina and, like everyone, she was caught up with Sonny's high spirits and good humour, but some days Rebecca quietly observed Gene and Sonny returning from being out walking by themselves or canoeing by themselves and she would think…maybe, maybe all is not lost.

Then, just before they were to return to their respective homes, one morning when Gene and Rebecca and Wyatt were alone, a blushing Gene said, 'I have an announcement.' Rebecca smiled peacefully at her daughter and Wyatt, while her heart jumped up and down saying, 'Hallelujah, about bloody time,' while in the next breath, Gene said she had accepted a two-year posting to Geneva.

'Geneva!' exclaimed Rebecca.

'Yes, Geneva,' echoed Gene. 'I'm going to work for the United Nations. It's an exchange program and the first time the Department has ever offered an overseas posting to a woman. I will be leaving in three weeks.'

It was a hard call for Rebecca to get over her disappointment and objections but rise to the occasion she did, for her daughter was no longer a child. She was an attractive woman, her hair a beautiful honey blonde, styled similar to that of Princess Grace. But where Rebecca's eldest daughter, Abigail, dressed in bright hues and patterns that caught the eye, her youngest veered towards plainer colours and simpler styles, perhaps that was what made her so suited to the business world.

Rebecca took a deep breath and smiled in a way Samuel would have approved. 'Aren't you a surprise package?' she said. 'What a fantastic achievement! What a fantastic opportunity. Well done you. We couldn't be more proud.'

And as she hugged her daughter, Rebecca told herself to look on the bright side: Gene was far from becoming a nun and she and Wyatt now had a reason to visit Geneva. Later she confessed to Gene, 'I'm sorry if I was a little shocked by your announcement. The truth was, well, I was a little shocked,' she admitted with a laugh.

'Me too,' chuckled Gene. 'You should have heard my stuttering queries when they told me my application had been approved. But carpe diem, right?'

'Indeed,' said Rebecca. 'What did they tell you when they told you your application had been approved?'

'They said I had proven myself in the profession and no doubt had decided to be a career woman.'

'Have you?' asked Rebecca. 'Have you decided to forgo marriage and children? I know it used to be hard for a woman to have both but one doesn't necessarily preclude the other nowadays. Look at Elsie MacGill, that famous aircraft designer.'

'She got married when she was nearly forty mother. I'm only twenty-five. I am the first woman to be offered this position in all of Canada and I'm not going to turn it down. This is not just about me; it's about the rights of women everywhere. It was only two years ago that women in federal public service were allowed to keep their jobs once they married. This is another milestone.'

'Hear, hear,' said Wyatt, clapping his hands, 'Becca, take a bow. You've raised an independent young woman. You should be proud.' Wyatt's calling her Becca had made it out of the bedroom long ago. Even her grandchildren now called her Granny Becca.

'Well,' said Rebecca, 'I can't take all the credit for that. Gene has always been mature beyond her years.'

Rebecca went to Ottawa to help Gene pack up her very avant-garde flat but mostly Gene gave everything away to charity, making Rebecca wonder if she were moving to Europe for good.

After that holiday Rebecca resigned herself to Sonny only ever being a son-in-law in her heart and that had to be good enough for her. Her first reading must have been wrong and she had to admit she had misread things over the years.

She and Wyatt never made it to Europe. He told her he'd been to Europe once too many for his lifetime. The only good thing about Europe had been the Dalton boys. He'd rather go to the Grand Canyon or Hawaii or the Caribbean.

Instead, in July 1960, after two years, they sent

Jonathan and Annabelle to Paris and Geneva while they looked after their children, like Lottie and Leonard had done for her and Samuel all those years ago.

The following April, after living abroad for more than two and a half years, Gene returned to Canada, the move like most things in Gene's life, surprising Rebecca for the report from Jonathan was that she was very entrenched in her European life. Geneva was a town of a similar size to Ottawa nestled amongst the Alps and close to Lake Annecy, the highest lake in Europe, the whole surrounds most scenic.

But Rebecca should have realised by now her daughter was nothing but unpredictable. Gene moved back in with her although Rebecca distinctly felt Gene would rather live alone, but there was Rebecca with a big empty house and only her living in it and not full time.

Mere days after her return Jonathan invited them over for dinner, a casual family get-together and a celebratory beef tourtière in Gene's honour. Wyatt was in town for the occasion. He and Rebecca were about to head off to New York to experience it in springtime, to ride through Central Park's falling cherry blossoms in a horse and carriage, to go to the top of the Empire State Building and to catch some shows on Broadway.

They walked down the long hallway in Jonathan's house into the living room and there was Sonny smugly sitting in a chesterfield armchair, his white smile lighting up his tanned face. He'd been single for the better part of two years and Rebecca had decided that Sonny was single like Morton was single. She no longer gave it a second thought. Over the years she'd come to see that Sonny could have just as easily been Wyatt's son, so common were their similarities – Wyatt at times needing his spacious emptiness to himself; Sonny needing to fly to an emptiness of his own choosing.

Two days later, the morning before they were about to jet off to New York, Rebecca was once more sitting around the breakfast table with Wyatt and Gene and in an ambience of déjà vu Gene cleared her throat and said, 'I have an announcement.'

Gene wore her hair longer again these days, almost to her shoulder blades and it was back to its natural colour, bleached blonde only from the sun. That morning half of it was secured at her crown in a narrow black bow. She looked very poised and elegant thought Rebecca.

She poured herself another cup of tea, while she smiled at her soon-to-be-twenty-eight year old daughter, all the time thinking what could it be this time, a missionary trip to the Congo?

'Well, out with it, girl,' said Wyatt, the patient saint for once not patient.

'I'm going on a holiday with Sonny. Just the two of us. I hope you don't mind.' She stared at them; her beautiful blue green eyes alight, while she nervously wrung her hands as if she were seeking their approval.

Suddenly Rebecca clutched her chest with her left hand. 'Wyatt,' she panted. 'Where are your heart pills?' Gene looked at her anxiously. 'How old am I? What's the date today?'

'The twenty-fourth of April. Mother what's happening?' exclaimed Gene.

'And the year?' Rebecca breathed out.

'1961. Mother!'

'Grab the calendar please, Gene,' Rebecca whispered hoarsely, 'just to be sure. I need to know how long I've lived for.'

Gene raced into the kitchen and returned with the calendar and while she was out of the room Rebecca winked at Wyatt while she started gasping, 'This can't be happening. This can't be.' And when Gene returned, Rebecca rasped, 'Here, give that to me.'

She reached for the calendar and reached for her blue pointy-framed glasses all the while her left hand was clenched to her heaving chest. And then she put her finger on the day's date and said, 'See this date, Wyatt, the twenty-fourth of April 1961,' she puffed. 'I know the day

252

now. I wondered if it would ever come.' She threw down her glasses. 'The day our Gene finally agreed to give Sonny Marlow a chance.' Rebecca could no longer contain herself, she burst out laughing, Wyatt likewise. Gene reached over and grabbed her mother by the shoulders and shook her in sweet vengeance for scaring her so, but she laughed as well.

43

Her mother was right. It had been ten long years. Ten years of her keeping her feelings for Sonny at bay while she lived her complicated, camouflaged life. In the beginning it may have seemed as if she had not been ready for love. But what it had been was: she had not been ready for loss.

It took her forty-two year old brother coming to Geneva with his happily married wife still years after the fact for her to realise she was already losing, by missing out on some kind of wonderful that could be in her life.

Before that fateful day in December 1950 she had no idea how bad nightmares could really be. But then they came. And stayed. On that trip north into the wilderness, they snapped at her heels like Cerberus. She endured them in silence, but even so they had a way of leaching into her days. Over the years she knew the best way to manage them was to be constantly busy: that by working, or skating, or hiking, even occasionally partying to the point of exhaustion, she could keep them at bay.

Like she had done in the past, she became an expert at keeping them to herself, while in one part of her mind, and soul, she would continue to tell herself: if something with Sonny is meant to be it will be. She tried not to bring her heart into it, lest she set herself up for eternal disappointment. In Geneva the demons finally disappeared from her life and she knew she was ready.

Until then it wasn't despite what she felt for Sonny, but because of what she felt for Sonny that she hadn't pursued him. He deserved someone better than her; someone not haunted by melancholia and images she couldn't erase; someone not inclined to be a zombie like her mother once had been; rather someone who matched his spirit.

She thought Kristina might have been that someone, even though that holiday at Parry Sounds was quite torturous at time, to see it all played out in front of her. But through it all, Gene still admired Sonny the most – and trusted him the most. In all her years she had never met a man like him. This man with fair wavy hair, honey coloured eyes and a perpetually tanned face from being outdoors thousands of feet above the earth, closer to the sun. This man with a generous heart who laughed and joked and smiled with ease, yet, Gene felt, was lonely around the edges. He was the one for her. And she liked to think she was the one for him.

That her friendship with Sonny had survived ten years was of great comfort. Come what may, she would always have that. She could count on him like a brother. But after ten years, what she worried about was, had the other survived too? And if it had, would it be short-lived? Would it be a softwood and burn quickly? Wouldn't that be poetic? To have held something so special – reserved for so long – only to discover it was a wine of classic vintage and reputation tainted by a bad cork. In her unguarded moments what Gene feared most was that Sonny was more like Morton than she gave him credit for. That he was more content in his bachelorhood than she was in her spinsterhood.

Before she left Geneva, rather than send Sonny a postcard like she did every now and then, she wrote him a letter telling him she was coming back to Canada and reminded him that years ago he had promised her she could kiss him another day and that the next time she saw him she would hold him to that promise. Could she have been any more brazen?

He hadn't replied. He simply had turned up at Jonathan's asking to keep his arrival a secret, which it had been. It was the best surprise!

The next day the two of them had gone walking in

Parc Maisonneuve and with a teasing smile on his lips which she matched in return, she let Sonny back her up against the ashen trunk of a silver birch and kiss her like there was no tomorrow: oh the pressure of his lips on her lips, his tongue on hers, sharing the same breath, breathless, her body, her heart, her insides all instantly warm and viscous like she'd drunk two glasses of Bordeaux.

That afternoon while he checked on the servicing of his plane and bought supplies, Gene raced around and bought an entire new wardrobe: a new blue one piece swimsuit with a wide halter neck; pedal pushers; a new pair of jeans; cotton blouses; a green evening dress, also with a halter neck; a simple white cotton dress with a swing skirt, softly shirred sleeves and tucked bodice; and her favourite: a polished-cotton, striped shirt dress with a full skirt and matching head scarf. It was a dress that reminded her of the northern lights – brilliant blue, magenta, yellow and green. It reminded her of fun.

The day her mother and Wyatt flew out to New York, she and Sonny flew west towards the Rockies.

'Where are we heading tonight?' she asked through the headsets as she sat next to Sonny in the co-pilot's seat.

'First stop, Lake Nipissing. There's a lodge there with several log cabins. This early in the season there should be plenty of rooms available.'

'Have you been there before?' asked Gene.

'No, but it sure looks pretty from up above.' He smiled at her and it was the same smile of ten years ago. Trust me it said, and she did.

The place was Memquisit Lodge on the northern shore of the lake's west arm. They chose a log cabin built in 1921 perched on a massive rocky buttress with its own dock, five minutes walk from the main lodge where they could dine if they were so inclined. Their cabin jutted out into the lake, screened on both sides by large black spruces as if it were the only house for miles.

Sonny carried their bags while Gene walked ahead

with the key. They were told it only had a double and a settee for bedding but they both decided it was the most beautiful cabin they had motored past. As the manager had waited for them to decide which lodge they would take Sonny looked at Gene with questioning eyes. She didn't hesitate. 'We'll take it.' She flashed Sonny a reassuring smile.

'I can sleep on the couch,' he muttered as he placed their bags inside.

'Oh,' Gene teased, 'Do you plan on sleeping?' She grinned at him but quickly turned away and looked out the window at the view.

'Can't fly a plane tomorrow if I don't sleep well tonight,' his voice barely a whisper. He was behind her, standing so close she could feel his breath on her neck and in the next moment his mouth was on her nape sending shivers over her skin. His hands grabbed her hips and pulled her back into him, setting in motion every lustful thought she'd ever had about him. One thing was answered; it hadn't taken long to stoke the embers in either of them.

'Maybe we should plan on staying here for more than one night,' she murmured.

She twisted in his arms and kissed him fully on the mouth, hungry for his touch, his taste, pressing herself into him, feeling him pressed up against her. He walked them back towards the table pushed up against the wall, sat himself down on the edge, spread his legs a little way apart and pulled Gene in closer, all the time his lips never left her lips, his hands never left her body, nor hers his.

Between kisses he whispered, 'I've got to get something out of my bag if we're going to do this.'

'You don't need to cover yourself,' she whispered.

'You have some other way to stop getting pregnant,' he said between more kisses.

'No. But I would be happy for you to be the father of my children.'

'I would be happy to be the father of your children

257

too but do you want children in nine months time?'

She kissed him some more while she tried to think of a reply. 'Not particularly. I'm willing to take my chance on you though. And put my trust in prayer. We may get some reprieve.'

He nibbled her ear. 'What do you think your mother might say if you were to return pregnant?'

'Oh I can tell you,' Gene whispered between more kisses. 'She said: "Don't hold anything back, Gene. Give that man everything you've got."' More kisses. 'And she couldn't help but add: "Wyatt and I would always welcome more grandchildren."'

'Your mother! Got to love her.'

Sonny tilted her back with one arm and swept his other arm under her legs as he lifted her and carried her to the bed. His bomber jacket on the floor somewhere, his shoes off, Gene unbuttoning his shirt as she sat on the bed, Sonny in his jeans, straddling her, kissing her while she removed his shirt and he pulled off her lightweight cardigan and then one item of clothing after another, till Gene, in her underwear, said, 'Can we move between the sheets?' And Sonny obliged, shoving the cover away so they were only between the sheets but not for long.

'It's daylight. I want to see you. I've waited a decade for this.'

He peeled off the last of his underclothes and hers, then flicked the top sheet off as he lay there facing her, running his arm down the side of her body while her fingers traced invisible paths across his chest as they stared into each other's eyes in wonder and in disbelief, that at long last they were at this place, this place that they could have been at years ago. And suddenly that knowledge hit them like a seismic force, hurled one against the other, hands and mouths clamouring, bodies and tongues and lips and eyes trembling and thrusting and tasting and weeping – an almighty ravishing that could not hold back the tide of years spent and wasted but wasted no more.

And through her tears and kisses Gene cried, 'I'm sorry, I'm sorry. I've loved you for years.'

And Sonny, hushing her, said, 'I know, I know. I'll just never know what took you so long.'

'It doesn't matter now, we're together at last.'

And they were.

That evening they feasted on each other as the long shadows turned into night. Once, after Sonny returned from the bathroom, he pulled Gene towards him and stroked her face as he gazed into her eyes. 'You didn't tell me you were a virgin.'

'What made you think I wasn't?' whispered Gene.

'I don't know, adventurous woman of the world that you are?'

'Not in everything,' murmured Gene. She pushed him onto his back and rolled over on top of his chest. 'How are you going to top that?' She grinned with delight.

He started to sing. *Oh, my love.* She lay atop of him smiling into his face, his eyes, while his adorable mouth, his dancing eyes smiled back into hers as he sang every word of *Unchained Melody*. His hunger, her hunger embodied in song. By the time he came round to singing the final chorus she was crying, but she was also singing. With him. For him. God speed.

44

They stayed three nights at Memquisit Lodge then flew west, stopping one night to camp at Pukaskwa National Park. The next afternoon they landed in Winnipeg, flying first over the Red and Assiniboine Rivers, and doing a loop around Assiniboine Park, which Sonny told her was bigger than Central Park in New York. Statuesque ash, elm and oak trees shimmered in new season growth, not just in the park but in elegant strands either side of the rivers. As they followed the path of the Assiniboine, Sonny pointed out the section where people skated in winter. It's longer than the Rideau Skateway he added.

Gene liked the sound of that. She grinned at Sonny. 'I missed skating in Switzerland,' she spoke through their headsets. 'The lakes didn't freeze over like here.'

Sonny's pickup truck was at the aerodrome where he'd left it over a week earlier. They drove to his house, a three-bedroom bungalow in River Heights, and that evening they drove to his parents to have dinner with Don and Elin.

As they left, Sonny wrapped his arms around Gene. 'Take a good look at Gene,' he said, 'because the next time you see her she'll be a different women.'

'Ja,' said his mother, 'How so?' Her so sounding like zo.

'She'll be Mrs. Sonny Marlow.'

Gene squeezed Sonny's arms with both her hands while he kissed her on the temple like Jonathan had kissed her for years. Elin started crying. 'Tonight you make me zo happy.' And all they could do was laugh at Elin who didn't look happy but was, and hug her and kiss her on the cheek.

'You'll make her even happier,' said Don, 'when you give her grandchildren.'

The next morning, while sunlit shadows danced on the windowpane, they lay together in bed, luxuriating in the intimacy they now shared. Sonny's arms draped around her arms, her head rested on his shoulder. He nuzzled her hair while she, ever so lightly, rubbed her hand across his chest.

'That's some scar you've got on your stomach,' he said, his voice gentle. 'How long you had that for?'

Trying not to tense, Gene replied, 'Since I was seventeen.'

'How'd you get it?'

'A doctor cut my stomach open.'

'What for?'

She rolled away. 'I had something inside me they needed to get out.'

'Which was?'

'You don't want to know.'

'You're wrong. I do.' He stared intently into her eyes. 'Lay it on me.'

Gene hesitated. 'Sleeping pills, if you must know.' Her eyes wavered as they tried to lock onto his.

'Jeepers, Gene,' he said. 'You wanted to end your own life?'

'Once there was a time…I was depressed.' She bit her lip. 'I was…I don't know what I was. But I hope I'm never that person again.'

'I hope you aren't either.' He reached for her hand and squeezed it. 'Why did you want to end your life?'

'I don't want to talk about it.' He looked at her pointedly. She really didn't want to be dragged back there, even now, even after all this time. It made her feel quite ill just thinking about it all. She closed her eyes. 'Please, Sonny. I don't want to bring that into the middle of what we have here.' Opening her eyes, she said. 'Maybe another day.'

'Okay,' he nodded. 'One day, I'd like you to tell me.' He brushed her hair back from her face as his fingers stroked her cheek. 'Come here.' He pulled her back so her head rested on his shoulder once more. 'Could you see yourself living here?'

Gene moved her head so she could look into Sonny's eyes.

'Yes.' She smiled. 'I could. With you is where I want to be.' She waited for a few seconds before asking, 'Do I have a choice?'

'If there's somewhere else you'd rather live, well, we could talk about that.'

'Here's good for now.' She smiled up at him then moved closer to kiss him. A little while later, she asked, 'Was that a proposal?'

'Did it sound like a proposal?'

'No.' She laughed. 'If it was, you need some practice.'

'Practice. Practice! I'll show you practice.' And before she knew it his body was smothering hers once more, showing her just how much practice he'd had over the years. The way he kissed her body was nothing short of worship. What he could do with his lips, his fingers, his tongue, his manhood made her realise what a deprived life she had been living. What her body could do in response bedazzled her. Even his throaty whispers and his orgasmic groans were a clarion call to her very own. She was fast becoming a wanton woman.

The physicality of his body enchanted her: the sparse light-brown hair on his chest, the hardness of his hips, the sureness of his shoulders, the way the two of them moved together, sometimes smelting as one, closer, closer, closer...could they merge inside each other? And at other times, when they were joined in union while their upper bodies remained wide apart, while she admired the fierceness of his male form and he revered the fineness of her female one ...oh, sweet Mary, that was arousal ad infinitum. The synchronicity of their eyes said it all.

Eventually – Gene didn't know how – they managed

to shower, eat, and pack up once more, taking a different route to the aerodrome; past an old airfield that Sonny told her had been used to train pilots back in the 1940s during the war. He pulled the pick-up over.

'Here's where I did most of my flight training.' He glanced at her. 'Here's where I learnt to do acrobatics. Do you want to see?'

'I'd love to.' After missing out on him for so long she wanted to fill herself with all things Sonny.

He put the pick-up back into gear. 'We'll pay close attention to the way we go so you can drive the truck back here by yourself. I'll come by, show you my tricks and then meet you back at the aerodrome.

Thirty minutes later Gene was back at the old airfield sitting on the bonnet of Sonny's truck, her hand above her eyes shielding them from the sun. Not long afterwards she heard a drone and swung her head around and watched a plane approach – but it wasn't Sonny's plane, it was a small vintage aircraft, an open cockpit biplane, with Sonny inside. She watched him fly by, then he put the plane into a steep ascent and when he was nearly several hundred metres above the ground he rolled it into a giant loop and then he reversed it and then he flew straight by, looped beyond the end of the field and flew back, corkscrewing all the way. How he managed to keep turning that plane and not lose sight of the horizon or the ground below him was beyond her. Her heart was in her mouth.

She knew that to master what he was doing had taken hours and hours of practice. He'd been born too late to be one of the original barnstormers, too late to be doing daredevil antics and aerial acrobats and crazy stunts that thrilled crowds of thousands but that day he thrilled her.

And then as he came to leave he wiggled the plane's wings as he approached her doing a final flyby and she laughed. It was as if the wings were waving at her saying bye-bye and then she saw that he had released an object, which came drifting down and then another one and another one: small, bright-coloured parachutes, one pink, one yellow and one blue.

She climbed the fence and ran towards the falling objects for she knew what they were: candies, from one of the original Berlin candy bombers and she knew Sonny was telling her he was happy. He couldn't be happier and neither could she. She ran and picked them up, waving her arms overhead as he flew by again but this time she noticed he was bringing the plane into land. She took a few steps back waiting for him to taxi towards her. When he cut the motor she ran towards him as he climbed down onto the ground and she threw her arms around him.

'Aren't you a clever man?' Her upturned face grinned into his.

'I'm not sure that qualifies as clever. Venturesome. I'd buy that.'

Gene smiled. 'That was a nice touch with the parachute candies.'

'Did you collect them all?'

'How many did you drop? I got three.'

'That's how many I dropped. Are you going to open them?'

'Now?'

'Yes, now.'

'Okay.' She smiled at him. 'Which one should I open first?'

'The pink one.'

Inside the pink one Gene found gum. Inside the yellow one she found chocolates. Inside the blue one she found what looked like sinkers, she wasn't sure, she pulled one of them closer to investigate and Sonny, said, 'No, they're not for eating.' And then wrapped up in blue tissue paper she found something else. A silver ring. A wide flat silver band.

She sighed as she looked down at the ring and touched it with her fingers. She wore no jewellery whatsoever.

'Gene,' said Sonny, his voice clear. 'Will you wear this ring? Will you marry me?'

She nodded. Tears blurred her eyes. She leant her face into Sonny's chest as he wrapped his arms around her. After a deluge of emotion rained down on her and pooled at her feet she managed to say, 'I know the value of this silver now.'

'That you do.' Sonny lifted her chin and kissed her on the lips, kissed her salty tears. 'Eli would be pleased.'

Gene phoned Morton. There was no answer – typical Morton. She called Wyatt's sister, now her Aunt Pearl, and asked her to ask Morton to meet them at six o'clock that evening at the southern end of Last Mountain Lake, near Lumsden Beach. Pearl told her she would be there if Morton couldn't make it, but Gene knew nothing would stop Morton from being there when they taxied up in the plane. It had been nearly three years since she had last seen her brother.

He grabbed her off the float and swung her onto the sand. After he hugged her he signed, "You are," and then he rotated his right hand around his face counter clockwise, from his lips and back again. "Beautiful."

'Thank you,' she smiled, hugging her brother again. He was quite a picture himself. Tall, muscled and tanned from working outdoors, his hair a dark blonde, his eyes a tawny gold, like their fathers had been.

'I don't think I've ever seen you happier,' he said.

'I don't think I have ever been happier,' Gene replied.

'Good.' He looked her up and down once more.

'Meet your new brother-in-law.' She beamed.

'Ah!' Morton exclaimed. 'That explains it. Congratulations,' He hugged Sonny. 'Finally!'

'That seems to be the standard response,' said Sonny, smiling in delight.

'We haven't done the deed yet,' said Gene. 'I want you to be my witness. Tomorrow. As soon as we can organise it.'

265

Marrying in the Catholic Church was not an option. Gene would need special permission from her bishop to marry a non-Catholic in her home parish, so they decided to forgo that idea and marry in a civil ceremony at the Registry Office with Paul, Wyatt's nephew, and his wife, Nadine, and Pearl and her husband, Jed, as well as Morton, in attendance. Pearl and Morton performed the duties as witnesses and then Nadine blessed their marriage with a reading from Paul to the Corinthians. But before Sonny could kiss his bride, Morton, said, 'Wait! I feel like I should be asking you, Sonny, to pledge an oath to take care of my sister. But I know you'll do that anyway, so forget it.'

'I will if you want it,' said Sonny. 'Go ahead – it will give us something to tell your Mom about.' They all giggled.

'Do you promise to love my sister as much as your father loved your mother?'

'Yes,' Sonny smiled.

'Do you promise you'll look after her and always be there for her?'

'Yes, I will always be there for you, Gene.' He was holding Gene's hands and his eyes were only for her.

'Gene, do you promise to love Sonny as much as Mom loved Dad? As much as Mom loves Wyatt?'

'Yes,' she answered, not taking her eyes away from Sonny's adorable face. How she loved this man. Her feelings for him swelled inside her, filling her completely.

'Well then we're good,' said Morton. 'Welcome to the family, Sonny.' He shook his hand and kissed Gene on the cheek. And just like that Sonny, her man, sans pareil, became her husband, and she his wife.

The seven of them dined at the flashest restaurant to be found in Regina, toasting their marriage with French champagne. It was an old bottle. Morton joked they had to chisel the dust off it before they brought it out to them and he probably was right. Somehow they had managed to cellar it just fine. Morton insisted on picking up the tab. The next morning Gene sent a telegram to her mother's hotel in New York and they decided to send a telegram to Sonny's parents as well – it would last much longer than a phone call. She did however phone Jonathan.

'Guess what Sonny and I did yesterday,' she said.

'Let me guess,' he replied. 'Got married.' She could hear his laughter down the line.

'How did you know?' She exclaimed.

'It was only a matter of time, Gene! A staggeringly long time,' he joked.

'I know.'

'Congratulations. Annabelle and I are so very, very happy for you. Put my brother-in-law on so I can tell him so.'

Next, she phoned Abigail who said she couldn't wait to tell Aunty Leise. An hour later they were airborne once more, bound for the Rocky Mountains, with a promise to spend more time with Morton on their return.

For Gene no other place in Canada – at least none that she had ever visited – matched the quiet and august beauty of the places Sonny took her to on their month long honeymoon.

It took them two days of flying and distractions before they arrived in Kootenay National Park. After being in the air for only three hours, when they were still in Saskatchewan, Gene spotted a lake and asked Sonny if they could land down there.

'What for?' he asked.

'Because I want you.'

He cocked his head and looked at her but didn't say a word, yet he put that plane down in record time. Seconds later they were lying in the narrow gangway next to the loading door, their bodies gyrating, the plane rocking, the water rippling all around the floats. Satisfied for another few hours, till they spotted another lake or waterway, till their bodies were thrumming and ready for more.

Lake O'Hara on the western side of the Great Divide,

west of Alberta and Banff National Park, was breathtaking: a natural rock amphitheatre, the seven waterfalls called the Seven Sisters heralding their approach. In the plateaus up above, a chain of small lakes – MacArthur, Opabin and Oesa – linked O'Hara with the ageless Biddle glacier. There, they camped for the better part of a week, walked down and back to the village of Field below, climbed up scree slopes to Abbott Pass hut perched between Lake O'Hara and Lake Louise, the lake her mother had visited years earlier with Wyatt – no wonder they had fallen in love. They stayed overnight at an altitude of nine thousand feet in the company of mountaineers recounting tales of expeditions to the Eiger and Kilimanjaro and debating which country would be the next to put a man on top of K2 in Pakistan.

They ate grilled lake and rainbow trout, fresh blackberries and bannock, which Gene made in memory of their trip together ten years earlier. They reminisced about the Cree people they had met, missions Sonny had flown since to Ellesmere Island with geologists, and how he had once flown back to Igloolik and tracked Rosie down, how she was married with two children.

For the first time, Gene found out the origins of Sonny's name, how he had been named after his mother's mother, who was called Sonya, how his mother had tried to call him Son-nee for years but his father had pronounced his name Sun-nee and Sun-nee had stuck. In turn, Sonny heard all about Gene's adventures in Europe, her trip to Paris, but mostly to other locations in Switzerland, and the walking club she belonged to. How she loved Interlaken. How she loved cheese fondue. She had bought a fondue set which was being shipped back with some of her belongings. She promised him when it arrived she would make fondue for dinner.

From above in the sky, and on foot, they caught glimpses of timid wildlife: hoary marmots, tiny pikas and placid mountain goats. They saw verdant larch meadows and pastel summer lupins. They sunned themselves on pebbled lakeshores and dipped themselves in frigid waters; water so soft, so clear, they were entranced by it except it was bone achingly cold, but nonetheless a ritual they underwent regularly, like making love, a cleansing for the next time they would come together. When they were by themselves, miles from anyone, they didn't bother with their costumes. Certainly Gene's nightie was still at the bottom of her bag.

Some days Gene would watch Sonny and think: he has elements of my father, Wyatt, my brothers all rolled into one but he is himself more. And she could not comprehend her own happiness or good fortune. Her life had changed so radically in such a short amount of time it almost felt like a dream. Her cup was overflowing.

Banff, Jasper, Mt Robson, Willmore, Kinbasket, Lake Louise, Medicine Lake, Maligne and Horseshoe: stunning lake after stunning lake. Mount Rundle, outside of Banff, was a marvel; a mountain of rock like a giant breaking wave from Poseidon, its curved peaks waiting to crash on the unsuspecting below. Slowly they zigzagged north over the cathedral Alps of the Rocky Mountains, one day Alberta, the next British Columbia. They may not have been married in a church but their marriage could not have been consecrated in a more holy place: the turquoise green of Emerald Lake, the lapis lazuli of Lake Peyto.

Elle aimait tout cela. Elle aimait tous de lui.
She loved all of it. She loved all of him.

45

Nine months after their honeymoon Gene conceived, just as she was beginning to wonder if she had prayed too hard not to get pregnant. She had spent the first few months of her marriage putting her touch on Sonny's home, now their home: painting rooms, new curtains, a few bits of furniture. She met other pilots' wives and their children but within a few months she realised she was not adjusting well to being at home with nothing much to do besides cooking, cleaning, grocery shopping, gardening and going for walks.

Fall came. The trees turned and lost all their leaves. The weather grew colder and the morning mist on the Assiniboine River was thick and eerie. Birds stopped by on their migration south: blue tits, nuthatches, thrushes and swallows. Sonny was coming and going – sometimes he would be away for up to a week or ten days and Gene wished she were flying away too. If he was just hauling cargo he would take her but they decided she wouldn't go with him if he were carrying people. If he was away for any stretch he'd return with a postcard for her and a handwritten message telling her something unusual or beautiful that he had seen and how much he missed her while he was away. He'd never give it to her. He'd just leave it somewhere in the house for her to stumble across. She loved coming across them, but she would love it even more if he weren't away for such long periods.

Gene would tell herself: this is my life now and it's just a matter of my getting used to it. But come Christmas when she still wasn't pregnant she went to Sonny, cuddled up to him in an armchair and said, 'I've been thinking.'

'Oh no, what have you been thinking,' he teased.

She paused. 'I want to do something outside the home. I'm not cut out for being at home day in and day out with nothing much to do.'

He was silent for a few seconds, then he said, 'All right. What do you have in mind?'

'I'm thinking I might train to be a teacher.'

'A teacher? How long will that take?'

'Not long, only a year. I have to do a year of education studies and some practical teaching blocks but because I already have my degree I don't have to start from scratch. I can be a history and geography teacher at a secondary school. I could even teach French if I had too. *Parlez Vous Francais*?'

'*Non*,' Sonny replied with a smile and shake of his head. 'It seems a lot of effort to go to when hopefully within a year, we'll have a kid.'

'Sonny, I'm used to a lot of work. That's part of the problem. And what happens if, heaven forbid we don't have a kid in one year's time. I'll go round the bend.' She paused for effect. 'I'm serious! From Geneva to here is quite an adjustment.'

'Okay, okay, my United Nations wife. So how's it going to work when we do have children?'

'I'll stay at home and look after them. But when they're at school, maybe I can be at school as well. I will still have school holidays off with them. I think it's a good idea. It will give us some extra money.'

'Are you worried I don't earn enough?'

'No.' She waited for him to take that on board. 'My brain is not being used and I'm conscious that I have an earning capability that's not being applied at this point in time when it could be. We could pay this house off sooner. We could help your parents out – send your mother back to Norway to visit her brothers while they're still alive. She never got to see her mother again.'

Sonny looked at her, weighing up the option. 'Okay,' he said. 'I'm happy for you to do whatever you want until

271

children come along. But when we have children I really want you, their mother, at home taking care of them, taking care of me.' He squeezed her when he said that last bit.

'Of course, I will,' Gene promised. After a few moments she added. 'Something that you don't know, Sonny, maybe because you were an only child, but children take care of each other.'

'Well let's hope we have more than one child.'

'I hope we do too,' said Gene as she kissed her husband's neck. 'Thank you.'

Gene didn't quite finish her diploma before their daughter Lindsay arrived. The first three letters were for Elin but the whole name was Wyatt's middle name. Gene wanted to honour him this way, an acknowledgement that he was a much-loved part of their family although he was not related to them by blood. Morton and her mother were touched by her choice of name and by her choosing Dalton for Lindsay's middle name.

After three weeks, Lindsay's blue eyes turned an intense blue-green, like her mother's, and grandmother's – no mistaking her heritage. Her hair was fair but strangely not a light fair like most toddlers but a darker colour, closer to both her parents. She was a good child but Gene really didn't know how she compared to other children. What she knew for certain was how much Sonny adored his little girl. His love for his daughter seemed to Gene to be her love magnified to the power of ten. Gene would wonder how that could be. She thought it was because Sonny was blown away by the miracle of Lindsay's arrival, whereas, because Gene had carried her inside, growing month by month, she knew Lindsay was a sure thing. Perhaps it did not seem so miraculous to her but Sonny, who was always a man of high-spirits, seemed to live his days in a heightened sense of elation, so in love and happy with his new family.

One night as they stood over Lindsay watching her sleep he told Gene he always wanted siblings. She knew.

She remembered that flash of insight she'd had as a seventeen year old, not long after they first met. It gave her the greatest joy to know she'd helped bring Lindsay into the world, into his life.

'I can't believe you didn't marry and have children before now,' Gene whispered, feeling, as she often did since her marriage, a mild sense of panic at how ridiculously fortunate she had been that he'd set his sights on her and then waited. Now that she was happily married she knew what she – and he – had been missing for so long. 'How come you never met and married someone else?' she asked, not for the first time.

'Because I got burnt badly the first time which slowed me down for years – Lesley, remember? Then I met you. Lost and unsure. Independent. Free thinker. Miss Auld Lang Syne – my long-standing friend. A girl who went on to become a woman on her own terms. No body else really compared. I knew I wanted you. It was just a matter of waiting until you knew you wanted me.'

'I know, but still?'

'You don't think what we have now was worth waiting for?'

'Yes! In a heartbeat, yes,' she said, emphatically. 'Sometimes I still can't get over the fact that you waited so long for me.'

He took her hand. 'That's why we're making up for lost time.' He led her towards their bedroom.

'At least you didn't have to wait twenty-five years like Abraham,' she teased. But in that moment she had a flash of Abraham: his first son by his handmaiden Hagar; his beloved begotten Isaac by Sarah; and then his six sons by his second wife Keturah, whom he married after Sarah died. Gene shivered, hoping she would be the one to give Sonny his own tribe of Israel.

But from that night onwards a sense of fear crept into Gene's life, a fear like the one that had haunted her for years – not for her life, but for the men in her life – for Sonny's. In the months before Lindsay was born Sonny made changes to his flying operations to ensure he would be home every night. He sold the Beaver, they paid off most of the mortgage and he gave some money to his parents urging his mother to go to Norway. Vun day, vun day she promised him.

He took a job with Transair, flying a Beech 18, mostly bush-flying on floats off the Red River in Winnipeg on what they called 'skeds' – scheduled runs – up the lake to Berens River, Poplar River and Norway House; to Island Lake, one of the largest native settlements in central Manitoba, about three-hundred miles away; and to St. Theresa Point.

In the winter months he flew on wheel-skis directly from the Winnipeg terminal to the northern settlements that lay along his sked run. Sonny would pull his twin-engine Beech 18 Expediter in among the big jet airplanes and help board his passengers: trappers, Indian Affairs officials, groups from government or mining outfits, and local residents who were coming to or leaving the city hospitals. Mostly, he hauled mail and freight. With that Beech 18, he handled virtually all the services north to Norway House and the other settlements on Lake Winnipeg and on Island Lake. There was the odd private charter. Only two mornings in three years did he turn back because his plane was getting too iced-up.

Sonny didn't mind changing to skeds; the flights were more regular, shorter and routine. What he especially liked was that he was home every night, and now he didn't have to do any maintenance on his own plane. When he parked the airplane at the Transair hangar, his shift was completely over.

He'd race home, rush through the door, embrace Gene, kiss her into a corner and say, 'How's my Snow Queen today? How's my little Norwegian princess?' Sonny used to love reading to Lindsay the Norwegian fairytales that were read to him as a child. First, though, he'd go and take a shower, sometimes, he'd shower with Lindsay but often he'd shower first and bath Lindsay while Gene got dinner ready for them. Sometimes all three of them would bath together. It was cramped but it was some of their best of times as their little girl stood on wobbly legs and poured water over their heads with a cup and thought it was the best game ever.

Most of Sonny's flights were in daytime hours because oddly his Beech 18 didn't have any navigation equipment. He could communicate via radio but there was no Automatic Direction Finder.

Gene was shocked when he casually mentioned there was no ADF indicator. 'How come?' she demanded. 'With all the communication equipment available, and Transair being such a large airline, surely they can afford to upgrade their equipment.'

'Well they don't,' he said, 'but it doesn't matter, I've been flying off maps for years. Besides they're not 100% reliable. Mountains, shorelines, electrical storms can interfere with radio signals.'

'You can't tell me you're more safe without an ADF.'

'No I can't,' he said. 'But I can tell you, you have nothing to worry about. I can still communicate via radio. And where I'm going map reading is easier. There are trees for start. Way up north in winter you could never tell if you were landing on terra firm or ice.'

Gene was not at ease. As much as she tried to fight it, thoughts of something happening to Sonny, like how something had happened to her father, plagued her mind. But Sonny kept on reassuring her, telling her his winter flying was much easier now as the aircraft was kept in a hangar overnight. It was warm when he started off in the morning. She had no idea what a treat that was he told her. Only if he got caught in one of the northern settlements and was told it was snowing in Winnipeg did he have to stay overnight and then warm his engines up with blow-pots.

He told her this was the most civilised, easy flying he had done for years and besides, he could fly in worse weather than most pilots as he'd done so much flying in the Arctic where the conditions were far worse. If he were grounded somewhere overnight he would call her if he could or ask whoever he was speaking to at Winnipeg radio to call Gene for him, which people always did, except one night someone who promised, forgot, and when Sonny turned up the next day Gene was ropeable.

'Do you want to know what sort of night I've had?'

He knew straight away what sort of night she had had. Gene was completely on edge and it took him over an hour of apologies and soothing words. 'Why didn't you call Tom to see if I checked in?'

'I did. Three times. There was no answer.'

He was sorry about that. Sorry about everything. And she knew he thought he had done the right thing but the thought of him having gone down somewhere, bleeding, broken, frozen, left her terrified.

'Gene,' he said. 'You've got to get a grip on this. I'm one hell of an experienced pilot. You know that don't you?'

'Yes,' she admitted.

'Well don't think the worst anytime I'm late. Think something's come up. Think there's a reason for this. You've got to do that. Don't feed your anxiety with more anxiety. Promise me you won't get in a flap.'

She tried to take comfort in Sonny's experience and prudence. But one day she was having afternoon tea with a group of pilot wives while Lindsay was playing in the next room with a group of children and one woman started talking about the Beech 18, referring to it as "The Widow-Maker" and Thelma said, 'My husband says you have to watch them all the time. You have to wheel it on apparently.'

'What does that mean?' Gene asked.

'I don't know. It's just what he said.'

That night Gene asked Sonny to explain what the term meant.

He squinted at her for many long moments. Finally he said, 'It means you have to fly the plane onto the runway when there is still sufficient airflow over the wings to actually be flying. The opposite is a process called a stall. A stall occurs when not enough air flows over the wings to keep the airplane aloft, and the whole weight of the airplane settles onto the wheels.'

'Go on,' said Gene maintaining firm eye contact.

'If you are flying a plane that you need to wheel on then that means you have to bring it in at a fair speed. If you land at low speed, you basically lose control and the plane will bounce down the runway.'

'So what does the Beech do that you fly?'

'It lands relatively fast,' Sonny said. He paused, swallowed. 'Do you have a problem with that?'

'Do pilots have problems with those types of planes?'

'Only if they don't know what type of plane they're flying,' Sonny joked.

'What's it like landing on water?'

'Like any plane – you've got to pick your water.'

Gene had also heard that sometimes one of the engines failed. 'What do you do if one of the engines fail?'

'You fly slower,' said Sonny, shrugging his shoulders. 'You hope you don't have floats on as you'll be dragging.' He came up to her and pulled her into his arms, 'Gene, what's the matter?'

'Nothing,' she said, shaking her head. 'I just wanted to understand something. That's all.'

'You can come for a flight with me one day when I do a mail run if you like.'

'Maybe,' she said, wondering would she be brave enough to take their daughter up in an airplane?

Weeks later she got a phone call from Madge, who was laughing away. 'That husband of yours, he's something else. Always got a solution to every problem.'

'Oh yes. He's resourceful,' said Gene.

'He knows how to get himself out of a pickle.'

'Yes,' said Gene not knowing what Madge was talking about but knowing the essence. 'He's very clever,' she said, 'and, modest. You know he downplays everything.'

'Oh yes,' said Madge. 'I bet he does. I know he doesn't deliberately flirt with danger and I mean no disrespect by this, Gene, but what Philly comes home and tells me, I can't help but laugh. He just turns it into one tall tale of hilarity.'

'Well tell me his latest tall tale because when Sonny walks through the door all that's on his mind is getting down on his knees and playing with his daughter. Any talk of work goes out the window.'

'Well,' she said, her voice full of juicy overtones as if she had forgotten to whom she was speaking, 'yesterday the latest drama was his retractable wheel-skis malfunctioned. He was coming down from Sandy Lake on wheels apparently, when he looked out and saw that one ski was down. He'd have to land on one wheel and one ski! Can you imagine that?'

'I'd rather not,' said Gene.

'Anyway, he flew past the Control Tower and radioed Tom who confirmed one ski was up and one was down.'

'"Shit a brick," he said, then a few seconds later he said, "Maybe I could head north to St. Andrew's airport." Apparently he said something to the effect, "With all that construction going on there's lot of mud and water everywhere. The plane will take a mud bath, but hopefully it won't turn over."

'But before he headed north he did another fly over and then he radioed back to the tower. "There's a piece of snow," he said, "along runway 31, it hasn't quite melted away, looks like the snow-blowers have blown it into a ridge about twenty feet wide and maybe three hundred feet long. I'll bring it down there."

'"Well just give us fifteen minutes to get everything organised," the operator apparently radioed back. Out came the fire trucks, the first aid people, everyone was on standby worried he might flip it. Everyone, that is, except Transair.'

'That would be right,' said Gene.

'Anyway, he let the other ski down and landed

perfectly with the two skis on this little bit of snow. No damage to anyone. No damage to any property.'

In her mind, Gene sighed. 'I'm sure Transair was pleased about that.'

'Why yes, only a little job for their mechanics. He's some man your husband,' enthused Madge. 'Where did you find him?'

'I've got my brother to thank for that,' said Gene, smiling into the phone, thinking you wait Sonny Marlow. But later that day after she calmed down she thought, he should have told me but he didn't tell me because he knew I'd be worried and now I am. How could I have prevented this situation from happening? And soon after she had her answer. She was going to extricate herself from this circle of pilot wives. She would say hello to them at Christmas parties and work functions but she was not going to be a lamb to the slaughter.

And that is what she did. Inch by inch she withdrew herself. The only person she would visit would be Elin or Sonny's cousin, Sylvia, and one day when she was with Elin, she asked her, 'Do you ever worry something might happen to Sonny? Did you ever worry something might happen to Don through all those years?'

'Every day, every day,' she said. 'But I just put all my worries together and send them up to God in prayer. And he listens.'

Gene smiled, remembering what Sonny had told her years ago. 'He does seem to listen to you. Keep praying, Elin.'

By virtue of proximity, Gene became closer to her mother-in-law than her mother in those early years of Lindsay's life. Sonny's mother had wonderful round cheekbones, made more obvious by her white blonde fringe that hid her broad forehead. She had strong healthy looking teeth, clearly where Sonny inherited his from – all thanks to lots of cheese, Elin claimed. Gene and Elin shared a passion for cheese, which Lindsay was quick to appreciate. As soon as they sliced a piece of cheese for her she ate it and put her hand out ready for another one.

'More, Farmor,' she would say, farmor being the Norwegian word for grandma on the father's side – father's mother.

At times Elin would call Gene and say, 'How about you bring my granddaughter over to me today and you go off and do something with a girlfriend.' Gene would go to a movie by herself. Sometimes on a Saturday Elin would say, 'Please, will you bring my granddaughter over to me today and let her stay overnight while you and Sonny get busy on making another one.'

Sometimes on these days, Gene would go with Sonny to the Winnipeg Flying Club or go out dancing. He was quite a dancer her Sonny. He could sing, he could dance, he could fly a plane, he could make love to her till she would cry out, 'I'm going to need a week to get over this weekend.'

And he would jokingly reply, 'All right, take a week, but that's all you're going to get.'

Not long after Lindsay turned two, Gene cajoled Sonny into letting her do her final six-week practical teaching block which she was unable to complete due to Lindsay's birth. Convincing Elin to look after Lindsay for six weeks straight was child's play. Convincing Sonny was a different matter, however when Gene miscarried he could see it would be good for her to have something to take her mind off things for a while. The strategy paid off.

In July 1966 just a month short of Gene's thirty-third birthday, their second daughter was born. Shane's birth coincided with Elin and Don taking their long overdue trip to Norway. This time, Rebecca and Wyatt came to look after Lindsay and the household for those first few weeks while Gene lived on hardly any sleep.

They named their little girl after the movie, Shane, that had come out years earlier, and which they had seen together on one of Sonny's visits out east, when Gene was at University. They gave her Sibonne, Gene's nanna's maiden name as her middle name. But mostly they called her Shane because when they decided on the name they had both been hoping for a boy.

46

One afternoon, a week after Shane's birth, Gene sat propped up on top of her and Sonny's bed, a pillow on her lap supporting Shane as she nursed her infant daughter and listened to her mother recount her trip out east. Her mother was wearing a pale blue summer dress with cuffed sleeves that came just to her elbow, set off by a narrow apple-green belt. Her hair was pulled into a high bun. She really did look like a pretty picture of summer thought Gene who felt the complete opposite.

Wyatt and her mother had spent two weeks with Morna, Gene's grandmother, and Esther, her aunt, at Bonavista, then Rachel, her other aunt, and her husband had accompanied Rebecca and Wyatt to Second Chance, staying for three weeks. It was Rachel's first trip back to Second Chance in over forty years and in honour of the occasion she brought as a house-warming gift: a home-made hook rug she and her daughters had spent all winter making. What a grand time they'd had, said her mother – took them back to the time when they were sisters growing up in the house together. Just when Gene thought her mother had finished talking all about their trip to Newfoundland, she made the observation that although it was great to have sisters growing up perhaps the reason she married Samuel so young was because she never had any brothers.

With her mother's admission hanging in the air Gene told her something she hadn't uttered aloud to another soul. 'I was hoping for a boy this time. A boy like Joel, in his image and his spirit to remind me of the brother I'd lost all those years ago.' She paused. 'Did you ever hope for something different than what you got?'

'Gene,' said her mother, her voice low in warning. 'Don't go saying that. The wee one will sense it and take it to heart. Be happy you have a girl. The two will grow up to be great friends.'

'How does that stand to reason? I'm better friends with my brothers than I am with my sister.'

'Well all my brothers died before they were six years old. I only had sisters who lived and Rachel was my best friend.'

'Mom, you're misunderstanding me.' Gene tried to hide the irritation in her voice. 'That's not what I'm saying. I was merely asking you if you ever longed for a boy when you were pregnant?'

Her mother sighed. 'Only the first time, when your father was away in the war. I missed him terribly and wanted a boy so I would feel like I would have more of him with me once the child was born. But after that I never cared. I just wanted a baby and I didn't care if they were a boy or a girl. All I wanted was for them to be healthy and to live.' Her mother swallowed before continuing. 'I can remember when you were only six months and I was breastfeeding you one night and this refrain kept on pounding in my head: lost one, kept one, lost one, kept one, lost one, kept one. I was gripped with fear and thought for sure I would lose you and so I went ahead and had another baby but it was Joel that I lost. It wasn't till years later that I saw a different pattern to the one I saw back then.'

Gene only half heard that last line. She was stuck on "lost one, kept one, lost one, kept one." 'Who were the babies you lost?'

Her mother looked at her and inhaled deeply. 'My first baby was a boy Samson. He lived for three days. Then Abigail. Then I had a boy we called Henry. He lived for one day only. Perfectly healthy but died that first night. Then Morton. Then you. Then Joel.'

'What happened to Samson? How did he die?'

Her mother stared at her intently. Her eyes were

piercing in that way they could be sometimes. After some moments, she said, 'He was drowned.' And Gene thought that odd – the "was drowned" rather than "drowned.' Next she heard her mother say, 'By my father, his own grandfather. He was mad.'

Nothing could have prepared Gene for that. 'Mad, as in crazy or mad, as in angry?'

'Both.'

'What did he do? Steal your baby away from you and drown him?'

'More or less.'

'He drowned your son!'

'Yes.' Her mother's voice was weary.

'Where did this happen?'

'In Newfoundland, at the place where I grew up.'

'What a bloody bastard!'

'Yes. I thought the same at the time, though I did not know the words. It's so far in the past, Gene. Nearly fifty years ago. Samuel and I forgave him eventually but we never saw him before he died, I couldn't bring myself to.'

'At least you had Jonathan shortly after. You forgot Jonathan in your list, Mom.'

Her mother looked at her and it was a second or two of silence, like the second or two that would have felt like a minute or two for people in the war, in Berlin or Cologne, crouched in their shelters as they heard bombs whistling down wondering if they were going to be hit or spared. Nothing they could do about it but gaze into each other's eyes and hold on, yet knowing it was a life or death moment.

'Jonathan's not my biological son,' her mother softly said. 'He wasn't Samuel's son either.'

And all Gene can think is: No. No. Take that back, take that back.

'I'm sure you knew that growing up. The first time we met Wyatt it came up. Don't you remember?'

And all Gene can do is frown at her mother and shake her head in stupefaction.

284

'His father was Matthew, your father's brother, who was killed in the war, and his mother was Matthew's wife, Lenore, who died of the Spanish Flu when Jonathan was only ten months old.'

Suddenly Gene wishes she could wind back time, wishes she could tell her mother: "Don't tell me! I don't want to know!" She wishes that was one secret her mother had kept to herself, something she could have shared with the angels or the ferryman.

The love Gene had for her brothers surpassed all others. But if she had to own it she would say she loved Jonathan just marginally more than she loved Morton and that went way back to the time when she needed him the most, to the time when he was not just her brother but her father also, a replica of their own father. And it was knowing that he was their father's deputy, their father's flesh and blood, his shape, his voice, his smell that helped Gene survive the most turbulent times in her life.

And here her mother was telling her he was none of those things.

Gene started to cry. 'I wish you had never, never told me that. Please. Please,' she begged. 'Never tell Jonathan. Never tell Morton.'

'Calm down, Gene. You're getting carried away. Jonathan knows he's adopted. We told him when he was five years old. He's always known. He's always been fine with it.'

Gene just stared at her mother, utterly dumbfounded. 'Why did you keep it from us then?'

'I never deliberately kept it from you. Your father and I always planned to tell you children when you older but then,' she paused, '...events happened and it never seemed important after that. Jonathan felt like our son in every sense of the word and we loved him as our own. No different to any of you children.'

No different! thought Gene.

'Can you leave, Mom? I don't want you here anymore. Thanks for ruining my life, again.'

Gene dismissed her mother with a single turn of her head and refused to glance back in her direction. How could Jonathan not be her brother? Her mother was left with no choice but to quietly walk out of the bedroom.

47

Years ago when Jonathan was twenty-five, Rebecca had told him about Samson. One night when the two of them were alone together around her kitchen table in her house in Montreal, not long after she had met Wyatt in fact, she told him there was something she wanted to share with him. Something she and her father decided they would tell him one day – tell him and only him – so that he would know at the deepest level just how much he had meant to them both.

She had and they had cried together over that story and if anything it had brought them closer together. Rebecca never had any intention of telling any of her other children so why had she said something that day? Was she hoping her disclosure would bring her closer to her daughter? Certainly that day it hadn't. Maybe over time…

Rebecca walked into the kitchen where Sonny and Wyatt were drinking coffee while Lindsay sat on Sonny's knee drawing with a crayon on a piece of paper on the table in front of her. Her father held her in place with a hand resting against her stomach.

'Sonny,' she said, 'I'm sorry I have upset your wife. I didn't mean to and I regret it but nothing I can say or do can change it.'

He and Wyatt gave her a questioning glance.

'What happened?' asked Wyatt.

'We were having a conversation about children, all the children I had. I told her the ones I lost and the ones who had lived. In my telling I omitted to mention Jonathan, which caused some confusion. I told Gene the truth, that he was adopted.'

'Is he?' Sonny was equally stunned.

'Yes,' said Wyatt. 'But he's not some stranger's child. His father was the best of men, Samuel's brother.'

'So actually he's her cousin,' Rebecca confirmed for Sonny's benefit. 'I don't think that bit sunk in. She just couldn't get past Jonathan not being her brother.'

Sonny looked from one to the other. 'Jonathan knows this?'

'Jonathan has always known. I thought the kids knew it in a round about way, but then I also thought it was immaterial. He is my son, our son, their brother.'

Sonny exhaled deeply. After a few moments he said, 'Don't worry I know how she can be. We'll just give her a bit of time. Let her get used to the idea. She'll settle down.'

But that night Gene refused to join them at the table for dinner. And when they got up the next morning Sonny was uncomfortable in a way they had never seen him before.

'I'm sorry, but she's being adamant. She doesn't want you in our house anymore.' He looked ashamed as he said those words to her, his mother-in-law. 'I don't want you to leave. It's just her. I've tried to talk sense into her but she won't listen.'

'It's okay,' said Rebecca. 'We can leave, but I hate to leave you with everything.'

'Would you mind going to stay at Mom and Dad's place for a few days and taking Lindsay with you, to give Gene some space?'

Gene wasn't keen on that arrangement but Sonny put his foot down.

Rebecca didn't go in to say goodbye to her daughter. She just stood at the door and said, 'Gene, I'm sorry for upsetting you. We'll be back in a few days. Why don't you call Jonathan and have a talk to him?'

But when she got to Don and Elin's place Rebecca didn't wait for Gene to call Jonathan. She called him herself, told him everything that had gone down. And while she and Wyatt played with her granddaughter all Rebecca could think of was Gene's, "again." When was the first time she had ruined her life? When she had been a zombie after Samuel and Joel disappeared?

Seeing, or rather imagining Gene in a state of turmoil, stirred up all manner of thoughts and feelings in Rebecca that she wished she could share with someone, and oddly the person she most wanted to share her bitter ramblings with was Samuel. He would know the right thing to say to settle Gene and make her see sense. Jonathan would help too though – he always did. Eventually she talked to Wyatt. She should have known all along she could have talked to Wyatt.

48

Mere hours after her mother and Wyatt left, Jonathan phoned Gene himself.

'How's my newest niece coming along?' he asked her.

'She's doing well,' she replied but didn't elaborate.

'What about you?'

She didn't reply. Couldn't.

'Gene,' he drawled, 'you are my sister. Not my one and only sister as there is Abby as well but the two of you are my sisters like Morton is my brother and Joel was too. We are family. I have never seen myself as not part of this family, of us not being one and the same. Even Grandma Crowe, Mom's mother, treated me like her biological grandchild.

'It never upset me that I wasn't born to Mom and Dad. In fact I felt so special because I knew I had two sets of parents who loved me. Mom and Dad could not have loved me more than my real parents. I knew that. I felt that. And I had cousins galore and grandparents who adored me, and siblings who worshipped me and I have wanted for nothing.

'Put this aside. For me, for yourself, for the sake of everyone. You know what you mean to me. I couldn't love you more.'

After the phone call Gene wished she could have said, 'Well I'm glad it didn't rock your life but it rocked mine.' It was as if something was missing that would never come right again.

And from that day on anything and everything about her fragile hormonal state amplified and deteriorated.

'Gene, Gene, what does one have to do to get a smile out of you?' Sonny would ask her.

She would open her mouth and clench her teeth in a forced expression that was more grimace than smile. She was in a bad place. These were her children, her own flesh and blood, and she wanted to be the best mother for them yet she felt like an abject failure.

She feared for her daughters' lives and she feared in different ways depending on the child. When she walked into a room she saw danger everywhere: a drawer not closed that could be pulled out and topple on Lindsay, a pair of scissors lying on a bench, wooden blocks on the floor that she could stumble over and break an ankle or a wrist. Anything and everything about their home was a hazard. She needed to lock the doors to make sure Lindsay didn't run outside and on to the road. With Shane she feared for her every breathing moment. She walked a constant path to her bassinet checking that she was breathing. She'd wake her up when she was sleeping just to make sure she was breathing. Her fear for Shane overwhelmed her like nothing else.

She got to the point she couldn't change Shane's nappies for fear she would stab her with the pin. So she just left her in soiled clouts, until some capable adult – Sonny or Elin – walked through the door and was able to manage that job without injury.

Some days she thought the best thing she could do for her children was to leave them alone. She would sit by the window and stare outside, sit on her hands so she wouldn't be tempted to do anything with them. She'd just rock back and forth.

Then at night she would rise from her bed and go downstairs to the laundry in the basement to wash nappies, do the ironing while Sonny and the children were asleep – at a time when Lindsay couldn't come along and grab the power cord and drag the iron down on top of herself and burn her flawless little body. She'd go into the kitchen and clean the stove, empty the fridge or the garbage and sterilise the bins.

At some point Sonny would come in and say, 'Gene,

it's the middle of the night. Can you just leave that and come back to bed or go read in the lounge. I've got to get up and work tomorrow. I need my sleep. I don't need this racket.'

He was right. But she couldn't sleep, and with him home and the children safe and asleep, it was the only time she could do anything useful around the place. Some nights when she knew Sonny was deep asleep she would sneak out and go for walks around the neighbourhood, how she used to walk around the grounds of Freshwater all those years ago.

Sonny did his best not to be angry with her. He would say to her, 'Gene, you've got to snap out of this. Ever since your mother told you about Jonathan, you've gone down hill. It's crazy.'

'Well I must be crazy then,' she retorted.

'I didn't say that. All I'm saying is that you've made this mean too much. You've lost perspective. You love Jonathan. He loves you. Nothing has changed between the two of you. Just forgive your mother for the way she told you and get over it.'

'I'm not sure I can.'

'What, forgive your mother or get over it?'

She couldn't answer him because what she wanted to say to him was: that's not what this was about. It was about something else. But she couldn't put words to the something else without painting herself as someone who was incapable of so many things including being home alone with her children. Many days she thought her children and Sonny would be better off without her. Some days she thought she would be better off without them.

49

The phone call came around eight o'clock at night. Rebecca and Wyatt had not long returned from Toronto where they had spent thanksgiving with Abigail and Will and their four children. It was Sonny. 'Becca,' he said, 'I need your help, Jonathan's help, Wyatt's help. Gene needs your help. She's not coping. I told her you're coming and she hasn't objected. Can you come back again? I know you haven't been home for long.'

She told him she and Wyatt would be there the day after tomorrow.

They arrived on dusk. Rebecca followed Sonny inside to the kitchen where he was hastily trying to tidy things up. His fair wavy hair was dishevelled as if he'd run his hands through it umpteen times, trying to decide what next.

'Where's Gene?' she asked.

'In the bedroom lying down. I've been putting her to bed every night when I come home. It's as if someone has died and she is mourning their death. She's gone all torpid.'

'I was like that once,' Rebecca admitted. 'After Samuel died. Jonathan will tell you I was a zombie for two years. I checked out for hours each day while the kids were at school.'

'How did you beat it?'

'It took Jonathan losing his temper at me, and Gene having a mishap at school. I just had to make some decisions, commit to some changes and find my long lost will power.'

'I don't think Gene could take me losing my temper at her.' They were all talking in lowered voices.

'So what happened two days ago that made you call?' asked Rebecca.

'I had to overnight up at Island Lake. Came home to Gene sitting in the lounge staring out the window and Lindsay crying because Shane had been crying all afternoon and she couldn't stop her crying. Gene was so out to it, as if she couldn't hear Lindsay's and Shane's crying. It was like she was in some state where she could block it completely. I don't how she could ignore all that hullabaloo. I honestly couldn't have. Lindsay was telling me Shane was stinky and she was. She was filthy. She had poo right up the back of her neck, all over her back, in her hair. I don't think her nappy had been changed in two days, her body was so red in places. God knows when Gene last fed her. Lindsay was crying telling me she wanted cheese please. Milk. I opened the fridge and there was no milk, no cheese.

'And so I phoned Mom. Dad answered and said Mom has been in bed with the flu for three days and hadn't been over to check on Gene. But then Mom came to the phone and said, "Yes, Sonny, every time I come over Shane has a dirty nappy. And Gene always tells me she must have just dirtied it. But a mother knows these things. But what can I do or say. I just change her nappy, give her a bath. With your help and my help she'll get there." She said she thought Gene was just having a hard time of it. Some women do apparently.' Sonny looked at Wyatt who blinked in agreement.

'Where are the girls now?' Wyatt asked.

'Lindsay's with my cousin, Sylvia.' He inhaled deeply. 'Shane's…Shane's in hospital.' And with that Sonny started to cry. And in that moment Rebecca felt the pangs in her own heart. Something had broken inside her normally imperturbable son-in-law.

She went over and hugged him. 'It will be all right, Sonny,' she murmured. 'It will be all right.'

'I know. I know.' He backhanded his cheeks. 'We've just got to get through this somehow.'

'What is she in hospital for?'

'Sylvia and I took her there. We wanted to make sure she was okay because she just wouldn't stop crying. Turns out she has a urinary tract infection. A four-month old child has a urinary tract infection! No wonder she's been crying her head off – all that burning every time she pees.'

'There. There,' said Wyatt who had come to rest his hand on Sonny's shoulder. 'She's getting help now. You did the right thing.'

'I had to call you.' Sonny was trying to suppress a sob. His fists were thrust tightly under his armpits as if he were trying to keep all his emotions in lockdown. 'I'm sorry. I don't know what to do about Gene. I can't be here. I'll lose my job. I've already called in sick yesterday. I need help in looking after the girls. I need help with Gene, but I don't even know where to begin.'

'Let me spend some time with her,' said Wyatt. 'Don't you worry about her. A lot of women get the baby blues but sometimes women succumb to a depression that's much worse and that sounds like Gene.' His eyes told Rebecca nearly everything she needed to know.

A few days later Rebecca and Wyatt brought Shane home from the hospital, telling the doctor Shane's mother was in bed, doing poorly. They didn't mention her mental state. They brought Lindsay back on the same day. They didn't want her home beforehand, worried about her little sister being in hospital.

Gene withdrew and became distant from everyone, even her own children. She rarely spoke to any of them.

One night, around midnight, Rebecca woke to raised voices. She came out to Sonny standing in the kitchen, wearing jeans and a navy pullover, his hands outstretched, pressed firmly onto the kitchen bench, an empty tumbler and scotch bottle beside him.

'What's up?' she asked.

He glanced at Rebecca and straightened up, turning to face her. 'Gene accused me of having a relationship with an Indian woman up at Inland Lake.'

'Goodness,' said Rebecca. 'That's quite an accusation. Is it true?'

'No! The only Indian woman I've ever had a relationship with was Kristina. You met her.'

'Yes,' said Rebecca. 'She was a lovely girl.' Rebecca wondered if at that moment Sonny wished he had married her instead. 'Why did she come out and say that, do you think?'

'She told me she heard it on the radio.'

'The radio!' Rebecca exclaimed in a loud whisper.

'Yes,' said Sonny and when Rebecca looked at him she looked at a Sonny she had never seen before – a man overcome with worry and fatigue.

'I think she might be losing it. She's starting to get things out of kilter. We've only made love once since Shane was born. She's lost interest in it. I feel like she's trying to push me away. Almost as if she wants me to go off and have an affair, because then she'll feel less guilty about not wanting to have sex with me. Honestly, Becca, I can't work her out anymore.'

Rebecca walked over and patted his shoulder. 'I know what that's like, Sonny. Sometimes when Gene was a teenager I couldn't work her out. Just hang in there.'

Wyatt decided they needed to get Gene out of the house, that with some distance she might get some perspective. They talked about taking Gene and the girls to Wyatt's farm. But then Rebecca erred. 'Look, I don't mind going there, but why should Sonny be denied his children because Gene's in such a confounded state?'

'It might help,' argued Wyatt.

'Can we try something else first?'

'Righto,' said Wyatt. 'Let's just get her out of the house here, interested in something. Who knows when she last laughed.'

'How long does it take for that Valium to start to work?' asked Rebecca.

'Weeks,' said Wyatt. 'Months.'

The next morning they suggested to Gene that she get up and have a shower as Wyatt would like to take her to a movie. Rebecca would stay home and look after the children. Rebecca was already looking after the children feeding Shane bottled formula every few hours. Gene seemed to have forgotten completely about the responsibility of an infant daughter almost as if she no longer had one. At least that is what Rebecca and Wyatt had surmised.

'No, I can't go with you, Wyatt,' Gene said. 'I can't leave my children at home with Mom.'

'Why not?' Rebecca asked.

'Because they might not be safe.'

'With me!' Rebecca exclaimed. 'Why for heaven's sake do you think that? Were my kids ever not safe growing up with me?'

'You could be like your father. You could go mad and harm my children.'

'No Gene, on my life I will never do that. You're worrying unnecessarily. Let Wyatt entertain you for a few hours.'

At two o'clock Wyatt finally managed to get Gene into his car. At home Rebecca and Lindsay played together with Shane for a little while and then when Shane got sleepy, Rebecca put her in her cot and said to Lindsay, 'What would you like to do now petal?'

Lindsay replied without hesitation. 'Play hide and seek.'

She hid under a bed, Rebecca hid on the porch, Lindsay climbed up and hid in the cement laundry tub, which Rebecca gave her ten out of ten for best hiding spot. Next, Rebecca hid in the wardrobe in the guestroom, and then when it was Lindsay's turn again Rebecca found her sitting on a chair looking out the window.

'Have you had enough of hide and seek, Lindsay?' she asked. ' Don't you want to play any more?'

'I am playing Granny. I'm hiding like Mom hides

every day. You don't have to go anywhere to hide. You just hide inside yourself.'

Rebecca stifled a gasp. Her granddaughter, a miniature version of her quiescent mother. 'Come here, child. That's not a game for you. That's no fun.'

Another night, Rebecca hears noises and gets up. She feels a cold draught and comes across Sonny as he is walking into the kitchen, pulling on his sage-green cold-weather flying suit. 'Gene's gone somewhere. She left the back door open. I've got to go find her.' It was December. Already there was a foot of snow on the ground.

'Wyatt and I'll go looking for her,' she tells him. 'You stay here, in case she comes back.' They find her three streets away. She's wearing her winter outdoor boots and thick duffle coat.

Rebecca puts her head out the car window and calls out her name but Gene either doesn't hear her or refuses to hear her. They drive ahead, stop the car, get out and walk up to her. 'Gene,' says Rebecca. 'It's time to go home and back to bed.'

Gene looks straight through her.

'Gene, do you understand? Can you hear me? I'm talking to you.'

'I don't know who you're talking to, lady, but my name's not Gene.'

'Oh,' says Rebecca, throwing a look to Wyatt. 'What's your name then?'

'My name is Silas Crowe.'

Rebecca blanches. Wyatt comes to her aid. 'Okay, Silas, we need to bundle you back in the car,' he says.

Back at the house they try and get 'Silas' to take a sedative but 'Silas' refuses.

'Okay, Silas,' says Wyatt. 'Tell me where were you walking to?'

'To the stage.'

'Where were you walking from?' he asks.

But Gene just stares through them as if they are wisps in the air.

Hours later when they at last retire to bed, Rebecca said to Wyatt, 'I feel so responsible for all of this. I should have never opened my mouth. All these crazy things she's coming out with I planted them in her head.'

'No,' Wyatt said. 'You gave her nuggets of truth. She was the one who turned them into seeds and planted them. You can't hold yourself responsible for what she's doing. If you were doing it to her, forcing her to march the streets at night then yes you would be responsible for that, but you're not. So, she's picked up some things you said, but she could have just as easily have flipped over something someone else said, or what she imagined they said. Like what she accused Sonny of.'

He rubbed his eyes. It was late and Rebecca could see he was tired and worried too.

'Be that as it may, Wyatt, I still feel responsible. This madness, my father had it. I've given to her somehow. It runs through my family. How have I managed to dodge it so far? Will I dodge it? Oh, Wyatt, promise me you'll tell me if I ever end up going mad.'

'It's not that easy. In a demented state people can't see it for themselves. They don't believe what people tell them.'

'Well, we will have to have a signal that you show me that says to me: "I'm not sane. I'm not thinking clearly, I'm not acting clearly. I need help. That I know I have to trust you implicitly and forego all my thoughts."'

'Would you recognise such a signal?'

'I'd like to think I would.'

'What do you think could be a signal that would do that for you?'

Rebecca thought for a while. 'My father's bible,' she announced.

'But you have it with you all the time. It wouldn't stand out.'

'I'll put it in the glass cabinet in the hallway when I go home and there it will stay unless you get it out and hand it to me. Will you promise you'll do that for me please, Wyatt?'

'I promise,' he said, 'but I don't think I'll ever be needing to do it. Come here, Becca." He reached for her to fold her in his embrace.

The next morning Rebecca calls Jonathan and tells him everything.

'We need to do something Jonathan,' she implores. 'She's not getting any better. The Valium Wyatt prescribed for her seems to be having no effect at all. She needs help but none of us knows what sort of help to give her. It's different to when she was seventeen. She was lucid then. She's not now. Delusional is what she is now.'

He tells Rebecca to leave it with him. He'll call back in a day or two.

But before he does, the following evening Rebecca wakes up in the middle of the night and it's almost too quiet. Earlier she thought she heard a trickling noise but now everything is muffled. Still, something in her being is on edge. She slips out of bed. Wyatt stirs beside her. She walks down the hallway to the end of the house. There is a line of light under the bathroom door and the thinnest wedge on the side where it is not closed properly. Slowly Rebecca pushes it open and sees Gene kneeling by the bath, holding a fully clothed Shane up to her shoulder.

She hears Gene whispering, 'Go to sleep now. Sleep in peace.' Beside her the bathtub is half full of water.

Quietly Rebecca walks in, crouches down next to her daughter, her knees pop in the process, but Gene is oblivious to the noise. 'Can I hold the baby please for a little bit?' she says.

Gene ignores her.

'Gene, may I hold Shane please?' Rebecca says.

Gene continues to ignore her.

'Silas,' she says. 'Please can I hold the baby for a minute?' And with that Gene turns and hands over the baby. After a few moments Rebecca says, 'She's hungry I'm just going to get her some milk.' Wyatt, who is now behind her, helps her rise. Slowly she walks out of the room as Wyatt says to Gene, 'Silas, you need to take your medicine now.' He pulls Gene up and takes her back to their room and makes her lie down while he gives her a tranquiliser to make sure she doesn't wake up again that night.'

A shaken Rebecca, clutching her granddaughter to her chest, goes to the phone and this time she calls Jonathan in the middle of the night. He arrives at midday. Together he, Wyatt and Sonny sign the paperwork to have Gene committed. Along with Jonathan, Sonny escorts his sedated wife on a commercial flight back to Montreal where they drive her to Freshwater, hoping that place will once more work a miracle on Gene.

50

After one long week Sonny returned. Rebecca thought he looked haggard, though Sonny said it felt good to be home. She and Wyatt popped out to a coffee shop so he could spend two hours in his own home alone with his children. At six o'clock they drove back to the house for dinner – spaghetti and meatballs – that Rebecca had prepared earlier. Afterwards, Sonny read to his girls and put them to bed while Rebecca and Wyatt did the dishes.

Then, when he joined them around the kitchen table, he pulled out a piece of paper and handed it to Rebecca. 'Does any of this mean anything to you? Gene rambles all the time but these things she keeps repeating.'

Rebecca read the lines out loud for Wyatt's benefit.

The iceberg. The emblem.
Bromo knows the enemy.
White is black and black is white
Ice is white and ice is black.
The head, the head, always the head.
Same with Jesus.
Cardinals are red. Cardinals are empty.
Stop Silas. Save the children.
Joel is frantic. Joel is so little.
Where is my brother?
Why is Abigail safe?
She is the adopted one.
Where is Sonny? Save Sonny. Sonny safe.

Rebecca's hands shook as she laid the paper on the table. 'Some of it has meaning.'

'Which parts?'

'Where do I start?' She paused. 'The day Samuel, and Joel disappeared we'd gone out to see a giant iceberg. I went out with Samuel first, just the two of us, then I took the girls out and later Samuel took Morton and Joel. Morton was the only one to ever return and to this day he has never told us what happened to Samuel or Joel.'

'Who is us?' asked Sonny.

'The rest of the family. I'm sure if he had, they would have told me.'

'Gene told me her father and Joel drowned. She never mentioned anything about an iceberg.' He paused. 'Though come to think of it, she did say once that seeing an iceberg was the last thing she wanted to see. I just took that as a Titanic-type fear thing she had. And I presumed that your husband and Joel died swimming, got caught in a rip or something. I didn't realise they were on a boat and that Morton was with them.'

'He was. He became mute afterwards. First time I heard him speak was at Wyatt's place about four years later.' Out of the corner of her eye, Rebecca could see Wyatt nodding in confirmation.

Sonny swore softly. 'Gene told me Morton learnt sign language to communicate with a friend, Andrew, who was deaf and she learnt too.'

'That's true. And that's how she and Morton communicated for most of their lives until Morton left home.'

Sonny pushed the paper back towards Rebecca. 'What else?'

'Stop Silas. Save the children.' She raised her eyes towards Sonny. 'We all know what that's about.'

'What about the bit about Abigail?'

Rebecca shrugged. 'I don't know. All I can think is that Gene would rather Abigail be adopted than Jonathan as she's closer to her brothers than Abigail. After Samuel's death Abigail spent two years in Toronto with her grandparents rather than move with us to Montreal. That's the only thing I can think of.'

'When she tried to kill herself with sleeping pills at seventeen, what was the reason?'

Rebecca's eyes rested on the clean kitchen sink while she took her mind back. 'She told us it was because she didn't want Morton to go away and leave her at home. She didn't know how she was going to cope without him. They were like twins speaking their own private language. And she was the only one who knew Morton was planning on going to Saskatchewan with Wyatt. She didn't raise it with Wyatt or me because she was waiting for Morton to raise it with us first. And I think she couldn't cope with that anxiety. It happened just after Andrew was killed in a car accident. Morton had good reasons for wanting to move away from Montreal and Gene knew they were good reasons, but she couldn't cope with the thought of being home alone with me and nothing much to look forward to.'

'That's what Jonathan told me,' said Sonny. 'But do you believe that, Becca? How could being at home with you be that bad?'

'In her defence, Sonny, I was not the best company at the time. I was very self-absorbed in my painting and I didn't understand that she was as desperate and downhearted as she was. I understand painful things can happen to people that make them want to end their life. Trust me, I do. I've been there. When I was eighteen I had an experience like that but the circumstances were of the most egregious and provocative kind, as you know.' Her voice trailed off. 'But with Gene she had six months of psychiatric treatment and it never revealed much. She stuck to the story about Morton and to be honest she put it behind her fairly quickly and once she returned from that trip up north with you, we all felt she was truly well again.'

'You know who knows but is not speaking?'

Rebecca's eyes darted from Sonny's to Wyatt's back to Sonny's. 'I tried to get him to talk to me once, in the early days but he wasn't forthcoming. He was just too upset so

I stopped. I always believed if he wanted me to know he would tell me.'

Wyatt reached across and grabbed Rebecca's hand. 'Maybe Becca, he doesn't have to tell you. He just has to tell Gene's doctor.'

'Exactly,' said Sonny.

Rebecca pressed her lips together. She inhaled deeply and exhaled deeply. 'I'll ask him then.' That night she put a call into Morton. She knew he hated using it but with Wyatt not there it was up to him to pick up. When she finished reading and talking he told her he would call Gene's doctor in the morning. He did more than call. He caught the train east to be with his sister.

A week later Jonathan phoned and told Rebecca this was all going to take much longer than a couple of months. 'We need a plan around how we are going to help Sonny and the girls and Gene. Abigail and I've been talking. We don't want all this to fall on your and Elin's plate. It's too much for the two of you. I know you have Wyatt and Don's help but even so. We need to spread the load.'

'I know, I know,' said Rebecca. 'But Elin maintains she's more than happy and capable of looking after them.'

'I'm sure she thinks that. But she's your age, Mom. You need to convince her to let other people help so when she has her grandkids with her she can enjoy them. We don't want to see her in an early grave because of Gene.'

'No,' Rebecca agreed.

'Abigail said she will take them for as long as you need her to. Charlie is ten now. Her kids virtually look after themselves and she said they would all be happy to help her take care of Lindsay and Shane. Annabelle and I are in the same boat. Speak to Sonny and let me know what you come up with.'

The only problem with Abigail or Jonathan taking Lindsay and Shane was that Sonny wouldn't get to see his girls. But Rebecca convinced him that he could talk to them at night and having a break for a few weeks here and there would be good for him. He came round eventually even though he said Jonathan was already doing enough for Gene without taking on their kids.

In the end they agreed Rebecca and Wyatt would look after the children for six weeks, then Elin and Don for six weeks, then Sonny's cousin, Sylvia, who had come by and offered to help out would take them for six weeks then Abigail for seven weeks with Sonny taking holidays for the fourth week to join them so he would only go three weeks without seeing his children.

51

After a few weeks Gene realised that her doctor was once again Doctor Trantham. But this time he had a second, younger doctor, Doctor Lewis, working on "her case" as they told her, as if she were a Dragnet file that they needed to solve. Bet they weren't interested in just the facts, ma'am.

'Did you come out of retirement for me?' Gene asked.

'I haven't retired yet,' Doctor Trantham smiled at her warmly behind his glasses. His hair was much shorter and thinner, and entirely grey. 'We've been talking to your brother, Morton.'

'Where's Morton?'

'He's staying in Montreal with your brother, Jonathan. He comes to chat with us when he visits you.'

'My brother Morton visits me?'

'Yes,' they told her.

'I must be asleep when he comes. Can you tell him to come at night time?'

They smiled at her but Gene was not convinced they would tell him.

'Morton's been talking to us about icebergs.'

'What icebergs?'

'The iceberg that killed your father.'

'Who said anything about an iceberg killing my father?'

'Your brother, Morton. He's very concerned about you and wanted us to know that the two of you are the only two that know of the circumstances of your father's death and your brother's disappearance.'

Doctor Lewis cleared his throat. He had a brown moustache and a mop-top hairstyle like he was one of

The Beatles. 'He explained to us that he told you about this years ago not long before you tried to commit suicide with an overdose when you were seventeen. Do you remember any of that?'

'I remember my brother should learn to keep his mouth shut.'

'Then? Now?' asked Doctor Lewis.

'Always. There are things people are better off not knowing.'

'Is that what you thought at the time?' He queried.

'I didn't want to hear it then and I don't want to hear it now.' Gene stood up and started pacing the room. She wanted to walk out the door but Doctor Lewis was sitting right in front of it blocking her escape. She looked at the window, wondering how far it was to the ground.

'Gene, you are safe in this room,' said Doctor Trantham. 'Have no fear. We will not tell anyone what we talk about. You will be okay sitting down but if you want to stand that's up to you.' He waited till she went and leant against a wall, her hands behind her back. 'What did you feel when Morton first told you what happened?'

'Horror. Helpless. For my father, for my baby brother, for Morton – that he was burdened with this for years. I wanted to take it away from him, from myself. I wanted to get rid of the story. Lose it from my head…my memory…my body. There are certain things I can't do any more, places I can't go to, things I can't see because of what Morton told me. Because of what I've done.'

'Have you made this story go away before?'

'Yes. I moved away from my family. Rarely saw them. By not seeing them, I didn't see the others – the missing ones. Slowly over the years some of the thoughts and nightmares left me and then when I hadn't seen anyone for two years I met up with Jonathan again and I knew it would be a kind of test whether they would be with me for life or not and when Jonathan came to visit me in Europe, they didn't come and I thought I had beaten them for good.'

'Where are they now?' asked Doctor Trantham.

'They are back.'

'What are they?'

'The image of a man, his brains and blood oozing out of his skull trickling all over my fingers while I try and hold his head together. The look of regret on my father's face. The image of my brother, his eyes wild and terrified trying to swim towards me. The image of a baby swirling below just out of reach. All in the same water and each time it swells it's a different colour: burgundy, blue, black, white. Which one do I save? But I can't save any of them.'

'You talk about your hands holding your father's head together but you weren't on the boat that day. It was Morton by himself. You were on land with your mother and sister.'

'Oh, I was there,' said Gene, adamant. 'I saw it all. I still see it all.'

'Who is the baby floating in the ocean?' asked Doctor Trantham.

'Samson.'

'And who is Samson?'

'I'm not sure. He's either my brother or my twin son.'

'I didn't know you had given birth to twins or a boy. When was this?'

'Just a little while ago. I gave birth to twins. A girl and a boy.'

And what happened to the boy?'

'He was drowned too.'

'Who drowned him?

Doctor Trantham is looking at her with keen interest. Doctor Lewis is watching her closely also. 'I think I must have.'

'You?'

They are quiet, then Doctor Lewis asks, 'Where were you when this happened?'

'In the boat. Always the boat.'

Then Doctor Lewis posed a question. 'Do you

309

wonder how it was that you weren't drowned along with all these people who have been?'

'All the time. I wish I had been. Then maybe I would be at peace.'

52

The week before Rebecca and Wyatt are due to leave Sonny's Jonathan calls with an update. Gene is talking to her doctors. But she's not making any sense. Events in her mind are garbled. They have her on high-grade TCA anti-depressants for people with severe depression but it doesn't seem to be having much effect. They are recommending a twelve-week course of ECT – electroconvulsive therapy.

There is a long silence over the phone. Is Rebecca screaming across that silence? She wants to. She wants to say: "Electric shocks to the brain! No! No! No! They don't even do that to animals. That's what they do to criminals on death row. Please don't let them do that to my daughter!"

'Mom?' Jonathan says, 'Are you there?'

'Yes,' she stammers. After a few more heartbeats she says, 'I'll tell Sonny and get him to call you.'

'There's one other thing you should know.'

She waits. 'Yes?' she says at last.

'Morton has broken his silence on what happened to Dad and Joel. He told me a few weeks ago. Apparently he told Gene the night Andrew died. The doctors think that was a contributing factor in her suicide. I will tell you if you want to know. I thought I would leave it to when you come back home if that's what you decide.'

'No,' says Rebecca 'I don't want to know.'

Jonathan says he thought as much. 'I think that's the right decision.'

Two days later Sonny comes to her. 'Would you mind if I asked Jonathan what happened to your husband and son? Just the barest details, so I can understand what causes Gene such distress. I will respect your wishes if you say no. I know I was not family back then.'

She looks at him wondering where this will lead and where this will end. 'You are family, Sonny,' she tells him. 'It is your call. But I don't want to know.'

When Rebecca firsts visits Gene at Freshwater it is late March. The room is centrally heated and Rebecca feels as if an invisible haze of desert air drapes over them. It is too hot and stifling. She peels off her overcoat, her scarf and her cardigan. She looks at Gene bundled up in bed, wearing a thick woolly jumper. 'Aren't you hot? Do you want me to open a window?'

'No,' she says. 'I'm cold. It feels like the world is constantly cold and dark. It feels like I'm in a glass room that doesn't get any heat. I see people but I can't touch them.'

Rebecca reaches out and grabs her daughter's hand.

'Can you feel that, Gene? I'm touching you now.'

'No,' says Gene. 'I can't feel anything,' says Gene her cold hand holding her mother's warm one.

Another time when Rebecca visits the days are warmer and longer. She brings her spring daffodils and jonquils to freshen up her room. A nurse comes and takes them away to put in a vase.

'How are you feeling?' Rebecca asks.

'I hate the food here, Mom. I don't know how they make it taste so bad but they do. It's bitter and salty. Can you bring me some food next time you come?'

'Sure, honey,' says Rebecca. 'Every time I come I'll bring you some treats. I'll get Annabelle to bring some too.'

The nurse returns and places the flowers on the trolley cupboard next to Gene's bed. When she leaves, Gene reaches over, pulls the flowers out, throws them on the floor then raises the vase of water to her lips and drains it completely.

'Here, let me fill that up again,' says Rebecca. 'There's

a jug on the other side of your bed you know.' She points to the pale blue and white plastic Tupperware jug.

'I didn't see that,' mumbles Gene.

'I'll get you one you can see.' Rebecca goes and asks if they have any clear glass jugs. They tell her they don't allow them because patients could break them and then use the glass to cut their wrists. It has happened before. It is a safety precaution.

'Okay,' says Rebecca, realising she is in a different world. 'My daughter is thirsty. She finds the food salty. Has more salt been added to her diet or something?'

'No. That's a side effect of all the treatment she's on. It affects the taste buds.'

'I see,' says Rebecca. She pauses, hesitates. 'I know you have a lot of patients and you probably do this already but can you please go to her a few times a day and make sure she drinks a few glasses of water for you. I'll look after her the days I'm here.'

The next time Rebecca visits there is a three-panelled room divider against a wall. Jonathan had brought it in hoping it would give Gene something to look at and think about. On it are tacked photographs of family members, drawings from Lindsay as well as two sets of handprints of each child and their ages below: Shane nine months. Lindsay, four years, six months.

'Shane's crawling. She's pulling herself up. She'll be walking by the time she's one year old,' Rebecca tells her. Gene nods but doesn't say anything.

53

Sonny comes to visit her and it is his face she yearns to see the most, yet it is his face that causes her so much pain. To look at its drawn state, the dark circles under his eyes, but mostly not to see his easy smile and hear his easy laugh makes Gene feel sorry for Sonny Marlow, sorry that he ever had the rotten misfortune of meeting Gene Dalton. How she wishes she hadn't gone north that summer with her brother.

But he is good this man of hers. He puts on a brave act. Gene apologises for everything.

He says the past is the past. 'Let's just focus on getting you well. Getting you out of here and getting you home.'

She asks him to come and lie down behind her and hug her. That way she won't have to look at his broken eyes.

'Gene,' he whispers, 'Tell me you don't want to end your life. Tell me you don't want to go down that path again.'

'I don't want to end it, Sonny. But I don't know if I want to live it either.' They clutch each other's hands as he kisses her nape and together they wet the pillow with their tears.

She doesn't remember much about icebergs any more. The cause isn't the thing, she tells her doctors. It's the effect that she's stuck with. 'When I was five I lost my father and my baby brother, Joel. At the same time I lost my next brother up, Morton. Even though we are close he was never the same again. Then the losses continued with his friend, Andrew, which resulted in Morton moving half a country away. And this year I lost my eldest brother. He's not my brother. He is adopted. Every man I have ever loved I end up losing. And the one I fear for the most is my husband, Sonny. I fear I will lose him too.'

'What about your children? Do you have fears around them?'

'Yes. If I love them, I will lose them.'

'Okay let's look at this more closely. At what you haven't lost. You haven't lost your mother. You haven't lost your sister. You haven't lost your brother, Jonathan, even though he is adopted. You haven't lost your brother, Morton. He has chosen his path in life. You haven't lost your husband and you haven't lost your children. You might be scared of losing them all but you haven't lost them yet and there are no reasons why you should lose them.'

One day Gene looks up at the wall divider and it is full of photographs of all the people in her life still living. The people she hasn't lost...yet. And she knows one thing. It's not the drugs making her sick. It's the fear and anxiety she feels over what might happen to them. It's almost as if she lives her life finding out they have all just died. Every day, the same feeling. She dreads bedtime. Sleep eludes her and in this building where they keep her there's no escaping outside. So many doors are locked. And there are so many guards and sisters on duty. Near daybreak sleep manages to track her down and when she wakes, she wishes she hadn't. Straightaway she feels nauseous again when in fact what she should feel is hunger.

One day when her mother is visiting Gene asks her, 'Why did you tell me that about Jonathan?'

Her mother doesn't answer immediately. After a little while she says, 'Because I couldn't lie to you about him. When you pointed out I had forgotten him I thought you must have forgotten he was adopted. I was just trying to set the record straight. But you know it's not important. I lost Samson when he was three days old and I met Jonathan in Toronto three weeks later when he was three days old. From the earliest of days I had a special bond with him. Everyone knew it. He knew it. That's why on her deathbed his mother said she wanted me to be the mother of her son. And of course I wanted to. It was as if it was ordained.'

'I've decided he is my brother. He's not adopted. You never told me that. And I never heard it. Because I want him to be the brother I have always loved and held in such high esteem.'

'As you should. He has not done a thing to lose your love and respect. I can't imagine him ever doing anything to upset you.'

Gene asks her mother why she thinks she lost three of her boys.

Once again she takes her time in answering. 'I don't know if there is a reason why. I don't think I will never know. After I lost your father and Joel I used to think it was because God was a jealous god and he was pure male. It's all there in the book of Genesis in the Garden of Eden. He blamed Eve. Think about it. The snake tempted Eve. She didn't have to accept and then having tasted the forbidden fruit, she didn't have to share it with Adam. The buck stops with her and so God banished them from the Garden and he made it difficult for her to have children, but more than that I felt he was an angry God and a jealous God. And when he says, 'thou shalt have no other gods before me', what he is saying is thou shalt have no other men before me – that I shall be revered above all others. And so what he has done to me, and maybe my mother? Take away from us the men we love. Good men, innocent young boys. And I could never accept that as an act of a loving God. That was the mark of an evil one, a selfish one. I have struggled in my faith because I can't abide with this someone, somebody else, some thing always being first. It's give and take in my book, but in his, I felt it was all take…that was my view on the world for the first few years after your father died. Until I turned the corner. Until I realised he had not taken everything. Until I accepted that perhaps I had been given more than most and I needed to be grateful for what was left and what was still to come in my life.'

'Well at least you had Jonathan.'

'I had Jonathan. I had you and Abigail but I didn't have Morton, not then.'

'At least he survived.'

'You don't think God tried to get to him. Or something else?'

Gene hangs her head. Something had gotten to her brother. In all her life she had never known him to have a girlfriend or a close friend after he lost Andrew. Perhaps Wyatt's nephew, Paul, was his only friend. If she was good at keeping her distance from people, Morton's abilities were on par if not even more adept.'

'Did Aunty Esther or Aunty Rachel lose any children?'

'Not that I know of.'

'What about Grandma Crowe?'

'What I know of my mother is she had a child that was stillborn, a baby that came early after she had a nasty fall and then two boys who drowned. All up she had seven children and only the girls survived.'

'What about her siblings? Did any of them die at a young age?'

'I don't know, Gene. I could ask if you want me to.'

'No, it doesn't matter. It's not important.'

But it was. The next time her mother came to visit, Gene said, 'I'm like you. Your mother was cursed. You are cursed. And I am cursed.'

'Do you really believe that?'

'Absolutely.' It was a force outside her control. How did she have any hope of beating it? She will bring nothing but heartache and bad luck to her husband and children. Like her mother did before her.

Sonny comes to visit again, says he is staying in Montreal with Jonathan and Annabelle and this time he's brought the girls east with him. Tells her they just celebrated Shane's first birthday. He pins a photograph of a little girl sitting on someone's lap, her eyes looking at a cake covered in hundreds and thousands and pink and blue icing. 'Annabelle made the cake,' he tells her.

'What do you tell Lindsay about me?' Gene asks.

'I tell her Mommy's not well. She's in a special hospital where children can't visit her. I tell her that her Mom will come home again when she's well. That she can do drawings for me to give to her Mom and maybe one day her mother will write back to her. Do you want to do that, Gene? Do you want to write Lindsay a short letter, a little "hello, I'm thinking of you?" Do you want to write on a birthday card for Shane?'

'She won't be able to read it.'

'Well, what about something for Lindsay?'

'Maybe one day.'

54

Over the weeks and months Rebecca looks at Sonny and thinks: You are one amazing man. His determination, his energy, his spirit around his children fills her with pride and love. The way he waltzes with his girls and sings *Can't help falling in love*. He is such a wonderful father. She tells him he is doing a great job.

'We will not go down in a blaze of melancholy,' he replies.

But one day after he returns from seeing Gene and talking to her doctors he is upset and full of self-blame. 'I didn't see it before. But I see it now. I gave Morton a promise to look after his sister and I didn't. I am responsible for the mess she's in. She couldn't handle the strain of my flying. I know. She tried to tell me but I didn't want to hear it. I should have been there for her. I should have stopped flying and become a mechanic or a farmer working outside on the land so she could keep her watchful eye on me and I could have joined her for each and every meal.'

'The hell you should have,' says Jonathan. 'That would have eaten away at your soul, faster than everything that's eating away at Gene's. You were meant to fly, Sonny, and we all know that. Even Gene if she were honest and compos mentis enough to admit it.'

'I can go back to flying on the weekends, just as part of the club. I don't need to fly every day.'

'Sonny, you were born to fly, like I was born to be a doctor. At this point in time you have to do what's right for yourself and your daughters. When Gene is well enough to join you again, then you can talk about what changes you might want to make. But we don't want to see you living on a diet of guilt. For some strange reason Gene's already indulging herself at that banquet.'

'That's right, Sonny,' Rebecca adds. 'Don't blame yourself for where Gene's at. We don't blame you. If we blame anyone, it's ourselves – for not looking harder last time, for missing the signs.'

'It's not about blame. It's about healing,' Jonathan says, and that was the last word on the subject.

Some days Rebecca would go with Sonny to visit Gene. She would observe him trying to nurture a new spark of life in her. It would break her heart to see Gene not respond. God knows what it was doing to him. 'I'm going to take a walk,' she would say. 'Give you two some time to yourselves.'

One night at home, Sonny tells her, 'Some days I wish she would get angry at me or upset, throw something at me even. Anything would be better than her being petrified and indifferent all the time.' Rebecca nods in agreement. Anything would.

But one day she arrives and Gene is no longer in her room. She is dressed and in the common room playing cards with other patients, her eyes, alive. 'Mom,' she calls out when Rebecca walks into the room, 'Do you want to play 500 with us?'

The next time Rebecca visits, Gene is back to staring out the window, in her nightie, unkempt and uncaring about her physical appearance. Her eyes flash their demented state. And Rebecca feels her own body flag at the sight of her…so mercurial.

It takes over a year before Gene is ready to move out of the main building into one of the houses. Several months later she announces she would like to have a trial period away from Freshwater. She'd like to go and be with Morton and see how she handles being out in the world again.

They want to encourage her in this yet at the same time they worry she is not ready. More than that, they worry that far away from everyone's watchful eye, she might summon the energy and inventiveness to do something drastic, to commit the unspeakable. They are warned that when patients are on their way back up you have to watch them the most. Gene was standing at the window of vulnerability.

Rebecca has weeks of nights being on edge; how she was when she found Gene kneeling at the bathtub on the verge of drowning Shane. She has weeks of vicariously living and breathing Morton's strain, weeks of feeling Sonny's pain.

He's hurt that Gene did not elect to come back home to him. He tells Rebecca he was prepared to move the girls to Sylvia's or his mother's, for however long it took, to let Gene ease herself gently back into their world.

'You know why she's gone to Morton's place, don't you?' Rebecca says to him. 'It's because it's easier for her. She feels less of a failure in front of Morton's eyes. Less pressure. She feels a failure in front of her children, in front of you. Don't take it personally, Sonny. It's not that she doesn't love you enough. It's because she loves you so much, that she can't face you.'

Rebecca hopes that Gene being around Morton and his huskies will heal her in a way that Wyatt's huskies healed Morton. She hopes many things.

55

At Wyatt's place – now Wyatt and Morton's place – Gene became Morton's twin, shadowing him, doing almost everything with him.

He said to her: 'Don't you want to rest?'

'Morton, I know sleep's important to my recovery, I know I'm not to get too tired, but honestly I've spent so many months resting I feel I've atrophied. I want to move. I want to fall asleep from physical exertion rather than medicate myself to escape my own mental bleariness.'

She worked with Paul and Wyatt out in the field, driving the tractor. She loved the sun on her skin, she couldn't remember the last time she spent so much time outdoors. She'd go with him in the pick-up when he went to town to get supplies. They'd go fishing on a lake. They'd go riding on the old push bikes that their mother and Wyatt rode all those years ago, letting the dogs pull them along like Sooty and Flint did back in their Montreal days.

Sometimes, Gene would laugh with the thrill of it and that was a good feeling: the wind in her hair, on her face, the steady speed, the slobbering happiness of the huskies – the simple innocence of it all. She needed to laugh more. It seemed such a foreign emotion. She helped Morton tend the veggie garden, which he'd mastered quite well, recalling how he used to help Grandpa Dalton, particularly in those months after their father was lost to them. They cooked dinner together. They went to the occasional movie; neither of them was that interested in the television, preferring to listen to the radio, read or do crosswords in the evenings.

Gene flicked through Wyatt's Canadian Medical Association Journals. She picked up her personal journal. Doctor Trantham suggested she take note of all the things she felt capable of doing, all the things she was grateful for. There was so much she wanted to say about Sonny but she feared putting those thoughts to paper, as if, like her mother, she was tempting fate, tempting God, by drawing attention to what a rare man he was. But she thought those thoughts while she asked herself: what would it take for me to be able to go back to Winnipeg and be his wife again, be a mother again? She was hopeful about being his wife. She thought she could do that. Being a mother, she didn't know if she were up to that yet. Would she ever be? She phoned him occasionally and Jonathan too. They phoned as well from time to time as did her Mom and Abigail and Elin. Not too often, not too regularly. She asked them to give her some space and they honoured her request.

One night in one of the medical magazines she came across an article on birth control and she tried to not hide from her personal experience: that the most terrifying thing about being a mother was when Shane was so young and helpless, so dependent and vulnerable. I thought I was doing okay with Lindsay, she thought, but when Shane came along I couldn't cope with the two of them. I don't think I could cope with more children.

She read on with interest about the oral contraceptive pill but afterwards she thought: I don't want to be taking more pills. I've taken enough for a lifetime and they say I will have to take anti-depressants till the day I die. Later she came to a section on a permanent procedure called a tubectomy – female sterilisation. That's it, she thought. It would give her the surety she needed...but how could she ever raise that with Sonny?

When her mother phoned a few days later, she asked to speak to Wyatt. They had a very long conversation, a very good conversation, and a very comfortable conversation. He was completely non judgmental. She loved that about him. Yes, he knew someone in Regina who did such operations. Yes, he thought it would be a good idea for her to go and talk to the doctor at least. He would place a call.

Morton took her to the appointment. When she came out, he asked her how it went.

'It went well. I think I want to go through with it.'

'What will Sonny think?'

She didn't want to think about what Sonny would think. She knew. 'Ah, Morton, I don't really want to tell him. This could be our secret.'

'You don't think your surgery scars will give it away?'

Gene chewed her lip.

'I just think, Morton, that sometimes the fewer people know things the better.'

'You can't not tell him, Gene. He's your husband. You can't not talk about it with him.'

She let out a large sigh. 'I know.' She bit her lip. ' I just don't know how. He always wanted to have a big family.'

'Do you think that's what he wants now?'

'I don't know, but if I go through with this I'll be making sure he never has a big family.'

'Just talk to him, Gene.'

She rang the doctor back the next day and booked herself in for the surgery in three weeks time. A week later, Morton asked, 'Have you spoken to Sonny yet?'

'No,' she replied.

'Do you intend to?'

'Yes, I intend to. I'm just not ready yet. I thought I might send him a letter. I've made a few starts on it.'

'Gene, you're running out of time. Do you want me to call him and talk to him about it?'

'No!' she snapped. A few moments later she said, 'I can't imagine you would enjoy doing that.'

'You're right I wouldn't.' He paused. 'What about Wyatt then?'

She inhaled. She exhaled. 'It'll be fine, Morton.'

Her brother didn't bring it up anymore. She knew he

wouldn't. He was so accepting. That's what she loved about him, why she had come there in the first place. But she also knew she loved Sonny and even though she was being purely selfish with this decision she knew she could not go through with it until she had talked to him about it. Two nights before the operation, she phoned him.

'Hi, Sonny, it's me.'

'How're you doing, Gene? Morton looking after you okay? I miss you. We all do.'

'I miss you too. Did you fly today?'

'Yes, went to the end of Lake Winnipeg.'

'How was that?'

'Eight people one way, six the other. Pretty straight-forward. A storm chased us home, but I landed before it arrived.'

'Where are the girls at the moment?'

'They're here actually. They've been with Sylvia for a few weeks. I picked them up tonight. Your mother and Wyatt will be arriving tomorrow as well. They're going to stay for a few weeks then they're hoping to come your way after that.'

Gene smiled into the phone. Even though she hadn't been able to call Sonny till now she had rung Wyatt and her mother telling them of her plans and asking if they could go spend some time with Sonny, to help him come to terms with everything if needs be.

'Please thank Sylvia for me.'

'Will do.'

'Sonny, I've been doing a lot of thinking, mostly about coming home to you, easing into things perhaps with the girls.'

'Great!' said Sonny, 'We can ease all you like.'

'Working with Doctor Trantham I've had to look inside myself and understand what I need to do to make that work.'

'Aha.'

'For good.'

'Yep.'

'And I think I've got some answers.'

'Okay.'

'See, I think in the beginning I was doing okay as a wife.'

'Gene, you were doing more than okay. Remember what we had?'

'Some of it, yes. After all this treatment, Sonny, there are some blanks.'

'Sure, I understand.'

Gene could faintly hear his breathing down the line. 'And I think I did okay with Lindsay in the early days.'

'That you did.'

'But when Shane came along, it was all too much.' Gene hated admitting that. Hated how pathetic it sounded. That she, an intelligent woman who had worked for the United Nations, participated in and held her own in committees attended by people from all over the world, interviewed delegates, prepared papers and recommendations, worked on some massive projects with some incredible deadlines, could not manage the daily schedules of a baby and a toddler. What was wrong with her! Even after all this time, it took all her might not to hang up on Sonny in abject mortification and self-disgust.

'I don't think I helped as much as I could have.'

'Sonny, it wasn't you. It wasn't that really.'

'So how do you feel about the girls now?'

'Tentative. Quietly hopeful that one day I will be a good mother to them. That we can all go bike riding together, maybe have a pet dog or two.'

'That all sounds promising.'

'Yep, it does.' Gene took a deep breath. She had to get it out. 'But here's the thing, Sonny. I don't think I can cope with any more babies – I'm open to trying sex again, I hope we can get that part of our life back – but I don't want to go through this hell again – and I don't think I could enjoy having sex with you while I feared I might get pregnant.' She paused. 'You know I could never have an abortion.'

Silence.

'Sonny, are you there?'

'Yes, I'm here.' A few moments later he said, 'Well, we could use rubbers. You could go on the pill. There are ways to manage things.'

'I know but they all carry some risk. I don't want to be popping any more pills and I'm sure you don't want to use a rubber for the rest of your life. It would wear thin pretty quickly.' She laughed lightly at her own joke.

'That it would,' said Sonny dryly. 'But seriously, Gene, in a few years when you're back on your feet and the kids are at school you might have a change of heart.'

'I'm sorry, Sonny. I don't think so. I want a permanent solution.' She paused and waited. 'I feel very strongly about this.'

He left out a deep sigh. 'I know. And I understand why you feel that given all you've been through. We can talk about this some more when you come back home. We don't need to make a decision on it right now.'

'Well that's just the thing…I wanted to have this all sorted before I come home.' She took a deep breath. Exhaling she said, 'I've booked in to have an operation the day after tomorrow.'

'For crying out loud, Gene!'

It was the first time he had ever gone close to swearing at her. She deserved it. She deserved far worse.

'Don't you think we should have talked about this a little bit more before now?'

'Well, that's what we're doing now.'

'How would this talking have worked if I were away on an overnighter?'

'I would have called you tomorrow night. That's why I phoned tonight.'

'Gene!' he exclaimed. 'You're impossible at times. Impossible!'

'I know.' She waited a little to give him some time to let off a bit steam. 'I'm sorry. I'm so terribly sorry.' She genuinely was, but she could see no other way out. 'Look, you may not have a tribe of kids, but you've got two. That's better than none. That's better than one. The girls have each other. They won't be alone.' But here it came. She took another deep breath. 'Sonny, if your having more kids is a deal breaker, then I understand, and I will step aside. I've been a poor excuse for a mother and a poor excuse for a wife and if you would rather take your chances on someone else, I completely understand and completely absolve you.'

'Don't carry on like that.'

'I'm not carrying on. I know what a big sacrifice this is for you to give up what you most want. And I'm telling you that I understand that, and I am prepared to give up the second thing I most want – because if I'm honest with you, the thing I most want before you is my health back – but after that, I'm prepared to give you up if you think you will be happier with another woman and more children, or if having a bigger family is something you absolutely need in your life.'

'Gene, if you are being honest, don't you think being happy with yourself, and being with me – being happy with me – is part of you getting your health back?'

'Yes,' she sighed. Then some moments later she said, 'However, Sonny, I don't want my mental health and my happiness to be dependent on you. I want to find it from within somehow.'

'I support you in that wholeheartedly. But suppose I took your offer seriously… whether I would be happier with another woman is a big if.'

'I know.'

'Would you be happier with another man?'

'No,' she whispered, the lump in her throat so close to the top. 'I was not thinking of making a life with any other man.'

'What would happen to Lindsay and Shane if I were to make my life with another woman. Where would they live?'

She hadn't expected him to call her bluff. But it wasn't

328

a bluff. This wasn't a game. 'They could live with you. I would like to see them from time to time.' She paused. 'Is that what you want to do?'

'I don't think so.' After a pause he said, 'What about fostering one or two Rosies? Do you think you might be up to that down the track?'

'If they were like Rosie that wouldn't be hard.' She waited to see if he had anything else to add. Then she said, 'So, Sonny, are you okay with this procedure?'

He exhaled. 'Gene, if I'm honest, no. It's been hoisted on me! Do I think that perhaps it is the right thing for you – yes… the right thing for us – maybe…the right thing for me – who knows? I'd like some more time to think about that, that's for bloody sure. I feel I'm being shafted here.'

'I'd like to get well, Sonny. I'd like to put the pieces together that are going to make it easier for me to come home and make home work. I'd like to do that sooner rather than later. I'm sure you'd like that to happen soon rather than later too. Yes?'

Sonny let out an exasperated sigh. 'What can I say?'

He sounded so defeated. Part of her wished she could ease his burden. Part of her wished he would say: 'Okay, Gene, go ahead, this is for the best. I support you in this.' But he had had no time to come to terms with this – and that was all her doing. It was unrealistic to expect his support.

'Where are you having this operation?' he asked.

She took that as his tacit approval. There could be no going back for her, for him. 'Regina General Hospital. I'm being admitted at 8 am on Thursday morning. Hopefully a standard procedure.'

'I hope so,' he said. 'I'll talk to you when you come out then.'

'I'll ask Morton to call you. Tell you how things went.'

'Thanks.' Seconds later he said, 'Gene. I love you! Even though sometimes it's really hard.'

'I know, Sonny. Thank you. I love you too.' Her voice

broke on her last words. She had to hang up the phone before she turned into a blubbering mess. Even then she was one.

Two days later when she came to in her white hospital bed, in a ward she shared with only one other woman, Sonny was there – with flowers, but without a smile.

'I hadn't expected to see you,' she said, shaking her head lightly to dispel her grogginess.

'There's got to be some perks to being a pilot.'

She smiled wearily at him, but then her smile faltered. 'Oh, Sonny, I'm sorry.'

'Me too,' his eyes watering for what might have been. He laid his arm across her chest, pressed his face into her neck; the two of them sharing the same ragged breath. They stayed that way for a long time, till Gene faded off to sleep.

After three months away from Freshwater Gene decided she needed to return. Her compunction over having the tubal ligation operation, while perhaps helping her in the long term, had dinted her spirits. She asked for another round of ECT. She told her family: I wanted to see if I was strong enough, and I was for a while.

But her words were the most encouraging words Gene had spoken in over two years. For in her admission they knew she had started down the road of taking care of herself.

The childcare routine they established in February 1966 was now a regular part of everyone's life. When Lindsay started school, Abigail left her family for six weeks and came to stay with Sonny to help. They shuffled things around so that Abby's next block fell in the school holidays; in that way Lindsay and Shane would join her family each summer holiday. Those six weeks in every six months were a normal part of life for everyone. Gene was largely oblivious to the machinations that happened outside Freshwater that kept her family ticking over.

When Rebecca visited Gene she saw the handprints of her granddaughters becoming progressively larger and multi-dimensional on the panel. Each time Gene received a new print she would cut around them with small children's scissors and paste the previous sets of hands on top of the latest set to show how much the girls had grown over time. Down the side were the numbers one to eight and a corresponding date and age for every three-month period.

56

Sonny whispers to her, 'Gene, remember our honeymoon? Remember Lake O'Hara? Get well and we'll go there again with the girls.'

'I'm starting to get well,' she tells him, 'I'm starting to feel better.' And it's true she does feel stronger.

'Sonny, I want to tell you, you are a good man, a good husband, a good father to our children.' He is with her again. She gets to say out loud the words she's been practising.

'Thank you.' He waits. 'Is there more? Is there a but?'

'I know you will have looked after the girls better than I could have possibly managed. Although I am a woman, I know you are more capable than I when it comes to being there for our children. Now that I am coming back to myself, I see this. I want you to know how reassuring that is. How implicitly I trust you with the girls. I wish I could be you. Some days I don't know if I can even be half of you.'

'Gene, remember Rosie? Remember how she turned that trip of hers down south to the sanatorium into an adventure. She learnt English for a start. Learnt to read and write. I suspect she made dozens of friends. And even when she got to Moose Factory and hitched that ride with us, she was still months away from seeing her family again but she didn't let it get her down. She had no regrets. We all found her adorable. She was our morning sunshine. And you may say that's just her personality. But I think it's more than that. It was her. She simply did what she could, where she was with what she had. And that's all I ask of you when you come home. You don't have to be perfect in anything. Just do your best and we will be pleased with that. Just be your happiest and you'll get happier. Love your children and they will love you in return and that will make a world of difference to you.'

'I don't know if I'll ever be one hundred percent well, Sonny, but I feel better for now. Can you live with me not being one hundred percent?'

'I can live with you being your best, which is not you being perfect. It is you trying every day in little ways to stay well.'

Her mother comes to visit and expresses surprise that she's started taking down the photographs and the girls' paintings.

'I'm getting better,' she tells her and smiles for her benefit, trying to warm her eyes to the idea. 'I'm preparing to leave. I've started packing.'

'Well done, Gene.' Her mother gives her a hug before launching into her latest news – Jonathan's news, well actually his son, Matthew's, news. She obviously can't wait to tell her. After finishing high school and spending a year trying to get into a professional hockey team Matthew had a change of heart and decided to go to McGill and become a doctor, hoping one day to be a medical advisor to a hockey team.

'He's been accepted, Gene! He will be the fifth generation of Dalton men to do medicine at McGill! The University has told us we are in their record books! Isn't that exciting? Your father would be so proud. The Dalton name will live on forevermore at McGill.'

'Good for them,' says Gene flatly, trying to think of what that means for her, who was once a Dalton but is no more, and is now a Marlow, a name which will be no more.

That thought sends her into a mild panic. One step forward, two steps backward.

'Gene, it wouldn't hurt for you to be a little excited, would it?' chides her mother. 'Wyatt was thrilled.'

She tells whoever visits she misses music.

'What happened to your singing?' Jonathan asks. 'I hear you've been spending time with the sisters in the chapel. Are you singing in there? Please tell me yes. I don't want to hear you've been crying,' he jokes. 'Join the choir and invite us to hear you sing on your last Sunday here like how you sang farewell to Rosie.'

She does spend time with a certain sister in the chapel. Sister Ursula. She asks, 'If you can't change something, does freedom and peace of mind, come from accepting it? Should you keep fighting to change something or put your energies into putting it behind you? Moving forward?'

'Yes,' the Sister says, 'Acceptance is the key. And forgiveness. Strangely often the person you have to forgive the most is yourself – for how you've treated others, for how you've treated yourself. I've talked to many people who have sat where you're sitting and what seems to happen for many people is their minds get stuck on replaying certain events over and over again, and what people in your situation often do is they think everyone else's mind is working the same way, playing over those same scenes and events in their heads. Therein lies people's shame, their incapacity to move forward. But the thing is other people have long forgotten and forgiven you your transgressions. And it's just a matter of asking God to hold your hand while we forgive those people, while we forgive ourselves and ask for God's eternal forgiveness and blessing on our life.'

She asks Sonny to bring her a recent photograph of the girls. She wants to see them.

And when he brings it she is sadder than ever. Two steps forward, one step backwards.

She looks at what they are wearing and the simple beauty of her daughters ruptures a part of her heart. The two of them are wearing matching dresses. Sonny tells her Elin made them for the girls. One is white with tiny blue flowers; the other is white with tiny green flowers.

'Looking at this photograph I can imagine a picture of you with one girl on each knee,' Gene says through her tears as she squeezes Sonny's hand and lets him pull her head towards him and kiss it.

'I thought if I gave you a photo like that you would know how much you were missing out. You might see them as my girls rather than your girls or our girls.'

'Do you have one of you and the girls together?'

'Yes,' he whispers.

'Can you send me a copy of that when you go home please? I'd like that one most of all. How old are they now?'

He tells her. She writes it down in her journal, the journal she has worked really hard to keep – under lock and key – but she has kept it, nonetheless. She writes the date:

30 May 1969. Sonny came today and brought a photo of the girls. Lindsay is six years and six months. Shane is two years and ten months.

She tells her family she has set a goal to be well enough to leave Freshwater by her thirty-sixth birthday at the end of August. Sonny asks would she like to come home in time for Shane's third birthday at the end of July.

'If I'm up to it I will,' she says. 'But I can't promise. Please don't make any plans. No party or anything.'

She asks Sonny to bring her her bank savings passbook next time he comes, or perhaps he could post it to Jonathan. She says she wants to buy gifts for some of the staff who've been so wonderful to her.

'I'll give you the money right now.' He pulls out his wallet.

'No! I need to do this myself. I need to pay for it with my own money. You've paid enough. All this treatment.'

'Everyone has pitched in, Gene.'

Next time she sees Jonathan she says, 'I've asked Sonny to send me my savings passbook but I think he's forgotten. Can I borrow some money so I can buy some presents for a few people around here?' Her brother hands over fifty dollars. She catches the bus to Lachute by herself, walks around town, does her shopping, has lunch and catches the bus back: small and gradual steps. She is feeling stronger, more sure of herself.

When Sonny comes next he tells her he wants to take her away for just a few days by herself, just the two of them, before they go home. He suggests going back to the Lodge at Lake Nipissing. Maybe they can start over again.

She tells him that sounds lovely. She says she wants to catch the bus to Montreal by herself and walk to Jonathan's place. Sonny tells her he'll meet her at the station. She tells him she can walk the three kilometres by herself. She needs to do this.

'Annabelle is going to make poutine for your homecoming dinner,' he says.

Gene smiles. 'She better make a double batch. I'll eat one whole dish myself.'

He tells her he has arranged for his mother and Sylvia to take the girls in the afternoons so when she gets back to Winnipeg she can ease back into motherhood.

'Sonny,' she says to him, 'you are the most thoughtful husband.'

'I'm trying to be more thoughtful,' he replies.

Her second last night at Freshwater, she asks Sonny to stay with her, to sleep in the same bed, to hold her and hug her. She even kisses him and lets herself surrender to all that she feels for him. She cries and tells him she is sorry, that she loves him. Over and over she sobs out her lament.

'Sonny, do you forgive me for my past? Do you forgive me for all I've put you through?'

He tells her yes and he is earnest. She can see it in his eyes; she can hear it in his voice.

'Will you forgive me my future?'

'Will you forgive me mine?' he asks in return.

It's like another night they've shared in another bed but this time they sleep in a single and they don't have sex.

The next morning as he is stroking her hair he says, 'Gene, are you sure you're ready to come home?'

'Yes,' she smiles wanly. 'I'm ready to leave. I just wanted to leave all my tears here, not take them forward in to my new life.'

'All right then.'

He takes most of her belongings, books, photographs and drawings with him and when she kisses him goodbye, when she presses her head next to his she says, 'Sonny, please remember, through all this, through everything I've been through, everything I've put you through, even though at times I am impossible, which I am, even though we still may have some rough days ahead, please remember I love you. Please never forget that.'

'I know Gene, I do Gene,' he says, as he strokes her cheek in farewell. 'See you tomorrow.'

In her diary she writes out the words to Edith' Piaf's *Non, Je Ne Regrette Rien* completely in French. And then in English the words. *Gene it starts with you. It starts today.*

To not look back. To have no regrets. If she could, she would make that her motto for life. In that one thing, Sonny would be proud of her.

Hiding Out

Vancouver, Canada, July 1969

57

When Gene had not turned up to Jonathan's place by four pm, Sonny was uneasy. He told Annabelle, 'to hell with it,' he was going to go to the bus station. 'Can I borrow your car?'

Fifteen minutes later he spoke to the customer service lady behind the bookings desk. 'Had the bus from Saint-Placide arrived on schedule?'

She picked up her clipboard and looked down the page. 'Yes it did,' she said. 'Got in at one twenty five.' She eyed Sonny up and down.

'Well, did you see a woman, yay high,' he indicated with his hands, 'with shoulder-length, light brown hair, intense blue green eyes, carrying a small duffle bag, step off the bus?'

'I'm sorry, mister, I didn't. That doesn't mean she didn't arrive. Hundreds of people step off buses here every day and I hardly notice them.'

He wrote out his name and telephone number at Jonathan and Annabelle's, along with a description of Gene and her name. He asked the lady to call if she saw someone that fitted that description. She assured him she would. He went back to Annabelle's hoping Gene would have turned up but as he drove he had a corrosive feeling in his gut that that was not the case.

He called Rebecca. She told him she would go immediately to the Notre Dame Cathedral and see if Gene was there. It was a place they used to go to when they were young. It had significance, a place of celebration but also a type of memorial. She would ring Sonny when she got back. Annabelle took the car and drove up to Mont Royal Park. She remembered Gene telling her she used to go there years ago with Morton and the dogs.

While she was out, Sonny phoned Freshwater to see what he could uncover. The sister on duty told him: 'I'm sorry you have the date wrong. She didn't leave today. She left yesterday. I know that for a fact because I helped move another woman into her room yesterday afternoon.'

'Are you sure?' Sonny asked, 'because the information we have is that she was leaving today.'

'Who told you that?' the sister asked.

Sonny had to stop and think about that. Where did the information come from? Was it only Gene? 'Can you please check your discharge records and tell me what they say. I'm happy to wait.'

After ten minutes she picked up the phone. 'Mr. Marlow, I'm terribly sorry but at the moment we can't find her discharge records. There is no signature or document in our files from her doctor or the patient. I'm sure it's just a matter of Doctor Trantham or Doctor Lewis not handing over the paperwork. May I take your number and phone you back with the information you are seeking.'

He gave her the number, but in the space of that ten-minute wait he knew it was a lost cause. His wife could be anywhere. She could be floating with the swift running water of the St Lawrence Seaway. She could be at the bottom of Lac des Deux Montagnes. She could be halfway to James Bay, or on her way to Lumsden, Saskatchewan. The possibilities were endless. What was clear was she had meant to deceive him. She had meant to deceive Jonathan and everyone. What wasn't clear was what were her plans beyond that? Had she lulled them into a false sense of optimism? Was she dead already? Did she want to go away and truly get well by herself, away from their hopeful eyes? Or did she simply want to vanish from all of their lives and put this completely behind her? Nothing about it made sense. The last time he had seen Gene she had moved him with her sincerity and her remorse and her loving. Was that an act? Or was she saying goodbye in the only way she knew how?

Jonathan came home from work. Rebecca came over as well. Annabelle sent their four children upstairs while the adults stared at the centre of the table in silence, trying to comprehend what Gene had done. Mostly they felt numb. Oddly, none of them wanted to fight it. They would do nothing to track her down. If she was running away, they wanted to let her run in peace. But after talking things through they decided if she had decided to end her life, they would want to know about it. In the end Jonathan and Sonny went and filed a missing person's report. They stressed they didn't want it broadcast as an emergency bulletin. They only wanted it disseminated in the event the police needed to identify a woman or a body. In that case they would like to be informed. All they knew was Gene would either turn up or she wouldn't. She would either write or she wouldn't. They knew zip.

58

One would have thought a woman who set out to live her life with no regrets would have been more stoic about it but, in those first forty-eight hours after leaving Freshwater, Gene cried more than she had ever cried in her whole life.

She cried over her family – her mother, Wyatt, her siblings. She cried for herself and the bad card she had been dealt in life. There were flashes when she was angry at the world, angry for being born to her mother, wishing she could have been born to someone else.

But mostly she cried over Sonny and Lindsay and Shane. Of knowing she wouldn't see her girls grow up. Of knowing she was walking away from the one man who loved her deeply, whom she loved deeply, of an experience she knew would never come again in her lifetime. Days earlier she had packed their photos away because she couldn't bear to look at their faces – at what she was leaving behind. The only thing that kept her from jumping off that bus and going back was her willpower and the voice inside her that said: this is for the best. This is how you love someone by setting them free. This is what Mary did when Jesus ascended to heaven. This way their lives will be whole. I am the poison apple that has descended from the poisonous tree and I will spoil their lives if I am in it. Taint it. Poison it. Destroy it. Something will happen to one or more of them. And they deserve better than that. They deserve the best of life and I hope one day they will find it.

On the third day of that bus journey that took her right across the country from Vaudreuil to Vancouver, she started to enjoy the scenery and part of her felt good about the decision to head west to British Columbia. All of Sonny's whisperings had reminded her of B.C. and how beautiful it had been. Maybe somewhere in that province she could make a new life for herself. She had travelled in camouflage after stealing a full nun's habit from Sister Ursula. She felt bad about that, but perhaps the good sister would reason it had gone to a worthy cause.

In Vancouver Gene found a phone booth, flipped open a phonebook and looked through the church listings. When her eyes read the Sisters of the Child Jesus in North Vancouver she made her decision. She asked a passerby for directions and caught a local bus.

Through a peeling wrought iron fence she could see two sisters pruning plants in a garden. She walked up to the gate and called out to them. One came over. Gene introduced herself and said she had travelled from Quebec and would like to join their order. Sister Marielle took her inside to the main building, sat her down and said she would go and speak to the mother superior.

Before Sister Eugenia, the mother superior, invited her into her office she asked her would she like a cup of tea. 'Yes,' Gene replied. 'I'd like that very much.'

'Which order do you come from?' she asked. She was a small woman with mossy green eyes and rivulets of broken capillaries across her cheeks.

'I'm not from any particular order,' said Gene. 'Though I'm wearing the habit of the Grey Nuns.'

The woman's head seemed to freeze with that admission.

'You best wait till the tea arrives before you tell me your story,' she said. 'How long have you been in Vancouver for?'

'Oh. About two hours,' Gene smiled.

Underneath her black gown Sister Eugenia's shoulders shook. She must have thought that rather funny.

Tea arrived along with oat biscuits. She offered one to Gene.

'Perhaps later,' Gene replied. She was hungry but she needed to get through her story first and plea if she had to. 'When I was eighteen years old I wanted to be a nun but my mother wouldn't let me,' Gene explained. 'I did three years of Enquiry in Montreal whilst I studied history and geography at McGill University. After my degree I deferred to my mother's wishes – not that she said so in explicit terms but I respected her sentiment. You see she had lost my father and one of my brothers fifteen years earlier and I think she feared losing me to some institution, even though she worshipped in the Catholic church and sent us to Catholic schools growing up.

'After my studies I moved to Ottawa and took a job with the Department of Internal Affairs. A few years later I accepted a posting to Geneva where I worked for the United Nations. Some years after that I returned to Canada.' Gene stopped to take a breath and pray for forgiveness. Now came the part she had to lie about. 'There was a man whom I knew for many years and we had feelings for one another. He pursued me and wanted for us to marry and have a large and loving family. He was a very good man but after much soul searching I didn't think I was suited to married life. My sensibilities lie elsewhere. During our friendship I studied for a Diploma in Education in Winnipeg but he expressed the notion that he wouldn't be happy for me to teach once we'd married and had children. I put my teaching plans on hold while I tried to determine my path in life and I came to the conclusion that it would be best for me to follow what I see as my calling, to move away so this man will be free to meet someone else and have a happy loving family. I know it is something he yearns for.'

Gene wet her lips and coaxed herself to keep going. It would be over and done soon.

'I decided to come here to the west of Canada as I thought it best that I do not cross paths with him and my family as I want to dedicate myself to a life of serving God without distraction.

'My mother is of advancing years and my elder brother and sister live close by so I feel she is well taken care of.' Gene swallowed. 'Though at times I feel my family still thinks they know what's best for me, when what's best for me is to do what I am best suited to doing. What I am capable of doing.

'Yes, I'm not worthy of wearing this cloth and veil. I have not earned it. I borrowed them from a friend and I will be returning them. I have not taken my first vows, let alone my finals. But it did protect me on my journey westward. I felt safe in it and people left me alone. Travelling by myself I'm not sure I would have felt so secure without it. I am happy to surrender it if that is your wish, but I hope one day to be so attired and in service of the Lord.'

Gene paused and hoped that the face she has mastered growing up was still serving her well in her mid-thirties. She did feel utterly wretched lying about Sonny, but this Gene knew for certain: to become a nun, one must be Catholic, female, unmarried, and sane. Being a virgin wasn't necessarily a prerequisite. Women of the night could go on to redeem themselves and become nuns. Married women, divorced women, women under the age of eighteen could not become nuns. Gene could only tick a few of those boxes. It was so absurd it was almost laughable. She could lie and say she was a widow. But she could never say that, that would be tempting fate.

Without asking Gene if she would like another cup of tea the Mother Superior poured her one while she considered her reply.

'May I ask how old you are?'

'Thirty-six in a few weeks.' Gene replied.

The sister stirred her tea. Silently she placed her spoon on her saucer. 'I think you have had sufficient life experience to know what is your calling. I don't believe you will have made this decision lightly. Your arrival here however without a letter of introduction from your local bishop, suggests your departure was made in haste. I want to welcome you here but I also do not want to be hasty nor do I want you to be hasty. You will need a period of reflection before you are able to freely commit. But,' and with that she smiled, 'that is why we have the processes we do.'

Gene smiled in return. She felt order and frameworks rather suited her.

The sister continued, 'I think it's wonderful you have a background in history and geology studies and a teaching diploma. You need to determine whether teaching is your calling and whether that is teaching per se or teaching as a Sister in our parish school.

'Now, as it has been almost two decades since you did your process of enquiry I suggest you enter our order as a postulant, however because of your previous association, I suggest you undertake this process over nine months. The time it takes for a woman to carry a child, no?'

Gene nodded.

'At any time should it be deemed that you do not have a religious vocation or you are unsuitable to this community, you will be asked to leave. Once you have completed your postulancy, the community will determine whether you are allowed to enter the novitiate as a member of our community. If you are received as a novice, you will spend two years preparing for first vows, learning about the community's history and theology, being formed spiritually, and perhaps preparing for some form of ministry.

'In effect your first novitiate year will be your canonical year and in your second year you will have the opportunity to engage in pastoral work. For you this could be teaching…but you will have plenty of time to decide if that is your course. Your non-canonical year is still very much directed towards formation in the life of the community and growing in relationship to God.

'Towards the end of those two years you will prepare for your first profession of vows. You will receive specific training on what the vows are, how they are lived, and so on. Typically during this time, novices make a retreat in preparation for vows. Thereafter, you can be admitted to first vows. You may renew these yearly or every three years up to nine years. At this point you must make final vows or leave.' She folded her hands on her lap. 'Do you have any questions?'

'Yes,' said Gene. 'I understand and accept with grace everything you have told me. My questions are more of a basic nature. May I live in the convent while I undertake my postulancy?'

'Yes, of course you may, my dear.' The sister smiled gently in understanding. 'I will have Sister Clara take you under her wing. She will find some suitable clothes for you to wear if you don't have some with you. Once you become a novice you can once again wear a habit – our habit,' she said pointedly, 'except as a novice you will wear a white veil. The dark veil is reserved for nuns who have taken final vows.'

59

Sonny could get over Gene deceiving everyone else but not her deceiving him.

He was the one, the only one who used to be able see inside Gene, to what she was thinking. From the very first time he sat opposite her he could see her mind ticking over and from that day forward he seemed to have a sixth sense as to what Gene was thinking. He could read her like a book, but not anymore. That stirred him. That he was losing his edge.

Her betrayal. Her abandonment shook him to the core of his being.

He would have preferred Gene telling him outright that she wanted to go away by herself to some undefined place for an undefined period. He would have preferred her telling him to his face it was over between them.

But in one breath to kiss him and tell him how much she loved him, then to walk away. That, he couldn't quite handle: that lack of honesty.

But what if she had actually decided to end her life. How could she tell him that? Sonny didn't want to dwell on that possibility for he had no comeback, only wrenching pain.

Four days later he arrived back at his home in Winnipeg. And there, in his letterbox, he found a small parcel – for him – from Gene – posted from Freshwater on the last day he saw her.

Part of him felt like pelting it across the front yard in anger. Part of him felt like cradling it like it was the last-born chick of the passenger pigeon. What he did was make himself go inside, pour himself a double scotch, sit at his empty table and drink it straight down. Then he opened it.

Inside he found three handkerchiefs: a pink one with Lindsay's name embroidered across the centre, a yellow one with Shane's and a blue one with his name on it. Tucked inside his blue one was Gene's wedding ring, made from the silver Eli Silver had given her nearly twenty years ago.

Sonny, Sonny

My heart, my life, my love.

Please forgive me. Please understand me. And please be free.

I came so close to coming home, Sonny, really I did. But in the last few weeks, more than ever I came to see that a brighter life for you, a brighter life for the girls, was a life without me.

You are a one in million man, Sonny. You deserve the best and I am far from the best. You deserve a large family. You deserve your name to live on forevermore. You deserve sons that will fly in formation with you up in the skies – sons that I can no longer give you.

This is what I want for you, Sonny. And I think if we can be completely honest with each other, in your heart, this has long been your dream too. If you could achieve your dream, wouldn't your spirit truly soar? I remember how you were when Lindsay was born, how excited you were, so jubilant and so in love with the world. I can but imagine how thrilled you would be with a newborn son in yours arms and your life.

What's stopping you from having this life, Sonny? What's stopping you from realising your dream? It is me who is stopping you; or rather it is your loyalty and devotion to me, your unfailing kindness, your sense of morality that you would never abandon your sorrowful wife, no matter how sick and testing she is. Sonny, I applaud you for your conduct. I honour you for the man you are. But I will no longer stand beside you and let you ruin your life.

And lest you think otherwise, I have thought of the girls in all of this. I am not their entire life: more than anything you are their life and their life is the life you and Mom and Elin and everyone has been able to create for them in my abysmal absence. I have not given them a wonderful life and walked out of them – granted with Lindsay we did have three beautiful years – but I'm sure she's had some beautiful years since I've been gone. I pray to God that she has, just like I pray to God there's a good woman out there, with an overflowing heart ready to love you and the girls like her very own. Because how hard is it to love you?

How do we make this happen for you, Sonny? For there are no words that I can use to convince you, there's no reasoning I can lay down before you that will have you agreeing with me. And so I have taken the decision that I can no longer be in your world. I don't know how longer I can be in this world either, but please know, that wherever I am, you and the girls are always in my heart and prayers.

I hope one day you will be in a happy place and want to wiggle your wings once more in that beautiful way you do. Fly up in the sky, Sonny. Take the girls with you, and drop your parachute candies out of the window. And as you watch them drift slowly to the ground, please know that that is not air inflating the fabric. That is my love for you all, even still.

Gene.

60

Over six months had passed since Gene left him, left them all, and Sonny still had trouble getting his head around it.

To sit at his own table and accept that his own wife had deserted him – even with the best, most misguided intentions – did not come easy to him. Nor did the fact that he had lost someone who had been one of his closest friends for more than twenty-years. To think you knew someone that well but didn't know them at all: to share such intimacy, such heartache, and for it not to count for anything in the end disturbed him deeply.

His mother-in-law was back with him, helping with the children for another six weeks. Wyatt would be joining her next week. The rotating schedule of caregivers continued ad infinitum. Aside from Gene's disappearance, though, nothing much about their lives had changed. It was as if she was still in Freshwater except now, no one visited her; except now, no one talked about her – except for tonight.

'Do you think she's still alive, Becca?'

'I don't know,' his mother-in-law replied. 'I wish I could tell you one way or the other. I wish as the woman who brought her into the world I knew this. But I don't. Maybe over time I will.'

'I'd like to know she was alive. That she was all right. I'd like not to think the alternative.' He sipped on a hot toddy.

'Yes.' Rebecca sighed. 'Oh, for a sign.' A little later she murmured, 'I had held out hope that maybe she would contact Morton. But she hasn't.'

'Morton seems quite nonplussed about Gene's

disappearance. His attitude is quite extraordinary,' noted Sonny.

'That's because disappearing, withdrawing is second nature to him. He doesn't see it as the end or anything out of the ordinary.'

'Do you think I should tell Lindsay?'

'That's up to you. If you tell Lindsay her mother's gone but you can't tell her where to, that might just add more confusion.'

He decided that conversation would be some time off. He would go on doing what he'd always done, getting them to do painted handprints for their mother. He'd already started adding to Gene's cut-outs. He'd found that artwork in Gene's bag. He'd found everything in Gene's bags. He doubted there was anything she took with her to wherever she was going. As if that was a sign that she had no need for it. Thoughts like that just tore him apart all over again.

'I always knew she was different, different to all the other girls. She never talked about settling down, getting married and having children. As if she were at peace with that and believed it would happen in good time and it did. She was one of kind. That's what I loved about her so much: her strength in the face of her own vulnerabilities; her self-possession; her self-reliance. With Gene I always knew I could have my life and she could have hers but we could also have one together. It's the loss of our shared life that I'm struggling with the most. That she lost sight of that.' He rubbed his eyes then dragged his hands across his face. 'With her leaving, her disappearance, I've lost what was going to be ours too and some days that cuts me up the most.'

Rebecca reached out and touched his forearm. 'I know, Sonny. I know what that feels like, truly I do. When Samuel disappeared the future I imagined with him, took for granted even, was vanquished; there was no hope, no possibility of that ever coming to pass. And I grieved for that too. For you, I think that's the question you have to ask yourself. Are you going to hold out and hope or are you going to accept that she's gone? I hope and pray she's alive and one day she will come to her senses and come back.' Rebecca took a sip of her tea. 'But I don't know, Sonny. Most days I think she's not coming back, at least not any time soon.'

'I always thought my love could save her.' His voice was still so raw, in reflective moments like this. He saw the way his mother-in-law looked at him, as if she could see the weeping rawness inside him. He wished he could stanch it. He still had some way to go to get over his long gone wife.

'I know.' Rebecca's voice was full of empathy. 'We all thought that. Your love, our love, the love of her children. But it wasn't enough. Some days I think the only love that could save her was the love of her father and brother who disappeared from her life when she was five.'

Rebecca got up, washed their cups, dried them, put them away, while he sat motionless wondering how his life had come to this.

'I have something I want to say to you, Sonny.' He swung his head towards her. She was leaning back against the kitchen sink.

'When you're ready, I want you to find another – for yourself and for your daughters. I think that would be for the best. I will love her as my own, as I have loved you and will always love you. I will continue to be a part of your life. I want to. I will be here every six weeks, every six months till the day I die but there will come a time when you need to let Gene go, say goodbye, remember the good times you had by all means, but give yourself permission to love again, like Gene has given you, to have the life you deserve, to be the man you are born to be. You're not the Sonny we know. We all know that and we know why but we want you to find your way back to him.

'And don't be shy about things. If you meet a woman and you want to take her out on a date, you take her out on a date, whether I'm here or not. I want you to call me from the office and tell me you're eating out with a friend. I don't want you to be uncomfortable about it. I look upon you as my son and I want you to be happy. I'm just eternally sorry my daughter has caused you such misery.' Her voice broke on misery. He watched her swallow down that stone in her throat.

'She gave me two beautiful daughters, Becca. Nothing can take them away from me.'

Months later Lindsay did ask him, 'Dad, is Mommy still in that hospital?'

'No,' he said. 'She's gone away.' He was determined he would not lie to his children.

'Where to?'

'We don't know.'

'Is she coming back?'

'We don't know that either.'

Then one morning weeks later Lindsay said, 'Dad, I don't mind that Mommy's gone away but I wish she could send us a postcard now and then. Granny always sends us postcards when she goes on holidays.'

He bent down to hug the innocent miracle that was his daughter. It was all he could do.

61

Those first twenty-one months of life in the convent community were structured and organised. The only free time Gene had were three afternoons a week between three and five p.m. and after eight o'clock in the evenings. Every other waking moment was full – thank God! Her days consisted of morning prayer, breakfast, readings and time for reflection, morning class (scriptures, rules and constitutions, theology, founding life, liturgy and music) – the sisters were delighted to discover her singing voice – midday prayer, community lunch, private study, prayer, reading, assigned tasks, duties, adoration of the blessed sacrament, supper, more study, then compline. Then collapse!

In her evening free time Gene would pore over the teaching syllabus for secondary school French, History and Geography as set out by the Catholic Independent Schools of the Vancouver Archdiocese. In her mind, she practised standing in front of a group of students, practised what she would say to them in each subject as they worked through the set topics. She wanted to prove to herself that she could master the skill of pedagogy. She felt there had been so many things in her life that she had been mediocre at, even dismal: being a wife, a mother, a cook, a daughter. In teaching she wanted to excel. It would reassure her that she had made the right decision.

Months earlier she'd written to the Manitoba Board of Education asking them to reissue her diploma in teaching as it had been "misplaced" in her move west. That piece of paper jumpstarted her life as a teacher in British Columbia. It was something from her old life, yet it was also something of her new. She was proud of it, but she knew better to show pride. Her small room in the novice dormitory was noticeably minimal: the only decor, her biblical and scholastic texts. She had no possessions and didn't miss them. Well, except one.

Not keeping that last photograph of Sonny and the girls had been her biggest wrench. But that photograph would be the one thing that would make her crumble. Day in and day out she did her all to not think of Sonny or Lindsay or Shane. When her mind stumbled over the word Shane she would find that the saddest of all. That she never got to experience her youngest daughter, to see her smile, to see her reaching out to her mommy. She had memories of Lindsay but none of Shane. Her daughter was a stranger to her and she to her daughter. But at night just before she succumbed to sleep she would pull that picture into view in her head. She wished she could have seen it with her own eyes. Her last prayer each evening was for her husband and two daughters: that they were in some way living a life she had paved for them.

In the 1971 spring term, Gene attended Marian High School in Burnaby as a teacher's aid. She enjoyed being out of the convent, seeing more of Vancouver's green vista in her daily travels. She enjoyed the snow-melted rivers and the bright bustling harbour and the mountains covered in conifers. It all reminded her of her time in Switzerland, when she was also alone, far from family, but mostly managing to forge a life for herself.

After her probationary three months she was given her own class the following school year. Undeniably some days she found stressful but she would tell herself, I have to be able to handle this. I have children who will be teenagers one day. And with them in mind she would try to be the kind of teacher they would look up to, a teacher that would inspire them to study history and travel to foreign countries through all that she revealed and the stories she told. Teaching gave her a framework to talk about life but not her life. At the end of each lesson she would say, 'Any questions, queries, comments or complaints?' She'd wait a second or two for any response. 'Good. I'll see you all next time.'

A part of her came alive in that classroom in front of those young people eager to learn more of life, to taste and feel it. Something about it reminded her of that trip she'd made with Jonathan and Sonny years earlier.

When school finished each day, Gene liked to stay in the last classroom she had been in and write up her notes, mark papers, prepare for the following day. In an empty classroom she felt free – quite a different feeling to being in the confines of the convent grounds. She realised there was something in that that needed further exploration but for now her life was in order. It was busy, full, and mostly she was content with that. On a few occasions she had the opportunity to watch the sun set over the Pacific Ocean, a first for her, and something about its warm orange globe submerging into the sea filled her with a deep sense of peace.

The other novices and women in her community seemed to accept her. She knew she had to continue to walk a fine line between being reflective and meditative, between contributing to theological discussions and being part of the order. If she were to stray she could be asked to leave and that thought more than anything motivated her to fully embrace her new life. One day Sister Eugenia said to her, 'Sister Eva – Gene had chosen that name for herself when she had been accepted as a novice – you don't receive or send any correspondence. It is permissible to write to your family.'

Gene bowed her head in front of the Sister. 'Thank you. I pray for them and trust in God.' Every night I pray for them, her heart pounded. The sister smiled, nodded in return. Suddenly Gene had a flash of Elin praying for Sonny and her girls and that comforted her.

62

One of the cleaners at the school in Burnaby was a native woman named Mary. One day after school she walked into Gene's empty classroom singing Carol King's *Way over yonder*. At the time Gene was crouched on the far side of the table, picking up some papers she had dropped. She listened to her singing all the while remaining in a crouched position until the woman had finished the last line.

'Where's yonder?' Gene asked.

The woman was so startled she screamed, dropped her broom and as her frightened eyes found Gene's wimpled head she yelled, 'Don't you go scaring me like that, Sister, or I'll yonder you.'

Gene burst out laughing. She laughed so hard she had to place her hands on the table and hide her face while she tried to find some composure but there was nothing she could do but surrender to mirth. The woman came up to her and helped her stand. 'I'm terribly sorry, Sister, for speaking to you like that. Please forgive me.'

'No,' said Gene. 'I'm sorry for scaring you so. There's nothing to forgive. I'm Sister Eva.' Gene held out her hand and that was telling for Gene, for it was the first time she had held out her hand to someone in...she couldn't remember how long. Normally she just nodded and bowed her head.

'I'm Mary,' the woman smiled at her. Her face was round and friendly and familiar. She reminded Gene of Rosie except she had a good eight or nines inches on her. In fact Mary was around five foot eight, a similar height to Gene. Her hair was shoulder length and layered in that modern style, many women wore.

'And may I ask you again where yonder is?'

'Yonder is Kitisak. Way up north. A few hours south east of Prince Rupert. Paradise. The home of Haisla Indians. Me.'

'What's taken you so far away from home?' Gene asked.

'Work. So I can save. So I can send money home to my father.'

'Do you live in Vancouver by yourself?'

'No, Sister Eva. With my husband. He drives a taxi. You ever need a taxi, you let me know.' She smiled at Gene.

'Thank you,' Gene said. 'You're very kind. I don't often have need for a taxi.'

'You're quite new,' she noted. 'Do you enjoy your days teaching teenagers?'

'Mostly. We're all learning together. I guess it's the same as being a first time mother.' She paused. 'Do you have children, Mary?'

'No, Sister, I ain't been blessed yet.'

And in those few words and a fleeting glance Gene had a measure of the woman's heartache. 'I'll pray one day you will, Mary.'

'Thank you.' Her eyes held Gene's in gratitude. 'I best get back to my cleaning. Sorry to disturb you.'

'Anytime, Mary, and please feel free to sing while you're cleaning my classroom. I like singing.'

From that day on their five-minute conversation became ten-minute, became twenty-minutes with a cup of tea and slice that Mary would bring with her.

Gene learnt all about Mary's older sisters and brothers living back on the reservation, how her mother had died of cancer, how they had opened her up and she was riddled with it and they could do nothing for her. How one day Mary hoped to return to Kitisak and raise her kids there once, God willing, they came along. How her husband had worked as a deep-sea fisherman in waters off the coast of Alaska but how he had given it all up to come south with her because she needed to leave after her mother had died. Her father, Ken, had given her his blessing to leave, but extracted a promise that she would return one day. So much of Mary's story Gene could relate to.

With Mary, Gene shared nearly everything about her life, how she had lost her father and youngest brother in a boating accident. She told her about her mother and Wyatt and her sister and two brothers, their children – her nieces and nephews – her working life, her travels abroad. Everything except the fact she had been married and had children whom she had walked out on. Part of her so wanted to have the solace of having a friend she could share her deepest darkest secrets with. However she couldn't tell this wonderful warm woman of her biggest failing. Not out of shame or guilt but out of a sense of wanting to preserve and uphold Mary's longed-for dream of motherhood. But more than that, Gene's husband and daughters were the one remaining treasure of her life that she wanted to keep for herself, as if they were her only earthly possession that she didn't want to part with or share with another soul.

Other days they talked and sang music. Mary saying she edited her repertoire to ensure they were suitable songs to be singing in the presence of a nun. John Lennon's *Imagine*, George Harrison's *My sweet lord. I don't know how to love him*, which Mary told her was from the musical, Jesus Christ Superstar. *If you could read my mind. Take me home country roads. You've got a friend.*

Then one afternoon she sang a song that that pierced Gene's heart in so many places she had to race out the door to hide her tears.

Later, she walked the corridors till she found Mary cleaning another classroom. 'Sorry I had to leave,' her voice just above a whisper. 'Who wrote that song you were singing?'

'James Taylor. The song's called *Fire and rain.*'

Gene had seen the fire and the rain. She'd felt it too.

The fire of electric shock. The rain of the cold showers. Days of brightest sunshine when all Gene felt was cold and bleak and miserable inside and wondered how the world could be so mean to her in its taunting. The third line of the chorus about finding a friend was Gene's life before she met Mary. She worried it was Sonny's life still.

And that last line… *but I always thought that I'd see you again*…was it not their personal anthem, Sonny and hers? What happened to *Non, je ne regrette rien?*

'It upset you,' Mary said.

'It…um…I think if ever I were to meet James Taylor I would hug him.'

Gene learnt that song. She learnt them all. Her after-school hours with Mary were the highlight of her week.

Another school year passed. Gene spent her whole break in retreat and came out to make her first vows before school started again. August once more, another birthday passed and Gene wondered about her children, about Sonny. Each and every one of their birthdays she remembered. She felt like sending them birthday cards. Some days she felt like sending them postcards like she and Sonny had exchanged postcards years ago, even if they were unsigned ones. But she never did though. She had walked away. She had encouraged him to take another. She had wanted them to have a better life. How dare she interrupt it with a random card?

She was back at school, back to spending a few hours each week with Mary, finding out she had yet another miscarriage. Gene hugged this woman who had become her close friend, her dearest female friend ever, while she cried over the fickleness of her womb, the hollowness of her loss. Gene had only ever miscarried the once. But Mary had miscarried eight times.

Another day Gene asked, 'Have you ever thought about adopting?'

'Many a time,' Mary replied. 'But Billy tells me when we're done trying we'll do that. He tells me it has to be my call, because it's my body taking the toll.'

'How's that body going?'

'It's getting on, Eva. I'm thirty-three.'

'Still time,' Gene smiled encouragingly.

One day Mary told Gene she was a kindergarten teacher, once.

'Really?' Gene replied, 'Where was that?'

'Up north. I trained down here after I finished school. My dad said one of his kids had to go to university and as all the others had managed to avoid it, it was left to me.'

'Did you enjoy being a kindergarten teacher?'

'Yes,' she said. 'For many years.'

'You didn't want to teach kindergarten when you moved here?' Gene asked.

'No,' Mary said. 'Being around other people's kids all day reminded me too much of what I was missing.'

Over the next summer break Gene worked in pastoral care. Some days Mary would join her, working with a group of volunteers and other Sisters doing food hand outs to the homeless on the Downtown Eastside, helping clean out at the shelters and soup kitchens. She met Billy, Mary's husband. The three of them had lunch together on several occasions. Gene wished they could have shared a dinner. She wished she could make fondue for them to thank them for their friendship.

The leaves turned amber; the hockey posters went back up. Mary came to Gene and told her that she and Billy were going home for Christmas and going home for good. Her older sister was having one more baby and she'd asked Mary to come home and be there for the birth. Time, she told her, to know what birthing was all about so she would be ready for her own.

'Good for you,' Gene smiled at her while her heart shouted: "Not good for me!" 'I will miss you,' Gene said. 'I will miss our songs and our singing.'

'And I will miss you,' said Mary. 'Please come and visit me one day. I want you to fall in love with the place. I want you to move there.'

Gene promised her she would. Said she hadn't had a holiday in years. One was certainly overdue.

She put on a brave face when it came time to say goodbye to Mary. Afterwards, her world was muted. The music slowed. Joy faded. That year, Vancouver's winter, which although always damper and warmer than winters out east, was by far one of her bleakest ever as the days shrivelled and her life diminished.

She was worried she might slide to a place she did not want to slide to. She gave herself a stern talking. She gave herself over to prayer. In the end she sought out Sister Eugenia's counsel.

'I thought I had been living in lightness,' she told her. 'But now I'm wondering if I have been living in darkness. My friendship with this humble woman seemed to burn bright like a flare illuminating areas of my soul that I didn't know were in shadow. I thought I was whole in my love of Jesus, in the fellowship of this community, in my teaching but I am lonely. It is as if her light was showing me a path I should follow, a path back to my earthly family. And here I stand bereft and confused. I'm sorry, Mother, I think I let this friendship mean too much to me. I have a sister but we were never as close. I perhaps didn't make a lot of effort and neither did she. With Mary I found the sister I always wanted. But a younger sister, and I didn't see it coming. She seems to have stoked family instincts, dare I say it – maternal instincts – that have been dormant for years.

'Eva,' Mother Superior said. 'Don't be sorry. God sent you Mary. Never bemoan or regret the people God sent to walk beside you and hold your hand. It's one of his miracles. Be accepting. Be grateful you understand why they were put there, the flashes of insight they offer.'

'I don't fully understand that insight,' said Gene, 'but I want to.'

'All in good time,' said the Sister. 'Come and talk to me, whenever you need to talk.'

Mary, bless her, missed her too. She started sending

her letters. For the first time ever at the convent, Gene received correspondence. Mary wrote about how much she loved being back with her family, how her father was in a good place and had rediscovered his love of falconry, and how her nieces and nephews were wonderful characters. She and Billy had made the right decision coming home. She didn't think she ever wanted to go away again.

Gene wrote back telling her about her students, about the slow and minute changes in Vancouver, for there was nothing she could write about her brothers and sister, her nieces and nephews. Occasionally she'd include something from National Geographic – that was her one indulgence. The Italian who managed the newsstand she walked by to and from school wouldn't hear of her paying for it. Gene felt her letters were hollow. Nothing like the letters she used to send back home from Switzerland. Every few letters Mary would include a cassette full of songs taped from the radio and Gene would play a few songs on a tape deck at school at the end of the day when only the cleaners were around, as if she were putting the music on for the cleaners' benefit, not her own.

One day while Gene was walking back from school to the convent, she passed a primary school where a man was playing basketball with two girls who were about seven and ten – around Shane and Lindsay's ages. She stopped to watch them bounce the ball around each other and try and shoot for hoops.

'Dad, new rule,' the eldest girl said once she'd managed to wrestle the ball from her father. 'You're not allowed to use both hands. Only one.'

'Am I'm being penalised? What for?'

'Because you're too tall.'

'But there's two of you and only one of me.'

'That doesn't count.'

'So I'm only allowed to bounce the ball or throw the ball with one hand?'

'Yes, and defend as well.'

'And what happens if I do all that and still beat you?'

'Try it,' she grinned.

They were having so much fun and they weren't even playing. And in that moment Gene wanted to yell out: 'I'll play with you. One adult and one child against the other.' She wanted to throw off her robe and pull on a pair of track pants. All of a sudden she was in the midst of this everyday family scene, but was it everyday? How many fathers played ball with their daughters? Not that many that she ever saw. She was reminded how her father played with her, and how Jonathan played with her. And she knew Sonny would be a man who played with his daughters as well.

And in that moment she was immensely happy and immensely sad. Without warning her heart faltered, her eyes squeezed shut almost of their own volition, as if her body was trying to erase what she'd just felt, what she'd just witnessed. But on this day other parts of her were stronger. 'My God, what have I done? What am I missing!' screamed her implacable soul, as she opened her eyes and her lungs sought to imbibe life.

Gene went to speak again to Sister Eugenia.

'I need to go and see my earthly family. The people I spent time with before I came to Vancouver. I can't make my final vows until I'm sure I'm on the right path.'

'I don't want you to make final vows until you are sure, Eva. You go with my blessing and you will be welcomed back with my blessing if that is your decision. You will not be the first Sister to leave and if you return you will not be the first Sister to return. Our door is always open.'

This time Gene didn't steal away. She walked out into the world wondering what sort of woman she would become. What – if any – sort of wife, mother, sister and daughter she would become? And would she – one day hence – make some more happy memories that would stay with her always?

Sunny Skies

Winnipeg, Canada, July 1974

63

Five years after Gene watched the retreating back of her husband she glimpsed it again. He still had the same posture: erect but at ease. That made her smile. It also made her heart twinge for she had to remind herself he was no longer her husband. For all she knew he could have had their marriage annulled on the grounds of desertion. He could have remarried, had more children. Her last letter gave carte blanche for him do whatever he pleased. So many contemplations now that she was out in a wider world where buildings were where they once weren't, and billboards advertised what they once didn't, while she thought about what she could hope to achieve from her endeavour.

Forgiveness? Absolution? Was that too much to hope for? Friendship? Permission to see her girls? Meet them. Be a part of their life if nothing else. Permission to see Elin and Don again? Would they want to see her again? Were they still alive? She had abdicated so many rights. She was below zero as a starting point. Would her children want to know her? Would Sonny want to let her into their life again? How would she feel about him when she stood in front of him? More importantly, how would he feel? Angry? Defiant? She prayed that the same man who once flew a poor Eskimo girl hundreds of miles out of his way would be as charitable towards his former wife.

She had gone first to their old house, stood across the road and watched who came and went. She knew she wouldn't be going and knocking on the door. That was too much of an imposition. What she discovered was Sonny no longer lived there. She crossed the street after

371

all, knocked on the door but the strangers inside were renting and had no idea who Sonny Marlow was let alone where he might live.

A thought came to her that she hadn't considered: he may not even live in Winnipeg anymore. Perhaps she would be forced to call his parents after all? But then she found his name and number in the phone book and his new address in Crestwood. Calling him, however, was way too confronting – for him and for her. Instead she decided to call every aviation company in Winnipeg.

The first call she placed was to Aquila Airlines. It was a new airline – she couldn't remember it from eight, nine years ago. The woman who answered said, 'Yes Mr. Marlow works here. It's his company. Buts he's not here at the moment. Can I get him to call you.'

'No, it's fine,' Gene said, unprepared for her efficiency. 'Is he away for a while?'

'He's away for a few days on family business. Back in the day after tomorrow.'

'It says here you do private charter and regular flights. Do you have a timetable and a price list?'

'I can send one out to you.'

'Maybe I can pop by and pick one up.'

'Suit yourself. Do you want me to make an appointment for you to see Mr. Marlow at the same time?'

'Oh no, no. I heard he was a good pilot that's all. Knew I'd be safe to go with his company.'

Two days later she went to the Winnipeg Airport. Walked along one of the back streets till she saw the sign for Aquila Airlines. She was once again wearing her nun's habit. Pulled it out from the bottom of the bag. She didn't think she would be doing that so soon but in the circumstances it seemed to provide the safety net she needed. She went inside and started a whole new conversation with the lady behind the counter, there was none of the, "I was the lady who phoned the other day." After the woman handed her their brochures, Gene went and sat in the corner of their reception and looked at their schedules and price list. After a few minutes she heard Sonny's voice call out to the woman behind the counter. Keeping her eyes down she heard him walk towards the bench. He made some joke. So like Sonny. She glanced up and there he was eight feet away with his back to her. She glanced back down then looked up again to see him walk away. After a few minutes, she walked up to the woman herself, quietly said she would have a think about things and turned and walked out the door with her head lowered.

Two hours later she phoned, asking to speak to Sonny Marlow. Oddly she was calmer than she expected. Seeing him had been the right thing to do. Some of her nerves had been replaced with a warm optimism.

'Yo. Sonny here.'

'Sonny, hello. It's Gene.' She smiled into the mouthpiece. She even smiled with her eyes, doing her all to make her greeting a warm one.

There were a few seconds of strained silence. 'Gene, huh. That's different.'

'I know.'

'Where are you calling from?'

'Winnipeg.'

'How long you been in Winnipeg?'

'Oh, about three days.'

'Where'd you come from?'

'Vancouver.'

'Been there all this time?'

'Yes.' Her voice was almost inaudible. 'Yes,' she repeated, louder this time.

Another few seconds of silence. 'What are you calling for, Gene? Just to say hello?'

'I'd like to meet you for a coffee. See how you're getting on. Find out how the girls are doing?'

'After five years, you want to meet me for coffee?'

'Yes.' She tried to sound enthusiastic as if she were saying: 'Of course!'

'Why, now, after all this time?'

'Well,' she drawled, 'if you meet me for coffee I'll tell you.' She waited. She didn't want to think about what he might be thinking. 'Is there a problem meeting me for coffee?'

'No,' he said. 'There's no problem.' He paused. 'Where and when do you want to meet?'

She told him where she was staying but she also said where and when they met was completely up to him.

"I'll meet you at two o'clock tomorrow at Angelos on Portage. I've got a run in the morning.'

'Two o'clock tomorrow it is. Thank you, Sonny. I look forward to seeing you.'

'All right.'

She was at Angelos ten minutes before two, scouting the place for a booth that would allow a certain amount of privacy. This time she wore clothes she bought at a charity shop the afternoon before: a knee-length purple A-line skirt and a lilac button blouse. Still thin after all these years. Her hair pulled back in a bun. Not a scrap of make-up on her face – she didn't own any.

Sonny arrived, pushing the glass door inwards. He glanced to the right and saw her. He didn't smile just strolled on over. God give me strength, she said to herself for the hundredth time. Part of her really did feel like fleeing.

She stood and smiled, pressed her hands into her thighs. He was wearing olive-coloured corduroy trousers and a checked shirt. So much about him was the same except for the sideburns that were now longer and thicker, and his hairline that had receded just a tad at the temples. But he still had a full head of blonde brown hair, which gave him a very youthful edge – at odds with the faint furrows across his tanned brow. She didn't know whether to hold out her hand, step forward and kiss him on the cheek or hug him. He didn't seem to know what to do either. In the end they gave each other the smallest smile as they nodded in greeting. She was so grateful he showed, so grateful that asking him to meet her had really not been that difficult after all. He could have rebuffed her outright. He could have hurled all manner of vitriol at her...perhaps he wanted to do that to her face.

'Thank you for coming,' she said.

'Well you came all this way. It's the least I could do.'

He sat down, placing his hands on his lap. He looked calm, whether he was or not she couldn't tell. But he seemed relaxed and patient as he waited for her to say something.

'I don't know where to start,' she said, suddenly feeling overwhelmed at the enormity of her actions.

'Well, Gene, you better start somewhere. You dragged my ass over here.'

She told him then that for the last few years she had been working at a Catholic co-ed school in Vancouver teaching History, Geography and French to senior students.

'I see,' he said. 'Now that you are teaching, do you like it?' he asked.

'I do,' she replied.

'What do you like most about it?'

'The people I meet. The stories I hear.' She paused and with the faintest smile said, 'I made a friend.'

He looked at her and the way he looked her she could tell she hadn't prefaced that right. Before she could explain, he said, 'Well I guess if you lived, that was always on the cards.'

'No. No. It's not what you think,' her voice implored.

'Do you have any idea what we've all been through? Me! Your mother! Your brothers, your sister. Wyatt. My parents! We didn't know if you were alive or dead? Can you imagine the hell we've all been through?' His voice was raised. He was angry. Still. Deservedly angry, she granted. 'I would have thought you could have turned up with an apology. Not a tra-la-la, I've got my life together again and everything's swell.'

'Everything's not swell.' She tried to keep her tone even.

'No you're right. It's not.'

He picked up the menu but after a few seconds he tossed it back down.

She swallowed. 'Shall we order something?'

'I guess we have to.' He exhaled loudly. 'What will you have?'

'I'll have an iced tea.'

'Want anything to eat?'

'Surprise me.' She smiled at him. There was nothing forced about it. Despite his hostility it was so good to see him again.

When he returned from the counter and slid back into the seat opposite she tried again. 'You've moved. I went back to our old house but there are strangers there and they didn't know where you had moved to.'

'I figured if you wanted to track us down someone as resourceful as you would find a way.'

'As I did.' She smiled a hopeful smile. She wanted to say: doesn't the fact that I tracked you down count for anything?

'Well I guess I'm easier to find than some.'

She ignored the barb.

'It can't have been that hard. I'm in the phone book after all.'

'I know,' she said.

'I'm surprised you didn't call at home.'

'No, Sonny. I wouldn't do that to you. I don't know your personal circumstances. I don't want to make things any more difficult for you than they are already.'

The corner of his mouth moved in the slightest of acknowledgements. 'Have you recovered?'

'Yes,' she nodded. 'Been well for the better part of five years.' She smiled. 'Sounds like I'm telling you I've been sober for five years.'

'So who's this person you've become friendly with?'

'A Haisla woman who worked at the school.'

376

'I see.'

'She's left now. Gone back to her home in Kitisak, near Prince Rupert.'

'And?'

'And I hope to see her again one day.'

Sonny nodded at her, but his eyes were questioning.

'Her name is Mary and she is the first real female friend I've ever had.'

'Well, good, I'm pleased for you.'

'You would like her. She has shades of Rosie in her. She's a good singer. She brought music back into my life again.'

'That's gotta be good. I'm pleased for you.' And she had to admit he sounded as if he were. There was no biting sarcasm.

'But not only that, Sonny, she and other people made me realise I had to come back...that I wanted to see you again, see the girls again...somewhere along the way I started to hope that perhaps there is something I can salvage from the wreckage.'

'It was a wreckage all right.'

'How are the girls?'

'Fine. They're with Abby. I dropped them off on the weekend. They'll spend the rest of the holidays with her.'

Five days ago was Shane's birthday. Gene hadn't bought her anything because she wasn't sure when she would be seeing her. 'Did Shane have a good birthday?'

Sonny's eyes widened a little in surprise. 'Yes, she did. Your mother was there. Insisted on making pancakes with maple syrup.'

'That's Mom.' Gene smiled weakly.

'What did you get Shane for her birthday?'

'Not what she wanted.' He took a swig of his coke.

'Oh. What did she want?'

'A kangaroo! As in a real, live, jumping, hopping kangaroo. She was a bit put out with the stuffed one I bought her.'

Gene could not help laughing.

'Where did she get that idea from?'

'Skippy the Bush Kangaroo! You know, that Australian TV programme?'

She shook her head. 'I haven't watched any television for years.'

'Yes, well normally I wouldn't see it either, but Shane has insisted – more than once – that I leave work early so we can watch it together.'

'Has she got you wrapped around her little finger?' Gene took a sip of her drink.

'Not exactly, but it is quite a good programme. It's about this young boy called, Sonny, believe it or not, who lives with his dad who is a park ranger. His mother died when he was young and his best friend is this kangaroo called Skippy. There's also this helicopter pilot called Jerry – whom Mom thinks is a dead ringer for me.'

'Does she?' Gene smiled.

'Anyway, Shane just wants to live in Sonny's world and she wants me to learn to fly choppers. I'm sure she thinks once I do that, then having a pet kangaroo will be the next logical step.'

Gene laughed. 'I wonder if all girls her age are into Skippy?' she mused.

'Do you know how old Shane is?

'Yes, Sonny. She just turned eight.'

'Good,' he said, with the barest of nods.

'Do they see much of Abby?'

'They see her for three months every year. Six of those weeks she comes and lives with us here in Winnipeg.'

Gene hadn't expected that. She didn't know what she expected. But she hadn't expected that. Her sister's devotion and kindness stuck in her throat. Eventually she managed to ask, 'What is Lindsay like?'

'She is the best girl. She is so mature. She's got a real head on her shoulders. Born with initiative. Shane has the keen eye of an observer. She has initiative too. If Lindsay misses something Shane steps in and does it. They never argue. They never complain. They are the best of friends.

I'm so proud of them and the way they've turned out.'

Gene felt her self relax a notch. Such good news, such relief. 'I'm pleased,' she whispered, her eyes downcast. Without looking at Sonny she asked, 'Have they suffered for not having a mother?'

'No, not that you would know. There's always been a female figure in their life. Week in and week out, whether it be Abby or your mother or my mother or Sylvia. Who do you think reared the girls?' His voice was raised again.

She had to lift her eyes to look at him.

'I couldn't. I had to put money in the bank for groceries, pay medical bills, keep a roof over their heads.' He sighed and shook his head in weary exasperation. 'You have no idea.'

She was right. She didn't. After a few moments she asked, 'Do you think they have what I had?'

'Did you think you had what you had when you were eight and eleven?'

Slowly she shook her head. 'It certainly didn't appear then.'

'So the answer is no. They're strong girls the two of them. Not that you weren't, Gene. Your willpower, your strength is probably more impressive than anyone I've ever met.'

'You have no idea what that took to do.'

He glared at her. 'You're right, I don't. Go ahead and enlighten me so I do.'

Yet another impasse.

'Well?' he asked, his cinnamon brown eyes suddenly far from warm.

'One day I hope to be able to tell you.'

'You said that to me once before. Thirteen years ago if I remember correctly. Right before we got married. I'm still waiting to hear that story from you.'

'Will you let me see the girls?'

'One day I might be able to let you.'

'When do you think that might be?'

He ignored her question.

'Where did you live in Vancouver?'

'In North Vancouver.'

'By yourself or with other people?'

She hadn't planned on telling him her circumstances straightaway. She didn't think they were relevant. Yet at the same time, she didn't want to lie to him. She could say: "I'll tell you another time," but how was she going to get him to give an inch if she wasn't prepared to?

'I lived in a convent,' she admitted at last. 'The Sisters of the Child Jesus.'

'All that time?'

'Yes.'

'What did you do, become a nun or something?'

'Something.'

He looked at her, waiting.

Gene sighed. 'After some time I was accepted as a novice. I studied and served for two years before I took my first vows. I have another seven years before I have to make my final vows of commitment.'

'How did YOU become a nun?'

It was hard not to maintain eye contact with Sonny as she said, 'I wasn't completely open and honest.'

'Hail, Mary, forgive me Father for I have sinned.'

'Please don't mock me! It was the best path for me to take at the time. It helped me get to where I am today.'

She looked at him, his fire quelled for now. 'You didn't answer my question. When do you think I might be able to see the girls?'

'When I decide that will be in their best interests.'

'How long will you take to decide?'

'Well to set the right expectation up front, it won't happen in the next week or the next month. It mightn't even happen in the next year. I want to make sure you are absolutely on the straight and narrow, won't flit in and out of their lives again. There will be no rejecting them a second time, Gene. You can abandon me. I can't stop you from doing that. But I will not allow you to hurt our daughters like you hurt me and the rest of your family.'

'I never meant to hurt any of you, least of all you.' Her voice was just above a whisper.

'Yeah? The odd piece of correspondence, Gene – how hard would that have been?'

She couldn't answer him.

'How long did you take to make your vows at that convent?'

'Two years.' She wished she could have fudged that answer.

'Well now you've got some idea. Two years to make absolutely sure you want to be a part of their life. Two years for me to decide that it's healthy for all concerned.'

'So am I just meant to wait around while you play God?'

'No! You're not meant to wait around. You're meant to prove to me that I can trust you again to do the right thing by our children.'

'All right,' said Gene. 'How do we go about that?'

'That, I'll have to think about. If you move from where you're staying, call me at the office, let me know how I can reach you.' He stood up. 'Don't call me at home.'

'Don't worry, I won't.'

'I'll get this,' he said. Gene looked down at the red laminated tabletop. The ice in her tea had melted. She hadn't even touched the orange cake he ordered for her.

'I'll see you, Sonny,' She called after him.

'I'll see you, Gene.' He walked away without glancing over his shoulder.

64

When Gene first moved to Winnipeg to live with Sonny, she didn't take in much of Winnipeg, for she was too busy taking in Sonny. Something of Winnipeg reminded her of Toronto, but flatter and with a smaller skyline. Now, years later, what she realised was Toronto didn't necessarily represent a happy time in her life. She was happier in Montreal, Ottawa, Geneva and Vancouver, happier with the people around her, the hills and the trees. She worried that part of her depression and condition after Shane was born was environmental. With all the elm trees in full bloom winter seemed a long way away, yet she worried that winter might be her downfall.

Based on these reflections she decided this time to make her life in Winnipeg different to her previous one. She found a ridiculously small flat on the top floor of a two storey building in Rue Valade in Saint Boniface. It was a lot smaller than others she looked at but given she had lived in a room barely bigger than a cupboard at the convent it actually was a step up. What the studio apartment had going for it was a large window overlooking a small green park and, beyond that, trees lining the river, creating a sense of the world outside coming inside. St Boniface she chose because the suburb was French speaking and Catholic. Perhaps it would remind her of happier days in Montreal and Switzerland.

The neighbourhood was close to the Red River, a hospital, a university, and the St Boniface cathedral, which she had always admired for its understated Romanesque architecture. However to her dismay, she discovered it had been destroyed by fire in July 1968. The sacristy and the dramatic façade with its large, round, now glassless window were all that remained. Behind it stood a modern church built and opened only two years earlier. There was a large graveyard close by, in one corner a statue of a missionary talking to a voyageur. She would often stop and admire that, particularly the voyageur's pony-tailed hair. Part of her wished she lived in an age where men wore their hair long. She found that look romantic and liberating, such a contrast to the missionary's blunt cut.

In her neighbourhood was also the former Grey Nuns' residence, now the St. Boniface Museum, the oldest building in Winnipeg, and reportedly the largest oak-log building in North America. Being close to the home of so many nuns for so many years was comfort to Gene, reminding her that that was still an option should nothing eventuate with Sonny and her daughters.

Did she have hopes of reconciling things with Sonny? In her craven way she hadn't wanted to think about that. There were so many unknowns. Did she want to have a physical relationship again with a man again or had her time in the convent vanquished the idea? Would she have amorous feelings towards Sonny...anything approaching how she felt when she left him? He was still, undeniably, a very handsome man. She could face the simple truth of that. And she couldn't deny the frisson of seeing him again. It had been so good to look into his face again.

What did he see when he saw her? Going into the change rooms at the charity shop the other day had been the first time Gene had seen herself in a mirror in years – since she was at Morton's back in 1968. Her hair when loose was halfway down her back. It hadn't seen the sun in years. It was much darker these days, more a mousy brown. Now that she wasn't wearing her wimple, she plaited it into a ponytail most days and often wore a scarf over her head as she wasn't used to her head being bare. Her eyes were still clear and blue, perhaps her most striking feature courtesy of her mother. Her cheekbones were pronounced and her teeth were in good shape. She was quite thin, the result of eating simply and walking lots. She had faint lines around her mouth and eyes that she couldn't recall ever seeing before. What did she expect? She was forty-one after all.

More important than appearances were feelings. She wondered what Sonny felt when he saw her, when he thought of her? Not a lot if their first meeting was anything to go on...but then she decided their first meeting was nothing to go on.

Still, she remembered the conversation they'd had on the eve of her operation, and the letter she'd sent him when she fled Freshwater. It was highly possible he had moved on to someone else, highly understandable. Some day she had to find the courage to ask him if there had been another woman or women in his life. Was there one still? She sensed he was not going to be forthcoming on that front.

And what of her children, who were strangers to her? She was so intrigued by who they might be. At times when she had been teaching in Vancouver, talking to a student, she'd catch herself thinking: I wonder if one of my daughters is like you? Bright, eager, timid, excitable, natural, relaxed...so many possibilities. Would they like her? Would they want anything to do with her?

All she knew was she wanted them in her life in some way and that way had to be mostly on their terms.

She hadn't planned things that well, coming back as she had, yet, she told herself, how could she? She didn't know what Sonny's reception would be like. All the schools were closed for the summer holidays; she couldn't approach any till two weeks before school started. As a secondary teacher in a Catholic school, she had earned only a small stipend: she hadn't minded at the time as most of her living expenses were taken care of. But now she needed to be able to provide for herself.

She found a part-time summer job working in the Winnipeg Art Gallery café from ten to four p.m. daily. She phoned Sonny and left a message regarding her new arrangements and told him, if he wanted to see her, best he come by when her shift was finished. She didn't have a phone at home.

Eight days after they first met, she saw him waiting outside the gallery as she was leaving. He suggested they go to Stephen Juba Park; pick up some sodas on the way. They sat on a park bench overlooking the river. He asked her if her place was furnished. She said the previous tenant had left a small table and two chairs. She'd bought a second-hand bed. She was going to buy a cassette radio.

'Is that a good idea?' he asked.

'Why not?' she countered.

'Forget it, Gene, I'm just teasing you.'

'I have some tapes I want to play.'

'Good.'

She told him the café job was hopefully only temporary. She'd like to get a teaching job if she were to stay on. He told her, if she wanted to see her children she had to stay on and make a commitment to being there.

She nodded slowly as she stared out at the river. She watched the mallards and their ducklings, and thought, oh, to have your uncomplicated life. She wondered if she would be able to see this through. 'Sonny,' she said. 'Do you remember you once said to me, we could talk about living somewhere else? Is that out of the question?'

'For now it is.' He paused. 'What were you thinking?'

'Nothing specifically. But I have wondered of late, what will happen if I discover I don't enjoy living in Winnipeg – how do I reconcile that with being with my, our, children? If it didn't work for me, would you let the girls come and visit me on their school holidays if I chose to live somewhere else?'

He exhaled loudly. His leg moved ever so slightly, lightly tapping his toes while he considered her request. After several moments he said, 'That's not outside the bounds of possibility in the distant future. But I can't give you a time on that. You need to get to know them first and for them to be comfortable with you before you go dragging them off to another part of the country.'

'I guess that's fair enough,' said Gene.

'That's more than fair enough. I'd say that's generous. Do you have any memories of what you tried to do to Shane?'

Gene stared at Sonny in confusion. She shook her head. 'What did I try and do to Shane?'

'Drown her when she was a baby.'

Gene's mouth was agape. Was Sonny really talking about her?

'If it weren't for your mother waking in the middle of the night, Shane wouldn't be alive today.'

'I'm sorry,' and her voice was sad; sad for a strange sick woman she didn't know, sad for one distraught husband. 'I don't remember that at all.'

'Believe me it happened.'

'I believe you,' Gene mumbled.

'The other saving grace is Shane has no recollection and Lindsay didn't see it happen.'

Gene turned the can of drink around in her hands and glanced at the opening. It was like a single daisy petal. 'What do they know of me now?'

'I haven't talked to the children about you in over three years. What was the point? Four years ago Lindsay asked me one day if Mommy was still in the hospital and I told her no. She asked where you were and I told you had gone. Gone where, she said, and I told her we didn't know. Shane never talks about you.'

Gene glanced at Sonny then lowered her eyes to the can in her hands. Was she expecting too much?

'You ready to answer all their questions?' Sonny asked.

She raised her head to look at him. She nodded slowly.

'You ready to answer all mine?'

She stopped nodding. She tried not to stammer when she asked, 'Are you still thinking two years before I meet them again?'

'Haven't changed my mind on that, Gene.'

'How do I gain your trust?'

'For starters, I want us to have a weekly appointment with a family therapist.'

'Okay,' drawled Gene. 'What for exactly?'

'So you understand what being part of our family is all about. So you understand what being a parent is.'

'Sonny, I have worked with children for the last four years. It might surprise you but I got on well with them and had a very positive relationship with many of my students.'

'What does that prove, Gene? That you can teach. That says diddly-squat about your ability as a parent.'

'Okay,' she drawled again. 'Do you have someone in mind?'

'I've found someone we can try.'

'So we have a weekly appointment with a family therapist. What else?'

'We have another weekly catch-up just the two of us. Just talking, getting to know each other again.'

'You want to be my friend or is there some other purpose?'

'I don't know, to be honest. I'll be watching you closely that's for sure.'

Gene sucked her cheeks in every so slightly as Sonny continued. 'But I imagine you don't have many friends here. You never did. Suppose you might need one from time to time. Be a bit mean to expect you to stay the course without any support. But you better work out how you stop yourself from sliding backwards. You better get some other people in your life besides me or you'll be living a pretty miserable existence.'

When Sonny had finished she asked, 'How are your parents?'

'They're doing fine, thank you. But I wasn't meaning them.'

'I think I understand what you are saying, Sonny. You're telling me your life has moved on and you're with somebody else, is that the case?'

'Does the thought of that bother you?'

She didn't know how to reply. She hadn't truthfully asked herself that question; she had only generally skirted the issue. 'I don't hold it against you, Sonny. It's what I urged you to do. I wanted you to be happy, remember?'

'I remember everything, Saint Gene.'

He left her there sitting on the bench.

65

Every Monday at four-fifteen p.m. she would meet Sonny at a therapist's office in Elgin Avenue. Every Thursday afternoon at four p.m. Sonny would meet her outside the art gallery and they would adjourn to a café or a park bench depending on the weather.

At their first session with Shelby, their therapist, Sonny told her point blank Gene had been absent from his and her children's life for five years. She had been in an institution for three years before that and had tried to drown her baby girl, which had led to her hospitalisation.

They spent that first session talking about why Gene wanted to have a relationship with her girls again, what sort of relationship did she see herself having, what did she feel was missing in her life that prompted her to try and reconnect with her children. There were some 'I don't know exactly' responses from Gene. The therapist told her that was okay, they would revisit these questions more over the coming weeks. In the next session they talked at length about the eight essential responsibilities that parents must adhere to in order to foster their child's physical and emotional wellbeing:

1. Provide an environment that is safe
2. Provide your child with basic needs
3. Provide your child with self-esteem needs
4. Teach your child morals and values
5. Develop mutual respect with your child
6. Provide discipline which is effective and appropriate
7. Involve yourself in your child's education
8. Get to know your child

Sonny said they had missed one. 'Have fun with your children.'

That was so like Sonny, Gene thought, slightly amused, but she quickly moved on and said it was difficult for her to do all those things because Sonny was forbidding her access, making it impossible for her to meet, let alone get to know her children.

Sonny countered her argument with his own stating she had abdicated responsibility for her children years ago by walking out of their life and not keeping in touch. It wasn't a right that automatically returned to her when she snapped her fingers and said I want my children in my life, I want to be part of their life.

The therapist acknowledged Gene's objections and needs but also said, given the circumstances, Sonny had a point. 'Gene,' she asked, 'are you learning about your children through your husband?'

Reluctantly Gene conceded. 'Yes, he is telling me about them.'

'Well I think slowly, slowly is the way to go. We'll keep working things through and I think it would be helpful to set some targets and associated rewards, such as if Gene gets to x point, then you, Sonny, will tell the children that their mother has been in touch and is keen to get to know them again. This is something we have to manage carefully on both sides in order for it to go as well as possible.'

One day when Gene turned up for their session, she discovered Sonny had phoned ahead and said he couldn't make it. To Shelby, Gene said, 'Sorry to cancel on you.'

Shelby replied: 'It's fine, Gene. We're not going to waste this session. I was going to suggest some individual sessions with the two of you. Come on in.' Once Gene had made herself comfortable Shelby suggested they talk more about what drove Gene to come back to Winnipeg.

Gene told her about Mary, how Mary had brought music back into her life and true friendship and how joyful that had been. It had been a catalyst and made her see that she wasn't as happy as she had tried to be in her new life. 'Partly why I came back was I want joy in my life again,' Gene said. She told Shelby about the family she saw playing basketball and how much she wanted to be a part of it. 'I wanted that sense of contentedness and completeness – that feeling I had with Sonny and Lindsay in those early years. That feeling that everything was right and at ease.'

'Your daughter, daughters,' she corrected herself, 'have grown up since then.'

'Yes.'

'They won't need you in the same way as when they were babies. They're likely to be quite self-contained and self-centred.'

'Oddly,' said Gene, 'it was their needing me that I didn't cope so well with. When Lindsay was about two years old I felt like we were over the hardest part. She was very independent. Not clingy. I went and did a six-week practical teaching block and my mother-in-law helped look after her during the day. I was busy but I was happy. I had the variety of my job. I had my little girl to come home to. Sonny would come home to both of us and we all delighted in each other's company. He'd always been an exuberant man but when he became a father he seemed to blossom in a way I had never seen before. He was beautiful. Our life was beautiful, joyful.'

'Are you hoping Sonny and you can get back together so you can have that type of life again, that type of joy?'

Gene's heart skipped a beat. 'Who said anything about getting back together again?'

'Me. I'm trying to understand your motivations.'

Gene laughed dryly. 'I wish you luck there. I don't even know my motivations.'

'I see,' said Shelby. 'I think there are things not clear for you yet.' She topped up their glasses of water. 'Hopefully through our sessions they will become clearer.'

Gene wondered how it was that before she left Vancouver she thought things had been.

'Can I ask you, how much of your returning to Winnipeg was about you wanting to see your girls again and or see Sonny again, versus you wanting to make some amends for the way you had treated them in abandoning them, the hurt you caused them?'

Gene tried hard not to blush at Shelby's question, for in all their discussions to date, not once had Gene talked about making amends for what she had done. She struggled to understand how her making such a sacrifice, her standing aside so Sonny could have a better life was a bad thing. But perhaps it was the way she went about it. Shelby was giving words to something she hadn't voiced herself; graciously assuming that was the case. It was the case, wasn't it? After some time Gene said, 'I think it was both.'

'Okay,' said Shelby. 'I want you to think about that more over the coming weeks. Think about how you are making amends or want to go about making amends.' She reached for a jug of water and refilled their glasses. 'Let's change tack,' she suggested. 'When you left that institution years ago and left Sonny, did you still love him?'

'Yes!' Gene's response was instinctive and unequivocal.

'So tell me what happened to that love?'

'What happened to that love?' Gene shook her head, trying to make sense of what she had done. 'I think it became like a fragile egg that I had to wrap in cotton wool and put away in a safe place and not ever bring out to look at lest it might break and what was inside might run out, slip away and I would never be able to put it back together.'

'Do you still love your husband?'

'I have feelings for him of course. He has always been a good man.'

'So it would appear. But do you still love him?'

'I don't know!'

'You don't know or is it you don't want to have any expectations, which is totally understandable, Gene.' Softly she said, 'Where is that egg now?'

Gene sighed deeply as she shook her head. 'I don't know.'

'Are you hoping you can find it, bring it out again? That it will be what helps bind you and Sonny together again, bring your family together again?'

'I don't know what to hope for. I don't know what Sonny wants. We've only had a few hours together since I've been back and as you can imagine they haven't been all "happy families". I get the impression he has moved on from me. Sometimes I sense he is with someone else. Most likely he has been. I basically told him to forget about me and find someone else to love him. So, I don't feel I have any right to ask him questions whatsoever. He doesn't owe me anything. I'm the one who owes him something.'

'What do you feel you owe him?'

'A better life.'

'With you?'

'I used to think without me. But now I don't know anymore.'

'Why do you say that?

'Because when we were good we were very good.'

Shelby's eyes met hers in quiet understanding.

After a few moments Gene offered her a summation. 'I think by coming back here I'm trying to give us another chance. Give him another chance. But that sounds crazy. Perhaps if I'm honest I want him to give us another chance. I want him to give me another chance: first and foremost, another chance in his life, in the life of our daughters. I don't know if that means another chance at being the mother of our children exactly, or even another chance of being his partner. And I guess I don't just want that chance. What I want is it to be a happy, joyful experience. I want the chance to work out in some way. I know there's no guarantee that it will.'

'You're right. There's absolutely no guarantee that it will.' Shelby paused. 'If he's unavailable or not open to that do you think you could still have a relationship with your daughters with him just being on the periphery?'

Gene didn't answer immediately. 'I'd like to think that I could. Is there any reason why I couldn't? I mean I should be capable of doing that don't you think?'

Shelby nodded slowly. 'Do you want to?'

'Y-es.'

Her hesitancy did not go unnoticed. 'You sound a little unsure.'

'I don't know them at all really. I only know Sonny. And I'm not sure they will want to have a relationship with me. I know I will be an outsider for some time, which is fine I don't need to be the centre of attention – in fact I hate being the centre of attention.'

'You will be an outsider. No matter what happens, you will be. You won't have the same standing as Sonny in their eyes. They will always defer to him, so it will be a challenge for you to have the same intimacy, the same respect and authority. They love their father. They will be very close to him. They won't be close to you. They may not even love you – certainly not at the beginning.'

Shelby paused for a few moments, giving Gene time to process all she had just said.

'You will be ranked low down on their list,' she continued. 'When children are young they tend to rank their parents the highest followed by their siblings – that order can change as they grow older, but that's the gist of it, followed by their grandparents then their friends, again those two tend to swap as they get older. That is the world you will be entering. I don't mean to discourage you. In fact, I encourage you. I want you to enter that world. I just want you to be aware of how it will be and to prepare for how you will overcome the disappointments, for children being children there will be disappointments aplenty.

'They will take their lead from their father, but remember they believe that in his life, in his eyes they come before you. And in your situation that has certainly been the case. If you and Sonny were to patch things up it's possible that for some time you will be viewed as a stepmother, as their father's new wife.'

'I think given where we are that's not about to happen.'

'Who knows,' said Shelby her tone ambivalent. 'What I think is more important is to be aware of how these things could play out and for you to remember that you are the adult in this relationship. It is your responsibility to act like an adult and not to overreact to anything; it's your responsibility to be compassionate and understanding. It's possible they could resent you coming back into their lives and trying to steal their father away from them. They could resent that you have more feelings for their father than you have for them.'

'So what you are saying is, it would be better that I put my relationship with them ahead of any relationship I have with Sonny?'

'No, Gene, I can't advise you one way or another. You are an adult and Sonny's an adult and in situations where both adults want to maintain their relationship or get back together it's important that they put their relationship first and the kids fall in behind. But where two adults are not in that space and never will be, it's important that each adult has a healthy relationship with their children, the best possible relationship, even if they only have the barest platonic relationship with each other. You know some kids amaze you with their maturity. They're thrilled when their parents get back together again. It makes them feel whole and grounded like nothing else.'

Some time later Gene said, 'I don't know how to move forward on any of this. It feels as if it's all in Sonny's court.'

'No. It might appear that way but it's in both of your courts. You both have to open up to each other. Tell each other what you think, what you hope for, what you want. Contrary to what you might believe, disclosure can be quite liberating. It can be quite powerful in transforming situations.'

Gene walked home via the Payfair supermarket. She bought a tube of condensed milk and sucked it completely empty by the time she got home. The purchase and her consumption were quite out of character for her. By the end of that tube she realised she hadn't set out for Winnipeg to redress her wrong doings; she had set out for Winnipeg thinking she could pick up her happy family life with Sonny again, like she had when Lindsay was a toddler. She hadn't really thought of Sonny or her kids at all, of what they wanted out of their life. They were like the tube of condensed milk. She was still trying to suck the life out of them without giving any life in return.

66

Throughout fall, as the loons called out through the morning mist and the passerines and herons and flocks of kingfishers flew southwards, Gene managed to pick up some relief teaching. In October, after a very quiet Thanksgiving, she received a letter of offer for a full time teaching position from Miles MacDonnell, a local high school. It was a 12-month maternity leave contract that started after Christmas and was likely to become a permanent position. She was delighted. The school offered classes in French immersion and she would be teaching History and Geography in French. It was six kilometres away from her flat. She would be able to walk there and back most days. It felt good to land that contract. It brought greater certainty to her life, when other parts were still uncertain.

When next she met Sonny and told him of her full-time job he was genuinely pleased for her. 'Well done,' he said. 'Hopefully you will make some friends amongst the teaching staff.'

'Yes,' Gene replied, 'and maybe amongst the janitors as well.' She longed for a friend like Mary.

'Do you have a lot of preparation to do for the role?' he asked.

'Yes, a fair bit. Plus, I've got some other projects I want to tackle before I start.'

'Good,' Sonny said, without inquiring any further. So she made some inquiries of her own. She wanted to know what the girl's favourite colours were.

'Lindsay loves blue, an intense light blue, turquoise colour. She says it reminds her of the sky and I'm forever up in the sky so it reminds her of me. But I think it reminds me of her eyes, your eyes, your Mom's eyes, hard not to miss.'

'I don't know what you're talking about,' said Gene, straight-faced, but tongue in cheek.

'Now Shane,' continued Sonny, 'I'm not sure what her favourite colour is any more. For years she loved yellow. She loved The Wizard of Oz and the yellow brick road, but now that she's into Skippy, she likes everything bush green.'

It was early November. There wasn't much bush green about. But on that day she was more concerned with Lindsay rather than Shane. Her twelfth birthday was coming up. 'What are you giving Lindsay for her birthday?' she asked.

'Well, she's talking about wanting to get her ears pierced. I thought I might let her. What do you think? This year or next year, when she's a teenager.'

'Up to you, Sonny, it's your call. I'd say she's old enough to look after them.' After a few moments she said, 'Can I get her something for her birthday?'

'How am I going to explain that?'

'It can come from you. I won't write a card or anything.'

'Gene...'

'Please!' her voice almost pleading. 'Let me. Does she like to read?'

'They both do.'

'I thought I would buy her a book. And one for Shane as well.'

'We'll see.'

When next they met Gene handed over two brown paper bags. On one she had written: Lindsay. Inside was a copy of The Princess Bride, with an exchange card and an embroidered bookmark: a strip of blue turquoise with white tassels, with her name and birthdate 18.11.62 embroidered in white.

Inside the parcel addressed to Shane was a copy of

Watership Down and another bookmark: hers a strip of green and her name and birthdate, 23.7.66, stitched in yellow to match the tassels.

'Maybe this will make her more interested in rabbits, rather than kangaroos,' said Gene. 'Though you may have to read it with her.'

'Thanks,' said Sonny.

She wondered if he would pass it on. Although she didn't want to pry, when next she saw him she couldn't refrain from asking what they thought of the presents.

'I'm sorry to say they were more interested in the books than the person who bought them.'

'That's fine, Sonny.'

'I told them a lady I knew thought they might like them, but I doubt they even heard that.'

'That's okay,' said Gene.

'We got Lindsay's ears pierced in the end. She now has sterling silver sleepers in them.'

'Very grown up,' said Gene. 'And how was her birthday?'

'It was a quiet affair. We just went to Mom and Dad's. I offered to take everyone out for dinner but Lindsay thought it would be easier on everyone if we went to Farmor's place.'

'Easier for your mother to cook for everyone?' queried Gene.

'Easier for Mom and Dad not to drag themselves out at night was what Lindsay was thinking...not have them walk through the snow and chill to a restaurant.'

'Oh, I see,' said Gene. 'That's very considerate of her.'

'That's the way Lindsay is. Always thinking of everyone else.' Their eyes met, the phantom of Lindsay between them. 'I'm sorry I couldn't invite you, Gene. I know we get together and have our catch-up sessions, and we don't end up in a screaming match—'

'That was never us.'

'I know. But I need some more time before I'm comfortable with things. And, you see, the girls are really

399

in a good place right now and I'm not sure I want to upset the applecart.'

'It's fine, Sonny,' she said. 'We're making progress. Slow progress.' She smiled. 'How are your Mom and Dad?'

'Dad's hearing not so great these days, all that time in planes. He wears hearing aids. Another reason why Lindsay thought it would be easier at home rather than in a restaurant – he finds all that background noise troublesome with his hearing aids. They're not the best technology.'

Gene nodded, wondering how bad his hearing really was. 'Does he still fly?'

'Occasionally he does a run for me. Most days he still tinkers with planes though, can't keep him away.'

'And your Mom?'

'She's does pretty well, all things considered. A bit of arthritis in her hands and toes, worse in winter, but mostly she says she can't complain.'

'Do they hate me?'

Sonny frowned at her. 'No one hates you, Gene. No one has ever hated you. Though I will say that any parent finds it hard going when people hurt their children.' He stared pointedly at her. 'Mostly, I think no one really understands you, that's all.'

'Do you understand me?'

'I think I understand you more than anyone, but that doesn't mean I always understand you. And even when I do understand you, it doesn't mean I necessarily agree with you. Do you get my drift?'

She nodded. 'I used to think you understood me better than anyone. It was hard to hide from you.' She immediately regretted saying that.

'Not too hard, obviously.'

'Did you look for me?'

'No.' He paused. 'Jonathan and I went to the police initially to provide your details in case a body was found. We thought suicide was a very real possibility…none of us wanted to think of that, that you were in such a bad place that you wanted to end it all.'

She was glad Sonny was looking at the table. If he raised his eyes to her she didn't know how she could maintain eye contact. That must have been hellish for him. For everyone.

'Your disappearance was clearly no accident,' he continued. 'If you were running, we weren't going to chase you. If you were going to top yourself, you clearly wanted us not to interfere, maybe save us from witnessing any of that.'

He looked at her then, his eyes searching. Mercy me. She didn't know where to start. All she could manage was a barely audible, 'Thank you.'

It was late November and nearly dark out. Neither one of them had mentioned the Christmas decorations that had started to appear in shop windows, for where would that conversation lead?

But Sonny being Sonny asked. 'What are you doing for Christmas?' She turned the question on him to buy herself some time in replying.

'What are we doing for Christmas? We're actually going to Montreal to have it with Jonathan and your Mom. I'm taking my folks as well. Abigail and her family will all be there too. Wyatt's getting on in years – he's 83 now. You mother asked all of us to come if we could manage it, even Morton who never likes to leave his dogs, asking him to get Paul to look after them. He's not too happy about that, but he'll be fine when he gets there. I suspect he will probably bring two across in the car if I know Morton.'

Gene agreed. 'Hard to separate him from his best friends.'

'They are, aren't they?' said Sonny, before taking a slug of his coffee. 'Did you know your Mom and Wyatt celebrated their 25th wedding anniversary back in July?'

Gene shook her head. That milestone had escaped her.

'Well they did, and they never had a party, so we're going to do something for them between Christmas and New Year.'

'That will be lovely, I'm sure.'

'Yeah. So that's what' we're doing for Christmas. If you wanted to rock up, I'm sure you'd be welcome, but I think you should make the approach and travel under your own steam. I can give you the money for a plane ticket or a train ticket if you can't afford it.'

'What an invitation,' said Gene, thinking did that come across as thinly veiled sarcasm? I hope so! 'So what you're saying, Sonny, is: while you're not yet comfortable introducing me to the girls you'd be happy for me to meet the girls if I were with Mom and everyone in Montreal for Christmas.'

'That's the gist of it. I don't believe it would be my place to stand between you and the rest of your family. In fact, I want you to reach out to them and maybe this will be the carrot you need to do that.'

That will be the way to do it, my foot, thought Gene. 'You know, Sonny, I might just find that a little too much all at once.'

'Suit yourself.'

'Is that a neat way for you to absolve any guilt you might have over me spending Christmas alone here in Winnipeg?'

'Whoa! Don't you dare try to make me feel guilty for abandoning you for one miserable Christmas! That's below the belt don't you think?' He glared at her for a few seconds before placing his right hand on the table, palm up, almost as if he were reaching out to her. 'Gene, I would rather you not be alone for Christmas. No one should be alone for Christmas and that's why I came clean with you. So if you're not going to go east, what else do you have in mind?'

She had nothing but she wasn't going to tell him that. She did not want Sonny's pity. 'I haven't thought it through. I don't think I want to go away as I really do want to be well prepared for when I start teaching. I thought I'd go to midnight mass obviously and do something with some church folk the following day. Don't worry there will be people more lonely than me on Christmas day.'

The next time they met for their non-Shelby catch-up Sonny took her to an ice hockey store.

'Christmas shopping,' he said by way of explanation.

'Of course,' said Gene, happy to join him for this activity. 'Are you buying the girls skates for Christmas?'

'No.' He paused. 'I'm buying you skates for Christmas. I dug out your old pair last week and I'm sorry they were so rotten I had to throw them out.'

'Sonny, you don't have to buy me skates for Christmas.'

'Why not? Did you make a pledge to yourself when you went west to give up skating as well?'

'No,' she said, feeling uncomfortable about the amount he was about to spend on her, uncomfortable still about many things.

'Do you not enjoy skating any more?'

'No, I imagine I would. It's just, well, I can buy my own skates.'

'Too late. I'm buying them for you. I want you to enjoy skating this Christmas, enjoy doing something at least.'

So he was feeling guilty about Christmas. But she thought better of bringing it up. 'This complicates things, Sonny. I have no idea what to get you for Christmas.'

'You don't have to get me anything. Your coming back from the dead, that's enough. Right now, knowing that I'm not in anyway responsible for you leaving the world, is a good enough present for me.'

'Oh, Sonny,' she whispered. She reached out and squeezed his arm before walking away to the back of the store. She needed some time.

In the end, the pair of skates she let Sonny buy her

was made from kangaroo leather, apparently standard boot material since the mid-sixties because it was more durable.

When the attendant told them that, her eyes met Sonny's.

'Poor Skippy,' he said.

Gene tried really hard not to laugh, but she couldn't help it.

After he dropped her home, she walked up the stairs, let herself into her flat, closed the door behind her, dropped her parcel on the floor and went over to the window to pull the heavy drapes. It was well below freezing. But before she did anything she stared out into the mute darkness. 'You're still one hell of a man, Sonny,' she said out loud to the silent expanse. 'How am I meant to get through all this and not be attracted to you, not have feelings for you? How am I meant to not love you a little, not hope a little, especially when you're coming from such a good place, wanting to do right by our children, when you're a decent man, a caring man?'

And from inside her came a reply: 'The same way you managed when you were eighteen, when you steered your own course for ten years.'

'Really? Really!' she answered back. 'So much has changed since then.'

Her reply: 'So how did you manage to lock all your feelings inside for the last five years – all your feelings for your children, and especially him?'

The next time they met up, Gene gave Sonny a Christmas wreath for their front door. It was made from twisted cane, had conifer leaves of different hues of green woven through as well as pine cones, fake red berries, and nine small mobiles hanging off it – three each of planes, elks and kangaroos.

'Where did you find this?' Sonny asked.

'I made it,' she said.

'Even the kangaroos?'

'Even the kangaroos. Cut them out of a picture book and built them up with lots of glue and paper and dipped them in resin.'

'How like you Gene. It's one of a kind,' Sonny said, a smile lighting his eyes.

'It is,' she smiled in return.

67

When Sonny returned from Montreal in the New Year Gene politely asked him how his trip went.

'Very good,' he replied. 'Going there was the right thing to do. It was what my head needed.'

'To get away?'

'Yes, that's right.'

'Are you saying that it was good to get away from your business or from me?' she queried.

'That's exactly what I'm saying. From you.'

'Huh,' she replied. 'What am I meant to make of that?'

'Make it of it what you will. I was glad to not be in Winnipeg thinking of you. I was glad to get away and get some perspective.'

'Well maybe you know a little bit about how I felt going to Vancouver.'

'You got all the perspective you needed at Freshwater,' he said dryly.

Gene sucked in her cheeks. Best to let that slide she decided. 'Did you tell anyone in Montreal of my presence here?'

'Not a soul. That ball is completely in your court.'

She slowly nodded her appreciation.

'So, how was Christmas?' he asked.

Smiling, she said, 'I broke in my boots.'

'Good.'

And that was the end of all talk of Christmas. She was half expecting Sonny to give her a complete rundown of everyone and everything; perhaps he was waiting for her to ask, so ask she did. 'Everyone fine back east?'

'Everyone was fine.'

They stared at each other, not saying anything, until

Sonny leant across the table and in a low voice said, 'Gene, if you want to know what's going on with your family, find out yourself, pick up the phone.'

'I don't have a phone,' she replied.

'Whatever. I'm not going to be the one that drip feeds you information so you can feel less bad about not being in contact with them. You don't want me to tell them about you – fair enough. But I've decided I'm not going out of my way either to tell you about them. We, Lindsay, Shane and I have a great relationship with all your family. We relate to them – get it?' He stared at her pointedly. 'It's up to you.'

Aside from that minor showdown the weeks rolled on. Sonny and her were getting on as well as ever, not really going over much old ground, just talking each week about the events of the past week, what the girls had been up to, what they'd done on the weekend. In talking to her about the girls he was very open. Any question she asked, he would answer – anything and everything. She was certain that before long he would revoke his extreme proclamation that he wanted to wait two years before he introduced her to Lindsay and Shane.

It was a good thing she was able to remain so optimistic for that winter in Winnipeg had been biting, reminding her she was back in the icy cold heart of Canada – far away from the mild-by-comparison, coastline. She splurged and bought herself a pair of sorrels and a knee-length, Woods arctic-down parka so she could get through the minus ten days of January, and the minus twenty nights. Though it was a rare occasion for her to venture out in the evening.

By late April, the snow had all but melted and the days were slowly warming. Sonny and her had planned to go walking in a park but a shower had intervened, so they were back at Angelos where they had first met nine months earlier.

'The holidays are coming up,' Gene said by way of an opener.

'They are.' Sonny paused. 'I guess you know more about that being a teacher and all.'

She laughed lightly, took a sip of her hot chocolate. 'Do you have any plans for the girls?'

'I do actually. I'm taking six weeks off and taking them on vacation to British Columbia. Something we've always talked of doing as a way of celebrating Lindsay finishing elementary school. They're really looking forward to it. We'll call in and see Morton for a few days over and back.'

'Oh…' It never seemed to amaze Gene that her siblings were a part of her children's life but she wasn't. After a pregnant pause she said, 'I was hoping maybe I would get the opportunity to meet them this summer and spend some time with them.'

'Sorry, Gene, but I have been looking so forward to this trip myself and planning it for a few years. It's something I really want to do with just the two of them. For all the time she's been at school the longest break I've ever spent with Lindsay is two weeks. It's all I could afford until I built up the business and got it to the point where I now have two partners and we can afford for me to have this break. I'm not changing these plans for you. I'm sorry.' He looked at her with eyes that were sincere and soft and brown.

She glared back. She felt hurt and frustrated. Could he see that in her eyes?

He must have because he flinched then turned his head away from her to look out on the street. 'What do you suggest I do?' he asked after some moments. Turning back to her he said, 'Take them to visit you in British Columbia? Tell them I've just heard where you're living.'

She stared at him – the impossibility of that. 'How would it be if I happened to be at Morton's when you visited?'

'You want to go visit your brother – by all means –

I'm sure he'd love to see you – but do you think that's going to win any favours with your daughters? You're not exactly reaching out to them that way.'

'Well maybe I could write to them and tell them I'll be at Morton's. Tell them I heard they were coming through and I would love to meet up with them again.'

Sonny tapped the menu on the table weighing up his options. After a little while he stopped. 'I'm sorry, Gene, in this I am going to be utterly selfish – your doing that could really throw a spanner in the works and spoil their holidays, when they have been talking about this for the past year. This is a time when you need to put their needs ahead of your own for a change.'

'I do do that, Sonny. I have done that for years, although it may not seem that way to you.'

'Nope, you're right. It doesn't. Enlighten me as to how your vanishing from their life, the girls being motherless, is putting their needs ahead of yours.'

She wanted to tell him, but she felt that if she did he would think she was crazy once more – still – when it wasn't the case at all.

After a while Sonny asked, 'What will you do over the summer? Did you have any thoughts or plans that don't hinge around the girls?'

Gene shook her head. 'Don't worry about me.'

'See, there's my problem, because I do.'

'Well, let me see my children!'

'Not yet. Do something else this summer to take your mind off them. Go visit Jonathan. I'm sure he'd love to see you. Catch up with Abigail – she will fill you in on your daughters.'

Gene stared at Sonny unable to respond.

Eventually she sighed. 'I might go visit a friend in British Columbia – Mary – the woman I told you about. She's just had her own setback.'

'What's that?'

'She has tried to have children for years. She and her husband, Billy, have talked about adopting but kept on putting it off, putting it off hoping they would one day be lucky and she would carry a child to full-term, so they never explored adoption. Now, when they have decided they would, she's been told she's too old. They won't allow women over thirty-five years of age to adopt.

'And she's thirty-five.'

'Yes,' said Gene.

Sonny cursed. 'It's the Air Force and me all over again! How did she take that?'

'They're trying to work it through with their local priest. She's trying to put a positive spin on everything but I think it has really knocked her for a loop.'

'Where does she live?'

'Kitisak, way up in the north.'

'How do you get there?'

'I don't know. By bus, I guess. Train.'

The next time he met Gene for their one-on-one session he pulled up in a station wagon. 'Is the dual cab in being serviced?' she asked.

'No,' he said. 'This is for you. So you can go visit your friend, Mary, over the summer holidays.'

'Oh,' said Gene. 'Goodness.' She was taken back. 'Does it belong to a friend of yours?'

'Nope, I bought it. The registration papers are in your name. It's yours. I figured you could do with some wheels.'

She walked the six kilometres to school and back each day and was happy to do so, but the car would certainly give her some freedom to go further afield. 'Sonny, I...I don't know what to say.'

'You could try, "Thank you."'

'Thank you.' She looked at him. 'Is there a catch?'

'Nope. No catch. I just wanted to help you out with your summer holiday to make sure you could do something you enjoy that's all.'

She smiled her appreciation. Part of her felt this was her consolation prize for not getting her daughters. 'I hope I remember how to drive.'

'I hope you do too. Do you need a practise run?'

'Yes,' she said. 'I think I do.'

He sat in the passenger seat while she drove to Birds Hill Provincial Park and back, all the while thinking but saying nothing about wanting to see her girls more than she wanted a car.

She wrote to Mary and she got a reply back urging her to come for the whole holidays. She went for four weeks all up, including one week driving there and one week driving back, camping along the way. When she returned home she was restless and frustrated that she could be spending this time with her daughters. She thought of Sonny constantly, wondering where he was and what he was doing with them. She felt herself going stir crazy being in her small apartment in the height of summer and with no one to do anything with.

She went to the Pavilion Gallery Museum in Assiniboine Park to see the Winnie the Pooh exhibition. That reminded her of her childhood, and her daughters. She walked around the city past the state legislature building with its Golden Boy atop, representing the spirit of youth – somehow that managed to remind her of Sonny. The grand staircase on the north side with the life size statues of bison in bronze also reminded her of Sonny, of their first trip up north. There was no escaping him. She packed up and took herself camping at Lac du Bonnet for a week and then another exploring Whiteshell Provincial Park. When she returned there was a postcard from Sonny from Kitisak of all places.

'*Gene. Trust the car went well. We have just spent two nights at Kitisak – not by design but navigational error on my behalf...obviously meant to be. I have to say your friend's little town is rather charming. I hope you enjoyed your time here. The girls have certainly loved their holiday. Sonny.*'

Something about Sonny's postcard irked her. She

411

knew it shouldn't have but it did. He was free to go wherever he wanted with whomever he wanted but she wasn't. The injustice of that weighed heavily on her mind.

When he returned they met in a coffee shop at four-thirty on their normal Thursday afternoon. He handed her what looked like a shoebox. Inside was a life-sized loon, a decoy made of finely woven sedge. 'I thought you'd like this,' he said, ever so softly.

Last fall she'd told him how she enjoyed waking to the call of the loons; how comforting that was. He'd obviously remembered.

She touched it with her forefinger. 'It's lovely.' The sculpture was life size, a simple natural form, but that wasn't the point.

She pushed it aside. 'Sonny, you can't keep buying me off like this, stalling for time.'

'I'm not buying you off and I can stall for time. We had a deal if you remember.'

'I remember, but it seems to me the deal isn't that reasonable.'

'Your actions weren't reasonable, Gene.'

'How long are you going to keep punishing me?'

'How long are you going to keep punishing me?'

'How have I punished you?'

'By your withdrawal. By your lack of disclosure. By your Gene-knows-best approach to life. By your complete lack of apology.'

'I apologised before I left!'

'Is that what you were doing? Apologising in advance for something people aren't aware of, for actions that have yet to be committed, is NOT an apology – it's a mark of deviousness – it does not absolve you.'

'Who am I meant to apologise to?'

'Well there's your mother and Wyatt for what you put them through, your siblings and their partners for the worry and disruption to their lives, me, the girls, my parents, my cousin Sylvia – all those women who have had to carry the load of mothering the girls because you absconded. You should be grateful for all they have done for you.'

'I am grateful,' said Gene.

'You have a funny way of showing it.'

'How can I show it when you won't let me get in touch with your parents?'

'I'm not stopping you from contacting your own family. Start there.'

'I will contact them one day.'

'When?'

'When I'm ready.'

'Of course,' he nodded. 'Well then, you can understand I will let you see the girls one day when I'm ready.'

'Why can't I see them now? I could drive round to your place tonight.'

'If you want a good relationship with your daughters you won't do that. Tell me why you didn't want to have a relationship with them five years ago.'

'I wasn't well.'

'Bullshit. You told me you've been mostly well for five years. Why didn't you want to have a relationship with your girls back then? What was the problem with them?

'There was never any problem with them. There was only ever a problem with me.'

'Which was?'

'I didn't want to lose them like I lost Joel.'

'You didn't want them to drown?'

'No, it wasn't about them drowning as such.' Gene bit in to her lips, as she tried to order her thoughts. 'I was looking back at my journal the other night. The one I kept under lock and key at Freshwater.'

'And?'

'One of the phobias that was running through my head, possibly even before you and Jonathan had me committed, was that I wanted to remove myself from the girls. I wanted you to take them away from me. I didn't want the responsibility of them. I didn't want to get close to them and lose them like I lost Joel. How Morton was lost to me for years. I didn't want that profound attachment and that unbearable separation.'

'Keep talking,' said Sonny.

'That's it,' said Gene. 'I don't know how I can explain it any better. This fear of losing them grew into something bigger as I feared I could lose you too, like how Mom lost Dad, and I couldn't cope with that. I couldn't cope with the thought of loving you all and losing you all so I walked away to try to avoid the pain that would come from losing any or all of you. And tied up with all of that was this unforgiveable thing I had done: having a tubal ligation, denying you having more children with me – denying you the possibility of having a son or two. By walking away, I attempted to fix both problems by giving you an out.'

'Gene, I got over not having any more kids, not having a son faster than you by all indications, for I was with Lindsay and Shane as they grew up and they were great kids, with great spirits. And if that was my lot in life, that was my lot. I got my head around that. On the holidays just gone Lindsay told me she wants to learn to fly and I'm going to teach her. I have every faith that if she and Shane are meant to be pilots one day, then they will be. And in twenty years time I will most likely have son-in-laws and grandchildren too. So all your talk about my non-existent legacy, our legacy, was moot as far as I was concerned. I'm not saying it wasn't a difficult decision for you to make, something that cut you up badly, but let's face it, you had made the decision, you had gone through with the operation. There was no looking back. You were the one who needed to accept the decision you had made and live with it.

'I have lived with it', snapped Gene. 'Every damn day since.' Gene always felt she had been in a no-win situation. Not because of Sonny but because of who she was. Having more children would do her head in.

Denying Sonny more children did her head in. She was right back where she was six years ago. She took a deep breath in, held it for several counts and when she exhaled she tried to let it go, tried to let it all go.

'You know your "damned-if-you-do", "damned-if-you-don't" view is what you are putting on yourself,' said Sonny.

So like him to read her mind just like that!

'Granted, that was a difficult few weeks we went through,' he continued. 'I was torn at the time, absolutely. But in the end I did not NOT support you. I did realise it was necessary for you, and I did not want you to suffer again like you had suffered – and as you said, it wasn't like we didn't have any children. So you're the one who has to shake that mentality. For god's sake shake it now, and shake it once and for all, so you can put it behind you.

'And that other fear you have of losing us – where did that get you? It was three decades since you lost your brother and father, surely you would have come to terms with that by your mid-thirties? You hadn't lost anyone since. And by your actions all you did was lose all of us when you walked away. You lost us for five years. We lost you for five years.'

'Yes, but you all lived!'

'You think your walking away has something to do with us still being here today?' She could hear the cynicism in his voice. 'What did you do? Make a secret pact with the Devil.'

She ignored him.

'Oh, that's right, pardon me,' he jeered. 'I forgot you were a nun. I should have said with God.'

Gene felt like throttling him. 'I didn't make a pact with anyone.' She was doing her all to keep her voice under control. 'But yes, I did think that I needed to walk away to ensure your lives would be safe from harm, safe from me.'

'Safe from you in what way?'

'Because I was cursed.'

'Are you still cursed?'

'That remains to be seen.'

Sonny looked at her and Gene felt the way he was looking at her was if he was trying to determine if madness still lurked inside. She had to convince him otherwise. 'Don't you see, Sonny? My mother was cursed, her mother was cursed – if you talk to Grandma Crowe I'm sure she will tell you all about it.'

'Your Grandma Crowe died over five years ago.'

'Oh...well...' Gene paused for a breather. 'How old was she?'

'Ninety-eight.'

'I hadn't thought.'

'I can tell,' Sonny exhaled. 'Never mind. Go on.'

'Well, I'm sure if you talk to Mom she will tell you all about what happened to Grandma Crowe. She will tell you all about her own life if she hasn't done so already and I am the woman in the next generation who is also cursed.'

'Gene, the only way you are cursed is by thinking you are cursed. Those women just had bad luck, like a lot of people have historically had back luck particularly with medical practices not being what they are today. Jonathan will tell you that I'm sure. But you think you are cursed. Shit, you should have been with me in Berlin, then you would understand cursed.'

'You can't compare what happened to my family to what happened to those people over there! You can't compare the fears I have for my loved ones, the loss I felt, to what those people endured day in and day out. They lived in a time and place where they expected danger, where they expected death and destruction. I didn't and still it found me. My world was benign. It was utopia and then it was shattered, just like it could be shattered again at any moment. Don't you think that's way more momentous, way more tragic?'

'No. Tragedy is in the eye of the beholder, just like beauty. Why do you think your pain and your tragedy are sovereign? You're sounding like the Gene I met twenty something years ago. You're looking at life as if it's threatening, as if it's over, when it's abundant and full of potential. Pick yourself up and get on with it like millions of people around the world have.'

'That's what I'm trying to do, Sonny.'

'Well, good. Keep trying.'

'I will, but maybe you could cut me some slack for leaving you and the girls like I did. Remember, your grandmother sent your mother away to a place where she could be safe. How is that so different to me leaving my daughters in your competent hands?'

'That's a question you'll have to answer.' He got up and left.

She was left feeling numb and upset. She was never comfortable arguing with anyone least of all Sonny. There were times in her life when she had to grit her teeth and be as persuasive and diplomatic as she could, when she worked in foreign affairs and for the United Nations. She didn't like it then either but she had managed. But this was different. This was personal.

Mutely she stared down at the crunched paper inside the shoebox while she tried to calm her breathing and let the tension go. After some moments she detected a hint of colour behind the white tissue. She moved it aside and there was a photograph of Sonny, Lindsay and Shane – it must have been taken on their recent holiday. Sonny was leaning up against a rock with one arm round each girl; Lindsay came up to his chin, Shane his chest.

She picked it up but it blurred on her and she had to put it back down, lean her head against the back of the seat and squeeze her eyes shut as unwanted tears trickled out of the corner of her eyes.

68

Gene thought about Sonny's closing remarks. Was she to infer that his grandmother would have gone with her daughter, his mother, if she could have? Or was his point that his mother was twenty years old, not pre-school age. Regardless of the answers she came up with, it didn't change the fact that she felt Sonny was trying to punish her for her actions, and that he wouldn't concede any ground until she had done something or some things…she wasn't sure what, but she was getting increasingly tetchy about it.

The weeks dragged on. The temperatures started their downhill slide and with it her mood. She wondered whether she should go see a doctor and ask to be put back on anti-depressants. She had been too ashamed to renew her prescription when she had run out at the convent – and for the most part she had got by with out the medication.

Now her patience was wearing thin. She wondered whether she should see a family lawyer. How would that all go down, particularly if Sonny really decided to play hardball? Who could she get to testify on her behalf? Sister Eugenia? Impossible. Her school principal? What could he say about her? Sadly, she was a woman with very few options.

'When can I see my children?' She demanded as soon as Sonny sat down at their next weekly catch-up. 'This has gone on for long enough.'

He glared at her. 'When you stop asking. But you know what? You can see your mother and Wyatt soon. They're going to be in town in two weeks and staying with me for six weeks through to the New Year.'

So like him to change the subject. 'Have you told them yet that I have moved back to Winnipeg? That I got in touch with you, wanting to see my daughters. I'm more than happy for you to tell them that.' As if he would!

'No, Gene. I haven't mentioned your name to them in years. But I have to say I find your lack of charity towards your parents and siblings at odds with your being a nun.'

Gene exhaled, not wanting to have this conversation with Sonny. She realised she had to make some attempt. 'Walking away as I did was an all or nothing deal. I didn't want to have them in my life and not you three. I wouldn't have been able to do it. I must be a failure in their eyes on so many levels. Even now. How can I tell them I've come back to be a mother to my children when I'm still failing at that? When I haven't got that sorted yet.'

'Don't think like that. Think of whether you would you like to see her? Them?'

'Come on, Sonny, one step at a time.'

'How hard is it for you to get in touch with them? Face them? I would have thought I would have been the hardest one for you to face.'

Ah, Sonny, there you are wrong, Gene thought...and suddenly she went from being angry at him to wanting to reach out and hold him in the most heartfelt embrace. I loved you the most. I missed you the most – your spirit, your optimism, your strength. Ever since I left you my life hasn't been whole. I've always known that and I got by for as long as I could on my own. Mary went some ways to filling that gaping hole but when she left I couldn't go on living without you...could she tell him that?

'I let you down, I know. I let everyone down.'

'Well then do something about it! This is not a game you and I are playing, Gene. It's not a set of chess. I'm not bargaining your family for the girls. I'm just trying to appeal to your conscience. They are your family. They're adults. They've all grown up. Your mother is growing old. They don't need protecting from you like our daughters do. That's not to say they still haven't had their hearts broken. They have. You can do something about that. You might be able to convince them to convince me to let you see the girls sooner. It might make me view you in a more favourable light.'

Aha, thought Gene, so there is a test I have to pass. 'You're being mean to me, Sonny, the way you are holding your power over the girls over me. I was never deliberately mean to you.'

'I'm not being mean to you. At least that's not the intention of my actions. I am denying you, yes. I have disappointed you, yes. But my actions are not aimed at getting back at you. Not aimed at deliberately hurting you. Though I recognise it may have hurt and disappointed you not being able to see your children last summer holiday. I knew I was being selfish. I told you that back in April – that was always going to be our holiday – plus there has been an element of wanting to see what you might do, how you might act if life presented you with some unexpected and difficult challenges.'

'The way you're testing me is not fair!' Gene exclaimed. The waitress behind the counter at the far end of the café was looking up at them. Gene gave her a thinly veiled smile.

Sonny barely glanced in her direction before he said, 'Maybe it's not, but it's acceptable under the circumstances.'

'How is it acceptable?' Gene tried not to raise her voice, but failed.

'Do I need to spell it out? How you say one thing and do another!' He leant towards her as he tried to control his anger.

'What was the problem with you telling me to my face that you didn't want to be with me anymore? You know you still could have lived here in Winnipeg and seen the girls now and then. We could have worked something out...if we're speaking honestly here, Gene, as you wrote in your infamous farewell letter...what was so hard about telling me to my face that you didn't love me any more?'

She shook her head in fierce refusal. 'It was never a case of not loving you!' her voice adamant.

'So you say, but that's where I stop buying what you're telling me, because people who love each other, work through things, even if they don't want to be married to the other person anymore, even if they decide not to be together? So was that what it was a case of? That you didn't want to be married to me any more? You returned your wedding ring after all!'

'No, Sonny, the fact that I didn't want YOU to be married to me anymore, that I didn't want YOU shackled to me any more, is a different thing altogether to ME not wanting to be married to you any more. It's a different thing to ME not loving you anymore.'

'I don't get the way your academic mind works, Gene! What kind of wife who proclaims to love her husband, who proclaims to love her children and love the father of her children, does not want him to be married to her anymore? Where's the love in that? For all your warped theories, Gene, and all your guilt, and all my patience and understanding, I can't get my head around that.'

'It's an eternal struggle isn't it? Trying to get one's head around something so big?'

They stared at each other in exasperation, in heavy silence, until Sonny exhaled. 'I'm so sick of your bloody cop-out nonsense.' He paused for the faintest instant. 'After we first met, I waited for you for ten years, while you were off doing your thing, getting your head together, doing God knows what.'

'I never asked you to wait for me.'

'So you'd rather I didn't wait for you.'

'Sonny!'

'Can't have it both ways, Gene. You knew I was waiting for you. You knew I had nearly given up on you when you wrote that letter from Geneva. You knew that your ship may have sailed without you, so long you had left things.'

'Yes... I... did. That was the risk I took. But, Sonny, I was always thinking of you and putting you first.'

'Bullshit! You were just sorting out your head.'

'Are you waiting another ten years?' Gene asked, a contemptuous edge to her voice. 'Waiting for me to sort my head out so I'll be good for a few more after that.'

'I don't mean to disappoint you, Gene, but I have no expectations any more when it comes to you. I don't sit around in disbelief any more. I don't grieve but I admit there was a time when I did. You want to know when?'

'When I was in Freshwater,' she said flatly.

'Hell no! When you were in Freshwater I was still hoping and praying every day you would get well and return to us. I didn't grieve then. What did I have to grieve for? It wasn't a case of woe is me.

'No, it was the cold calculating way that you left. That you thought so much of yourself that you couldn't think of me for just a little. That you couldn't confide in me where you were at, what your needs were, that you couldn't trust me that we could work out a solution together. Yet you had the gall to warn me about the rough days coming my way.'

'Sonny, please believe me. I am truly sorry.' And she was. She had been truly sorry then but he had no way of knowing it and she was truly sorry now, now that she could clearly see that after all this time, after all her overtures, the pain was still there, etched in the lines around his mouth, in the seeping sadness in his eyes. She reached out her hand to squeeze his but he jerked it away.

'Sorry? Don't you think that's a little too little too late?'

He was right. Supremely right. She hadn't apologised since she'd been back. She remembered last August when she returned Sonny saying that she could have apologised. Why did she not come holding her apology in her hand like a gift? My God she had pride. Where all her husband had was pain. Visible pain.

'I wanted kids for so long and then when we had them

I hardly got to enjoy them because YOU weren't there to look after them! You caused me so much stress because I constantly worried about the safety and the wellbeing and the happiness of our children because you were absent! I know you were sick and couldn't help it, but even so that's what you denied me. And then you vanished – deliberately – without a trace – and that upset and stressed me in countless other ways. Not to mention everyone else. Until one day I woke up and said, "Screw you, Gene. You're not going to be denying me anymore," and I said, "Good riddance." Good riddance to the hollowness you left us with. Good riddance to my bare unwanted love because what was the point. You're not the Snow Queen – you're the Ice Queen – when it comes to emotions. Not all of us have your skill in denying their emotions, denying their love, their loss, their pain, their grief. I'm not you. You're a paradox. Some days I used to think you struggled; that you lacked a certain internal fortitude but I think yours is the strongest of all. What affects normal people doesn't affect you. You've lost the common touch of those basic emotions. Instead you let something that is not such a big deal blow right out of proportion so it swamps your life and everyone's life around you.'

'Jonathan not being my brother was a big deal.'

'For a moment in time but it meant Jack Squat! What I would have given to have Jonathan be my older anything – hell it wouldn't have bothered me whether he was related to me by blood or not.'

'You've got him.'

'I have and I'm grateful for that each and every day. But I'm not talking about Jonathan per se, I'm talking about how you take something and make it mean something else – and we are all left to suffer in the dark and in your wake, suffer for what we don't know, whatever it is you carry around inside you that you can't seem to shake, you can't seem to talk about and never apologise for. It poisons you, Gene. It's like something terminal inside you. It's as if when they cut you open they left that thing inside you. Whatever that thing was. You went to Freshwater but you didn't spew it up. You went back a second time. Seems to me you still haven't expelled it. You've got to expel it and then maybe you can live a semblance of a normal life, maybe then you can appreciate what you have rather than bemoan what you don't.'

'I spent hours, years, speaking to those people at Freshwater.'

'And where the hell did that get you? Did you talk to the people that matter? This is what I mean when I said to you last year, the first time I saw you, that you have to prove to me that I can trust you. That trust cuts both ways. YOU HAVE TO TRUST ME. At this juncture in your life you are in a position where you have to totally trust me and one way or another, Gene, you are going to be forthcoming in that trust.'

'How many times do I have to tell you I trust you implicitly! I always have. When I was seventeen, I trusted you with my stories. When I married you, I trusted you with my life. When I left, I trusted you with our girls. How can you say I don't trust you?'

'Easy. Because to this day I still have not heard from your lips how you got that scar across your stomach. What prompted you to commit suicide? You know it was your brother who had to slice open your stomach and break every hospital rule in the book to save your life. Can you imagine the horror of that?'

'What are you talking about? Jonathan didn't operate on me!'

'The hell he didn't. You owed him the truth for saving your life, not some cock and bull story about not wanting Morton to leave.'

Gene was reeling from Sonny's bomb. In a daze she muttered, 'Seems to me you know more details than I do.'

'Bullshit, Gene. Today, I bared my pain to you. But after twenty-five years you can't bare yours. Some love that. Some trust.' He was standing, pulling on his duffle. 'You can get this one for a change.'

She threw down a tenner and raced after him. He was already out the door. It was almost dark, the air chill. Graded snow lay all around them. Faint streetlights blurred up ahead.

'Sonny, wait!' she called. But he kept walking. She ran after him. 'Sonny, come back!' She walked behind him looking at his back feeling all the hurt he felt inside, all her hurt.

'Sonny, please,' she begged. She didn't know if he could hear her. She didn't know what to do. All she knew was she had to somehow, some way fix this.

On Portage Avenue, in the cold blue light of a winter's night, a mezzo soprano voice echoed off the Tyndall Stone of the buildings, carrying through the still air to the tall structures up above, pealing like carillon bellows. And the voice Gene heard was her own. *Ave Maria Gratia.*

After the first verse she switched to English lest he not understand the words. The cold invaded her feet. In her circular breathing the chill air scourged her nostrils. But her pain was insignificant to his. He stood ten metres away. But his back was no longer to her as she continued to sing:

Ave Maria! Ave Maria!
Maiden mild!Listen to a maiden's prayer!
Thou canst hear though from the wild,
Thou canst save amid despair.
Safe may we sleep beneath thy care,
Though banish'd, outcast and reviled -
Maiden! hear a maiden's prayer;
Mother, hear a suppliant child!
Ave Maria!

People at the bus stop across the street were no doubt staring at her but she didn't care. When she finished she and Sonny walked towards each other.

'The last time I sang that song,' she gasped, 'was on the day I learnt how the people I loved had died. How the man I loved had his head crushed and how his life and his soul bled out of him. It was something you never want to hear.'

'I know,' Sonny said, his voice tender. He placed both his gloved hands on her shoulders. 'Thank you for at long last telling me yourself. Jonathan and Morton told me about Joel and your father. I'm sorry, Gene.' He squeezed her shoulders. 'It must have been awful hearing it. It must have been beyond awful for Morton to have lived it.'

She nodded slowly, her whole body trembling. 'Did Morton tell you about Andrew?'

'Yes,' he sighed. 'That was tragic too. Your poor brother, seeing that happen to his best friend.'

'He was my best friend too,' said Gene. 'He was also my fiancé.' And with that Gene started to cry like she was still on that bus bound for Vancouver.

69

Sonny drove her home. Inside he cranked up the heating and made a pot of tea while she went to the bathroom. When she came out, he was standing at a gap in the curtains staring at the blackened night.

'Where are the girls at the moment?' Gene asked.

'With Mom and Dad. I have them go there every Thursday afternoon as I never know how long we're going to be. I don't want to be watching the clock every time we get together.'

Her eyes met his. 'Thank you, Sonny. Have a seat. Excuse the spartanism.'

'Do you spend much time here?' he asked.

'Yes,' she said. 'The outlook is quite pleasant during the day. But I often venture out. Some days I skate up the Red River, walk through the parks in daylight, sometimes through the city on a Sunday when few people are out.' Just a few days ago she'd walked past the law courts noticing the snow all over its stairs, only a two-foot wide section cleared on one side for people to walk up and down. Further along, the line of conifers outside the Land Title's building were heavily laden with snow, while the leafless elm trees on Broadway matched the pewter sky, their bark more grey than brown. She rather liked the slumbering stillness of such days, as if the world and winter had drawn a truce.

'How do you spend your nights?' he asked. 'There's no television. Your nights must be so long.'

'I don't need a television. I listen to the radio. Do crosswords. I borrow books from the library. I read a lot actually. I mark assignments, exam papers. Prepare lessons.'

'I was expecting something like your place in Ottawa.'

'That was a different life.'

'Do you have many visitors?'

'Every morning.' Gene smiled at him. 'Two cedar waxwings come feed off my windowsill.'

He smiled at her. 'Remember when we first met and we talked about our happiest memory. Do you have any new ones?'

'Yes,' she smiled. 'Of singing with Mary in school like teenage rebels hoping we wouldn't get found out.'

'What were you singing?'

'Would you believe *Hooked on a feeling*?'

Sonny seemed to think that was rather funny. A nun ooga-chaking. 'Am I meant to believe she was a bad influence?'

'No,' Gene said, in all seriousness. 'She was the best of influences. I hope you get to meet her one day.'

'I hope so too.' He picked up the loon he had given her a few months earlier. 'Any others?'

'Yes,' she drawled. 'Of a picnic we had once, you, Lindsay and me. How she fell asleep in my arms and I fell asleep in your arms. And you fell asleep with your snow queen and princess as you used to call us. We were all so content.'

'We were, weren't we?'

In the soft light Gene thought she could see compassion in his eyes.

'Do you have any happy memories of your time with Andrew?'

She nodded. 'Sit down. I will tell you.' She poured the tea and held a cup in her hands as she looked down at the opaque liquid. 'You know Andrew was deaf. He was the reason Morton learnt to sign. Me too. Morton and I grew up in our own world but Andrew was very much a part of it. Certainly when we were young he was, then, in the early teenage years he and Morton were as thick as thieves. After we first got the husky puppies, it was like I got dumped in favour of them. I was on the outs for a

428

few years, boys being boys more or less, being more comfortable with their own gender and their own fun. But after a few years the three of us found our way back together. They would invite me out on runs or we would go ice skating together or play cards. Sometimes we would go and see a sub-titled film.

'When they left school Morton and Andrew both got jobs working for the Montreal Gazette as typesetters. Andrew would do the early shift, clearing up from the night before, resetting all the blocks and starting on his columns. He'd start at eight in the morning and finish at four in the afternoon. Morton would start at two in the afternoon and finish at ten in the evenings, typesetting the front-page stories. Then he got offered a journalism cadetship though he still worked the same shifts. Some nights Andrew would go and meet him after work and they would go to a pub or a bar. Only on the weekends would they spend time together with Sooty and Flint. Instead Morton would take them out in the morning. And Andrew would come by in the afternoon and take them out. We gave him a key to our house as Mom used to work in the postcard business in the afternoons and sometimes I would be late home from school with choir practice or having to find something in the library or pick up something from Annabelle's.

'But often it would be Andrew and I who would take the dogs out for a sprint. He'd let me ride Morton's bike while the dogs pulled me along and he would run beside me. Sometimes we'd swap. Or we'd leave the bike behind and take the dogs on a romp up to Mont Royal. One day I must have told him we had a new song we were learning in the choir. *Ava Maria*. How beautiful it was. And then one afternoon when we were in the cathedral practising I looked up and there was Andrew sitting two thirds of the way back in the pews, watching me, watching us with his jet black eyes and his jet black hair. When I saw him, he grinned at me and shook his head as if he were saying, "What took you so long, Gene, to spot me?" There was something about him that hinted at mischief, what I think I loved about him so much.

'The next time we were up at Mont Royal resting on a park bench he asked me what it was like to sing. He said I looked so happy when I was singing, did I know that? And I said, "No, I didn't know I looked happy."

'He asked me if I would sing for him and could he touch my throat while I was singing so his fingers could feel the vibrations.

'I laughed to hide my discomfort at the idea. I told him, "I can't sit here and sing with your hands on my throat staring at me while I sing."

'He told me to close my eyes. So that is what I did and when I finished I opened my eyes and he was looking at me in this way I couldn't describe. He was mesmerised and I was mesmerised. With him, with his face because for the first time I saw it differently and his hands resting on my clavicle, his fingers on my throat suddenly were the most sensual things I had ever experienced and without words being spoken we kissed. And we kissed and we kissed and it felt as if we were meant to be together. We always had been. We always would.

'And from that day on every afternoon when I didn't have choir practice, Andrew and I would be together. We lived for the afternoons. Some days we'd only take the dogs out for a quick sprint and then he would take me riding on the bike, me doubled behind him. He'd take me to cafés. We'd go to the botanical gardens. We'd go to a curling rink. We were inseparable. I'd come home and Mom would be back at her paintings or in the kitchen and I would help her cook and we'd have dinner together, some days Andrew would stay for dinner as well, and then she would return to her canvases or do the ironing or read while I would return to my school books. Our romance was ours entirely.

'Then, one cold December day while we were huddled together in a café drinking chocolate au lait, he asked me if I would marry him when I finished school and I said I would marry him the very day after school finished. We were so eager. I wouldn't even be eighteen. A child bride. And I thought this is how it must have been for my mother when she first met my father. It felt so right. Afterwards we walked down to Le Vieux Port and watched the sun set on Marché Bonsecours. Across the water it glowed orange, and the city lights were purple and green and red – I remember it so clearly – and he asked me to sing *Ava Maria* for him again. But this time I leant back into him and he had his arms around me, his fingers tucked under my scarf as we looked out over the frozen waterway at that historic building, the heart of Montreal for so many years, and I sang for him once more.

'Later that night Morton came home to tell me Andrew had been crushed to death between two cars, his head split like our fathers. And I was incapable of helping Morton bear his loss for I was too consumed with my own.'

'I had no idea,' Sonny whispered.

'Why would you?' Gene whispered back. 'We never told a soul. You are the first to know.' She inhaled deeply then took a sip of her tea before continuing. 'There was something exquisite about keeping our love secret. Or maybe falling in love so unexpectedly was exquisite.' She sighed. Her eyes met Sonny's. He gave her a sad little smile. 'Because we had been so selfish with our love, how could I tell people afterwards? I would look like a complete fraud. People would think I was hijacking my brother's misery or making it up for attention.'

'So yes, I couldn't handle what happened to my father and brother. I couldn't handle Morton having to have witnessed it all. His helplessness. I couldn't handle Morton leaving me because then I really would be left with no one. But mostly I couldn't handle hearing how Andrew came to his untimely end. I couldn't handle my life without him. I just wanted to be with him. And so that is what I tried to do.'

'And this is what you were trying to get over when you came up north with us?'

'Yes.' Gene chewed her lip. 'In Freshwater I came to the conclusion that I couldn't let myself love people with abandon, for when I did, they were taken away from me. And then shortly after –mere weeks – I met you and started to have feelings for you. That wasn't right. It wasn't safe. For me – but mostly for you – your life would be in danger if I were to fall in love with you. But also it wasn't right that I could feel for you in the way I felt for Andrew…not in the same way, but in a similar way. That was a betrayal to him. And I couldn't reconcile that inside. I think it took me years to realise that Andrew was called home for a reason and that reason was so that I would be free to meet you. It was like he was an angel leading me towards you. It was his parting gift. I know we are the ones who ultimately have to save ourselves.' She paused. 'But I also know now that in our darkest days the right people come along to help us. I couldn't see that back then but I see that now.'

Sonny reached across and squeezed Gene's hand. Then he stood up and pulled her to her feet. He led her across to her single bed. 'Lay down,' he whispered. 'Let me hug you like we did on that picnic blanket that day.'

Hours later when she woke he was gone.

70

Gene stopped asking when she could see the children, and Sonny stopped saying not yet. Instead he started to bring them into her life in novel ways. He brought her photographs for her to pore over, their school reports, and then one day he brought her something quite remarkable. What he called their yearbooks. Something Abigail had implemented way back as a kind of shared memory for the girls, given that they didn't have a constant mother in their life.

It had an entry for each six weeks of the girl's life: written by their carer summarising what they had done during that time as a way of conveying important information amongst the group of women who raised Lindsay and Shane, and for Sonny as well. Dental appointments. Doctors' appointments. Sporting events, adventures they had gone on, any significant school achievements. There were entries from their daughters as well, journal type reflections. It was a voyeur's goldmine. How farsighted of Abigail. Sonny told her she could only have them for two weeks because he had to return them before they were noticed as missing.

They stopped their sessions with Shelby. Sonny stopped meeting Gene after school. Instead he would meet her for dinner one night a week, take her out or come to her little flat and she would cook for them both. She told him she had joined the St Boniface Church choir and invited him to come to a service one Sunday. Bring the girls. He said one day he would do that.

She told him about Mary. How at long last she and Billy had been recognised as being eligible for adoption and they were on a waiting list.

'That's great news,' he said. And he was enthusiastic for her friend as if he had known her personal struggle throughout the years.

And then one get together in early December, no different to any other time they got together, as they were eating veal cordon bleu, one of her favourites from her time abroad, Sonny asked her if she would like to join them for Christmas. Would she like to spend some time over the break with her daughters, with his parents and catch up with her mother and Wyatt?

Slowly she shook her head as she gave him a wry grin. 'I can't believe your timing.'

'Good or bad?'

'Both. I've made other plans. Thank you for the invite but I'm going to see Morton for Christmas, heading out on the 23rd December as soon as school finishes and won't be back until the 3rd of January.'

'What prompted that?' He paused. 'Did I wait too long to ask you?'

Gene chuckled. 'No, Sonny. I need to go see him and tell him about Andrew. He needs to know the real reason I attempted suicide. God knows he's been carrying around the guilt of what I did for too many years. Before I see anyone else, before I talk to anyone else, I need to do right by him.'

'I'm impressed,' Sonny said.

'I haven't done it yet!' she replied, laughing ever so lightly. 'But I will. We're going sledding with eight of his dogs on Diefenbaker Lake as well. I'm really looking forward to that. Those skates you bought me last winter won't know what hit them.'

'I'm jealous,' he said, his eyebrows raised, his mouth pressed together in a firm line. He really did look a little put out. 'What I wouldn't give to go sledding with Morton and his dogs?'

'How about next year, you let me look after the girls for Christmas and you head off with Morton? I'd be happy to give you some time off to relax and enjoy yourself for a week or two. Have your own adventure.'

'I'd be happy to take the time.'

Gene topped up their glasses with orange juice while she tried to rally all the insouciance of her earlier years. 'Sonny, it occurs to me, now that I'm heading off to see Morton, that perhaps we should cover off something.'

'Yeah, what's that?'

'Well,' she ventured, 'we haven't specifically talked about it in all the time I've been back, however I'm wondering, in the interests of developing greater trust between you and me,' she paused momentarily to catch his eye, 'if you can level with me about something.'

'About what?'

'Well for starters, that photo you gave me of you and the girls, taken in British Columbia when you were on holidays, I was wondering who took it.'

'I don't know, some camper. Why?'

'Part of me thought, thinks,' she exhaled, 'gosh, this is hard for me to say…that you have a lady friend that you took on holidays with you. And I figured when I'm at Morton's, if he lets something slip, I would rather have heard it from you than him.'

Sonny's face was unreadable. He picked up the napkin and wiped his mouth before placing it back on the table. 'You're wrong. We have spoken about this when you first came back. You assumed I was with somebody and I asked you if the thought bothered you and you didn't give me a direct answer in that typical way that you do. You said something along the lines that you wouldn't hold it against me, that you had encouraged me and you wanted to me to be happy.'

'You didn't give me a direct answer at the time either.'

'Do you want a direct answer?'

'I'd like to know where things stand.'

'Go ahead, ask away.' He slowly twirled his glass on the table but his eyes did not leave her face.

'Have you remarried?'

'Do you think I would be here in your flat if I had?'

'Have you fathered any more children?'

'Not that I'm aware of.'

'Are you with anyone else?

'Not at the moment.' His eyes were intense, holding her own. 'You don't think my life has been complicated enough?

'What about back in July? Did you take someone with you and the girls to BC?'

'No,' he said softly. They continued to stare at each other. 'Aren't you going to ask me if I dated other women? If I've had female friends.'

Gene **really** didn't want to know anything about that. Once she knew she would never be able to un-know. 'No, Sonny, that's none of my business. It was your life.' She lowered her eyes. 'It's still your life.' She shrugged. 'You are entitled to do what you like.'

In an instant he was on his feet, looming over her. 'You know what I'd like?' his voice impassioned. 'Just once in your life can you be jealous? Can you allow yourself to FEEL that?' Both his hands pounded his chest. His cinnamon eyes glared at her in all their beautiful naked intensity. 'Show me you're jealous of the attention I may have given to another woman! Show me you're jealous of the affection I may have lavished on other women! Don't show me that you understand, that you don't care, that you can cope with it. I want you fired up! Do you remember what that is, Gene? I want you on fire with jealousy.' He was in a blistering rage, overcome with anguish. He grabbed his coat. Halfway towards the door he turned towards her. 'I want you to want me! Stop being a martyr and start being a woman.'

He was gone; the door left wide open; the frigid air rushing in behind him.

71

She didn't see him for six weeks, nor did she call. She was a debacle of emotions, thawing, rasping, slowly transforming.

She did, however, have a lovely Christmas with Morton. Not wanting to have a new memory of Andrew's death taint his home, Gene didn't tell Morton about Andrew until a week into her visit. She waited till they were away camping with the dogs, in a hut sitting round a log burner listening to the resin hiss and spit and the coal crack and explode.

He was nineteen when his friend was killed. He was forty-four now. His hair was sandy and still thick, always sticking up at odd angles over his head. He washed it plenty but it seemed to Gene he never bothered combing it. He'd leave that to when he got it cut. His skin was brown and lined, not that she could tell when they were rugged up with only their faces visible, however back at the farm she had seen his neck and was amazed at the creases the sun had scored into it over the years. But his eyes were the same, so like their fathers, his golden gaze.

They talked largely about her teaching life. She told him she was back in Winnipeg, talking to Sonny about seeing the girls. At times they reverted to sign language and that was a comfort to know it came instinctively to her even after all these years. But her brother had taken it to an art form when communicating with his dogs. To watch him parley with his dogs through signals and whistles was a rare privilege. She was proud of what an accomplished dog handler he'd become.

When she told him about Andrew, he told her, he was

glad Andrew had the chance to love a girl as special as her. She had not expected him to say that and his words made her sad, sad for her brother, thinking: you lived Morton but did you get to love a girl who was special? It was a relief to tell him and, unlike the night he had lain next to her and told her about her father, Joel and Andrew, when they lay down that night in their heavy duty sleeping bags, the yoke they shared was lightened.

Two weeks into the New Year that was 1976 she phoned Sonny at his work. 'Hi, Sonny. It's Gene.'

'Hi, Gene. How'd you get on?'

'It was good to see my brother.'

'It's always good to see Morton. Even though at times he doesn't have a lot to say.'

That made her smile. 'I made you all Christmas presents but I never got round to giving them to you before I went away. They're for winter, so it would be good to get them to you sometime.' She had knitted them each a woollen scarf. Sonny's was in muted browns, Lindsay's was in a blue blend of course, and Shane's was in shades of green.

'All right.'

'Sonny, can we start afresh?'

He was silent for a second or too, then he sighed. 'Yep, we can.'

'Are you free for dinner next Thursday week?'

'Wait a sec.' She waited. 'Yes, I can make it. I'll pick you up at six-thirty.'

'Okay.' She paused. 'Sonny, um, there's just one more thing.'

'Yep.'

'Although I have never shown it or said it, I have been jealous. Then. And now. Of Lesley who knew you at seventeen, through to Kristina in Parry Sound and the parade of girlfriends I never met. But oddly, jealous most of all, of my daughters, who've spent many more years than I by your side.'

438

When he came by he asked if it would be okay if they ate in. He'd brought takeaways.

'Fine,' she said, opening the door for him. 'What sort?'

'Moussaka.' He smiled. 'We've got aubergines.' He grinned.

'Where's the Greek restaurant in Winnipeg?'

'At my house. Lindsay cooked it. Abby– '

Gene started to cry.

'Now, Gene, don't get upset. It will taste good I promise. Abby taught her and Lottie apparently taught Abby.'

Gene nodded as she tried to stanch her tears while he patted her on the back. 'There, there. Can you whip up a salad? And stop crying or else I'll have to take you out dancing to cheer you up.'

'Is that a promise?' She laughed, as she reached for a handkerchief. 'How did you manage to sneak this out of the house?'

'There was no sneaking. I told the girls I had a meeting with someone. Could I take two portions please?'

'Who's looking after them tonight?'

'They're home alone: new year, new regime. After your mother left three weeks ago Lindsay announced she was old enough to look after Shane and herself in the afternoons until I came home. She insisted. I folded. Put my trust in her. She's mature and keen to be independent. So one of them calls me when they get in from school. If I'm not in they call Elin. If I've got an overnight then Dad will pick them up from school. It's working well.'

'I could look after them, Sonny.'

'I know.' He paused. 'Soon.'

'Are you sure they're okay?'

'Hell, yeah. They're fine to be left at home for a few hours. We've got great neighbours either side if they need someone in a hurry. I won't be gone long. I make sure they lock the house up after I leave. Your mother will ring them at seven thirty, like she does every night. I'll be home before nine.'

She looked at him.

'Seriously, Gene, trust me. Don't worry.'

'Okay.'

'So how about this,' he said. 'The other day I mentioned you to them.' His eyes twinkled.

'You did! What did you say?'

'I went to use the bathroom one night and it was a mess. They had girl stuff everywhere. I said to them, "What is this bombsite? How's a man meant to find his razor? What would I tell your mother if she were to come walking through that front door right now and see this paraphernalia everywhere? What would I say to her?"'

Gene smiled. 'What did they say?'

'Lindsay said, "Dad, you'd tell her: where have you been all our life?"'

'"Yeah," said Shane, "don't you know, that we've been waiting."'

Gene chuckled. 'Did they really say that?' she asked.

'Yep.'

'What a wonderful sense of humour they have.'

'That's my girls.' He looked at her. 'Our girls.' He paused. 'That will take some getting used to again, no longer being a sole parent.'

'I'm sure it will.' Our girls, she liked the sound of that very much, though part of her wanted to say: 'Define our.'

Another night a few weeks later, Sonny said, 'I'm serious about taking you dancing. But you might want to upgrade your wardrobe. You're walking around as if you're a woman in your fifties. Not thirties.'

'Forties, Sonny. I'm forty-three in August. You'll be forty-nine in a few weeks.'

'Steady on,' he cautioned. But then softly he said, 'You get my drift, though.'

She looked at him in his purple and green paisley shirt with its wide collar and open neck. He wore his hair long and wavy like it had been at the end of their ten weeks up north back in 1951. What did she look like to him? 'Where would we go dancing?'

'I don't know. Some pub. Some bar.'

'Don't you think we're a little too old for that?'

'Just go out and buy yourself some new outfits. Look at some magazines. Go into a music store. Look at Cher, Joni Mitchell. That country singer, Olivia Newton-John. Treat yourself. Surprise me.'

Next week when he came by she was wearing flared jeans, a white embroidered cheesecloth top and her hair was unbraided in a new style. For the first time ever she'd tinted her hair. For the first time in decades she had a fringe and wore faint smudges of blue eye shadow.

'Better?' she smiled.

'Better,' he smiled. 'Now I recognise you. Joni Mitchell eat your heart out.'

'Is that who you think I look like?'

'A little. You look more like my wife.'

'Oh!' She blushed and walked away into her tiny kitchenette but he followed and blocked her in the corner, his hands either side of the bench so she had nowhere to move, nowhere to look except for his teasing eyes, his teasing mouth and in the next breath he started singing *Forever in blue jeans*.

Gene laughed lightly, feeling as if she were gliding back over the years of her life, feeling free of control, free of care.

Sonny smiled but he kept on singing, each line more suggestive than the previous.

'What **are** you thinking, Sonny?' She couldn't help smiling. He was like the Sonny of old, knowing the words to every song.

'Oh, I'm wondering if you still kiss like my wife.'

'Kiss. What's kissing?' she murmured, turning her head away. She couldn't look at him and talk about kissing.

He placed his fingers on her cheek, turned her face back towards his and gazed solemnly into her eyes, then he kissed her – long and sweet – just their lips touching, slow and measured. He opened his mouth, and she hers, so they could once more savour the taste of each other, remember the way of each other, and before they knew it their finely-wrought fuse of love and lust and longing was ablaze, and they were kissing like they did that first time in Parc Maisonneuve. How could she have forsaken this? She really was insane!

When they broke apart, gasping, Sonny said, 'Now that's the Gene I remember.'

'Enough fire for you, Sonny?' she teased, everything about her suddenly warmer, pulsing.

'The more fire the better.' He peeled off his coat. 'So I was wondering…'

'Still wondering?' She arched a solitary eyebrow.

'Yes,' he drawled. 'Do you want to come back as the girls' mother or my wife or both?'

'Do I have a choice?'

'Just answer the question.'

Gene smiled tentatively. 'Can I say both then? Is that too much to hope for?' she gushed. 'Too much to ask?'

'No. It's what I hoped you would hope for.' He pulled her possessively into his arms.

Gene felt like she had just ridden over a bump in the road and her stomach was still lurching upwards while her body was crashing down. She pressed her face into Sonny's neck, breathed in the long-forgotten scent of him. Somehow, someway she had found her way back to him; her way back to herself; to them.

She started trembling with relief, with the enormity of that possibility, sensing any moment she was going to be overwhelmed by great gulping sobs.

'I hate to disappoint you,' he said, 'but I have this effect on every woman.'

Her erupting sob gave way to laughter. She tucked her wet face into him and continued to shake with relief and love and joy and tears. This man who knew when to be a clown and when to be a saint.

'I was thinking,' he said, as he reached for her hand. 'Why don't you get used to being my wife again first?' He led her out of the kitchen towards the single bed. 'Don't want to overload you with the pressure of teaching, wife duties and motherhood all at once?'

'Is that your academic opinion?' she teased.

'I just think we should master one thing before we move on to the next. Besides, you wouldn't want me to be in a rush to take just any woman I date home to meet the children – our children – would you?'

'No,' she whispered.

'Good, then let's take this slowly.'

They took it slowly for she felt like a virgin all over again. Everything about her body was tingling like a twenty-year old, to be living this miracle, to have his love in her life again, to be able to love him again. They forgot dinner that night.

The next time he called round she was wearing a pale pink tee shirt under a soft apricot day dress that had a round neckline fitted bodice and a full A-line skirt that bled into a darker tangerine at the neck and hem. She smiled and raised one eyebrow at him.

'You keep getting better with age, Gene. Shame that dress won't stay on you for too long.'

'Not so fast, Sonny.' She reached for her cardigan and her bag as she turned him around and marched him out the door. 'You're taking me to dinner. That way you'll have plenty of time to admire everything.'

Over their steak Diane and cabernet franc, Sonny said, 'I was thinking that before I re-introduce you to the girls we could maybe have a second honeymoon.'

'Like we were going to before I escaped?'

'Yes. But this time there's no escaping.' His tone was deadly serious.

Gene chortled as she tried desperately to control herself. 'Sorry, Sonny.' A reluctant smiled tugged at his lips. 'I'm not going to escape. I promise. I would miss you too much. I did miss you too much. I wasn't whole without you.'

'Good, I'm glad to hear it. Neither was I.' Gene reached out and squeezed his hand. He squeezed hers back.

'And this time we're not going to the Rockies. I was thinking of some place east where we could go by ourselves for four or five days in the summer holidays and then I could fly back and bring the girls in for a week or more with the two of us. What do you say?'

'I say, yes please.'

Sonny reached across to stroke her face. She placed her hand over it and held it there. Her heart swelled.

Later, as he was running out her door, kissing her goodbye, he whispered, 'Now, do you think my two year plan was not such a bad idea?'

'Yes. You were right, you're always right.'

'See, you just had to trust me.'

'I know.' She paused. 'I do.'

'Yeah, but it took you bloody long enough.'

After he left she went into the kitchenette to make a cup of tea. Walking past her dimly lit table with its petite vase of yellow primroses she glanced down and noticed a coin or was it a button on the table. On closer inspection she discovered it was neither. It was her silver wedding ring.

72

In the first week of July, 1976, thirteen-year old Lindsay and her soon to be ten-year old sister went to stay with their grandparents, Don and Elin Marlow, while Sonny took care of a private charter. The week before he had flown a couple to Lake Nipigon to explore the nearby Chimney Lake rock towers. He would fly back in and pick them up, then fly them onto Parry Sound. From there the couple would make their way back to Toronto. Meanwhile Gene would drive through to Parry Sound by herself. She and Sonny hoped that when they came to return home from Parry Sound the girls would drive back to Winnipeg with their mother so they could spend some quality time alone just the three of them.

In the station wagon Sonny had bought her the year before, Gene drove to Thunder Bay and Sault Saint Marie, almost backtracking the journey she and Sonny had made on their honeymoon. With the windows down, the air whipping the ends of her hair, her John Lennon sunglasses on and the radio blaring, Gene sang out her lungs like she had just been born, tapping the steering wheel and dash as percussion.

She camped by herself enjoying the last days of her second single life, savouring the flush green of the trees, the champagne light of dawn, the birds fluttering and tweeting, the fresh blackberries on the roadside, swollen with inky fruit. Her halcyon days full of joy and promise, overflowing. *Let Your Love Flow.* That was her. That was him. It was their season. And it was summer.

When she reached Parry Sound she walked up to Sonny and held her left hand out for him to kiss it, for him to see she was once more happily wearing his ring. In the early afternoon they flew towards Lake Nipissing where they had put down fifteen summers ago. This time Sonny was in a different floatplane. She remembered her first time in a floatplane – with him in 1951 when they headed north to James Bay with Jonathan and Joanie – and their flights during their honeymoon in 1961. She felt herself swirling in the happiest of memories. Forty-five minutes later she saw Lake Nipissing appear before her. Sonny showed no signs of adjusting the wing flaps and preparing to land.

'We're not going to Lake Nipissing?' she asked.

'No,' he smiled at her, his teeth gleaming. His gold-rimmed sunglasses defined his face. His brown bomber jacket, still hanging in there after all these years of wear, though with patches on the elbows, exuded his being. Suddenly she had a flashback of the day they had flown over the pod of Beluga whales years before.

She smiled in return. 'Surprise me then.'

After another forty-five minutes he brought the plane down on a long narrow lake, motoring up to a small wooden jetty. Behind it was a flat, grassed section between two silver birches and a small log cabin.

He turned the engine off and they removed their earmuffs. 'Does this place still look the same?' he asked.

For a moment or two Gene couldn't speak as she shook her head in amazement. 'Hard to believe it, but it does.' She turned to him. 'How did you know?'

'I asked your mother.'

'She knows you're bringing me here?'

'No. But I thought it would be the perfect place for us to start over again.'

She hugged him. She kissed him. 'It is. The most absolutely perfect place.'

On her second visit to the quaint log cabin on Lake Temagami's northwestern shore, Gene slept in the same rough-hewn bed that her parents had slept in thirty-eight years before. The one where her father lay in the middle of the night when Gene woke him to tell him there were strange men's voices outside. That night the only male voice Gene heard was Sonny's as he called out her name, 'Oh, Gene…Gene.'

Followed by her response in shimmering serenade: 'Oh, Sonny…oh, Sonny…oh…my…salvation, Sonny.'

Afterwards, in naked bliss, they snuggled together like two spoons. 'Sonny,' she whispered, 'did you really mean that bit about good riddance? What were you thinking when you said that?'

'I tell you what I was thinking.' He launched into *Don't give up on us.*

'You crazy man,' she chuckled.

'Crazy. You call me crazy!'

They laughed till she turned around, rolled him onto his back and lay on top of him. The curtains were wide open, the screened windows ajar as the ambient moonlight washed them in a soft lunar glow. They couldn't see everything but they could see enough: each other's eyes.

'Why do you love me so? After everything?'

'I love you because of everything,' he said, holding her hair back from her face. 'When I was twenty-four I fell in love with a seventeen year old girl who spoke of her unwavering compassion for Judas. It was as if she understood him better than anyone and could see her way to forgive him when nobody else could. I loved your perspective. From that day on I loved your pure Auld Lang Syne heart. I thought together we two would be unbeatable, as you would always find it within you to forgive me anything. I never realised at the time that it would be me having to forgive you for anything and everything.' He paused. 'You were meant to be my teacher, Gene Marlow.'

'No,' she whispered in denial. 'I am beyond sorry.'

He ran his fingers across her fringe. 'Why did you take so long to tell me the story of your life?' he whispered.

'That has been my eternal struggle, Sonny.'

'Struggle no more.'

'I don't know where to start.'

'Start with just one thing. Andrew.'

'All right,' said Gene, biting her lip for a few moments. 'I didn't want to betray Andrew's memory, the sacredness of what we had. I didn't want to inflict what I'd heard about him and Dad and Joel on anyone, like Morton had done to me. He had suffered too much for too long. He couldn't help it. I understood that. But I could help it. I had to. He carried the secret of Dad and Joel for eleven years when he was a child. I could carry it for longer when I was an adult.' She took a deep breath.

'But that knowledge and those images haunted me, for years they haunted me. Because his telling was so vivid. Because I loved them so deeply. I saw it all. I felt it all. It was harrowing. So many nights I'd go to sleep and I'd find myself in the horror of that boat or in the horror of being next to that car, trying to reach out with my hand to save Andrew, to save Dad. I'd scream myself awake and when I did it would feel as if I had blood all over my hands. I'd have to get up and wash them and the very last thing I wanted to do was go back to sleep lest I find myself back in the midst of that nightmare.' Gene bit her lip. 'Has that ever happened to you?'

'Once or twice,' murmured Sonny.

'Try hundreds of times, a thousand times.'

'Oh, Gene.' He squeezed her shoulders. 'That must have been terrifying. I'm sorry you had to live with all that.'

She nodded silently in acknowledgement. 'It felt so real every time. I'd wake up completely distraught then I'd slowly realise it was only a nightmare but then I knew it did actually happen to these people I loved.'

She bit her lip. 'I can't imagine, well maybe I can, what Morton has had to live with his entire life. With those broken nights comes this constant state of exhaustion that gradually becomes normal. You cope by living on borrowed energy, by being wired in a weird kind of way, hoping that eventually when it's time to go to sleep your body will be so exhausted that those nightmares will stay far away.'

'How long did these nightmares last?'

'Oh and off…about eight years the first time. Those spectres eventually left me in Geneva. I was finally at peace. I felt like I was seventeen all over again and my life held promise. That is when I decided to come back to Canada. That is when I wrote to you hoping that maybe we could make a go of it. Maybe I could at last live a normal life and be free from all that forever'.

'Why didn't you ever tell me?'

'Why?' She sighed. 'Because when I came back from Geneva the nightmares were gone. Thank, God. There was no way I was going to tell you anything and risk them coming back. And I never ever wanted to talk about the cause – how everyone died and what led to my suicide. When Morton told me, I felt as if I'd taken a silent vow to keep all that secret. He may have passed over the baton of knowledge, that was his prerogative, but it certainly wasn't mine to disclose to anyone.'

Sonny stroked her back. 'And the nightmares came back after Shane was born…after you found out about Jonathan.

'Yes and no. Even before Shane was born I was having mild panic attacks about you, about something happening to you. And then after Shane was born in the space of five minutes I found out about Jonathan and Mom's baby, Samson, who also drowned at the hands of her own father and that set me off.'

'But you came to terms with Jonathan being who he was.'

'Yes,' agreed Gene. 'You were right what you said last November that Jonathan not being my brother wasn't a big deal but it was for a little while. It's hard for you to understand how shocking and upsetting and unfathomable I found that. You have no idea how much I worshipped Jonathan when I was young. Without

Jonathan there wouldn't be a Dalton family. He was this beautiful, caring young man who held everything together and pulled us all through.' She swallowed. 'I finally got to the point where I was okay with him not being Mom and Dad's son because I rationalised he wouldn't be cursed like their other sons had been – which meant I wouldn't lose him.

'But hearing about what my grandfather did to Samson, seeing that little baby drowning, like Joel drowning, like my father drowning. I couldn't cope with that. I couldn't cope with anything.'

'We noticed,' said Sonny. His hands hugged her waist. His smiled was tender. 'And now we understand.'

Gene nodded. 'The fears just grew and grew. Everything I've ever told you about those fears I have about losing my loved ones, about losing the girls is true, is real and at the very heart of those fears is you.

'You, whom I met when I was seventeen and reeling but such was your spirit that it was impossible not to see your light and love. That evening at Moose Factory when you nearly kissed me I was relieved for you, because you had escaped, because hopefully you wouldn't have me jinxing your life and it wouldn't be viciously curtailed.

'And then when I was well and yearned for our relationship to manifest itself, it did. I couldn't believe my good fortune. We were thrilled to be finally together and in love. But at the same time I was ashamed of my scars and my Juliet-styled suicide. I didn't want you to think that because I did something as extreme and Shakespearian as nearly dying for love, that my love for you was not as poignant or profound or passionate. You, the great love of my life. You, whose life has been nothing but adventure and optimism and caring and coping.'

'And patience.'

'And patience. That too,' she smiled.

'And forgiveness.'

'How could I forget that most of all?' Gene ran her

hands across Sonny's warm chest, halting over his merciful heart. 'Your inspired life has made all those things possible in my life. It has made my life. It has made our family and I'm hoping that together we can restore our family. I'm hoping I can do that for you now. That you will see you are my heart, my life, my love.' She stroked his face. 'I don't know if you can make sense of that.' She shrugged.

'I can – now.' He pulled her face towards his and kissed her. 'That was one hell of a story. Thank you.' With his lips next to hers he murmured, 'Any more secrets?'

'No more secrets.'

'No?' He paused. 'Good.' He went to kiss her again but hesitated. 'Ever?'

'Never.'

'Promise.'

She kissed him in answer, kept kissing him, as she felt him harden beneath her. Sliding him inside she leant over him, her hands either side of his shoulders, moved with him, her every caress, her every undulation telling him she was sorry, she would make it up to him, over and over, she loved him, still, forever, that was her promise.

When she wakes his voice is more than a whisper. His version of *After the lovin'* fills her so completely, so gloriously. She cannot believe she can be so blessed to be living this life, to be loving this man, to have this man loving her – still – despite everything.

In daylight they canoe up a river and picnic under the shade of white pines. They dive off the jetty. They fish for walleye and trout. They play Scrabble. Gene wins every time.

They dance and sing to the cassette tapes they brought with them, Sonny in his swimmers, Gene in her tie-dyed singlet and navy briefs. *You to me are everything.*

They cook and sing. *You're my best friend.* They swim and Sonny sings *Don't go breaking my heart.*

451

Afterwards Gene, nearly drunk on love, stumbles, mumbles, 'I wouldn't live if I tried.'

Sonny spills his beer he laughs so hard. He drinks and sings. *Love really hurts without you.*

Not any more she promises him.

He sings Elvis, the King, his favourite, *Suspicious minds.*

And Gene says, 'Thank God we didn't let a good thing die,' as they kiss and kiss and kiss, revelling in the sensation of having their lips and hands on one another, their bodies joined as one.

At night when they lay in each other's arms Gene wonders if other people are ever this happy. 'Sonny,' she whispers, 'When we go back and settle down again, can we have a ceremony, a small party, invite all the family and you and I can do what we never got to do when we got married, say our vows, in front of everyone, in front of the girls and they can be a part of the service. I'd like that.'

'I'd like that too.' He kisses her neck and pulls her even closer.

'Have you told your parents about me yet?'

'No, I was going to tell them on the quiet when I go back to pick up the girls. I want to surprise them. I can't wait to see Mom's face.'

'She will cry,' says Gene, smiling.

'Yes,' agrees Sonny. 'She will be zo happy, zo happy.'

'Zo happy,' repeats Gene. 'Are you zo happy, Sonny?'

'I am zo happy.' He kisses her on the temple. 'You know, you were right?'

'About what?'

'There is something quite exquisite about a love that is secret. There is something exquisite about falling in love so unexpectedly.'

'I'll say. Something miraculous. Thank you.'

They kiss and their kisses are exquisite, as is their lovemaking.

The morning when he leaves to fly out Sonny jokes, 'How will you fill every waking hour without me, Gene? How will you cope?' What will you do?'

'I know exactly what I'm going to do.'

'You do?' He smiles at her, looking for the answer in her eyes.

She smiles at him, her silence prolonging the teasing.

'Are you going to surprise me when I get back?'

She shakes her head. 'Sorry, Sonny, the surprise is not for you. It's for everyone else.'

His brow frowns in question.

'I'm going to write to Mom, to Jonathan, Abigail, your parents, your cousin Sylvia, to Mary and to Sister Eugenia.'

'I'm only going to be away for a few days!'

On the jetty he pulls her into his arms for one final kiss before he steps into his plane. 'Happy?' he asks.

'Never been happier,' she tells him. 'Never been more grateful. I can't thank you enough for forgiving me, for loving me, for saving yourself for me, for saving me.'

'What else could I do? I love you.'

'I love you too.' She kisses him, squeezes him, holds him tight. 'What about you? Happy?'

'You'll see.' He kisses her again and brushes her face with his fingertips. 'I'll be back in four days with the two most gorgeous girls you ever laid eyes on. Look for me in the late afternoon sky.'

She stands on the jetty and watches him take off. She waves for a good minute. His plane rises slowly, circles once and circles a second time. The second pass he comes closer and jiggles his wings. Gene bursts out laughing. Her husband, the jubilant Berlin candy bomber and in the next moment she sees something falling below the plane, and another one, and a third. They are drifting down towards the lake. She wildly flaps both her arms above her head, flaps them to let her amazing man know she has seen them.

And with her hands skywards she sends up a prayer for the miracle of Mary and for the blessing of Sonny, how the two of them lit up her darkest shadows and in a flaring moment showed her what made life so worth living. She dives in, clothes and all, and swims towards the falling parachutes, swims towards him, towards the best of her life.

THE END

Resources

You can find more information about Sherryl and her books on her website: www.sherrylcaulfield.com.

This includes:

- Discussion Topics for book clubs on Come What May

- Frequently Asked Questions on Come What May

- Music links for the soundtrack of Come What May

On her website you can also sign up for her newsletter to be kept up to date with major book releases.

If you want to get in touch with Sherryl you can do so by:

Sending her an email to: info@sherrylcaulfield.com

Or by visiting her Facebook page: SherrylCaulfieldAuthor where she often runs giveaways, posts images from her books, provides project updates and chats to her readers.

Book 3 of The Iceberg Trilogy, Come Full Circle, will be released in 2015.

Acknowledgements

As with my first novel, considerable research went into Come What May, particularly as I knew very little about aircraft and bush pilots before I started. To that end, Bush and Arctic Pilot by A.R. Williams and other stories I found through Virtual Horizons magazine were of immense value and interest, as too was Sarah Ekoomiak's Life Story. Joseph Boyden's novels, Three Day Road and Into Black Spruce, helped to immerse me in the world of the Cree and life in Hudson Bay, and the films, Map of the Human Heart, and The Snow Walker helped with a sense of place. To the best of my abilities I have tried to accurately portray historical events, places and the odd Cree word I uncovered through my research. Any mistakes are entirely my own or have been altered for the purposes of fiction.

The inspiration to write The Iceberg Trilogy came about following a holiday I had to Canada one northern summer, and the inspiration for Sonny in part came from the father of a university friend. You can find out more about the inspiration for both Come What May and its predecessor, Seldom Come By, by reading the Frequently Asked Questions and various blog articles on my website: www.sherrylcaulfield.com.

Many people over many years have helped me shape this novel and the trilogy into its final form. To all of them I am incredibly grateful.

Specifically, for Come What May, I would like to thank once again my partner, Mark, and my sister, Anita, for telling me straight what they always think, for reading Come What May throughout its various iterations and for always being 100% behind my writing and publishing journey.

To the wonderful women from across the globe who helped me finesse Come What May – Ruth Schaffer, Carolyn Wood, Sandie Squires, Jane Brisbane, Gabrielle

Reinhardt, Svetlana Stankovic, and Katherine Hooten – thank you for being part of this journey.

I would like to single out my dear friend, Leah Sparkes, my Newfoundland guide, who has been so forthcoming in her support of my writing and in sharing historical aspects and life experiences in Newfoundland and Canada so I could capture the realities of life and the extreme seasons in that beautiful diverse country. Thank you, Leah!

Finally, thanks to my family and friends who have been tireless in their support of The Iceberg Trilogy. Thanks also to the many readers and bloggers around the world who have embraced Book 1 of The Iceberg Trilogy, Seldom Come By, especially Hildy Nightingale from The Book Bosses, Vee Carthens from Honey Lemon Tea, and Sheree Davey from The Eclectic Reader.

I appreciate your support very much.